She was a respectable, unmarried, probable virgin—his sisters' governess, his stepmother's companion. In a word: forbidden. Untouchable. Dangerous.

Some dangers were worth risking.

He drew her closer, one arm sliding about her waist, bringing her to him so that the small rounded breasts just brushed against him. A taste. Just one taste of those sweet berry-stained lips…

His lips touched hers and her wits whirled.

Warm, firm lips feathered and caressed, promising ravishment and yet teasing with light touches before settling properly…

His control shook as he felt the flowering of her lips, the softening as they opened. Quelling the urge to ravish her mouth, he took it gently. Honey, sweet wild honey, intoxicating—and her very hesitance, even clumsiness, seemed to make it all the sweeter. All the more dangerous…

With his final, fading shred of sanity and control Julian pulled back, breaking the kiss.

'This,' he informed her, 'is not a good idea.'

Author Note

Julian, Lord Braybrook, has been buzzing around in my head for some years now. He originally appeared in HIS LADY MISTRESS, and several of you asked if 'that rake who took Verity out onto the terrace' would ever get his own story. At the time I was writing A COMPROMISED LADY, and when Julian managed to muscle in on the action there too I knew the only way of dealing with him was to write his story.

LORD BRAYBROOK'S PENNILESS BRIDE

Elizabeth Rolls

First published in Great Britain 2009
Large Print edition 2009
Harlequin Mills & Boon Limited,
Eton House, 18-24 Paradise Road, Richmond, Surrey TW9 1SR

ISBN: 978 0 263 20674 6

Set in Times Roman 14½ on 15¾ pt.
08-0909-88518

Harlequin Mills & Boon policy is to use papers that are natural, renewable and recyclable products and made from wood grown in sustainable forests. The logging and manufacturing process conform to the legal environmental regulations of the country of origin.

Printed and bound in Great Britain
by CPI Antony Rowe, Chippenham, Wiltshire

Award-winning author **Elizabeth Rolls** lives in the Adelaide Hills of South Australia, in an old stone farmhouse surrounded by apple, pear and cherry orchards, with her husband, two smallish sons, three dogs and two cats. She also has four alpacas and three incredibly fat sheep, all gainfully employed as environmentally sustainable lawnmowers. The kids are convinced that writing is a perfectly normal profession, and she's working on her husband. Elizabeth has what most people would consider far too many books, and her tea and coffee habit is legendary. She enjoys reading, walking, cooking, and her husband's gardening. Elizabeth loves to hear from readers, and invites you to contact her via e-mail at books@elizabethrolls.com

LORD BRAYBROOK'S PENNILESS BRIDE features characters you will have already met in HIS LADY MISTRESS.

Recent novels by the same author:

HIS LADY MISTRESS
A COMPROMISED LADY

For Joanna Maitland,
who showed me such a good time
in Braybrook's territory, and beyond.

Chapter One

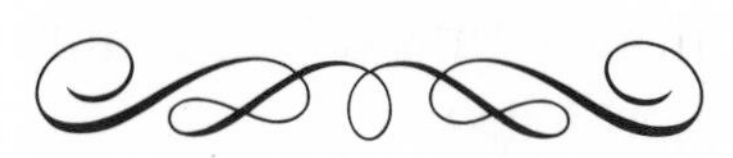

Julian Trentham, Viscount Braybrook, bit his tongue, figuratively speaking, and reminded himself that his stepmother, Serena, considered tact the best way to deal with his wayward half-sister. Telling Lissy she sounded like a second-rate actress in a bad tragedy was not tactful.

'But it *isn't* fair, Mama!' said the Honourable Alicia furiously. 'Julian only met Harry for five minutes yesterday and—'

'Half an hour,' said Julian, sitting down on a sofa. 'Long enough to ascertain that, apart from his post as Sir John's secretary, he has no prospects.' He eyed the tabby cat seated on Serena's lap out of the corner of his eye. The blasted thing was convinced he adored cats. It couldn't have been more mistaken.

'Five minutes!' repeated Lissy, 'and poor Harry is declared *unsuitable*. Whatever that means!'

'Amongst other things, it means you'd run the fellow aground inside of a month,' said Julian, unmoved. 'Have sense, Lissy.'

The cat stretched, brilliant green eyes fixed on Julian.

Lissy glared. 'I would not!'

Serena chimed in. 'Lissy dear, I feel quite sure that charming and pleasant as Mr Daventry may—' She made a grab for the cat, but it was already flowing off her lap. 'Oh, dear. Now, where was I? Yes, Mr Daventry, I am sure he is not at all well off, so—'

'What does money matter? And anyway, he *has* an income!' protested Lissy.

'Two hundred a year?' Julian suppressed a snort. 'And, no, money doesn't matter. Just as long as *you* learn to manage without it. Otherwise you will find it matters a great deal when the bailiffs take your furniture and the landlord kicks you into the street.'

'Harry has his *own* house,' said Lissy. 'In Bristol. He told me.'

'A man of property, then,' said Julian. He watched, resigned, as the cat strolled with offensive confidence towards him. His setter bitch, Juno, sprawled at his feet, lifted her head and then lowered it with a doleful sigh.

'Well, I wouldn't marry Lissy,' piped up six-year-old Davy from the corner, where he was endeavouring to put together a puzzle map of Europe. 'I'm going to marry Mama.'

Somehow Julian preserved a straight face. 'Excellent notion, old chap,' he said. 'Only not unless you want to land in Newgate!'

Lissy looked as though she might have giggled, had she not been trying so hard to look affronted.

The cat sprang into his lap and made itself comfortable. Very comfortable; its claws flexed straight through his buckskin breeches.

'Never mind, dear,' said Lady Braybrook to her youngest son. 'You won't want to marry me when you are old enough anyway.'

'No, indeed,' said Julian. 'After all, Lissy no longer wishes to marry me. Do you, Liss?'

'I never did!' exploded Lissy.

'You proposed to me when you were about five,' said Julian, reminiscently. 'It was most affecting.' He turned to Davy. 'Why don't you trot off to the kitchens and see if Ellie has something for you to eat?'

Davy leapt to his feet, scattering Europe to the corners of the drawing room, and decamped before his mother could veto this excellent idea on the grounds of education or indigestion.

As soon as the door shut behind him, Lissy burst out again. 'It isn't fair, Julian! Why should you have any say in it?'

'Probably because I am your guardian,' he said. 'For my sins,' he added. 'Calm down, Lissy. You're too young to be thinking of marriage.'

'I shall be *eighteen* soon!' she cried, making it sound like a death sentence.

'You turned seventeen less than three months ago,' Julian pointed out. 'You're not precisely on the shelf.'

'What if it were one of your rich, titled friends?' she countered. 'Like Lord Blakehurst?'

Julian blinked. 'Since he's married, I'd shoot him! Believe it or not, I would refuse my consent to any binding betrothal until at least next year.' The cat in his lap rolled, displaying its belly in furry offering. Resigned, Julian kneaded the shameless creature.

Lissy stared. 'But, *why?*'

'Because you're too young,' he said. 'And don't tell me again that you're nearly eighteen!'

Deflated, Lissy said, 'But we *love* each other. It isn't fair. Just because he isn't wealthy—'

'Lissy—Daventry can't afford to marry you!' He strove for patience and nobly squashed his instinctive, and more cynical, reaction. 'Not with bills like the ones sent to me from Bath last month,' he said.

Lissy blushed. He hoped some of his pithy comments on the advisability of keeping a check on expenditure had sunk in. 'It *is* unfair, though. If we cannot see each other, then—'

'I didn't forbid him the house!' said Julian irritably. 'For God's sake, Lissy! Stop acting as though you were in a bad tragedy!'

Serena coughed, and Julian gritted his teeth, remembering the tact. He added, 'He seems pleasant enough, and I believe I can trust *him* not to go beyond the line.'

'You mean, we may meet?'

He fixed her with his best steely glare. 'If he is invited to the same entertainments, then of course you will meet. He may call here. Occasionally. But you may not meet him unchaperoned, nor exchange correspondence. And I would make the same conditions for any man courting you, even if he were a veritable Midas!'

'I suppose you think you're being generous!'

He nodded. 'Yes. Now that you mention it, I do. And if at any time you are tempted to view me as a callous tyrant,' he added, 'you might care to ponder the fact that our father would have shown Daventry the door with a horsewhip, set the dogs on him, complained to his employer, and confined you to your room for a month. At least. And think—once you are twenty-one, I will be powerless to prevent your marriage.'

Faced with this very accurate summation, Lissy set her mouth in a mutinous line. In trembling tones she said, 'If you had the least idea about *love*, Julian, you would understand the *agony* of being obliged to wait!'

She swung around and stormed out.

Serena, Lady Braybrook, said, 'I thought we agreed to be tactful?'

Julian snorted. 'Tactful? Lissy needs a dose of salts!' He removed the cat from his lap. 'What has she been reading, Serena?'

Ignoring that as wholly unimportant, Serena regarded her stepson. 'Tell me, dear—when you were seventeen—'

'Yes, all right, very well,' said Julian hurriedly, recalling some of *his* youthful peccadilloes. He looked away from the cat, which was staring up at him indignantly. 'At least I never wanted to marry any of them!'

At Serena's choke of laughter heat flared on his cheekbones, and the cat took advantage of his distraction to reinstate itself with fluid ease.

'So I recall,' Serena said, still laughing. 'Is Tybalt annoying you? Just put him out.'

He grimaced. 'I think I can survive one cat.' Even if it was stretching its claws on his breeches again. Serena was fond of the thing. 'Was I that much of a nuisance?'

'Worse,' she assured him. 'Whenever news of your misdemeanours at Oxford and then, after you were sent down, London, reached us, your father nearly had apoplexy.' She smiled reminiscently. 'The worst was the rumour that Worcester was about to call you out for your attentions to Harriette Wilson.'

Julian blinked at this unabashed reference to one of his youthful follies. 'Dash it, Serena! Where did you hear that?'

'Oh, was it true, then? I told your father it was more than likely a silly invention and not to give it a moment's thought. Was I wrong?'

'He *told* you?' He hadn't even realised that his father *knew*!

Serena stared. 'Well, of course! How else could he ask my advice?'

'He asked your advice?' Julian tried, and failed, to imagine his father discussing his son's involvement with a notorious courtesan with Serena.

Grey eyes twinkling, she said, 'Frequently. Which is not to say he took it very often.' Her mouth twitched. 'Not intentionally, anyway.'

Julian decided he didn't want to know. 'Hmm. Well, I'm here now for the rest of the summer, and Lissy and Emma are off to Aunt Massingdale in the winter. Surely we can keep Lissy out of mischief until then.'

'You're staying until Parliament resumes?'

He shrugged. 'Mostly. I do need to see Modbury about some business. I'll go to Bristol for a few nights next week. Since I'm meeting with him I'll write first and ask him to find out something more about Daventry. This house, for one thing.'

'Yes, that surprised me,' said Serena.

'Modbury should be able to discover something if Daventry does own property,' said Julian. 'Apparently, Alcaston is his godfather and settled the income on him.'

Serena frowned. 'Alcaston? The duke?'

'Yes. He recommended Daventry for the post with Sir John,' said Julian. 'Will you be all right while I'm away? Are you sure you don't want Aunt Lydia to visit? Or—'

He broke off under the fire of Serena's glare.

'I may be stuck in this wretched chair, Julian, but as I've said before, that does not mean I require someone hovering over me the entire time,' she told him. 'And since that is exactly what Lydia would do, no—I do not want her to visit!'

'Very well,' he said. 'No Aunt Lydia.'

He'd have to think of someone else, because with her daughters off to Bath for the winter Serena needed a companion. He looked at her with affection. Her confinement to the *wretched chair*, as she put it, limited her physical independence. While he could see her point in categorically refusing her widowed sister-in-law as a companion—Lydia would fuss mercilessly and bemoan ceaselessly the unfairness of fate—who else was there?

'Julian—I don't want *any* well-meaning relatives fussing over me.'

'No. I understand that.' Sometimes he wondered if she could actually read his mind…he'd have to think of something else. Meanwhile he'd best write to Modbury and ask him to find out what he could about Daventry.

Chapter Two

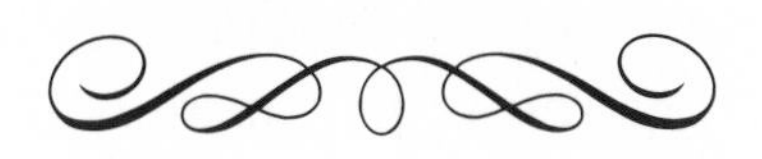

I think I've found the house you wanted, my lord. Only Daventry I could find. It's on Christmas Steps.

Yes?

Only thing, my lord—there's a young woman living there from what I could find out…a Mrs Daventry …

Good Lord! Julian stood at the top of Christmas Steps and wondered if he was insane even thinking of descending the alley. Modbury had thought so, and Julian could see his point. The alley was positively medieval, and so steep someone had actually built steps. According to Modbury it led down to the old quay, and at least once had housed the sort of establishments sailors on shore leave frequented—brothels and taverns.

You can't visit, my lord!

The hell he couldn't. Gripping his umbrella, Julian started down the slippery steps. There were two possibilities. Either Daventry kept a whore down here—it was not unknown for a woman to use her protector's name—

or he was already married. On the whole, Julian thought a conveniently distant wife more likely; a mistress was only convenient if she were close enough to bed regularly. Either, however, would settle Lissy's idealistic infatuation, if a description of the alley wasn't enough.

It was dark in the alley and a dank chill closed in, with a reek of cabbage, fish and sour humanity on the breeze rattling the shop signs. The old, timbered houses with their cantilevered upper storeys loomed over the street, holding light and fresh air at bay. A couple of seedy-looking taverns were the only hard evidence of the street's former reputation. There were few people about, but suspicious eyes followed him from doorways and windows. He consulted the address Modbury had given him—there, on the opposite side, just before the next set of steps between a fishmonger and an apothecary, was the house he sought.

A one-eyed, moth-eaten cat sheltering in the lee of the building flattened its ears and hissed, slinking away as he approached the open door.

A voice was raised.

'Now be sensible, missy. I got Mr Daventry's letter and it says, right here, "the house and all its contents"! See? *All* its contents. Not "all its contents if no one else happens to want them". So—'

'Well, I assume you're not planning to put *me* on the auction block along with my clothes and hairbrush as part of the contents!' came another voice. A prim, schoolmistressy voice a man would think twice about annoying.

The voice went on. 'And if you can make that distinction, then you should be capable of exempting the rest of my personal property.' Irony gave way to anger. 'And since Mr Daventry is my brother and not my husband, he owns neither them nor me!'

Blast! Probably not wife, then. Mistress remained a possibility…

The angry woman continued, 'When you return next week, you may *have* the house and all its contents because I shall have removed myself and *my* possessions to lodgings!'

Through the open door Julian could now see a large, beefy-looking man, in the old-fashioned knee breeches and frieze coat of a respectable tradesman. He had his back half-turned, but there was no mistaking the rising annoyance in the set of his jaw.

'Now see here, missy!' he growled, all attempt at reason abandoned. ''Twas unfortunate I misunderstood how things were, but there's no call to take that tone! I'll be calling in the sheriff and bailiffs if you remove more than your clothes and hairbrush. Everything, the letter says, and I've made a list, I have!' He brandished a piece of paper, presumably in his unseen opponent's face. 'If aught's missing, I'll have the law on you!'

It was none of his business, Julian told himself. Common sense dictated that he remain out of any legal brangle between Daventry and his *sister*. Only this wasn't Daventry…and exactly what situation had the man misunderstood?

The woman spoke again. 'You may leave, Goodall. I suggest you clarify your instructions with my brother. In the meantime my solicitor will call upon you.'

Goodall, far from being abashed, took a step forward, presumably towards the woman.

'Are you threatening me, missy?' His voice had turned thoroughly unpleasant.

'Leave!' Sister or not, the undercurrent of fear in her tone flung Julian into action. Three swift strides took him over the threshold.

'Goodall!' he rapped out.

The man swung around. 'Who the hell are you?'

'The lady told you to leave,' said Julian coldly. 'As an acquaintance of Daventry, I suggest you do so before I speak with the magistrates on his behalf about entering this lady's home and harassing her. Out.'

He strode past Goodall with scarcely a glance at the woman. All he could see was that she was of medium height, bespectacled and clad in dull brown. His attention was on the aggrieved Mr Goodall, and he deliberately interposed himself between them.

Goodall flushed. 'Now, see here—'

'Out.' He delved in his pocket and pulled out his cardcase. 'As for who I am…' He took out a card and handed it to Goodall '…I'm Braybrook.'

He gestured to the door and Goodall, his face now as pale as it had been red, swallowed.

'I'm sure…that is…I didn't mean—'

'Out!'

Goodall went.

Julian closed the door and turned to receive the heartfelt gratitude of his damsel in distress—

'I have no idea who you may be, but you will oblige me by also leaving.'

Frost glittered at him from behind unbecoming spectacles. And there was something odd about her direct gaze, something faintly disconcerting—as though she had the ability to see straight through. Right now he wouldn't have wagered a penny on her liking what she saw.

As for what *he* saw—the woman was a quiz. Her hair colour remained a mystery under an all-enveloping and extremely ugly cap. As did whatever figure she might possess beneath a gown remarkable only for its sheer shapelessness and being the drabbest brown he'd ever seen.

Any lingering hope of her being Daventry's doxy faded. No self-respecting doxy would wear the gown, let alone the spectacles.

And she faced him with her chin up, her jaw set, and her mouth a flat, determined line.

'No gratitude, ma'am?' he drawled.

Those queerly penetrating eyes narrowed. 'I'm reserving it until I know who you are, and why you entered my home without my leave,' was the icy rejoinder.

'Well, you won't discover either of those things if you kick me out into the street,' he pointed out with what he freely acknowledged to be unforgivable logic.

It seemed she concurred. One small fist clenched and the pale cheeks flushed. Otherwise her control held.

'Very well. Who are you?'

He supposed she could not be blamed for being suspicious. He took out his card case and extracted another card, holding it towards her.

There was a moment's hesitation before she moved, and then it was warily, watchful eyes on his face as she took the card. At once she stepped beyond his reach behind a settle before examining the card.

He watched, fascinated. There was something about her, about her face—what was it? Apart from that she looked cold.

She was glaring at him again.

'So, Lord Braybrook—assuming you are Lord Braybrook and not some scoundrel—'

'I'm obliged to point out that the two are not mutually exclusive,' he said.

She positively bristled. 'That I can well believe!' Then, 'Oh, for heaven's sake! One of my eyes is blue and the other brown! And now perhaps you will stop staring at me!'

One was blue, the other… So they were. He could see it now; behind the spectacles one eye was a soft, misty blue and the other hazel brown.

'And, no, I am not a witch,' she informed him.

He smiled. 'I assumed you weren't, since Goodall left in human form rather than as a toad.'

For a split second there was a flare in her eyes that might have been laughter. A lift at the corner of the mouth, which was, he suddenly saw, surprisingly lush.

Soft pink lips that for a moment looked as though they might know how to smile.

The impression vanished like a snowflake on water.

'Frivolity,' she said, as one who identifies a beetle, all the softness of her mouth flattened in disapproval.

'Ah, you recognised it,' he said with a bow.

This time her eyes widened, but she controlled herself instantly.

Intrigue deepened. What would it take to crack her self-control?

'Do all your rescuers receive this charming response?' he asked. 'It's true, you know; I am acquainted with Harry. As for my motives; I was coming to call on you and overheard Goodall. I interfered out of disinterested chivalry, Mrs Daventry.'

'Miss Daventry,' she corrected him.

He watched her closely. 'Oh? I understood a Mrs Daventry lived here?'

Her expression blanked. 'Not now. My mother died some months ago.'

'I beg your pardon,' he said quietly. 'My condolences.'

'Thank you, my lord. Will you not be seated?'

She gestured to a battered wingchair by the empty fireplace. The leather upholstery bore evidence of several cats having loved it rather too well. The only other seat was the uncomfortable-looking wooden settle opposite with a damp cloak hung over it. He took the settle and, at a faint startled sound from her, glanced over his shoulder to catch the surprise on her face.

'What?' he asked. 'You can't have thought I'd take the chair!'

Her mouth primmed. 'I've noticed gentlemen prefer a comfortable chair, yes.'

His opinion of Harry Daventry slid several notches. 'Then they weren't gentlemen, were they?'

Her mouth thinned further. 'And you are?'

He laughed. 'Usually. I'll warn you if I feel the urge to behave too badly.'

'Very obliging of you. May I offer you tea?'

Prim. Proper. As calm as though she entertained the vicar.

Tea, though. He didn't like tea at the best of times. And imagining the quality of tea he was likely to receive here sent shivers down his spine. His spine's concerns aside, however, good manners dictated acceptance. And Miss Daventry looked as though a hot drink would do her good.

'Thank you, ma'am. That would be very pleasant.'

She nodded. 'Then please excuse me. My servant is out.' With a graceful curtsy, she left through a door at the back of the parlour.

Julian took a deep breath and looked around the cramped room. This was what he had come for, after all: to judge Daventry's condition for himself. And if Lissy could see this, the circumstances to which she would be reduced if she married Daventry, it might give her pause for thought.

It was spotless, though, he noticed. Absolutely spotless. As though dust dared not settle in a room tended by Miss Daventry. Everything gleamed with care. Wood waxed and polished. Not a cobweb in sight. Against one wall was a bureau bookcase, crammed with books. Julian frowned. It was old now, but it spoke of one-time wealth.

Interesting. Other things caught his eye. An old-fashioned drop-sided dining table against the wall held a lamp. Brass candlesticks that once had been silver gilt. A battered wine table, piled with more books beside the wingchair. Every sign that the Daventries had once been well to do, commanding the elegancies of life and, in sinking to this address, had clung to a few treasured reminders. Perhaps the crash of the '90s had brought them down. He could even sympathise with their plight. His own father had steered clear of those shoals, but had not been so canny in recent years... Lord, it was cold in here!

His mouth hardened. Harry Daventry would not restore his family's fortunes at the cost of Lissy's happiness. No doubt Daventry's sister would be quartered in his household... His eye fell on the books tottering on the wine table—sermons, probably, and other improving works. He picked up the top volumes and his brows rose. Sir Walter Scott—*Ivanhoe*. He looked at the next couple of books, poetry. So Miss Prim had a taste for the romantical, did she? He picked up the final volumes—Miss Austen's *Northanger Abbey*. Serena had enjoyed that...

He set the books down, frowning. Contradictions lay hidden beneath the layers of brown sobriety and the cap. Strolling back to the settle and sitting down, he wondered what colour her hair might be. Not so much as a strand peeked from that monstrous cap. Mousy? It would suit the spectacles and that prim mouth with its iron clad composure. Although it wasn't quite iron-clad, was it? What would it take to breach it utterly?

She would return soon. Miss Respectability, laden with a teatray needing to be put somewhere... Below the window was a small tea table.

With a sigh, he rose, shifted the table, placing it between the wingchair and the settle. Good manners, he told himself. A gentleman did these things. It had nothing to do with Miss Daventry herself or wishing to show her that not *all* men were inconsiderate oafs who took the only comfortable chair, leaving their sister the wooden settle. Definitely nothing to do with *her*. It was simply the right thing to do.

He looked at the empty grate. It *was* cold, after all.

It was the work of a moment to lay a fire, find the tinderbox and have a small blaze going.

He had barely sat down again when the door opened and Miss Daventry came in bearing a small tray.

Shock sprang into those disquieting eyes as she saw the fire. 'Oh, but—'

Julian rose and took the tray from her, setting it down on the table before turning back to her.

She hadn't moved. She was staring at the little table as though wondering how it had arrived there. Then she looked at the fire. All the tension in her face, all the taut lines, dissolved, leaving her, he saw with a queer jolt, looking tired, yet as though something far more burdensome than the tray had been lifted from her.

Almost immediately she recovered, saying in her primmest tones, 'How kind of you, my lord. Please do be seated.'

She bent over the tray and poured a cup. 'Milk? Sugar?'

'A little milk, please.'

She handed him his cup, poured her own, and sat down, her back ramrod straight.

Julian took a wary sip, and acknowledged surprise. The tea, if one liked the stuff, was perfectly acceptable. And the teacups, although old and chipped in places, had once been the height of elegance and cost a small fortune. Yet apart from mentioning Alcaston as his godfather, Harry Daventry made no play with grand connections or past glory.

'Perhaps, my lord, you might explain how you know my brother.'

Miss Daventry's cool voice drew him out of his thoughts. Did she know about Lissy? If so, then it probably had her blessing. She was no fool. The advantages of such a match to her were obvious. She might make a decent match herself from the connection.

'Your brother has become acquainted with my sister.'

Miss Daventry's teacup froze halfway to her lips. Her face blanched. 'Your sister—?' The teacup reversed its direction and was replaced in its saucer with a faint rattle. 'Would your sister be Miss Trentham?'

'Yes. My half-sister.'

Spear straight she sat, her mouth firm and a look of mulish obstinacy about her chin. The air of dignity intensified, despite the pallor of her cheeks.

Hell! No doubt she would defend her brother's marital ambitions to the hilt. Why wouldn't she? Such a connection would be a lifeline for her.

His mouth set hard.

He had to protect Lissy. Nothing else mattered. Even if he had to batter Miss Daventry's pride into the dust.

'How very unfortunate,' she said, her voice calm. 'I trust you are doing all in your power to discourage this?'

Unfortunate? From *her* perspective? *He* had every reason to disapprove of Mr Daventry, but what possible objection could *she* have to Lissy?

With freezing hauteur, he said, 'I am at a loss to know how my sister merits your censure, Miss Daventry.'

'Never having met her, I do not disapprove of Miss Trentham,' said Miss Daventry. 'Merely of—' She broke off, staring. Faint colour stained the pale cheeks. 'I think I understand the purpose of your visit, my lord. A warning to Harry? "Stay away from my sister, and I'll stay away from yours." Is that it?'

Outrage jolted through him. 'I *beg* your pardon?' Thank God she hadn't divined his original suspicions!

She faced him undaunted. 'If that is not the case, I beg your pardon. I can think of no other reason for your visit.'

Could something of his reputation have reached Miss Daventry via her brother's letters?

'No doubt, Miss Daventry. However, I *am* a gentleman. Whatever you may have heard to the contrary.'

'Your reputation is of no interest to me, my lord,' she informed him, picking up her cup and sipping her tea.

'And what leads you to believe that I have a reputation, Miss Daventry?' His reputation, after all, was not the sort one discussed with respectable females.

She gave him a considering look over her tea cup before answering.

'Everyone has a reputation, my lord. All that remains in doubt…' she sipped, '…is the nature of that reputation. Naturally, since you are a gentleman, yours is not the sort of reputation in which I interest myself.'

'Yet you referred to it, ma'am.'

The brows lifted. 'I, my lord? Hardly. You alluded to the possibility that someone might have mentioned you in unflattering terms. Thus suggesting that, deserved or not, you have a reputation.'

Julian nearly choked on his tea. Did she dot every 'i' with a needle? Serena, he realised, would have been cheering the chit on.

She changed the subject. 'We were speaking of your sister, my lord,' she said. 'As I said, I do not disapprove of Miss Trentham. How should I? I have not the honour of her acquaintance. But I do disapprove of my brother's interest in her.'

'A fine distinction, Miss Daventry,' he said. 'Would you care to voice your objections?'

If possible, she sat up even straighter. Her chin lifted.

'There is a looking glass over the chimneypiece, my lord. Examine yourself in it. Bring to mind your home. Your estates. Recall your rank. Then look about you. Tell me what you see.'

He didn't answer. Her cold, blunt assessment rivalled

his own. The obvious, brutal response was that everything about her and this room spoke of impoverished gentility. But faced with her quiet dignity, he simply couldn't say it. Which was foolish beyond permission since the words had been on his lips.

After a moment she spoke again. 'Your silence is answer enough. Harry and Miss Trentham are from different spheres. You cannot wish your sister to make such a step. I assume that is what you are come to tell me, and also that you have refused to permit Harry to see your sister again.'

'Not quite, Miss Daventry,' he said.

He'd intended exactly that, but Serena had talked him out of it.

She stared and he felt the corner of his mouth twitch. That had rattled her.

'You *can't* approve such a match!' The disbelief in her eyes echoed in her voice.

'Naturally not,' said Julian. 'But my sister has a stubborn streak and in four years when she gains her majority, I will not be able to prevent the match. Your objections tally with my own. Your connection to the Duke of Alcaston notwithstanding—'

'My *what*?'

'Your brother's godfather, Alcaston,' said Julian, eyeing her spectacularly white face. 'Are you quite well, Miss Daventry?'

'Yes…yes, perfectly.' Some colour returned to her cheeks. 'He told you that, did he? It makes no difference, surely?'

'None,' said Julian. 'Your brother is still ineligible as a match for my sister, even with the income his Grace has settled on him.'

She nodded. 'So. You have forbidden Harry the house, and—'

'No. I have not.' Serena had pointed out that the fastest way to encourage clandestine meetings was to ban legitimate ones. He could see the logic, but…

'*No?* What sort of brother *are* you, then?'

That caught Julian on the raw. 'A good one, I hope!' he snapped. 'Yes, of course I could forbid them to meet! And where would I be when Lissy hoaxed herself into the role of Juliet and the young fools eloped?' Serena again.

'Lissy?'

'Alicia,' he said.

'I beg your pardon,' she said. 'I did not mean to tell you how to order your sister's life—'

'Ouch,' he said drily. 'I hope that I do not *order* my sister's life, as you put it.'

She flushed. 'I'm sorry, that was—'

'If you don't stop apologising, I shall start to think you are buttering me up.'

'Nothing, *my lord*, could be further from my intentions!'

'No. I thought as much,' he murmured.

That silenced her. If one discounted the draconian glare, which fairly scorched the air between them.

He grinned. He couldn't help it. He wished—oh, how he *wished*!—Serena could hear this exchange. He tripped on the thought—Serena would like this prim, outspoken woman. A woman who was about to be kicked out of her home…and Lissy needed a sharp dose of reality to convince her that life with Harry Daventry would not be love's young dream at all, but a nightmare. Yes. This might work. Two birds with one shot. He almost patted himself on the back. And then remembered that not only had Miss Daventry not accepted, but that he hadn't made the offer.

'Miss Daventry,' he began, 'I gather you intend to seek lodgings when this house is sold.'

'Until I can secure either a position as a companion or a teaching post.'

Better and better. 'In that case, I wonder if the offer of a position might be acceptable—'

'No! It most certainly would *not*!' she flared.

He stared at her scarlet face. 'I may live on Christmas Steps,' she continued furiously, 'but that does not mean—!' She broke off, biting her lip.

And he realised that—whether or not his reputation had preceded him—an unspecified offer from a gentleman might well be viewed with suspicion by a respectable female living on Christmas Steps.

'My stepmother requires a companion,' he said. And waited.

He was disappointed. Apart from her blush deepening, Miss Daventry maintained her composure, or, rather, regained it.

'Oh. I see,' she said. 'I cannot think, my lord, that you really want me as a companion for your stepmother.'

No explanation. No apology. She moved straight on from the potential quagmire of embarrassment. He had to applaud.

'Why not?' he asked.

'Only consider the consequences!' she said. 'If I were living in your house, Harry would use that to—'

'Precisely,' he said softly. 'You would be an unexceptionable reason for your brother to call. Most illuminating for Alicia.'

Her eyes flew to his. 'You mean—'

'Meeting you, knowing you must earn your living—'

'Would give your sister food for thought,' she finished.

'Yes.' She had caught the point in a flash. He added feelingly, 'It would also relieve me of the stigma of being thought a mercenary, callous brute by my sister, because offering you the position would signify my approval of you and, by extension, your brother.' But it would force Alicia to view Daventry in a different light—a young man who could not provide for his sister.

Another silence. She was thinking about it. He had seen enough of her to know that otherwise she would have rejected the suggestion out of hand. Miss Daventry had a mind of her own and reserved the right to use it.

'I doubt that I would be a suitable companion for Lady Braybrook,' she said.

If the lady in question were anyone but Serena, he would have agreed wholeheartedly. As it was…

'You would amuse her,' he said. 'Meekness bores her, and I think we can leave *that* out of your list of virtues.' An understatement if ever there was one.

Amused at her blush, he went on. 'An accident some years ago left her unable to walk. I want someone intelligent to keep her company. I was considering older females, but I think she would like you. You mentioned teaching—do you have any teaching experience?'

'Yes.'

'I have another sister still in the school room and a six-year-old brother. At present they have no governess, so you could help there.'

Miss Daventry looked sceptical. 'That will hardly answer once the summer is over and they require more lessons. I cannot be in two places at once.'

He shrugged, dismissing the objection. 'Once another governess is hired, you can be available on her days off, or if she is indisposed,' he said. 'Naturally, were you prepared to take on this dual—or should I say triple?—role, I would pay you accordingly. Shall we say, one hundred pounds per annum?'

While he did not precisely expect Miss Daventry to leap at his generous offer like a cock at a blackberry, she would no doubt be somewhat flustered. Most governesses or companions were lucky to receive a quarter of that.

The soft, rosy lips parted slightly and he felt a jolt of what he sincerely hoped was mere gratification....

'You cannot possibly pay such a ridiculous sum to a companion who relieves the governess,' she informed him.

The devil he couldn't! He bit that back, opting for icy civility. 'I *beg* your pardon, ma'am?'

'It is ridiculous,' she repeated, her mouth re-primmed.

It was, was it? Just how much more did the harpy want?

'Moreover,' she went on, 'it would be grossly unfair to the other governess, who might well be older and far more experienced, were I to be paid such an astronomical sum!'

His jaw dropped. 'You're complaining that I'm offering too *much*?'

She frowned. 'What did you think I meant?'

He shook his head in disbelief. 'Miss Daventry, permit me to inform you that most people would not concern themselves in the least if I offered too much. My offer stands.'

Her eyes narrowed. 'Fifty,' she said.

His mouth twitched. Good God! He was actually arguing—haggling like a merchant outside the Corn Exchange—with a potential governess, trying to persuade her to accept a higher figure!

'Miss Daventry, your scruples are admirable, but your value to me lies far beyond the companionship you will offer my stepmother, or whatever knowledge you may impart to my younger siblings.'

'But I might fail,' she pointed out.

'One hundred per annum,' he insisted, battling the urge to laugh at this dowdy, honest woman with her disturbingly pink, prim mouth and earnest mismatched eyes. 'If it helps, no one besides ourselves will know how much you are paid. Certainly not the other governess.'

'No. It doesn't,' she said at once. 'It is still unfair, whether the other governess knows, or not. *I* would know.'

He gritted his teeth. Damn the wench. Could she not strangle her scruples and accept his generosity? 'Miss Daventry, upon occasion I play cards. I bet. Shall we say twenty-five pounds per annum as a companion? A further twenty-five as a governess. I'll gamble the other fifty against you being able to dissuade my sister from marrying your brother.'

Her eyes narrowed again behind those frumpish spectacles. 'Very well, on one condition…'

He might have known it. 'Which is?'

'If I am still in Lady Braybrook's employ when your sister marries, the extra fifty pounds ceases. And should she marry my brother, I repay you—'

'Not bloody likely!' he said. And couldn't believe he'd said it. What was he about? He *never* swore before females, but something about this one tipped him on to his beam ends. As for Miss Daventry—the ladylike façade was in ruins, her mouth parted in shock.

'I *beg* your pardon?'

Sheet ice encased her voice. As for her eyes…that was it—the eyes were tipping him off balance. And she was angry, furiously angry. Beneath that calm exterior was someone quite different.

'Er, certainly not,' he corrected himself. 'Otherwise, Miss Daventry, it would not be gambling. Would it?'

Under his fascinated gaze the fiery creature was visibly subdued and closed away. Prim Miss Daventry stood in her place. 'I disapprove of gambling,' she informed him. 'You can hardly expect—'

'Damn it all!' he exploded. 'What I expect seems to be

going by the board! I *expect* you to accept my generous offer. I *expect* you to be ready to accompany me when I return to Herefordshire in three days. I *expect—*'

'Three days?' Fire licked through the cracked façade. 'I cannot possibly pack up this house in three days! Nor—'

'My man of business will handle it,' said Julian, pouncing on her implicit acceptance of his offer.

'Nor could I possibly accompany you to Hereford!'

'Why the d—why not?' he corrected himself. 'How will you take up your position if you do not?'

'Oh, don't be so literal!' she said. 'I meant I cannot travel alone with you. We should have to spend a night on the road.'

It was his turn to feel outraged. 'Dammit, girl! Believe me, I've no designs on *your* virtue!'

'It wouldn't matter a scrap if you did or not,' she said frankly. 'My reputation would be ruined either way! I am twenty-four, Lord Braybrook. I cannot travel with you alone.'

'You expect me to engage a *chaperon* for you?'

He couldn't quite believe it. Five minutes ago he had offered this impossible woman respectable employment and they had been arguing ever since. Somewhere he had lost control of the transaction.

'Of course not,' she said impatiently. 'I shall travel on the stage, and—'

'The deuce you will!'

'Lord Braybrook, I have frequently travelled on the stage—'

'Well you shouldn't have!' he growled, adding, 'And you won't this time.' Which was so illogical as to defy comprehension. Companions and governesses always travelled on the stage.

'Yes, I will,' she said.

Julian gritted his teeth in barely concealed frustration. 'Miss Daventry,' he ground out, 'I begin to see why you consider yourself unsuited to the position of companion!' The inescapable fact that she was perfectly right about the situation didn't help in the least. Nor the defiant chin that said she knew she was right, and that she knew that he knew… He halted that train of thought at once.

'Ma'am, I cannot agree to a lady under my prot—' one look at her outraged countenance and he corrected himself before the façade exploded in flames '—for whom I am responsible, travelling on the common stage. Or the Mail,' he added, before she could suggest it. 'You will travel with me!'

'Not unchaperoned!' she shot back.

'Very well!' he snapped. 'Will it be acceptable if a maid shares your room at the inn we put up at, or must I inveigle a Dowager Duchess into service? I've no designs on your virtue, but even if I had, seducing the governess in my travelling coach is *not* one of my favoured pastimes!'

Miss Daventry flushed. 'There is no need to be horrid about it. I am not at all concerned about *you*. Merely how gossip might construe it. I have no wish to find myself the object of vulgar curiosity and censure! A servant at night will be perfectly adequate. Naturally I will pay for my own accommodation and—'

'You will do no such thing,' he stated with deadly calm. 'As of this moment, Miss Daventry, I consider you to be in my employ. Any expenses incurred on your journey will be borne by *me*. Are we clear?'

For a moment the prim mouth took on a mulish set, but she dropped a slight curtsy. 'Yes, my lord.'

Discretion, ever the better part of valour, suggested it was time to beat a hasty retreat. Before he strangled her, or worse, swore at her again. Having solved several problems in one stroke, he was in no way minded to have his plans upset by Miss Prim and Proper deciding she could not enter the employ of a gentleman so dissolute as to swear in front of a lady, let alone allude to the possibility of seducing her in a travelling coach.

'I will bid you a good day then, ma'am.' He set down his cup and rose. 'I have business tomorrow and Wednesday. We will depart on Thursday. My carriage will take you up at seven a.m.' He bowed. 'If you do not object to starting early.'

She had risen too.

'I will be at the top of the steps outside the Chapel of the Three Kings. Will a trunk and valise be too much?'

He raised his brows. 'You will pack whatever you require. If it does not fit, a carrier will bring it.'

He held out his hand. A polite gesture to seal their bargain. Nothing more. For a moment she hesitated and then placed her own hand in his. Awareness shot through him. Her hand fitted his as though they completed each other. Startled, he met her gaze. Behind the spectacles her mismatched eyes widened, as though the same awareness had taken her. For a shocking instant their gazes linked as tangibly as their hands. Then her lashes swept down, veiling her eyes, closing him out.

He released her hand and stepped back. 'Good day, ma'am. My man of business will call.'

'Good day, my lord,' she responded quietly.

Having seen Lord Braybrook out, Christiana Daventry closed the door behind him with trembling fingers and leaned against it.

Had she run mad? What was she about to accept his offer of employment? What if he wasn't Lord Braybrook at all? And what was it about him that had broken her usual self-control? Not since she was sixteen had Christy lost command of herself like that. It hadn't done any good then, either. Not that she cared. She could manage without being beholden to anyone.

She fished Lord Braybrook's card out of her pocket, frowning. Anyone could have an elegant card embossed. Except, how could anyone but Lord Braybrook know of Harry's interest in Miss Trentham?

Miss Trentham, who, according to the perfunctory description in Harry's last letter, had blue eyes and black hair—Christy muttered a distinctly unladylike word—just like Lord Braybrook's. Indeed, if they were anything like her brother's blue eyes and raven hair, then Miss Trentham would be nothing short of a beauty. She had never realised eyes could actually *be* that blue, outside the covers of a romance from the Minerva Press. Or that penetrating, as though they looked right into you and saw all the secrets you kept hidden… Oh, yes. He was Lord Braybrook right enough. And she had accepted a post as companion to his stepmother and a sort of fill-in governess. It must be a most peculiar household, she reflected. Most ladies of rank would hire their own companions and the governess.

She snorted. It was all of a piece with his arrogant lordship. Marching into her home as though he owned it. Taking up far too much of her parlour with his shoulders…why on earth was she thinking about his shoulders? It hadn't been his shoulders that had forced Goodall to back down, it had been that stupid card with his name and rank on it. *Lord* Braybrook. A title and Goodall had been bowing and scraping his way out backwards. Where was she? Oh, yes. His arrogant lordship, telling her what to do, taking the beastly uncomfortable settle instead of the wingchair, taking the tray and moving the tea table for her—lighting a fire she could not afford, although if she was leaving on Thursday there was enough fuel to last.

At least she was warm now. It had been a kindness on his part. Of course some men were considerate, but she must not linger over it as though he had done it for *her*.

Drat him! Cutting up her peace, arranging her life to suit his own convenience, dismissing her concerns about propriety in the most *cavalier* way, and—

Well, he did come around in the end…

Only because he had to, or you wouldn't have accepted the position!

Which begged the question: why—despite his desire to have her give Miss Trentham's thoughts a more proper direction—did he still persist in thinking her a proper companion for his stepmother and younger siblings?

She had flown at him like a hellcat, been as rude as she knew how and argued with him when he showed a wholly honourable concern for her comfort and welfare on the journey to Hereford.

Why hadn't he simply retracted his offer of employment and walked out?

And why was she even bothered about it? Why not do as he suggested and accept his money without argument? In a ladylike way, of course.

The seething, rebellious part of her mind informed her that she was going to have trouble accepting any of his lordship's dictatorial pronouncements without a great deal of argument. Ladylike or otherwise.

In the meantime, due to his lordship's rearrangement of her life, she had not enough time for everything. Certainly there was no time for pondering the odd feeling that she had just made the most momentous decision of her life. Or had it made for her. As for the ridiculous notion that Lord Braybrook was somehow dangerous—nonsense! Oh, she had no doubt that to some women he might be dangerous, but she had heard the scorn in his voice.

Believe me, I've no designs on your virtue.

That stung a little, but when all was said and done,

she *was* a dowd. Perhaps a little more so than was necessary, but that was all to the good if it deflected the attention of men such as Lord Braybrook.

There had been that look, though, the feeling that he truly saw *her*, Christy, not merely Miss Daventry… She shut off the thought. Only a fool needed a lesson twice. The last thing she wanted was for him to notice her at all. Men seemed to have difficulty in comprehending when *no* was short for *no, I don't want to go to bed with you* rather than *no, you aren't offering enough.*

Crossly she pushed away from the door. She would not be sorry to leave this house. Once it had been happy enough, when Mama had been alive. But now it was filled with memories of nursing her dying mother. One must go on. And apparently, come Thursday, that was precisely what she would be doing.

As for Harry—was he mad? How could he imagine himself a suitable match for the Honourable Miss Trentham? A viscount's sister, no less! The least investigation… She knew the answer of course: his Grace, the Duke of Alcaston. The Duke's patronage had given Harry ideas dizzyingly far above his station.

Why could Lord Braybrook not behave like any normal man, forbid the match and see that the importunate suitor was denied the house? She had that answer as well; he thought it might drive his sister into revolt, and if his sister was as used to getting her own way as he was, then he had a point.

Unless… There was one way in which she might ensure Lord Braybrook could take that action without his sister uttering a word of protest. A single letter to his lordship would suffice. She looked at the bureau bookcase, hesitating.

Writing that letter would work, but at the cost of an appalling betrayal. Telling tales under a self-righteous cloak. And it was important for Harry to acknowledge the reality of his situation. Somehow she had to persuade him that his course of action was wrong. She needed to see him. Harry would ignore her letters to him. She must see him, try to persuade him of the wrongness of his intention to ensnare Miss Trentham or any other woman without telling her family the truth.

It might even ruin Harry if the truth were generally known. She wasn't sure, but she could not take that risk. As a last resort she might have to tell the truth, but it would drive a wedge between them and she had no other family. None that she cared to acknowledge.

And there was another consideration—the money Lord Braybrook offered. She did have some money. Enough to manage if she were very careful, and prices didn't rise. But there was little left over to hoard against illness or chilly old age. With this position, she could add to her meagre nest egg. Even if it were for a year or less, she would earn far more than she could in any other position, and she would save her keep as well.

She could pack up her books and take them with her. Braybrook had said his man of business would help; very well, she would ask him to sell the furniture bequeathed to her by Mama. It might not fetch very much, but every penny helped, and she was *damned* if she'd leave it for Goodall to sell on Harry's behalf!

Accepting Lord Braybrook's offer was the sensible thing to do. As long as she remembered her place. Separate. Apart. If only she could succeed in teaching Harry that lesson.

There was no real choice. She must go into Herefordshire and make Harry see the truth—that a greater gulf than mere money lay between the Daventrys and the Trenthams. If she failed, then, in the last resort, she must tell Lord Braybrook the truth herself.

Despite the fire warming the room, she shivered, imagining his disdain, the brilliant eyes turned icy. She stiffened her spine. It didn't matter. There was no question of her being upset by his contempt.

That sort of thing only hurt if one committed the folly of allowing someone too close. A warning voice suggested that in breaching her reserve and triggering her temper, Lord Braybrook had already stepped too close. She must ensure he never did so again.

Chapter Three

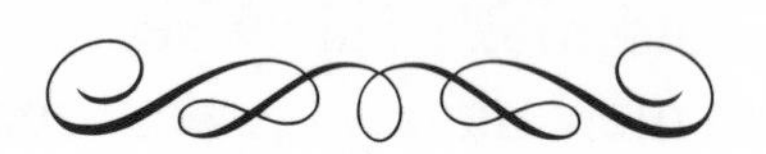

Three days later an elegant equipage pulled up St Michael's Hill to the Chapel of the Three Kings. Julian sat back against the squabs, still not quite able to believe what he had set in motion. On the seat opposite sat his valet, Parkes, stiff with disapproval, apparently determined to remain so for the entire journey. The news that he was required to sit inside, rather than on the box hobnobbing with his crony the coachman, had been ill received.

Not a chaperon precisely, thought Julian. For a young lady of quality, Parkes would be thoroughly inadequate. For the governess, however, his presence would dampen gossip. Besides which, Julian still felt uneasy about Miss Daventry. Something had sparked between them. Something dangerous, unpredictable. He found himself thinking about her at odd moments, smiling slightly at her stubborn independence.

He should have put her in her place, reminded her of the abyss between them. But that had been impossible with her cool façade shattered. They had spoken as equals. That must never happen again. No matter how much it piqued his interest.

She was just a woman with a temper that she had learned to control. Nothing more. There was no mystery behind the prim glasses that would not upon closer acquaintance fade to mundanity. In the meantime, it was safer to have Parkes, rigid and disapproving, on the opposite seat beside Miss Daventry. If nothing else, it would serve to remind her of the gulf between master and servant.

The carriage drew up outside the Chapel. Glancing out, he discovered Miss Daventry had foiled his plan to assist with her baggage. She was seated on one of a pair of trunks and accompanied by a female of indeterminate age and generous proportions. Julian wondered how the devil the pair of them had got the trunks up the street.

Miss Daventry had stood up. 'Goodbye, Sukey. Thank you for your help. I wish you would let me—'

'Oh, go on with you!' said the woman. She shot a suspicious glance towards the carriage and lowered her voice to the sort of whisper that could cut through an artillery engagement. 'Now you're quite sure all's safe? Can't trust these lords. Why, only t'other day—'

She broke off as Julian stepped out of the coach. Miss Daventry, he was pleased to note, flushed.

'I'm sure it will be all right, Sukey,' she said, darting a glance at Julian. 'Good morning, my lord.'

'Good morning, ma'am. My valet is within the coach,' said Julian, with all the air of a man setting a hungry cat loose in a flock of very plump pigeons. 'I do hope that allays any fears your friend has.'

The woman's eyes narrowed as she stepped forwards. 'Aye, I dare say it might. *If* so be as he ain't in your lordship's pocket, in a manner of speaking. If you *are* a lordship an' not some havey-cavey rascal!' She set her hands on her hips. 'I ain't looked after Miss Christy this long for her to be cozened by some flash-talkin' rogue! Why, only t'other day a chap persuaded a young lady into his carriage and had his wicked way with her. Right there in the carriage! An' her thinkin' it was all right an' tight, just acos he had another lady with him. Lady, hah! Madam, more like!'

'Ma'am, I assure you that I have no designs upon Miss Daventry's person,' he said with commendable gravity. 'Her brother is known to me and my only object is to convey her to her new position as my stepmother's companion.'

Sukey snorted. 'Easy said!'

'Sukey,' said Miss Daventry, 'I am sure it's all right. Truly.'

Clearly unconvinced, Sukey stalked to the coach and peered in, subjecting the scandalised Parkes to a close inspection. She stepped back, clearing her throat. 'I dare say it's all right.' She looked sternly at Miss Daventry. 'But you write soon's you arrive. Vicar'll read it to me, like he said. And keep writing so's we know.'

'Sukey—!' Miss Daventry appeared completely discomposed.

The older woman scowled. 'Can't be too careful, Miss Christy. You do like we said an' write!'

'Yes, Sukey,' said Miss Daventry meekly.

Julian blinked. There was someone in this world to whom Miss Daventry exhibited meekness?

'This is everything, Miss Daventry?' he asked, signalling to the groom to jump down.

She looked rather self-conscious. 'Yes. But one of the trunks is only books, so if there is not room—'

'There is enough room,' he told her.

The groom hefted one trunk into the boot along with the valise. The other trunk was strapped on the back.

Sukey came forwards and enveloped Miss Daventry in a hug. To Julian's amazement the hug was returned, fiercely.

Finally Sukey stepped back, wiping her eyes. 'Well, I'm sure I hope it'll all be as you say. You be a good girl. Your mam 'ud be real proud of you. You take care, Miss Christy.'

'I will. You have the keys safe?'

'Aye. I'll give 'em to that agent fellow. Off you go, then.'

Ignoring Julian's outstretched hand, Miss Daventry stepped into the coach and settled herself beside the valet.

Julian found himself facing judge and jury. He held out his hand. 'Goodbye, Sukey. You may rest assured that Miss Daventry is safe.'

Sukey accepted the proffered hand, after first wiping her own upon her skirt. 'I dare say. Miss Christy—

Miss Daventry—she's a lady. Just you remember that, my lord. I'm sure I hope there's no offence.'

'None at all,' Julian assured her.

He stepped into the coach and sat opposite Miss Daventry. They moved off and Miss Daventry leaned out of the window, waving until they turned the corner and she sat back in her seat. Her mouth was firmly set, her expression unmoved. Yet something glimmered, trapped between her cheek and the glass of her spectacles. Julian watched, wondering if her emotions might get the better of her, but Miss Daventry's formidable self-control prevailed.

Relieved she was not about to burst into tears, he performed the introductions. 'My valet, Parkes, Miss Daventry. Parkes, this is Miss Daventry, who is to be companion to her ladyship and also assist as governess at times.'

Miss Daventry smiled. 'How do you do, Parkes?'

'Very well, thank you, miss.' And Parkes relapsed into the proper silence he considered appropriate when circumstances dictated that he should intrude upon his betters.

Seated in his corner of the carriage, Julian picked up his book and began to read. There was no point in dwelling on the fierce loyalty Miss Daventry had inspired in her servant. Nor her obvious emotion at Sukey's protectiveness. Of course Miss Daventry had feelings. Nothing surprising nor interesting in that. Her feelings were her own business. He had not the least reason to feel shaken by that solitary tear.

On the other side of the carriage Christy watched as his lordship disappeared into the book. She had not bothered to have a book to hand. If she dared to read in a carriage, the results would be embarrassing. Especially facing backwards.

She steeled herself to the prospect of a boring journey. There was no possibility of conversation with the elderly, dapper little valet. He had all the hallmarks of a long-standing family retainer. He would not dream of chattering on in the presence of his master, even if Christy herself did not fall into that limbo reserved for governesses and companions. She knew from experience that her life would be lived in isolation, neither truly a member of the family, nor part of the servants' hall. Neither above stairs, nor below. An odd thought came to her of generation after generation of ghostly governesses and companions, doomed to a grey existence on the half-landings. Just as well, too. It made her preferred reserve far easier to maintain.

Her stomach churned slightly, but she breathed deeply and otherwise ignored it. It was partly due to tiredness. With all the work of packing up the house, she had scarcely had more than five hours sleep a night, and last night she had barely slept at all. She never could sleep properly the night before a journey, for dreaming that the coach had gone without her and she was running after it, crying out for it to wait, not to abandon her…

She wondered if she dared lower the window and lean out. No. It would be presumptuous, and she would become sadly rumpled and dusty. Not at all ladylike. She set herself to endure, leaning back and closing her eyes.

Leaving Gloucester midway through the second day, Julian knew Miss Daventry was not a good traveller. He had without comment lowered all the windows. Not that she complained, or asked for any halts. But he could imagine no other explanation for the white, set look about her mouth, or that when they stopped, she would accept nothing beyond weak, black tea. She hadn't eaten a great deal of dinner or breakfast either.

He knew the signs from personal experience, only he had outgrown the tendency. There was little he could do about it, he thought, watching her. She was pale, and her eyes were closed, a faint frown between her brows. Oh, hell! 'Miss Daventry?'

'My lord?' The eyes opened. He blinked, still not used to their effect. The shadows beneath them were darker today than yesterday. It shouldn't bother him. *Noblesse oblige*, he assured himself. Nothing personal.

'Miss Daventry, perhaps you might change seats with me?'

Somehow she sat a little straighter. 'I am very well here, my lord. Thank you.'

He was not supposed to feel admiration—she was the governess-companion, for heavens' sake! His voice devoid of expression, he said, 'I think "well" is the last word that applies to you at this moment. Certainly not "very well". Come, exchange places with me.'

Determined to expunge any misleading suggestion of personal feeling, he added, 'I cannot sit here any longer feeling guilty.'

Blushing, she complied, scrambling across past him.

'Thank you, my lord,' she said, still slightly pink.

He inclined his head. 'You are welcome, Miss Daventry.' Detached. Bored, even. 'Of course, should it be necessary, you will request a halt, will you not?'

She squared her shoulders. 'That will not be necessary, my lord. I should not wish to delay us.'

He raised his brows. 'I assure you, Miss Daventry, a brief halt will be a great deal more preferable than the alternative—won't it, Parkes?'

The valet, thus appealed to, permitted himself a brief smile. 'Indeed, sir. I've not forgotten how often you used to ask to be let down.'

Julian laughed at Miss Daventry's look of patent disbelief. 'Perfectly true, Miss Daventry. But I became accustomed eventually.'

A small smile flickered, and a dimple sprang to life. 'I fear I did not travel enough as a child then. I remained staidly in Bath.'

'Bath? I understood from your brother that your home had always been in Bristol.' Where the devil had that dimple come from?

Miss Daventry's pale cheeks pinkened again and the dimple vanished. 'Oh. Harry was very small when Mama moved to Bristol. And I went to school in Bath when I was ten. When I was older I became a junior assistant mistress.'

She subsided into silence, turning her head to watch the passing scenery.

Julian returned to his book, glancing up from time to time to check on Miss Daventry. He told himself that he was not, most definitely *not*, looking for that dimple. He had seen dimples before. But, really, for a moment there, the staid Miss Daventry had looked almost pretty. Spectacles and all. And her mouth was not in the least prim when she smiled. It was soft, inviting…

There was something about her. Something that made him want to look again… The eyes. That was all. Once he became accustomed to them, she would have no interest for him whatsoever. In the meantime she was suffering from carriage sickness and it behoved him to care for her. No more. No less.

Reminding himself of that, Julian reburied himself in his book, only glancing over the top every ten pages or so.

Aware of his occasional scrutiny, Christy tried to ignore it, repressing an urge to peep under her lashes. Her heart thudded uncomfortably; the result, she assured herself, of having so nearly revealed too much. Her pounding heart had nothing to do with those brilliant eyes that seemed to perceive more than they ought. It wasn't as if he cared about her, Christy Daventry. She was in his charge, therefore he owed it to himself to make sure she was comfortable. If she were not, it was a reflection on himself. He was being kind to her in the same way he would care for any other servant. Or his dog or horse. Admirable, but nothing to make her heart beat faster. *Noblesse oblige.* That or he was ensuring she wasn't sick in his beautifully appointed carriage.

But the bright glance of his blue eyes was hard to ignore. She was infuriated to find herself drifting into a daydream where his lordship's remarkable eyes were focused on her. And not because he was concerned she might be sick all over his highly polished boots.

Ridiculous! She knew nothing of him. Except that he was thoughtful enough to find a companion for his stepmother, kind enough to change seats with the carriage-sick companion, and sensible enough not to drive his sister into revolt. Heavens! She was rapidly making him out to be a paragon.

Lord Braybrook was no paragon. The lazy twinkle in his eyes, combined with unconscious arrogance, suggested he was the sort of man a sensible woman steered well clear of. Assuming he had not already informed the sensible woman that he had no designs on *her* virtue, as though the idea were unthinkable. And a very good thing too. Christy had a sneaking suspicion that when his lordship did focus his attention on a female, good sense might come under heavy fire.

Oh, nonsense. He was probably horrid on closer acquaintance, the sort of man who kicked puppies. Yes. That was better. No one could like a man who kicked puppies. Or kittens. A pity she was having so much difficulty seeing him in the role. Much easier to see those lean fingers cradling a small creature…rocking it.

She smothered a yawn. Such a warm day…rocking… like a cradle. No, that was the coach. It was beautifully sprung and she felt much better now, facing forwards. Far less disconcerting to have the breeze from the open window in her face and see the world spinning towards her and away, rather than just spinning away in front of her…rocking, rocking, rocking…

Later, some time later, she was vaguely aware of being eased down to the seat, gentle hands removing her bonnet and spectacles, tucking a rug around her, a light touch feathering over her cheek…a dream, a memory, nothing more. Christy slept, cradled in dreams.

She awoke in near darkness to a touch on her shoulder and a deep voice saying, 'We are nearly there, Miss Daventry.'

Dazed, she sat up. Strong hands caught her as the coach swung around a turn. Coach? Where…? Blinking sleep away, she clutched at the strap hanging down, and the hands released her. Some of her confusion ebbed. This was not Bristol. She was in a coach, with Lord Braybrook and his valet. Why had she been lying down with a rug tucked over her? And where were her glasses? Everything was blurred.

Worried, she felt along the seat. They must have fallen off while she slept. And how dreadful that she had dozed off in front of Lord Braybrook and been shameless enough to lie down! And her spectacles were probably broken if they had fallen to the floor.

'Miss Daventry—is something amiss?'

She flushed. 'My spectacles must have fallen off. I can't see without them.'

'Of course.'

He reached into his pocket and drew out a small object, offering it to her. Confused, she reached for it and he placed it in her hand. Immediately her fingers recognised her spectacles, wrapped in a handkerchief.

'I thought they were safer in my pocket,' said his lordship.

Her fingers trembled slightly as she unfolded the handkerchief, shaken by a memory of gentle hands making her comfortable. Had her dream not been a dream? Had he laid her down on the seat and removed her spectacles and bonnet? And tucked the rug over her? She swallowed. He must have. But the caressing touch on her cheek had certainly been a dream. Hadn't it?

'Thank you, my lord,' she said, putting the spectacles on. The darkening world came back into focus. 'You are most kind.' She schooled her voice to polite indifference. His *noblesse oblige* again. If she remembered that, good sense would prevail. Not the foolish dream of tenderness. She handed him the handkerchief.

He pocketed it. 'Not at all, Miss Daventry. We shall be at the house in a few moments. Your bonnet is on the seat.'

His cool tones revived her wilting common sense. She retrieved the bonnet, and attempted to tidy herself, securing stray tendrils of hair with hairpins before replacing the bonnet. She thought that she must be sadly rumpled after the day's journey and sleeping in the carriage, but there was little she could do about it.

Julian dragged his gaze away from her to look out of

the window. He could see the house now, lights glimmering in the dusk, its bulk dark against the deepening sky. Home. Concentrate on that. Not the impossible softness of her cheek under his fingers as he removed the bonnet and spectacles, not the jolt to his gut as he finally saw the colour of her hair, a rich tawny brown, rigidly scraped back and confined with a battalion of pins. Nor the queer protective sensation he had felt watching her sleep, her mouth relaxed and soft. Definitely not the odd pang he had felt when she awoke and sat up, clothes and hair askew, and that vulnerable sleepy look in her eyes.

She was in his employ, a servant to all intents and purposes. He had no business feeling anything for her beyond a sense of general responsibility. Indeed, to judge by her cool response to him, that was precisely what she expected and preferred.

She would neither expect nor wish him to be thinking about a little girl left at school in Bath. It was none of his concern. It should not come near him, let alone touch him. Ridiculous to feel sympathy for that long-ago little girl. He had gone to school himself at eight…memories poured back. His confusion at his first return for the holidays to find his mother gone. The servants' evasions of his questions. His father's bitterness and refusal to explain and the slow realisation that there was to be something scandalous, and expensive, called a 'divorce'. That he probably wouldn't see his mother again. And he hadn't. After the divorce she had married her lover and lived on the Continent, dying when he was fifteen. By then he had understood. His father's attitude had been quite clear when he married Serena as a matter of convenience to breed a couple of back-up heirs. Better to marry for reasons less likely to sour on one than love—property, connections and duty. One needed to like and respect one's spouse. Anything more was damned dangerous, and passion and desire were best served by taking a discreet mistress.

Still, he remembered the child's sense of abandonment and loss. Worse for a girl, of course. Boys were better able to cope with such things. Look at Davy, longing for the day he went to school. Not until he was ten, though. Serena had insisted and, since he knew his father had agreed, that was that. Besides which, he liked having Davy about the place. All of them, in fact.

Christy sat up straighter as they bowled up the avenue, the horses finding a second wind so close to their stable. They rattled over what appeared to be a stone bridge, under an arch into a narrow passageway and out into what must once have been a castle forecourt. Obviously someone had been watching for them, because as they drew up at the front door several people and a dog raced down the steps.

To Christy's startled eyes Lord Braybrook appeared to be surrounded by a mob as he stepped out of the coach into the light of the carriage lamps. She had the oddest sensation that thick glass reared up, allowing her to see, but slicing her apart from the bright circle.

'Did you bring us anything?'

'Why didn't you come back sooner? You *said* you would be back yesterday!'

Lord Braybrook fended off the barking black-and-tan setter, swung a small boy up into his arms and said, 'For heaven's sake, be still, you three! Get down, Juno. Anyone would think I'd been away for a month! How are you, Davy? Have you behaved yourself?'

'Yes.' The small boy nodded vigorously.

'Liar!' said an older boy of fifteen or so. 'He's been a little pest, Julian. He glued himself to the front steps last night so he wouldn't have to go to bed until you came home! The bottom of his nankeens is still there!'

'Yes,' chimed in the girl. 'And Mama made *us* pull him out of them when they wouldn't unstick! She said it was our fault he got the glue because we were supposed to be minding him!'

In the dusk, Christy had the distinct impression that his lordship was trying to preserve a straight face. Laughter bubbled up inside her.

'Davy?' His lordship's voice was mild enough, but something about it hinted at tempered steel.

'Well, you *said* you'd be back!' muttered the little boy.

'Hmm. I was delayed. Next time go to bed when you're told.' A stern voice, one to be obeyed, but affectionate. Caring.

'Oh, very well. That's what Mr Havergal said. *Did* you bring us something?'

'Who is Mr Havergal?' asked his lordship.

Davy shrugged. 'Just a friend of Mama's. Don't you

know him? He calls quite often.' He tugged on his brother's lapel. 'Did you bring us anything?'

'No. I brought your mama something instead.'

'Mama?' came the chorus from three throats.

Lord Braybrook put the little boy down, patted the dog, an elegant bitch, and turned back to the coach. 'Permit me to assist you down, Miss Daventry.'

Christy stood up, and discovered herself to be appallingly cramped from the long journey, her legs barely able to hold her. Carefully she moved to the open door.

A strong hand gripped her elbow. Heat shot through her. Shocked, she looked up.

The firm lips curved a little, not unsympathetically.

'I dare say you are a trifle stiff, Miss Daventry. I am myself.'

Christy took leave to doubt that. The wretched man had leapt down as lightly as a stag, without any hint of stiffness.

'I…thank you, my lord.' Tingling heat still spread through her. Folly! She was tired. Imagining things. She was chilled and his hand was warm.

He assisted her down from the carriage, steadying her as she stumbled a little.

'This is Miss Daventry,' he said. 'Miss Daventry, these are my youngest sister, Emma, and my brothers, Matthew and Davy.'

Christy summoned a smile, despite her tiredness. 'Good evening, Emma, Matthew, Davy.' The dog came and sniffed at her and she bent to fondle the silky ears.

'And Juno,' said his lordship. The dog returned to him, tail waving.

'Good evening, Miss Daventry,' said Emma politely.

'Good evening, ma'am,' said Matthew, bowing slightly.

Davy scowled. 'Did you make Julian late?'

Now she thought about it, she probably had. 'I am afraid so, Davy,' she admitted. 'His lordship kindly gave me an extra day to ready myself before leaving Bristol.'

Davy looked unimpressed. 'Mama was cross with me because of my nankeens,' he informed her. 'I had bread and butter for my supper, and no cake.'

Lord Braybrook stifled an odd sound and leant down to give his small brother a not unkindly swat on the behind. 'Don't blame Miss Daventry for your misdoings, scamp. Now, off with you. It's long past your bedtime.'

Lord Braybrook kept his hand close to Christy's elbow as they went up the steps into the mellow lighted hall, closely attended by Juno, who seemed to feel she must remain as close as possible to her restored master.

A butler bowed. 'Welcome home, my lord.'

'Good evening, Hallam,' said Lord Braybrook. The butler glanced at Christy but his well-trained visage betrayed not the least surprise or curiosity.

She stared about her. The hall was enormous. She had the impression of great age, a high-vaulted ceiling and pinky-brown weathered stone. A branching stone staircase at the back led up to a gallery

'Welcome to Amberley, Miss Daventry,' said Lord Braybrook.

Her response was lost in a startled exclamation from the back of the hall.

'Good heavens! Who is this, Julian?'

Two people were there. One a tall, slender young lady who must, Christy surmised, be Miss Trentham. Black curls, loosely arranged and confined with a pink bandeau, framed a vivid face with the family eyes. The other was an older woman, seated, her legs covered with a shawl, and a large tabby cat in her lap. An instant later, she realised that the chair had wheels—a Bath chair.

The woman was staring at her in amazement. And, she thought, disapproval. Her new employer. Lady Braybrook herself.

'Julian, what have you done?' This in tones of deep suspicion.

His lordship went to her, bent down and kissed her on the cheek. 'I suppose you will think I have been far too precipitate and should have discussed it with you, but—'

'No doubt!' said Lady Braybrook.

Lord Braybrook smiled. 'This is Miss Daventry, Serena—your new companion.'

If Lady Braybrook had looked puzzled before, she looked positively stunned now. Her jaw dropped and she said, 'But I told you! I don't want a companion! Even if I did, I would very much prefer to choose my own!'

Christy blinked. She had known he was autocratic—arrogant, even. Her lips set. Yes, she had definitely known he was arrogant! But this! He had completely bypassed his stepmother's views on the subject!

Anger, and hot embarrassment, overcame the little voice warning her that she'd better bite her tongue.

She lifted her chin and said in the sweetest tones she could muster, 'Thank you, my lord, for a most interesting, if wasted, journey. Perhaps next time you might have the goodness to take account of the views of *all* the persons involved before embroiling anyone else in your schemes. I do trust that I may be offered a bedchamber for the night rather than trudging back immediately!'

Chapter Four

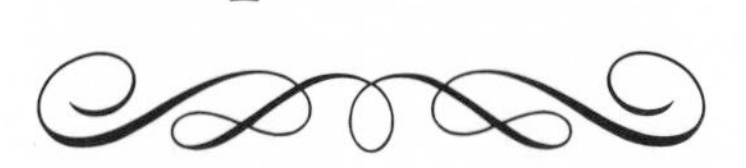

Lady Braybrook's eyebrows nearly disappeared into her elegant cap, but Christy didn't care. To hell with what anyone thought of her. She was tired after two days' travel, and now she had the journey back. She probably wouldn't even have time to see Harry before being bundled off and she would have to dig into her slender savings to stay at an inn while she found lodgings.

Then, 'Oh, well done, dear! Julian, for heaven's sake, stop standing there gaping and see that Miss… Daventry, did you say?'—a swift glance at Miss Trentham— 'Yes, have Miss Daventry's baggage taken up. She may have the guest chamber along from me. That will do very well.'

She held out her hand, saying, 'You must be famished, Miss Daventry, so do not worry about changing.' Bemused, Christy came forwards to accept the proffered hand.

'Lissy dear, show Miss Daventry where she may

wash her face and hands. Then bring her to the small dining parlour.'

Christy permitted herself to be led away by Miss Trentham and heard Lady Braybrook say in tones of steely determination, 'In the meantime, Julian, shall we discuss this privately? Matt—take Davy upstairs and see that he goes to bed.'

Miss Trentham smiled at Christy in a very friendly way as she led her out of the hall and asked, 'Are you really Miss Daventry? What a coincidence! I...*we* know a Mr Daventry. He...he is a most particular friend.' She blushed prettily.

'No coincidence at all,' said Christy. 'Harry is my brother. Lord Braybrook sought me out intentionally. Since he was under the erroneous impression that your mother required a companion, he thought of me.'

Miss Trentham's blue, blue eyes opened wide. 'But, surely *you* need not work?'

There was no scorn in her voice, only shock.

First trick to his lordship, thought Christy, following Miss Trentham down a passage. Probably the last one though, given Lady Braybrook's reaction to his high-handed efforts. She elaborated, feeling she might as well partially earn the quarter's wages that Lord Braybrook would undoubtedly insist she accept. 'But of course, Miss Trentham. Harry must make his own way in the world and I cannot be a burden on him.' Miss Trentham looked a little self-conscious, and Christy went on, 'At this stage of his career he has quite enough to do to support himself. Our—' She caught herself and went on, 'His godfather is generous, but it does not extend to supporting a sister.'

'Oh. I…I see.' The dazed tone suggested that Miss Trentham was gaining a whole new view of matters beyond Harry's good looks and charm. 'Here we are,' she said, opening a door. 'This is the garden room. Mama insists the boys come inside through this room and there are always soap and water here.'

Removing her bonnet to lave her face and hands, Christy thought Lady Braybrook sounded extremely practical. Kind, too, and probably a far more pleasant employer than her last. Christy sighed as she dried her face. She wouldn't be getting much of a reference out of this one either.

To Whom It May Concern:

Miss Daventry arrived to be my companion on Friday evening. After raking down my stepson, she returned to Bristol on Saturday morning.

Yours etc., etc.

As a reference, it had limitations, she acknowledged, re-pinning her hair. And as a position, this must be a record: dismissed before she had begun. Her hair as neat as she could make it, she turned back to Miss Trentham.

'Are you ready?' asked the young woman. 'It will be famous having you here, you know. Leave your bonnet. One of the maids will take it up to your bedchamber.'

Christy left the bonnet and followed Miss Trentham from the room. 'Ah, Miss Trentham, I believe Lady

Braybrook said that she did not want a companion. I dare say I shall be dispatched back to Bristol tomorrow.'

Leading the way along the corridor, Miss Trentham shook her head so the black curls bounced. 'Oh, pooh! Of course you won't. That is what is so particularly annoying about Julian—he persuades people to do precisely as he says! Even Mama. And he is always so...so insufferably certain that he knows what is best. Mama says he means well, but if you were to ask me, he's a tyrant!'

'Explain, if you please, Julian.' There was a distinct bite in Serena's voice.

Julian had wheeled her into a small parlour off the hall. 'A ploy,' he said, closing the door and turning to face her. 'The companion part is a blind. She's actually here to keep Lissy in order.' Bringing up a chair for himself, he explained his reasoning.

Serena's eyebrows rose. She was silent for a moment, thinking it over, and he waited.

'I see,' she said eventually. And he had the sneaking suspicion that she did see. Every single machination anyway. He hoped to hell she couldn't see the inexplicable attraction Miss Daventry held for him. Not that it mattered, because he wasn't going to do anything about it.

'I suppose she's dowdy enough for a companion-governess,' said Serena thoughtfully.

Dowdy? 'Nothing of the sort,' he said stiffly. 'She is still in mourning for her mother, Serena!'

Amusement crept around Serena's eyes and mouth.

'Oh,' she said. 'I see. Well, I dare say some of my own mourning garb can be altered to fit her. It will certainly give Lissy pause for thought.'

'She stays, then?' What the hell was that jolt of relief in his midriff?

Serena blinked. 'Oh, I think so, dear. I'm sure she will suit admirably. She's not at all mealy-mouthed, is she?'

'No.' Along with meek, that was the last adjective he'd use to describe Miss Christiana Daventry.

Christy tried not to let her shock show. Lit with more candles than she would have used in a year, the small dining parlour was somewhat larger than the entire ground floor of the Christmas Steps house. And, since these were wax candles, without the reek of tallow.

'Ah, here they are.' Lady Braybrook was already seated at a circular table with his lordship and Matthew, who both rose politely.

'Come and sit beside me, Miss Daventry,' said Lady Braybrook. 'I apologise for my lack of tact earlier. You must have thought yourself in a perfect madhouse! Unfortunately Braybrook did not see fit to apprise me of his intentions.' She glared at her stepson, who had strolled around the table to pull out a chair for Christy.

Christy managed to look demure and murmured her thanks as she seated herself. There was no faulting his lordship's manners, even if his high-handed assurance left a great deal to be desired.

'I beg your pardon, Serena,' said Lord Braybrook, sitting down again.

Christy doubted the sincerity of his lordship's contrition. And she observed that, far from kicking puppies, his lordship was obviously very fond of dogs. The setter, Juno, lay as close as possible to her master's chair, chin resting on a stretcher.

'Mama,' said Miss Trentham, 'Miss Daventry is Mr Daventry's sister!' Her eyes sparkled. 'Should I send him a note to say she is here?'

Christy caught Lord Braybrook's eye, and said, 'How kind, Miss Trentham. On accepting his lordship's offer, I took the liberty of writing to Harry myself.' Spurred on by malice aforethought, she added, 'I would be most grateful if you were to inform him that I have returned to Bristol and will write again soon.'

An odd choking sound came from Lady Braybrook. Christy turned quickly and her ladyship patted her lips with her napkin. Laughing grey eyes met hers.

'No, no, Miss Daventry. That will not be necessary. Now Braybrook has explained *all* the particulars, I am delighted to have you here.' She glanced at her daughter. 'Yes, Lissy, Julian explained the connection. A kind thought to assist Miss Daventry in this way. And so pleasant for me.'

Miss Trentham brightened. 'Oh, famous! You see, Miss Daventry—I told you Julian would talk Mama around. I'm sure Mr Daventry will come to see you as soon as may be.'

Christy had not the least doubt of that. His lordship was one of those annoying persons who always contrived to achieve their ends.

Lord Braybrook met her gaze blandly. 'Naturally, ma'am, when he does so, you must take a morning or afternoon off to spend with him. I dare say you have not met for some time.'

'No,' said Christy. 'We have not.' *Not since Mama's funeral.*

It had rained unrelentingly. And they had stood there, soaked to the skin, wondering if *he* would come. If he would have the decency…well, *she* had wondered. Harry had thought it unlikely. Indeed, unnecessary.

Don't be a peagoose, Christy. I dare say he has much to occupy him.

She would never forgive Alcaston for that. Never. Not to come to the funeral. Nor send so much as a wreath. Discretion, of course. That had been his reason for not attending little Sarah's funeral all those years ago…but she had foolishly thought that he would attend Mama's funeral. She shivered. If anything further had been needed to drive home the necessity of standing alone, that had been it.

'Miss Daventry?'

Horrified, she realised that his lordship was speaking to her and that she had been staring into space.

The bright eyes were focused on her, faintly frowning.

'I beg your pardon, my lord. I was woolgathering.'

Heat pricked behind her eyes, but she kept her voice steady. He was still watching her, with eyes that peeled away too many defences.

'I fancy Miss Daventry is very tired, Julian,' said

Lady Braybrook. 'I'm sorry, my dear. Your room will be prepared by the time you have finished your supper and you may go to bed. We need not arrange anything tonight. Do have some chicken soup. And, Lissy, please pass the rolls to Miss Daventry.'

As she helped herself to the soup and accepted a roll, Christy wondered what sort of establishment she had landed in. A greater contrast with her previous live-in situation could not be imagined. A sense of dislocation niggled at her. Rather than treating the governess-companion as a lesser being, Lady Braybrook treated her as if she were a favoured guest. If she were not on her guard, she would forget her place. Never before had that been a problem. Never before had she imagined herself belonging. Not caught forever on the half-landing. She *must* remember that, all kindness aside, Lady Braybrook was her mistress.

And Lord Braybrook her master?

She gritted her teeth. She was a dependant. Not their equal. If she could not remember that, how could she convince Harry?

Christy spent the next morning unpacking, or rather she spent twenty minutes unpacking, and the rest considering how best to fit into the household. Lady Braybrook, she discovered, did not usually leave her bedchamber until late morning, when a footman carried her down to the drawing room. This was explained by Grigson, an unsmiling female whose fashionable clothes proclaimed her Lady Braybrook's dresser, when she came to tell Christy that her ladyship awaited her in the drawing room.

Lady Braybrook was seated by a sunny window, the tabby cat enthroned on her lap. 'Thank you, Grigson. That will be all. Good morning, Miss Daventry. You slept well? You look much better this morning. Braybrook mentioned that you were uncomfortable in the carriage.'

Christy curtsied. 'Thank you, ma'am. I slept very well. His lordship should not have concerned himself.'

'Hmm. Well, I am glad you are feeling better. Do come and sit down and we can discuss your duties. You really only have Davy and Emma. Matthew is home from school, so you need not worry about him. Lissy has her French and Italian conversation and her music to practise. And she should do some sketching. You are able to help her with those?'

'Of course, ma'am.'

'Excellent.' Lady Braybrook beamed. 'With Matt on holiday, Emma and Davy need not have many lessons. Emma must practise her music and Davy must continue his reading, French and a little arithmetic, but until Matthew goes back, there is little point in more. Davy would play you up dreadfully, I dare say!'

'I assure you, he would not get away with it,' said Christy. And mentally kicked herself. Adoring mamas did not commonly like to know their high-spirited darlings needed discipline.

'Excellent,' said Lady Braybrook. 'From the way you gave Braybrook his own last night, I didn't imagine you would have any difficulty with Davy.'

Christy blinked.

The cat rose, stretching, all elegant muscle and sinew. Lady Braybrook made no effort to hold it, and it leapt down, stalking towards Christy.

She eyed it sideways, wondering if her pet's desertion would offend Lady Braybrook. Unblinking emerald eyes stared back.

'Ma'am, if you do not dislike it, I have given some thought to my role here—' She broke off as the cat sprang into her lap. Oh, drat! She could hardly tip the creature off and it had been so long since she had been able to have a cat.

Lady Braybrook smiled over her embroidery, as the needle continued to flash. 'My dear Miss Daventry, why should I dislike it?' A faint twinkle appeared in her eyes. 'After all, you have had more time to become used to the idea than I!'

Christy blushed, and petted the cat, who had settled down purring.

Lady Braybrook laughed. 'Oh, don't feel embarrassed. Believe me, I know how autocratic Braybrook can be when he is arranging everything for one's good. Maddening, is he not? Now, tell me: what were you thinking?'

'Well,' said Christy, 'I noticed this morning that you did not come down until quite late and—'

She broke off at Lady Braybrook's wry smile.

'These silly legs,' she explained. 'I take my bath in the morning, and of course it does take a little time. Such a nuisance…'

'Ma'am, I did not mean—'

Lady Braybrook chuckled. 'Of course not. Tell me what you have in mind.'

'I wondered if I taught the younger children in the morning, before you came down, if that would work?'

'An excellent idea,' said Lady Braybrook. 'Then I shall steal you for the rest of the day. Although after lunch you might accompany Lissy and Emma for their walk.'

'Naturally I would be happy to do so,' said Christy, 'but if I am to be your companion—' The amused look on Lady Braybrook's face stopped her.

'You have other duties, Miss Daventry,' pointed out Lady Braybrook.

Christy flushed. 'Lord Braybrook explained, then?'

'Braybrook,' said her ladyship, not mincing words, 'is the most devious and annoying man imaginable. I haven't decided if he is disguising your true purpose from Lissy, by pretending that you are my companion, or disguising your true purpose from *me*, by pretending you are here to help open Lissy's eyes!'

Christy found herself smiling. 'He used both arguments with me. Perhaps I am merely a convenient stone to be hurled at two birds.'

Lady Braybrook's lips twitched. 'He's not completely blind, Miss Daventry. I doubt he believes you to be made of stone.'

To this cryptic remark, Christy said nothing. There was something unsettling about the amusement in Lady Braybrook's voice. The cat rolled in her lap, offering his belly, eyes closed to blissful slits as she obliged and kneaded.

'Another thing, my dear. That striped creature is Tybalt—Tyb. He has an absolute genius for making up to people like Braybrook who loathe cats. If you dislike him, or he makes you sneeze, for heaven's sake, tip him off.'

Again the sense of dislocation swept her. She felt not at all like a dependant. Lady Braybrook was doing everything in her power to make an outsider feel at home. She had even given her one of the best bedchambers.

'Thank you, ma'am, but I love cats.'

Lady Braybrook smiled. 'Excellent. Braybrook, like most men, prefers dogs. I must say I have never worked out why so many women love cats, and men profess to loathe them, but love dogs.'

'That,' said Christy, caught off guard, 'might be because cats are independent, not slavish like dogs. Perhaps we women admire an independence and power few of us will ever know. Your Tybalt may sit in my lap, but he is the one conferring a favour. Cats are rather like aristocrats. They have staff.' Oh, dear. Should she have said that?

A ripple of delighted laughter broke from Lady Braybrook and she laid aside her embroidery. 'Oh, goodness. I'd never thought of that, but you are perfectly right. Although many women love dogs too.'

'And that,' said Christy, wildly aware that the conversation had somehow become far too personal, 'is because we are far more flexible than gentlemen and are capable of loving creatures for quite opposite reasons. Cats for their dignity and independence, and a dog for its loyalty.'

'Good morning, Serena. May I interrupt?'

Christy froze. As a lesson in the perils of unguarded conversation, this would be hard to beat.

Julian had enough sense to pretend he hadn't heard the comment about aristocrats and cats, but he was pleased to see he had been correct in his estimation that Serena and Miss Daventry would suit.

'Of course, dear,' said Serena. 'Miss Daventry was just observing how much you and Tyb have in common.'

Julian took one look at Tyb's current position, sprawled with considerable indelicacy in Miss Daventry's lap. He wasn't sure any reply was safe. His mouth dried at the sight of Miss Daventry's slender fingers kneading that furry abandoned belly. He'd never realised all the advantages of being a cat before.

Miss Daventry, of course, was taking no notice of him whatsoever. Although he thought there was a faint flush of colour in her cheeks.

Piqued, he said, 'Good morning, Miss Daventry, I trust you slept well?'

'Very well, thank you, my lord.'

Prim. Proper. Precisely what she ought to be. Not speaking until spoken to, evincing a becoming respect for her betters. But under the dowdy façade lurked quite a different creature. One who was not Miss Daventry at all. One who argued, and refused to be put in her place. Who sat kneading a cat's belly in a slow hypnotic rhythm that sent heat curling through him. Christy. That was the woman he wanted to know. And he wouldn't mind switching places with Serena's cat either. His body tightened. Hell! If Miss Daventry could read his thoughts, her cheeks would ignite in fury.

'Do you require something, Julian?' asked Serena.

He turned to her, realising that he had been staring at Miss Daventry. Somehow he had to relegate the woman to her proper place.

'No. I merely came in to see that you were well. I will be in the library if you require me. Just send Miss Daventry.'

Serena sent him a very straight look. 'Thank you, Julian. I believe I need not use Miss Daventry like a page boy. We will see you later, then. Good morning.'

Julian removed himself, before he could put his other boot in his mouth. It was the cat's fault. If the blasted creature hadn't been lolling in Miss Daventry's lap so brazenly, he would never have been such a fool.

His agent's reports would banish his wayward thoughts. Anything to rid himself of this fancy to find out what, beyond a sting like a wasp, hid behind Miss Daventry's prim façade.

At luncheon Julian congratulated himself on an excellent choice of companion. Serena seemed brighter, happier than he had seen her in a long while. Not that she was ever self-pitying, but he had thought for some time that she had lost something of her sparkle.

Miss Daventry was worth her hire for that alone.

'I think, this afternoon, Miss Daventry might accompany Lissy and Emma for their walk,' said Serena, sipping coffee. 'She must learn her way about.'

'We intended to ride this afternoon, Mama,' said Lissy. 'Of course, Miss Daventry may still come with us. May she not, Julian?'

He glanced up, trying not to appear at all interested. 'Miss Daventry ride? Yes, if she wishes.' As an invitation it left a great deal to be desired, but his unbecoming interest in Miss Daventry must not be indulged.

Miss Daventry cleared her throat.

Bracing himself for the inevitable, Julian said, 'I collect you have an objection, ma'am. Please state it.'

Miss Daventry's eyes narrowed. 'Not precisely an objection, my lord. An observation.'

Did she *have* to be so damned pedantic?

'Yes?' He didn't like the snappish tone of his voice, but Miss Daventry seemed not to notice.

'I don't ride,' she said.

'Don't ride? But *everybody* rides!' Lissy's disbelief was palpable.

'Not everyone, Miss Trentham,' said Miss Daventry gently. 'I have always lived in a town and we couldn't afford a horse.'

'But Harry, I mean, Mr Daventry rides. He told me he had ridden since he was a child—'

'Enough, Lissy.' Julian was at a loss to explain the revulsion sweeping him. This was precisely why he had hired Miss Daventry—to demonstrate to Lissy the gulf between them. To force her to realise all she would be giving up. Now, hearing Miss Daventry explain the reality of genteel poverty with quiet dignity, he suddenly didn't like it. The opposite side of the equation was laid brutally bare—Miss Daventry's humiliation.

He had never intended to rub *her* nose in the gulf between herself and Lissy. If he were honest, it had not occurred to him. And yet, he could see Lissy thinking, looking at Miss Daventry's dowdy appearance with new eyes, applying it to herself. And Miss Daventry seemed unperturbed.

Why wouldn't she be? She's had years to accustom herself to her station and you are paying her fifty pounds extra for the privilege of having her nose rubbed in it.

Part of him rebelled against this cold logic. Surely, even if only as part of her remuneration, she was entitled to some enjoyment in her life. It might ram the message home to Lissy all the faster, he told himself. Yes, that was it.

He looked across at Serena. She raised her brows, dearly.

'We still have Merlin in the stables,' he said, wondering what the devil was so entertaining.

She smiled. 'Dear Merlin. I dare say he will be glad of a little outing. By all means, dear. I'm sure it will be very beneficial.'

Beneficial for whom? wondered Julian. Something about Serena's smile had alarm bells clanging. He turned to Miss Daventry. 'Ma'am, if you would care for it, you may ride Lady Braybrook's old mount. He is very quiet, used to carrying a lady.'

Miss Daventry demurred. Of course.

'Thank you, sir, but I will be more than happy to remain with Lady Braybrook. I—'

'No, dear. Go with them,' said Serena. 'I would be much happier if you learned to ride. Lissy is for ever giving the grooms the slip when she rides out, but I fancy she will not be so rag-mannered with you! Especially if she knows you to be inexperienced.' She shot a glance at her daughter. Who blushed.

In one final attempt to avoid her fate, Miss Daventry said, 'But I have no riding habit!'

Serena—Julian silently blessed her—dismissed that with a wave of her hand. 'Oh, pish! You may have my old one. It will be a little large, but the colour will suit you. It's quite a dark blue, so you need not scruple to wear it despite your mourning. And there are any number of mourning gowns in my dressing room. Heaven knows I wouldn't fit into most of them any more.' She smiled ruefully at Miss Daventry, and added, 'I have a tendency to put on weight sitting in this horrid chair. It would be better, of course, if I were not so fond of cakes and made more use of my exercise chair.'

Julian looked at Lissy. His sister was watching Miss Daventry, an odd expression on her face, as the companion accepted politely.

Chapter Five

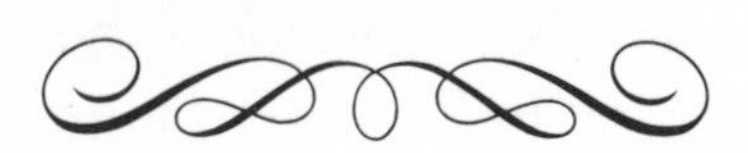

Christy frowned at her reflection. The riding habit was slightly too large, but the wretched thing was almost flattering. She had an observable figure. Most of her gowns deliberately disguised that. Wearing gowns in any way related to one's shape was, in the crudely expressed opinion of her former employer, 'asking for it'. Too-large gowns—which were easier to button up unassisted—the caps, and the spectacles all helped. Not that the spectacles were mere disguise—she would trip over her own feet without them.

No one looked beyond a dull, shapeless gown, the cap and spectacles. They saw only the dowdy paid companion or governess. It was safer that way.

Only she had the uncomfortable sensation that, like his lordship, Lady Braybrook saw Christy, not Miss Daventry. She had been right about the habit suiting Christy. The deep blue gave a little colour to her cheeks, although that might be the country air. She fingered the braid up the front of the habit. It was beautiful, so elegant. She had never worn such clothes in her life. Perhaps it didn't matter. She was still the companion-governess. Borrowed plumage did not make fine birds, she told herself as she went downstairs.

'There you are!'

Lissy and Matthew were waiting in the hall, which Christy had learnt was the Great Hall. Apparently Amberley was very old indeed and the Trenthams had been here for ever.

'You do look nice,' said Lissy, and Christy bit her lip not to smile at the new hint of patronage. 'The horses have been brought around. We have Mama's old hack for you. He's terribly quiet.'

'Not a slug, though,' put in Matthew. 'You could have ridden another horse, but Julian said it was better to be safe than sorry. He said he didn't want to bury you.' Not a hint of patronage there.

'An unwelcome expense, no doubt,' said Christy.

Matthew grinned. 'He didn't put it quite like that.' The grin turned impish. 'It was more the inconvenience.'

Christy peered over the top of her spectacles at him, in a manner she had found to be very effective with youngsters. They never seemed to realise it was a bluff; that without looking through the lenses she could see very little.

Even so, she could see Matthew's grin; and those blue eyes, very like his brother's, continued to twinkle.

'Julian's outside, with the horses and Emma and Davy,' said Lissy, cheerfully. Not at all as though this were the brother she had described as a tyrant the previous evening.

No doubt he meant to see them off, thought Christy, wishing she had not agreed to this ride. No doubt she would make a complete fool of herself. Wasn't one meant to learn to ride as a child? Probably little Davy was more accomplished than she would ever be.

Sure enough, when Lissy and Matthew took her out on to the front steps, Davy was already mounted on a chestnut pony with a pretty head and lively eye. Emma was mounted on a bay. His lordship stood close by, holding the reins of a tall black horse, and a lead rein attached to the bridle of a sleepy-looking dappled grey. Not a horse, really. More a large pony.

Grooms held two other horses. Mentally counting, and looking at the quality of the black horse, Christy came to a dead halt at the top of the steps as an appalling realisation struck her. She had assumed a groom would accompany the riding party and attend to her instruction. Apparently not. His lordship was dressed for riding. Which meant…she gulped…he was planning to teach her to ride.

Schooling herself to reveal nothing, she met his lordship's limpid gaze. And saw the glimmer of unholy amusement.

Drat him!

He knew, to a nicety, just how embarrassing she would find this and he was enjoying it!

His greeting confirmed it. 'Miss Daventry—I'm sure you understand that I prefer to ensure your safety myself.'

She smiled. Sweetly. 'I am very grateful for your lordship's condescension.'

His brows snapped together, and his mouth hardened. Then his gaze flickered to Lissy, listening avidly, and he said, 'Not at all, ma'am. Come and meet Merlin.'

Meet Merlin. As though the creature were of some account to him, like his dog. Christy watched, fascinated, as Lord Braybrook petted the old horse...something told her Merlin was no longer in the first flush of youth. His lordship's hands were gentle, rubbing the ears, stroking the arched neck. Then something was produced from a pocket and whiffled up out of his hand with an appreciative crunch and snort.

'Come.' His lordship spoke abruptly. 'Hold out your hand. Quite flat and still.' She obeyed and he placed a sugar lump on her palm. Horrified, she stared at it. Old though he might be, judging by the noise he'd made munching the last lump, Merlin had teeth. Large ones. In perfect working order. But before she could protest, or drop the sugar, soft whiskery lips took the treat with amazing delicacy. The teeth, again, dealt with the offering in a fashion anything but delicate.

A delighted thrill went through Christy. Without thinking she stroked the long nose and found it velvety. Liquid dark eyes blinked at her wisely, and then...that same velvet nose was shoved against her chest and rubbed up and down with great enthusiasm.

Caught unawares, Christy staggered back hard against an immovable wall. A wall with arms that steadied her effortlessly. A shocking warmth stole through her and for one heartstopping instant she relished the male strength surrounding her. A delight promptly banished by hot embarrassment, but before she could react, strong hands grasped her shoulders and eased her away.

'I beg your pardon, Miss Daventry,' said his lordship in obvious amusement. 'Merlin *is* a gentleman, but he is very fond of sugar. Are you all right?'

'Perfectly,' she said, ignoring her racing pulse.

Davy, from his perch on the little chestnut, said in pleased tones, 'Look, Julian! Merlin has slobbered all over her chest.'

Christy looked down. Sure enough the braided front was a mess. She gulped and met laughing blue eyes that were pointedly *not* looking at her…chest.

'Don't worry, Miss Daventry. I'm sure it will come off.'

'But, Lady Braybrook won't like—'

'Nonsense,' said Lord Braybrook. 'She always grumbled about that trick of Merlin's. He has slobbered on it before. Besides, she gave you the habit. It's yours now.'

Christy flushed. Besides the habit, Lady Braybrook had given her a number of gowns, saying she never wore them and that they were unsuitable for Lissy. They were even more unsuitable for the governess. Of course, a lady's maid was given her mistress's cast-offs, so perhaps it wasn't *too* improper.

'Can we go? *Please?*' begged Davy.

Matthew had mounted, and one of the grooms was about to put Lissy up. Christy gulped as the groom linked his hands for Lissy's booted foot and threw the girl into her saddle. Dear God. If he did that to her, she would go straight over the saddle and land on the ground.

'Miss Daventry?'

Lord Braybrook's voice sounded oddly distant.

'Is there…is there not a mounting block? I don't think the way Miss Trentham was—'

'I'll put you up, Miss Daventry.'

Unresisting, she was led around to the saddle. Balanced against Merlin's side, clutching the stirrup, she lifted a foot. His hands grasped her waist and lifted her. She gasped, and found herself perched on the saddle. For a moment his hands stayed at her waist, then dropped to her hip, steadying her. That was all. Wasn't it? Her body hummed, as if…as if he had caressed her. Nonsense! He was making sure she was safely in place. She sat up as straight as possible, and the disturbing hands released her. She sighed in relief, thinking her ordeal over.

Wrong. His lordship was busy arranging her right leg safely over the pommel, long fingers gripping her knee as he pushed it into position. She froze, desperately trying to ignore the intimacy of his touch. Ridiculous. He was merely showing her how to sit. There was nothing intimate about it. Then his hands were on her left ankle as he adjusted her foot in the stirrup. She had to remind herself that she was wearing a boot. That he was not really touching her ankle. More accidental touches as he shortened the stirrup leather. Then he caught her foot again.

'Keep your heel pushed down, Miss Daventry,' he instructed, doing it for her. 'That helps to keep your, er, *seat*, firmly in the saddle.'

That was a relief to know. She felt like a bug perched up there. Merlin seemed a great deal taller than he had from the ground.

'Now—your reins.'

Christy looked down at the reins. She had picked them up. She knew that much. But what should she do with them?

His lordship showed her. 'Just hold them lightly,' he said, long fingers guiding hers to the right position, and showing her how to shorten the reins. 'They are not to help you balance. Only to guide him. You must only feel his mouth. A light contact. And keep your thumbs on top.'

Her hands were gloved, but his touch felt just as shockingly intimate as it had on her legs. He stepped back and looked her over. She blushed.

'Very well. At least you don't have to be told to keep your back straight,' he commented. He walked around to his own horse and mounted with fluid grace.

Ridiculous to glow at such off-hand praise. Determinedly she sat even straighter in the saddle.

Merlin snorted and took a couple of steps. Stifling a gasp, as her balance shifted, Christy clutched at the saddle, but Merlin came up against the end of the leading rein and stopped. She straightened at once and glanced across at his lordship, but he seemed not to have noticed.

Any more than he had noticed how scared she was.

Stupid. It was years since she had fallen off that horse of Harry's, and Merlin was much quieter, but still…she forced herself to breathe deeply.

All women had waists, Julian reminded himself. Discovering Miss Daventry's waist under the slightly-too-large habit might have been a surprise, but not one that should have had his hands lingering, marvelling at the suppleness of the curve, and then drifting to her hip.

With a swift glance at Miss Daventry to assure himself that she was secure in the saddle, he tugged gently at the leading rein and put his own mount into a walk. Miss Daventry's face blanked as Merlin moved, but she gave no other sign, beyond sitting very straight and still.

He had been trying to believe that Miss Daventry must be as shapeless as her gowns. But she wasn't. She disguised her body as effectively as she hid her true nature. Under the dowdy clothes she was slender and lissom as a willow. She would be sweet, warm…*sweet*? Hell's teeth! If she knew what he was thinking now, and as he settled her in the saddle, she'd be a virago!

Miss Daventry might have an elegant figure and a neatly turned ankle, but she was a bundle of prickles. For which, he admitted, she could not be blamed. A wise woman in her position avoided drawing mens' attention, unless she wished for a career in the *demi-monde*. Governesses and companions always held themselves slightly apart.

A lonely existence…

'Where shall we go,' asked Lissy, bringing her mare up beside them. 'Miss Daventry, you choose.'

Julian noted that Miss Daventry looked somewhat startled at being consulted. She demurred.

'Oh. That's very kind, Miss Trentham, but I do not know this part of the country at all, so—'

'I like the river,' said Davy, hopefully.

Lissy sighed theatrically. 'Not the river again, Davy!'

'No, Davy!' said Emma. 'Not everyone likes waiting while you watch for trout that never appear.'

Davy scowled.

About to vote for the river and bring down a deluge of fury on his head, Julian was forestalled by Miss Daventry.

'A river? With trout? Real trout?'

Davy's scowl vanished as hope rekindled. 'And salmon. Really big ones,' he said, dropping his reins to demonstrate. He shot a glare at his sisters as he caught up the reins again. 'And they do appear. Julian owns them.' This last with great pride.

Miss Daventry's mouth barely twitched. 'Then of all things, that is what I should most like to see,' she said firmly. 'I had no idea his lordship was important enough to own fish and make them appear.'

Emma giggled, and Matthew shouted with laughter.

'There you are, Julian. When do you try holding back the tide?'

'As I recall,' said Julian, trying not to laugh, 'that wasn't King Canute's idea! The river then. Come along all of you.'

They rode towards the river, all thought of quarrelling forgotten.

He had to hand it to Miss Daventry. She had averted

a quarrel very neatly. Lissy was far too well brought-up to argue with her. He was amused to see that Lissy's attitude to Miss Daventry was just what he had hoped it would be. Sympathetic affection laced with pity. Which should be enough to have Lissy entertaining second thoughts about her infatuation for the dashing Mr Daventry. In his experience pity was a death knell to passion.

As for Miss Daventry, he listened with deepening respect as she took shameless advantage of Davy's momentary gratitude.

'Davy, what is the French word—' beyond a faint smile she ignored a groan '—for "fish"?'

His littlest brother stared, and wrinkled his brow. *'Pou...poussin?'*

'Nearly,' said Miss Daventry. 'That is a chicken, but it does sound similar. *Poisson.*'

They rode on towards the river and Julian listened in utter disbelief as Miss Daventry proceeded effortlessly to enlarge not only Davy's French vocabulary, but Matthew, Emma and Lissy's as well.

Talking about fish.

By the time they reached the woods, Christy felt a great deal safer on horseback. Lord Braybrook had insisted on keeping to a walk, but now permitted the younger members of the party to ride ahead.

'Very neat, Miss Daventry,' he said, as the youngsters raced off whooping. 'I had no idea Davy knew that much French.'

She smiled. 'You are paying me handsomely, my lord. I should use my time to the best advantage.'

'There is that,' he said. 'Sit up straight, Miss Daventry. We'll essay a trot.'

Before she could utter a word of protest, he had urged his mount to a trot. Trotting, she discovered, was a great deal harder than walking. Merlin bounced, and so did she. His lordship, she observed, riding astride, was able to rise and fall to the rhythm. In a side saddle she had no such option.

She gritted her teeth, sat up even straighter and tightened her right leg around the pommel. As far as she could see, she was going to earn every last penny of her one hundred pounds per annum.

They had not gone far before the younger members of the party were well out of sight around a bend in the woodland ride. The sound of pounding hooves and faint laughter floated back. Breathless from the bouncing, Christy managed to say, 'Should we not catch them up, my lord?'

He flicked her a glance. 'You'd break your neck at that hell-for-leather pace.' He frowned. 'If you wish to stop bouncing, sit straighter and keep your heel down. It will keep your…seat in the saddle.'

Her…seat was already so sore that the last thing Christy wanted was to have it in closer contact with the saddle, but she obeyed, and, sure enough, she bounced less. Whether or not she was any more comfortable was a moot point.

'I cannot but think that Miss Trentham will find

riding with me in attendance somewhat boring, my lord,' she said a few moments later.

'Probably,' he said.

She flushed, suddenly aware that he too must be finding the restricted pace a bore. 'I am sure if you wish to catch up with the children, that I will be perfectly safe. Merlin seems very quiet.'

His brow rose. 'Certainly not, Miss Daventry. Whatever my shortcomings, I have a little more consideration than that.'

Christy subsided. Surreptitiously she patted Merlin's neck, finding it warm and silken. Despite still feeling like a bug perched on top of him, she found that she rather liked Merlin. She liked the friendly way he occasionally swung his head and blew at Lord Braybrook's mount. And once or twice lipped at Lord Braybrook's breeches. At least, she assumed he was only using his lips.

It would be nice to ride him again.

She flinched away from the thought. Becoming fond of Merlin would be as foolish as becoming fond of Lady Braybrook's cat. Or feeling herself to be part of the family. This was not her place. The landing—that was her place; no matter how kind and considerate the family might be, she was not one of them. She would do far better to take her cue from his lordship's hauteur and remember that she was not riding for her own pleasure. That was incidental. His lordship had insisted because it made her more useful to him.

'Dare you attempt a canter, Miss Daventry?'

This appalling suggestion broke in on her thoughts just as they came out of the woods on to a sunny watermeadow.

'A canter?' He'd said *dare*, curse him! 'Of course, my lord.'

Something that might have been a smile flickered across that impassive countenance. 'Very well, then,' he said. 'Shorten your reins a little, but don't put any more pressure on his mouth. It is just to give you a little more control *if* you need it.'

Carefully she followed his instructions.

'Good. Now—sit up, and give him a kick.'

She did. Merlin remained in a trot.

'His ribs are quite strong. You won't break him,' came the comment.

She tried again. And found herself swinging along a great deal faster, his lordship's horse keeping pace beside them. It was…exhilarating. She could feel the wind rushing past, feel the power of the horse surging beneath her, part of her. It was like…like flying.

It was also a great deal more comfortable. Nowhere near as much bouncing.

'I'm doing it!' she said in breathless delight. 'And I'm not bouncing any more!'

'Merlin's paces are particularly smooth,' was the dampening rejoinder.

Killjoy.

'I *beg* your pardon?'

Blushing, Christy realised she had spoken aloud.

Buoyed by her delight, and determined not to be

cowed, she repeated obligingly, 'Killjoy.' And flicked a glance at him.

He was grinning. Laughing with her. Something leapt inside her, bubbling, part of the mad delight of the swinging motion beneath her and the glorious summer's day.

Killjoy? Julian fought not to laugh out loud as he rode beside her. He should have known. He'd taught both Emma and Davy to ride. How could he have forgotten that moment of joy on their faces when they first broke out of a trot? How could he have forgotten his own first canter? The sudden realisation of power coiled beneath him. The sensation that one had somehow harnessed the wind…

He set his jaw. He had not forgotten. But Miss Daventry was the governess. The companion. He had no business to feel her triumph so keenly. No business to note the flush on her cheeks, the sparkle behind the spectacles. Definitely no business remembering the firm suppleness of her waist, the dainty ankle in Serena's old boot. He took a deep breath and willed his blood to steady. He certainly had no business thinking of another way to bring a flush to her cheeks.

He rode on in silence, ignoring her, except for necessary instructions. For her part, Miss Daventry appeared to have taken the hint. She volunteered nothing further, but obeyed him in silence. Exactly the way it should be. Except she was still flushed, smiling. After half a mile he said, 'Sit up straight and feel his mouth by closing your fingers, then pull him in gently.'

He watched carefully as she obeyed, matching his pace to hers. Somewhat to his surprise, she managed quite well, Merlin responding to her hands. They came to a halt. 'Well done,' he said. 'In fact, I think we can dispense with this.' And he leaned down and removed the leading rein. Looking up, he met Miss Daventry's shocked gaze.

'But—'

'If he really decided to go, I probably wouldn't be able to hold him,' he told her. 'That was just until you felt in control. He's very quiet. You know how hard you had to kick to make him canter.' Seeing that she still looked slightly nervous, he said, 'Miss Daventry, whatever you may think of my duty of care to you, trust me when I say that I do not take risks with my horses!'

Behind the spectacles her eyes narrowed. Not a flicker of her mouth as she said, 'A point indeed, my lord.' But that blasted dimple was there—hidden laughter. Hidden pleasure beckoning unbearably.

With a curt nod to her to follow, he rode on.

The river slid and sparkled beside them, the wooded hills rising on either side. Further up, the river went into a gorge and they would meet the others coming back. Unless they took a track up into the forest, but he hoped they would wait before doing that. Being alone with Miss Daventry was dangerous. Not because he thought she had the least idea of entangling him, nor yet because he intended to entangle her, but because the curiosity to know what would happen if he did so, shocked him.

So where in Hades were his siblings?

Laughter and hoofbeats came from the trees and sure enough, a moment later, they appeared. The little group had been enlarged. Two young men now rode with them.

Julian recognised them. Harry Daventry and Ned Postleton—the squire's son—riding either side of Lissy. Neither man was bothering to look ahead towards where he sat awaiting them with Miss Daventry. Both were competing for Lissy's attention.

But as he watched, Lissy leaned towards Daventry and spoke, nodding and pointing with her whip. Daventry looked towards them and even at fifty yards Julian saw puzzlement on his face. Lissy said something else, and the puzzlement vanished. Every line hardened as he stared towards his sister. With a brief word and nod to Lissy, he spurred forwards, then pulled up beside them, his face grim. 'Good afternoon, my lord,' he said. The young horse he rode fidgeted, tossing its head and mouthing the bit.

'Good afternoon, Daventry,' returned Julian. 'I don't need to introduce you to our companion, do I?'

'No, my lord. You do not.' It was said between gritted teeth. Daventry turned to his sister. 'What are you about? What are you doing here? Why are you not in Bristol?' His voice indicated the complete opposite of delight. A surge of anger rippled through Julian. No matter how shocked the cub was, at least he could greet his sister civilly! He waited for Miss Daventry to annihilate the boy.

'Did you not receive my letter?' she asked in diffident tones. 'I sent it last week, as soon as I knew I was coming. It should have reached you.'

Daventry flushed. 'I…a letter came yesterday.' His scarlet deepened. 'I have been very busy. Sir John has had a great deal of work for me.'

There was just the slightest pause, before Miss Daventry said, 'Of course.' There was no hint of reproach or hurt in her tone, but Julian shot her a glance. Her mouth was more than ordinarily firm, controlled. As though she held something in check.

'Then this is a pleasant surprise for you, Daventry,' said Julian. He fought to keep anger from his voice. If Daventry chose not to open his sister's letter, it was no business of *his*.

'As you say, my lord,' said Daventry, his lips stiff. 'I should like to speak to my sister privately, if you—' He broke off as his horse danced and flung its head up at the approach of the rest of the party.

'Is this not a lovely surprise, Mr Daventry?' called Lissy. 'I told the others not to breathe a word when we saw you! Miss Daventry is to be Mama's companion and my governess. Oh, Miss Daventry, this is Mr Postleton.'

Davy scowled. 'She's my governess too! She's teaching me French.'

Lissy ignored that. 'And Mama says that when she is unable to chaperon me, Miss Daventry may do it, so I dare say you will see a great deal of her, sir.' She smiled at Harry.

Neither Mr Postleton nor Mr Daventry looked in the

least gratified by the intelligence that in future Miss Trentham's chaperon would have the use of her legs.

'Didn't know you had a sister, Daventry.' Postleton's eyes slid over Christy. Julian bristled as Postleton raised his hat, his eyes weighing up and assessing charms. 'Afternoon, ma'am.'

'Good afternoon, sir.' Miss Daventry acknowledged the greeting with cool good manners.

Julian edged his mount closer, for some unspecified reason wishing to shield Miss Daventry from Postleton's attention. The younger man's gaze swung his way and became a knowing smirk.

He turned back to Miss Daventry. 'Braybrook's mounted you well, I see.' His voice was all innocence, but Julian froze. Better not to react. It was possible that Postleton had made the remark innocently.

'As you see,' said Miss Daventry in an expressionless voice. 'This is Lady Braybrook's old hack. I have not ridden before.'

'Ah. Dare say you're not up to a gallop, then.'

Harry frowned slightly, staring at Postleton, but nothing in Miss Daventry's expression suggested that she saw anything suggestive in Postleton's remarks.

Postleton turned to Lissy. 'Miss Trentham, would you care for a gallop? Slow going when Braybrook's got your governess to consider.'

'Oh, well…' She glanced at Miss Daventry and then at Julian for permission. He nodded. 'Yes, you and Emma and Matt if he wishes it.' Postleton might indulge in crude innuendo over the governess, but he was not fool enough to pass the line with Miss Trentham of Amberley.

Postleton looked less than enthused at this addition to the party, saying merely, 'After you, Miss Trentham, Miss Emma.'

'Can I go?' pleaded Davy.

'No,' said Julian, and before his little brother could object, said, 'You are going to have a jumping lesson over that log while Miss Daventry speaks to her brother. Off you go. I'll follow, but no jumping until I say so. Not even by accident. If you can't stop Star, I'll put you on this leading rein and mount you on a complete slug for a month.'

Davy brightened and trotted towards the log.

Julian glanced at Miss Daventry, who said, 'I think you covered everything, my lord.' The dimple flickered.

He snorted. 'You have to with that one. Be warned, ma'am!'

Chapter Six

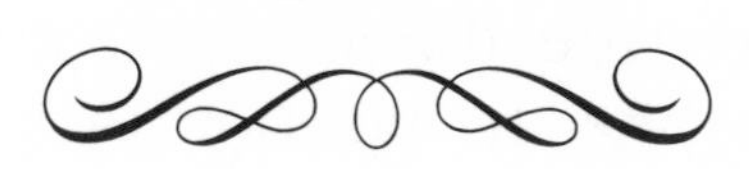

Christy watched for a moment as he followed his brother and then turned to her brother, who was staring at her, his mouth hard.

'He seems mighty familiar with you. Dammit, Christy! How am I supposed to support the character of a gentleman, if my sister is seen to be—'

'Seen to be what, Harry?' she snapped. 'Supporting herself and saving for her old age? What was I supposed to do when you sold the house? Starve politely?' She dragged in a breath, reaching for self-control at the same time. 'No. Don't let us quarrel. Shall we try again?' She managed a smile. 'It's lovely to see you. Are you well? Is that your horse?'

He shrugged, still looking annoyed. 'I'm well enough. And this is one of Sir John's youngsters. His Grace mentioned in his letter of recommendation that I was good with young horses. What the devil are you doing here, Christy? Why, of all positions, did you apply for this one?'

'I didn't,' she said. 'His lordship visited me. I explained it all in my letter.'

'*What?*' His jaw hardened. 'Why the hell would he do that? Dammit, Christy! His reputation—' He broke off. 'How did he find you? I suppose he's been nosing around—spying!'

She shrugged. 'I have not the least notion. But he called while your friend Goodall was there. We talked, and he offered me the position. After he had sent Goodall on his way.'

'He *what*?'

She held his gaze. 'Some of the contents of the house were *mine*, Harry. Goodall seemed not to understand that.'

'Dash it, Christy!' he said furiously. 'What need did you have for them if the house is to be sold?'

'None,' she told him. 'But I do need the money. I have arranged for their separate sale.' She saw no need to inform him that she had kept some of the smaller items their mother had left her, as well as most of the books. Better that he thought them sold and gone.

His eyes shifted a little. 'Well, of course I would have given you your share of the money. And that does not explain why you accepted this position!'

'Why should I not?'

'Because he's using you to get at me! Surely you can see that? *Leave my sister alone, sir, and yours is safe*—it's obvious!'

Christy thanked a benevolent deity that Harry had not realised the full deviousness of Lord Braybrook's plan.

'And I suppose he wants you to spy on myself and Al—Miss Trentham!' snarled Harry.

Christy bit her lip. She'd known he wouldn't be overjoyed to see her, but this bitterness…

'No more than any other governess or chaperon,' she told him, denying the small dagger of hurt. 'And what is there to spy on? You are always at pains to assure me that you are a gentleman. Therefore I can expect you to behave as one, can I not?'

'Dammit, Christy! That is not what I meant!' He changed the subject. 'How do you know Braybrook means honestly by you?'

'He has given me no reason to distrust him,' she said quietly. 'My bedchamber is two down from Lady Braybrook's own. I am to spend my days with either Lady Braybrook or with the younger children or Miss Trentham. Beyond my function within the household, he has no interest in me whatsoever. He is hardly the sort to threaten *me* because he disapproves of *you*!'

Harry snorted. 'And just how many governesses do you imagine Braybrook has favoured with a riding lesson?' he snapped. 'Not to mention a new riding habit! I know *you* would not have purchased such a thing.'

Christy flushed. 'Since her maid would have little use for it, Lady Braybrook gave it to me so that I could ride with her daughters. His lordship was kind enough to give me a lesson for the same reason. Apparently Miss Trentham is in the habit of giving the grooms the slip and riding alone.' She watched him, wondering…

Harry said nothing, but his shifting gaze and sulky mouth were answer enough. Easy enough for Alicia to know Harry's day off and ride out, or walk out if necessary. Especially with her mother chairbound. More anger at Harry bubbled up. She held it down. No need to say anything. It would be harder for Alicia to play that trick now.

'Now don't jag his mouth this time! That's it! Well done!'

Glancing over, Christy saw Davy bring his pony around, and canter back to face the jump again, blazing triumph on his face. She knew exactly how he felt. A glance at Lord Braybrook discovered an equal triumph and pride on his face, as he watched his younger brother. A rush of warm delight stole over her. Such a simple foolish thing—

'Christy! Are you listening?'

She dragged her attention back from his lordship. 'I'm sorry. What did you say?'

'That it would be better if you resigned. Returned to Bristol.'

She stared. 'On what pretext?'

He scowled. 'Anything. Say you've received a better offer. Or that you don't like the country. Lord knows you never have!'

'I've never had the opportunity!' she said. 'And I find that I like the country very well.' She did too. She had not realised how hemmed in, confined she had felt by town.

'Well, a better offer then.'

With the wage he was paying her, his lordship would know that for a lie instantly. 'As governess *and* companion I am being paid better than I could hope to achieve elsewhere. His lordship is not an idiot. Besides, where should I go?'

Harry was still trying to come up with reasons for Christy's swift departure ten minutes later when Alicia and the others came trotting back.

Alicia smiled at them benevolently. 'You must ride over on Wednesday, Mr Daventry,' she said. 'I am sure Mama will be able to spare Miss Daventry for an hour or so.'

'Wednesday?' queried Christy.

Harry scowled. 'My day off,' he said, not sounding pleased with Alicia's suggestion. At her startled glance, he forced a smile and added, 'Perhaps you could ask for Wednesdays off, Christy. Then we could meet for part of it. Sometimes.'

Summoning all her powers of diplomacy, Christy said, 'I shall mention it to Lady Braybrook.' Along with the information that it was Harry's day off. She could just imagine how many times he would fail to arrive at an arranged meeting with his sister and later plead an unavoidable engagement!

Lord Braybrook trotted up with Davy. 'We should be going home now, you four. You may ride ahead if you like.'

The four younger members of the party rode off, waving farewells.

Braybrook turned to Harry and Postleton. 'Good day,

gentlemen. Daventry, I'm sure Lady Braybrook will be amenable to you visiting your sister.'

Christy forced a smile. 'Thank you, my lord. I'll see you soon then, Harry.'

'Yes. Yes, of course,' he muttered.

She nodded to Mr Postleton. 'Goodbye, sir.'

'Say rather, *au revoir*, ma'am,' said Postleton, in an appalling accent, as he bowed extravagantly. 'French, y'know. I'm sure we'll meet again,' he said, as though he thought it a high treat for her.

Christy's temper jerked on its leash. 'I am a governess, Mr Postleton,' she informed him in tones of sweetest condescension. 'I *do* recognise the French language when I hear it spoken.'

Julian choked. Definitely time to go.

'Good afternoon, Postleton,' he said, in as urbane a tone as he could manage for the laughter welling up. 'Come, Miss Daventry. We had best follow those four.'

They set off back along the meadow at a trot. Once out of earshot, he said, 'I would advise you to be wary of Postleton, Miss Daventry. He does not always keep the line with…women.' With women he considered his inferiors would be closer to the mark, but he could not say that.

Miss Daventry snorted. No doubt she understood exactly what he had left unsaid.

He felt his mouth twitch. 'Could this be another reason why you consider yourself a failure as a companion.'

She pulled Merlin up. He turned, startled, to find her glaring at him, her cheeks absolutely scarlet.

'Do you think that, my lord?' Her contempt stung. 'Then I dare say that you will not be in the least surprised when I inform you that Mr Postleton, no matter how distinguished his lineage, or ample his fortune, is no gentleman to indulge in such innuendo with women present! Have you no regard for your sisters?'

That caught him on the raw. So she had understood Postleton after all.

'But they did not understand, Miss Daventry. You did. What does that say about you?'

Her eyes narrowed. 'Exactly what it says of you—that I am not ignorant. And that I cannot afford the luxury of being as sheltered as your sisters!'

She nudged Merlin with her heel and rode on. At a trot. Precisely as he had taught her. For some reason that irritated him.

'What the devil do you think you are doing?' he snapped, bringing his horse alongside.

'Going home!' She bit her lip. 'That is—back to Amberley.'

She said nothing further, but her colour remained high.

What was it about her that got under his skin? Ready to strangle Postleton himself, he'd ripped up at her for saying very much what he was thinking. She was right; innocence would leave her easy prey for men like Postleton. Or himself. What would it be like never to trust anyone fully? Never to let anyone close, because you did not really belong anywhere or with anyone. Damn it! He was becoming maudlin. He forced his mind back to practical matters.

She sat as straight as ever in the saddle, but something about the set of her lips reminded him that they had been out quite a while. She was going to be sore.

'Feel his mouth, Miss Daventry. We'll slow to a walk.'

They did so without mishap.

'Is he tired?' asked Miss Daventry, patting Merlin's neck. 'He's old, isn't he? I'm not too heavy for him?'

Unwilling approval stabbed through him. And wry amusement. Miss Daventry hardly weighed enough for Merlin to notice. He had noticed, though. Noticed how sweet she felt as he lifted her to the saddle. Noticed the faint fresh scent of lavender that hung about her. Lavender and something else that he didn't want to think about. Something that was Miss Daventry herself.

'No, Miss Daventry,' he said tightly. 'My concern is for you. You are going to ache quite enough.'

She nodded and they rode on in uncomfortable silence.

To Julian's relief, Davy awaited them on the other side of the woods.

'Star is tired,' he informed them. 'The others *would* go too fast.'

'Very wise,' said Miss Daventry, smiling. 'Do you call her Star for that pretty mark on her forehead?'

Davy looked affronted. 'Star is a *gelding*, Miss Daventry. Don't you know the difference?'

Now, how would prim and proper Miss Daventry get out of that? wondered Julian.

'I'm afraid not, Davy,' she said calmly. 'I am dreadfully ignorant about horses. You tell me.'

Davy's explanation of the differences between mares, geldings *and* stallions, not to mention their significance, was startlingly comprehensive. Julian concluded that Davy was picking up a good deal of information of a decidedly agricultural nature on his visits to the stables.

And all the blasted female did was nod and murmur encouragement from time to time. Quite as if none of this surprised her. Which he admitted, it probably didn't. If she'd understood Postleton's less than delicate insinuations, this should hardly stretch her understanding. And at least she wasn't enlarging Davy's French vocabulary on the subject.

By the time they reached the stableyard, Christy knew that she had been out far too long. She looked at the cobbles. Down, it always looked further, but how to dismount? Slide? Even as she wondered, his lordship dismounted, tossed his reins to a groom and moved towards Merlin.

Her body tensed, remembering his hands on her waist, her ankle. No. She kicked her left foot from the stirrup, unhooked her right leg from the pommel, and slid.

It was much further than she had realised and the cobbles a great deal harder. Her legs gave way, collapsing under her.

He caught her, hauling her against his chest before she actually hit the cobbles. Shocked, she clung to him, conscious of the mingled odours of horse, leather and warm, slightly sweaty male.

'What the devil did you do that for?' came the clipped, furious voice. 'I warned you that you would be sore!'

Annoyed, she pushed to be free, but her legs wobbled despicably and his lordship ignored her feeble attempt and kept an arm around her.

'You didn't warn me my legs wouldn't work!' she said crossly.

He snorted. 'Given that they must feel like chewed string, I didn't think it necessary!'

'Is Miss Daventry all right, Julian?' came a younger voice.

Matthew stood there, his jacket slung over one shoulder. 'Shall I help her up to the house?'

'Yes,' said his lordship. 'If you have seen to your horse.'

'Oh, yes. We walked the last bit to cool them down,' said Matthew. 'Take my arm, Miss Daventry.'

He held it out and Christy took it gratefully, trying an experimental step. Chewed string, indeed! She was furiously aware of Lord Braybrook hovering. Not exactly protectively, more like a hawk waiting to swoop. Her legs held and she tried another step.

'That's it, Miss Daventry, said Matthew encouragingly. 'You shouldn't have jumped down like that, though. Lucky Julian was there. I thought you would land on the cobbles.'

'Damned lucky,' came a mutter from behind her.

Determinedly Christy looked back and met the blue eyes.

His lordship's face was set hard. She repressed a shiver, trying to ignore the memory of his body, hard and powerful, pressed against her own. As though…as though he owned it.

'Thank you, sir. For the lesson, and your patience.'

The line of his mouth flattened even further.

'You're welcome, ma'am. Good day.'

He caught up Merlin's bridle and led him away.

Christy turned back to Matthew. She could recognise a dismissal when it slapped her.

Julian watched her go from the refuge of Merlin's stall. God help him, he could still feel the imprint of that slender body. Small breasts crushed against him, the faint, rising scent of lavender. And a wisp of escaping hair, curling around her brow. Tawny brown glinting gold. Startled, mismatched eyes behind the misleading spectacles, and soft, slightly parted lips.

He'd wondered what she would taste like. Not only wondered, but considered finding out. It would be better to see as little of her as possible. Not that there was any danger of seducing her, but he could do without the inevitable frustration of not being able to do so, if he didn't squash this inexplicable attraction.

Miss Daventry was dangerous. The more so because she had not the least idea of it. She didn't even realise the danger *she* was in. Not that she was in any danger. He was not, definitely *not*, going to seduce his step-mother's companion.

'Miss Daventry!'

Christy turned carefully at the autocratic summons,

conscious of stiff, aching muscles. She had spent the rest of the afternoon sewing and talking with Lady Braybrook until it was time to change for dinner. Now she wondered if she might have to eat her dinner off the mantelpiece. She could almost hear the creaking protest of overused muscles with every movement. As for the stairs, they were a penance.

'My lord.'

He was frowning at her. 'That is one of Lady Braybrook's gowns.'

She felt heat steal over her cheeks. No doubt he thought she was dressing above her station in this soft grey silk. Her skin flickered at his intent stare. She twitched the heavy embroidered shawl Lady Braybrook had given her, drawing it a little closer across her bodice.

'Her ladyship wished me to wear it.' Her ladyship had more than wished. She had ordered. On pain of being sent back upstairs to change, should Christy dare to rebel and appear in one of her old gowns? How could she refuse? She couldn't remember when she had last talked, really talked, with another woman apart from her mother and Sukey. It was frighteningly easy to believe, to pretend, that she belonged here.

Her last employer had considered her as more of an errand girl, only addressing her when she required something. Lady Braybrook's notion of a companion was far more…well…*companionable* than Mrs March's had been. It touched a chord inside her, an unacknowledged yearning that had been better left sleeping.

'And you obliged her.'

There was something odd about his voice, but she forced herself to respond calmly. 'As you see, my lord.'

Her tone was even, quite indifferent. Which, given that her lungs had apparently lost their capacity, was remarkable. There was nothing, she told herself, *nothing* about Lord Braybrook to make her breathing hitch.

She had seen handsome men before. Men with blue eyes. Well-dressed men. There was no reason in the world for her waist, hands and—her stomach fluttered—legs to remember how carefully he had settled her in the saddle. There had been nothing intimate about it.

'And the cap, Miss Daventry—'

'Is my own,' she informed him stiffly.

He didn't doubt it. Not for one moment. Serena wouldn't have been seen dead in the monstrosity. And not a scrap of hair was to be seen. For which he ought to thank every god in the pantheon. Three ruined cravats on the floor of his bedchamber were testament to his distraction over whether or not Miss Daventry's hair could possibly be as silken as it looked.

Clearing his throat, he gestured for her to precede him into the drawing room. And averted his gaze from the lure of her slight figure. *Voluptuous*, he reminded himself. He preferred voluptuous. Ripe, seductive, *womanly* curves. It would help enormously if he remembered that, rather than the supple curve of Miss Daventry's waist.

To his relief Serena, Lissy and Matthew were already down. Finding himself alone with Miss Daventry… His cravat tightened in the most unaccountable way, and he wondered what excuse he might have used for abandoning her.

'Ah. There you both are.' Serena smiled. Then frowned. Direfully.

Julian blinked. And glanced down to check that he hadn't forgotten some vital item of attire. Like his trousers.

'No, dear. *Not* a cap. Not with that gown.'

He choked back a laugh, and risked a sideways glance to see how Miss Daventry was taking this admonition.

Meekly. Not a flicker of rebellion. For some reason that irked him. She'd bristled like an angry cat when *he* mentioned it.

'Julian, for heaven's sake, remove it!'

Remove it—? Remove Miss Daventry's cap? His fingers itched.

Playing for time, he said, 'Remove what, Serena?'

'Miss Daventry's cap!' said Serena in pained tones. 'Now, Julian!'

Rebellion sparked then all right and tight. Miss Daventry clutched at the cap…just a split second after Julian's instinctive response to an order that would have made a troop sergeant jump.

The cap dangled in his hand, and Miss Daventry stared up at him in disbelief, minus the remnants of her dowdy disguise.

'Much better!' declared Serena.

Part of Julian's brain agreed. The witless part that took one look at the gleaming tawny coils of Miss

Daventry's hair and wanted to slide his fingers into it. The other part of his brain, the part that recognised Miss Daventry as Disaster-Made-Flesh, told him to return the cap without delay, and tell Serena to mind her own misbegotten business.

'Give it to me, Julian,' said Serena. Stunned, he obeyed. And groaned mentally as she shifted in her chair and sat on the cap. Not even the redoubtable Miss Daventry was going to retrieve it from there.

'And let that be the last of these caps that I see,' Serena said cheerfully. 'You may wear them at my age.'

Lissy giggled. 'But, Mama—Mr Havergal said they were repellant at your age too!'

Havergal again? Who the devil *was* this Havergal fellow?

He couched it a little more tactfully. 'Who is Havergal and what does he have to say to your mother's choice of headgear, Liss?'

'Nothing at all,' said Serena.

'Oh, he's an old friend of Mama's,' said Lissy. 'He plans to settle not far from here and rides out from Hereford to visit Mama every few days. Haven't you met him?'

'Not yet,' said Julian. An oversight he planned to correct very soon. He glanced at Serena. 'I'll look forward to making his acquaintance.'

'I'm sure you will soon,' said Serena, her cheeks faintly pink. 'Now where was I? Oh, yes. Miss Daventry—at twenty-four, a cap is an abomination.

And when you have such pretty hair, 'tis a crime to hide it. Isn't it, Lissy?' She favoured her daughter with a stern look.

Lissy blinked. 'Pardon, Mama? Oh, yes. Miss Daventry, you look much nicer without the horrid thing!'

She did. Years younger and damnably pretty. Even with the spectacles. None of which deflected him from the fact that Serena had purposely changed the subject. Whoever Havergal was, she didn't want to talk about him.

'If we are finished correcting Miss Daventry's lamentable taste in caps,' he said, 'perhaps we might have our dinner.'

Over the next few days Christy settled into the rhythm of the house. In the mornings before Lady Braybrook came down, she taught Davy and Emma. After lunch she walked with Lissy and Emma, practising French or Italian conversation, or sketching.

She saw little of Lord Braybrook. She suspected he had taken a dislike to her. He never spoke to her unless he absolutely had to. And she had not been asked to accompany him out riding with his sisters again.

On the afternoons he escorted his sisters riding, she remained with Lady Braybrook. When he could not ride with them, she accompanied them with an elderly groom called Twigg, who instructed her patiently and seemed to like her.

This was how it should be, Christy told herself, as she escorted Alicia and Emma out to the garden for some sketching practice about a week after her arrival. It didn't matter if his lordship liked her or not. For all his faults, he was too fair-minded to dismiss her if she did her job well. Since Lady Braybrook was happy with her, she was safe. After all, his plan was working perfectly. There were innumerable opportunities for Alicia to be faced with the reality of what marriage to Harry would mean…such as this sketching party.

'You know, we *have* sketched Amberley before,' grumbled Emma, as they walked across the park.

Christy was not about to be deflected. 'Excellent. Then we can compare what you have sketched. It's interesting how different people can all draw the same familiar scene and produce completely different pictures. And if you hunt out the old sketches, we can see how you have improved and how your style may have changed.'

Emma scowled. 'I'd rather go to the stables and draw one of the horses.'

This notwithstanding, she settled down and silence reigned while the three of them sketched. At length Christy called a halt and looked at her pupils' efforts.

She was hard put to it not to chuckle. Both sketches said as much about the artists as Amberley. Emma's was very exact, down to the precise number of windows visible and including every tree and shrub as well as a stray gardener. Alicia, however, had shown Amberley as a rearing mass of stone with a turbulent background of non-existent clouds.

'But it's sunny today, Liss!' protested Emma when she saw this.

Alicia glared. 'Who cares? Amberley looks so romantic when there's a storm coming. Like something in *The Mysteries of Udolpho*.'

Emma rolled her eyes. '*That* silly book?'

'It's not silly! You haven't even read it!'

'Only because Mama won't let me!' said Emma. 'Anyway, Matt said it was silly.' She turned to Christy. 'May we see yours, Miss Daventry?'

'Of course.' Christy passed her the book.

'But this is not Amberley,' said Emma frowning. 'You said "our home".'

'Amberley is your home,' said Christy. 'This is *my* home. Or it was. It is to be sold now.'

'Oh,' said Emma. 'Liss, it's awfully good. Do look.' She tilted the book to give Alicia a better view. Christy held her breath. She had drawn the house meticulously, showing its size, its position between the apothecary and the fishmonger, the very unaristocratic nature of the street. It was, above all, completely unromantic.

Alicia looked rather daunted. 'You lived *there*?' she asked, as though such a thing were unimaginable. 'But I thought…a town house, Mr Daventry said.'

'Well, it's in a town,' said Christy cheerfully. 'Right in the middle of Bristol near the quay. Rather noisy. Wealthy people live in Clifton for the most part. I lived in that house after I left school, although I became a junior mistress for a year first. Then I was at home with Mama before I took a live-in position as a companion out at Clifton. I came home to nurse her.' No need to mention the more unpleasant aspects of earning your own living. Such as being considered fair game by your employer's son. At least she did not have to contend with that here.

Emma was still examining the picture. 'Is that an apothecary beside your house, Miss Daventry?' she asked.

'An apothecary?' Alicia sounded stunned.

Christy nodded. 'Yes. Very useful when Mama was ill. And a fishmonger on the other side. Smelly, sometimes, but it was a very convenient house. Not so large as to require more than one servant to help with the housework, and close to all the shops. Shall we pack up?'

Alicia was notably silent as she packed up her sketching gear, nibbling at her lower lip, and frowning as though deep in thought.

'Is something bothering you, Alicia?' asked Christy gently.

Alicia flushed. 'Oh, no. That is one of Mama's old dresses, is it not, Miss Daventry?'

'Yes,' said Christy. 'Thanks to Lady Braybrook's kindness I shall not have to make myself new dresses for years. Quite a saving.'

Alicia's eyes widened. 'For—?' She broke off, staring past Christy. 'I…I think…is that not Mr Daventry coming towards us?'

Christy turned. Sure enough, Harry was striding towards them from the direction of the house.

Alicia went pink, casting a nervous glance at Christy. 'How…how lovely. I mean, for you, Miss Daventry.'

Harry bowed as he drew near. 'Good afternoon,

ladies. Lady Braybrook said I would find you here. Sketching, is it?' He bestowed an extra smile on Alicia.

Alicia smiled back, but Christy thought there was just a touch of reserve in her expression.

'We sketched Amberley,' said Emma, 'because Miss Daventry said that we should draw our home, only of course she drew *your* old home in Bristol. It's awfully clear. You can even see the apothecary next door!'

It did not appear that this information afforded Harry the least pleasure. 'Can you?' He looked at Christy. 'Lady Braybrook has given you permission to walk with me in the grounds. She says Miss Trentham and Miss Emma should return to the house.'

'Of course,' said Christy. She smiled at Emma. 'Perhaps you might take my book and pencils back to my room, Emma?'

She watched as the girls departed and then faced her brother.

'Why the hell did you do that?' he demanded.

She raised her brows. 'You don't think Miss Trentham deserves some inkling of what is in store for her if she marries you? Of course, had you not led her to believe that you owned a *fashionable* town house—'

He scowled. 'It's no business of yours! You'd be better off having a care for your reputation! People are talking about Braybrook squiring you around! Of course, I assured Sir John that there was nothing in it, but—'

'You *what*?' Christy's temper spilled over. 'How dare you discuss my affairs!'

Stubbornness crept into his expression. 'He's a rake.

Everyone knows that around here! Why, he's even got—' He broke off, and cleared his throat. 'Well, mum for that, but even though Sir John says Braybrook isn't the sort to seduce the chambermaids, let alone the governess, people are talking.' He gave her a scathing glance. 'Although you're not the sort to attract him, so there can be nothing to worry about—unless he was bored.'

'His lordship,' said Christy with a decided snap, 'appears not to have sunk to such ghastly depths of *ennui* as that!' She denied the ignoble urge to ask what it was his lordship had got. It was none of her business. Besides, she could hazard a very fair guess that his lordship had a mistress tucked away close by. Hereford, perhaps. That was how these things were done.

'Well, you might give a thought to *my* position,' growled Harry. 'It won't help my standing if people are whispering that my sister must earn her own living!' He went on. 'And there is no need for you to do so! His Grace would help you. If you would only—'

'No.' She cut him off. 'I want nothing from him! Harry—be sensible!'

He snorted. 'Sensible? I am being sensible! The quickest way to establish myself is by an advantageous marriage, and—'

'You cannot marry anyone without telling the truth! Let alone Miss Trentham, who is accustomed to all this!'

All this, she gestured to include, meant the pinkish-brown bulk of Amberley, the grounds and the woods stretching down to the glimmering stretch of river. And not just Amberley itself, but all it represented—Lissy's place in the world. A world from which she and Harry were barred.

In this world, being the illegitimate son and daughter of a duke made every difference.

She had always known that. No one had cushioned the truth for her. She had known it at eight when people pointed and whispered in the street. And at ten when she had gone to school in Bath with strict instructions that her 'father' had died and where they were from. That the Duke of Alcaston was Harry's very generous 'godfather'. And she had known it at eighteen when she had fallen in love for the first and last time. For some, love did indeed alter when it alteration found.

Although perhaps for Harry it was slightly different. He at least could make his way in the world and be known according to his own actions. She, on the other hand, would always be judged on her mother's status as a duke's mistress. Tainted. A potential whore. The sins of the mother were very definitely visited on the daughter.

Harry seemed to read her thoughts. 'And what came of it when *you* told the truth? If you hadn't been so high minded—'

'I told the truth!' she snapped. 'I prefer to manage honestly and upon my own terms. How will you support Miss Trentham?'

He shrugged. 'I daresay his Grace would increase my allowance if I married. Especially if I married well. And she has a dowry.'

Her teeth clenched.

'She has a dowry if her brother chooses to release it!' she said, not bothering to disguise her contempt for his attitude. 'And you have no claim on Alcaston at all. You cannot rely on him.'

'Since I was never fool enough to antagonise him as you did, I'm not worried he'll cast me off.' His mouth hardened. 'I see no reason why my birth should make a difference. As for Braybrook—' he shrugged '—he's fond enough of Alicia not to let her starve. He'll know damn well that it's better to help me than cast her off.'

Christy's fists clenched, but she said in a calm voice, 'I hadn't thought of that. How convenient for you that Braybrook is devoted to his family.'

Harry went scarlet. 'I didn't mean it like that! Just that—look, Christy, don't make such a piece of work of it. A good marriage for me would help us both. If I can persuade our father into settling some money on you, then you could live with us. You can help Alicia with the household.'

'How very generous,' she said carefully. 'This certainly puts things in a different light. I'll think about it.'

Harry looked relieved. 'You do that. You'll see it's for the best. It's not as if I'm going to seduce Alicia or elope. Her connections won't help my career if she's disgraced.' He pulled an elegant timepiece from his pocket. 'I must be off. An engagement in Hereford. Just thought I'd call on my way past.' He put the watch away. 'Change your day off next week. We could go into Hereford together. Sir John has a gig that I am permitted to use.'

She smiled. 'I am afraid not, Harry. Wednesdays seem not at all convenient for Lady Braybrook.'

Chapter Seven

Christy said goodbye to Harry at the stables and then walked up to the house. He was determined, then, to snare Alicia. The situation was worse than she had thought. She had believed that she could influence Harry, make him see the wrongness of deceiving Alicia and her family. She was a fool.

Perhaps she ought to be grateful Harry was clear-headed enough to see that an elopement or seduction would damage Alicia and by extension himself. Instead she felt sick. Cold calculation held him back, the realisation that a disgraced bride would be a burden. And inside her churned the knowledge that if he'd claimed more altruistic reasons for not seducing Alicia or eloping with her, she might not have believed him.

Her course was clear although she had time before she might have to act. Any hint that Alicia was likely to do something foolish, and she must tell Lord Braybrook the truth. Armed with that information, he would be able to forbid Harry the house and even the headstrong Alicia would agree he was correct to do so.

It would ruin Harry if Braybrook made the truth public. He would probably lose his position. And the story would travel. Even with Alcaston's support, it would be difficult, if not impossible, for Harry to find another position. It was even possible that Alcaston, to whom discretion was all, might cast him off as he had her…

She wouldn't come out of it well either. Her position here would be finished and possibly all other positions, unless she changed her name, which would mean she had no references at all… No. That couldn't be allowed to matter. Perhaps, since the truth would save Alicia, Lady Braybrook might agree to write her a reference under an assumed name? But what about Harry?

She opened the side door that led into the garden room and walked slowly back through the hallways that led to the Great Hall. Could she bring herself to ruin Harry so entirely?

The answer came easily—if it saved Alicia from a crashing mistake, then yes, she could. She could not bear to see the family torn apart by Harry's ambition and Alicia's folly.

There would be no point threatening exposure; Harry might simply pretend to agree and become more secretive. The knowledge that he was capable of using a girl's affections so coldly sliced deep. That was worse than the rest—if Harry had truly loved Alicia, then she would sympathise. But he didn't. Alicia was a means to an end and he had weighed her brother's affection for her in his plans.

She came out under the musicians' gallery and turned towards the main stairs. She must return to Lady Braybrook and the girls. Continue opening Alicia's eyes to the truth. Not just the life she would lead, but the far more bitter truth that Harry felt no affection for her.

'Miss Daventry?'

Startled, she spun around. Lord Braybrook rose from a seat at the huge oak refectory table to one side.

'My lord. I did not see you. Were you looking for me?'

He came towards her, frowning. 'Is something bothering you?' There was no suspicion in his voice. Only concern.

Something inside her tilted as he walked towards her. Quaked in fright that he read her thoughts and feelings so easily.

'Of course not!' she said too quickly, summoning a bright smile. 'Whatever should be bothering me? You will excuse me, my lord. I must return to my duties.'

'A family quarrel, perhaps? I saw your brother.'

Her smile froze and she spoke as coldly as possible. 'I do not believe that is anything to do with you, my lord.' The lie tasted sour. Her quarrel with Harry was very much his business. Should she simply tell him? Get it over with?

He reached out, carefully smoothing between her brows with one finger. Shock jolted through her. Then, lightly, he touched the finger to her lower lip, traced the curve.

For a moment she stood, unable to move for the torrent of sensation. Then she stepped back, her eyes lowered. She forced herself to concentrate on a patch of sunlight glowing on the Persian rug beneath her feet. 'Is that all, my lord?'

His hand dropped back to his side. 'I'll bid you good day,' he said. And turned, walking swiftly away.

She shivered as he disappeared through a door under the gallery at the back of the hall. Why had he done that? Worse, why did she feel as though a thousand chrysalises were hatching into butterflies in her stomach? Not just her stomach either—her entire body hummed, fluttered at the memory of his touch.

His reputation. He's a rake!

His touch had driven everything else out of her mind. No, not just his touch—he had been concerned about her. He had noticed her distraction. That was temptation itself.

It was not so much that she mistrusted him, but herself. Mistrusted the little voice murmuring that he had truly *seen* her. Enough to see her distress. As though it mattered to him. She could not afford to think that. The half-landings might be a trifle dull, but it was safer to remain on them.

He was going to stay away from Miss Daventry. Under no circumstances would he wait for her in empty passages. Nor would he risk finding her alone by coming down early for dinner. Or any other meal. Nor would he permit himself to wonder about what brought a frown to her brow or a worried look to her eyes. It was not his concern.

None of which resolutions explained why, the following morning, Miss Daventry's empty place at the breakfast table felt like a void.

Julian carved more ham for himself, refilled his coffee cup and glared at the empty place. Was she ill? And why was he wondering about it? He'd been insane to touch her yesterday—how could touching a woman's brow and lower lip with a single finger feel more intimate than—?

'Is the ham disagreeing with you, Julian?'

Serena's amused voice broke his reverie. And that was another puzzle—why the devil was Serena downstairs at this hour?

He shrugged. 'I merely wondered why Miss Daventry is not down.'

Serena's lifted brows had him adding hurriedly, 'After all, she's not much of a companion to you lying abed.' And immediately had to banish images of Miss Daventry lying abed, tawny tresses spread in silken abandon on a pillow—*his* pillow. He strangled the forming vision, cleared his throat and pulled his chair closer to the table.

'Since Lissy and Emma have gone to spend the day with Lucy Pargeter, we decided that Miss Daventry should have her day off,' said Serena. 'I dare say she is preparing to go out.'

'Out? Where?' And how? As far as he was aware, Miss Daventry could not drive so much as a gig.

At that moment the door to the breakfast parlour opened to admit Miss Daventry. Julian stared. She was wearing one of her old gowns, an unadorned grey cambric with a deep blue spencer. A plain straw bonnet hung from her arm by its strings. There was not a cap in sight, however, and the coiled tawny tresses seemed to capture every stray gleam of sunlight. A single wisp had escaped, drifting against her cheek

He swallowed, his fingers itching to tuck the wisp back, brush his fingers over the soft cheek, feel the warmth of leaping blood under her skin.

Not a good idea at all.

'Ah, Miss Daventry.' Serena's smile was unabashed. 'His lordship was wondering where you were. Have you thought where you might go for your day off?'

Casting a suspicious glance at Julian, Miss Daventry said, 'I thought to go for a walk, ma'am.'

Julian frowned. A walk sounded harmless, but what if she became lost? The forest stretched for miles.

Matthew looked up. 'There's a nice path up through the woods just beyond the village,' he said helpfully. 'Then you follow it back along the ridge and down to the river, and it brings you home the way we rode the other day. I'll draw you a map.'

Which put paid to Miss Daventry losing her way; Matthew's maps were generally very good, but still—

'That is easily a walk of four miles, Matt,' he said irritably. 'A great deal of it uphill. She will be exhausted!'

'Oh,' said Matthew, plainly crestfallen. 'Well, I suppose it's a bit steep, but—'

'*She,*' said the cat's mother, sweetly deferential, 'enjoys walking. And *she* is quite capable of deciding for herself how far she can walk. Thank you, Matthew. That sounds lovely. I shall take my sketch book and pencils.'

A very odd choking noise escaped Serena, but all she said was, 'You had better take food with you. And some water. I know that walk and a great deal of it *is* uphill.' She smiled. 'And you might like to take a basket with you for blackberries.'

'Blackberries?'

'Oh, yes!' said Davy, muffled by a mouthful of toast. He swallowed hastily. 'There's a jolly big clump just where you get back down to the river.' He added, 'Only you get a tummy ache if you eat more than you put in the basket.'

Miss Daventry's dimple made the briefest appearance. 'Do you?'

'You do,' said Serena, absolutely straight faced. 'A medically proven fact. And the juice is very hard to get out of clothing. Not exactly medically proven, but you might like to bear it in mind.'

There was that dimple teasing him again. Curse it, she wasn't even looking at him, so why should he feel so enchanted by it?

'Thank you, ma'am.'

And not just the damned dimple—laughter in her eyes and voice, and the corners of her mouth lifting into the loveliest smile, one that he could imagine stained purple with blackberry juice, lips as sweet and luscious as the most forbidden of forbidden fruit, softening, parting… What the hell was he *doing*? Indulging in erotic fantasies about Christy Daventry and blackberries was bad enough, but at the breakfast table with her and his family it was lunacy!

'Just don't become lost,' he said coldly. 'Searching for you would be inconvenient.'

'Your lordship is all consideration.'

He breathed a sigh of relief as the dimple vanished and prim Miss Daventry returned in glacial propriety. As long as he didn't think about melting the ice… He blocked that from his mind as Matthew explained the route, tearing a page from a small notebook in his pocket. Melting this particular glacier was out of the question. It didn't want to be melted. He had seen that yesterday. He had seen the flash of awareness in her eyes before she stepped back behind her walls.

Perhaps he could tempt her out again, but if she didn't want to play, then that was that. He was past the age where an uninterested woman was a challenge. Wasn't he?

He pushed back his chair and Juno, sprawled behind it, leapt to her feet, tail waving. 'Coming, Davy?' he asked. 'I'm looking over some crops this morning. You can come if you wish and your mother doesn't mind.' Davy's constant chatter would drive all thought of Miss Daventry out of his head.

Davy's face lit and he turned pleading eyes on Serena. "Mama? May I? Please?'

A smile twitched at the corner of Serena's mouth. 'Oh, I think I can manage, Davy. You may go.'

Julian eyed Serena. 'You won't be lonely?'

'Not at all,' she assured him, pouring another cup of tea.

He left it there. Every instinct shrieked that she was up to something. But what?

Davy finished his toast in record time, wiped his mouth and jumped up, giving no further time for speculation.

Julian grinned and held out his hand as his little brother came around the table. The small fingers that slid into his hand were sticky. Definitely sticky. He was going to end up with jam all over his breeches, no doubt. 'We'll stop by the kitchens for some food on the way to the stables.'

Unable to help himself, he glanced towards Miss Daventry. She was watching Davy with an odd smile. She looked up. For an instant their gazes held and then, still with that queer, twisted smile, she turned away.

For a moment she had looked...well, *longing*. But what would a woman like Miss Daventry long for? Riches? Status? Probably. Who could blame her? Her future was insecure in the extreme. He pushed the thought away, giving his attention to Davy's questions as they left the room together. But he could not quite banish the niggling question—*what would happen to her after she left Amberley*? For she would. One day she would be gone. Where would she go? What would she do? And why did the image of her alone in lodgings, eking out every penny, leave him cold and shaken?

* * *

Sticky with perspiration, damp tendrils of hair clinging to her brow, Christy forced her aching legs up the last of the incline. Lungs burning, she leaned against an oak at the top to catch her breath. Below her the track wound away down through the oak woods. She had come out on a broader track, a ride, stretching in either direction along the top of what she supposed was a ridge. Matthew had explained it all as he drew the map for her.

Just turn right when you reach the top. It will bring you to a lookout over the river after a couple of miles. You could eat your lunch there. Another two hundred yards on, you'll find a track leading you back down to the river where we rode that first day and you follow the river home. It's very easy.

Easy.

Except for the pull up that hill. Matthew's *a bit steep* didn't even begin to describe it. Taking out her water bottle, she uncorked it and had a couple of mouthfuls, letting it trickle down slowly. Goodness, she was hot! Her bonnet dangled from her arm by its strings. She had taken it off less than a third of the way up the hill. There was no point worrying about sunburn in the green cool of the woods, and the lining would be ruined with perspiration if she did not.

She was hot, sticky and, she suspected, rather grimy. Her hair was dishevelled, and her gloves were stuffed in her pocket. Ladylike Miss Daventry had remained at the bottom of the hill. Or perhaps back at Amberley. Up here there was no need for her. Up here there were only squirrels and birds to see Christy. A rabbit hopped across the path. She smiled—very well, rabbits too. She looked about. It was just a wood. Trees. But the sunlight slid through the leaves in dappled green light and there was such a feeling of freshness, of damp earth, of things growing and simply being. And it was all hers. Every sun-dappled scrap of it. In this moment the trees, the damp growing earth, the birdsong and the occasional scurryings of small creatures were all hers. She stood quite still, drawing it in, wishing she could remain right there, in that place and time. For a moment her whole being sang with joy and delight at merely being alive.

Still with that delight brimming over, she set off along the ridge for the promised lookout. She found it easily enough, a rocky outcrop where she perched high above the valley and could see the river far below, a shining ribbon slipping along towards its rendezvous with the mightier Severn at Chepstow, and at last the sea. All connected, all of a piece. Boats, like a child's bath toys, came and went as she munched her bread, cheese and apples. Apples that had grown in this same earth, warmed by the same sun pouring down on her head and shoulders. Folly to imagine that somehow she was part of it, but the idea lingered of being held, cradled, for once belonging. She should, she knew, put her bonnet back on—she was going to be sadly freckled, even a little bit sunburnt. She didn't care. Even her spencer had been discarded and folded away in the satchel. She couldn't think when she had enjoyed a day more. And all she had done was go for a walk. In Bristol when she had walked there had always been streets, noise and smells. Here she had the forest track and instead of noise, the song of birds and the occasional sounds floating up from the village below nestled in the trees on either side of the river. She watched a small ferry being poled across. Lady Braybrook had said something about organising a boating picnic for the children in a few days. She had no doubt that her ladyship would announce that she had absolutely no need for a companion that day and insist that she went with Lissy and Emma.

She sighed. That was the greatest danger of all. This affection she felt for all of them. Not just Lady Braybrook, but the children. Matt with his quiet scholarly ways, yet still with the streak of boyish mischief, Emma and Lissy, so merry and confident, and little Davy with his hero-worship of his eldest brother. Christy pushed away the memory of them going off together that morning, Davy chattering like a magpie and his lordship, dark head bent to catch all those whirling words, his little brother's no doubt sticky hand safe within his, and the dog at their heels.

Foolish sentiment, she told herself. It was not for her. They were kind, friendly, but they were not her family. Eventually she would leave and have to depend solely upon herself. That was constant. She had known it at eighteen when she had fallen in love—

No!

She grabbed the satchel and pushed herself to her feet. That bitter memory would not spoil this golden day. It would be over soon enough and she would have to wait for her next day off, which might be pouring with rain. Picking up the basket she had brought for blackberries, she set off.

Today there was only today, with no regret for yesterdays and definitely no worry about tomorrows. She was going to pick blackberries. She was going to enjoy the day's gifts and hoard the pleasure like a squirrel with a nut, every scrap of sunshine, every touch of the breeze on her hot face, every birdcall and every blackberry that didn't get as far as her basket.

Two hours later, picking blackberries, Christy acknowledged that one of the day's memories would be blackberry brambles. She wouldn't have believed how viciously the wretched sprays could cling. As for connected, the problem was to *avoid* being connected. They clung to everything, her hair, her skirts; her bare arms were well and truly scratched. Her basket was two-thirds full and that had taken an hour, although she admitted it might have been quicker had she not eaten so many. She loved blackberries and these, bursting with sunshine, were temptation itself.

She was slightly damp, having cooled her face in the river, but it was so hot she would be dry again by the time she reached Amberley. Although she would still slip in by the side door. She was a mess, but she was having so much fun. Never had she been able to roam like this for a whole day. Always she had been kept within doors, living in town. Either with her mother or at school or in her jobs. When she had gone out, it had been to do an errand. There had never been a chance simply to *be*. And blackberries had always been bought.

Moving around the patch, she saw a particularly luscious bunch over her head. Standing on tiptoe, she reached up, carefully lifting a prickly shoot out of the way…and felt it catch across the tops of her breasts through the cambric and linen of her gown and chemise.

'Bother!' she muttered and twisted around to release the clinging barbs. More snagged on her hair. With a curse she reached up to remove them. And froze as something on the ground caught her gaze. There, coiled lazily in the sun, was a greeny-coloured snake. She pulled back with a startled gasp, lost her balance and fell against the brambles. The snake didn't move.

One eye on the snake, Christy tried to pull free, but discovered that she was held fast. As soon as she loosened one set of barbs, another gripped with even greater tenacity. The snake appeared oblivious, until it suddenly uncoiled, raising its head. Briefly the forked tongue flickered and then with a rustle of grass and fallen leaves it slithered away towards the river.

Christy breathed a sigh of relief, and continued to battle the brambles, only to hear the sound of approaching hoofbeats. She muttered a curse as she twisted to look over her shoulder. Riding towards her on his tall black gelding was his lordship, sitting easily in the saddle as if he had grown there.

Spending the rest of the afternoon entangled in a bramble bush because she was too proud to call out would be stupid. Drawing a deep breath, she yelled. He raised a hand and his horse altered course towards her.

'Miss Daventry, is something—?' He broke off and the blue eyes widened. 'Ah.' He barely suppressed the grin, but swung down and came towards her swiftly. 'Are you all right?' His gaze fell on her scratched arms and his mouth set hard. 'What the devil were you doing to get that scratched?' Even as he spoke he fished an odd-looking tool out of his coat pocket, unfolded it to reveal a blade and began cutting her free.

'I was reaching for *those…*' she indicated the dangling blackberries '…and overbalanced.'

He gave a disgusted look as he caught a spray snagged on her hair, cut it and cast it away. 'Miss Daventry, the first rule of blackberrying is that no fruit is worth falling into the brambles for.'

'There was a snake,' she said, feeling foolish. 'I dare say it was harmless, but it startled me.'

'A snake?' He began to unhook a shoot that had caught across her breasts, the small barbs digging mercilessly. She froze at the shocking feel of his fingers, brushing with apparent uninterest over her breasts. Her breath locked in her throat; she looked down. The long, lean fingers worked carefully, detaching the clinging prickles. She swallowed. She felt surrounded by him, by the mingled odours of leather, horse and something warm, spicy and very male. This close she could see the faint dark shadow along his jaw, even though he would have shaved that morning. It looked scratchy, tempting, as though it invited curious fingertips. She clenched her fists, denying the thought, denying the sensation of his fingers brushing her breasts. Several layers of cloth should have muted his touch. They didn't.

His hands stilled. 'I'm sorry. Did I hurt you?'

'Wha—pardon?' She gulped. His right hand rested very lightly on her right breast. Heat rose, aching in both breasts.

'Your hands clenched. Did I hurt you?'

'Oh. Er, no. Of course not.' She forced her hands to relax. She wasn't used to being so close to a man. That was all.

He frowned as though not quite convinced, but continued. 'What colour was it?'

'Colour?' Frantically she pulled her senses back from the accidental caress of those long brown fingers. 'Oh, the snake—greenish. It was quite long, too. A yard?' No doubt he would think she was exaggerating and tell her that snakes didn't grow to that size.

'A grass snake, then,' he said. 'Harmless.' There was a ripping sound as one stubborn barb tore her gown, a small, three-cornered tear. His breath hissed in.

'Blast. Did that scratch you?'

'N…no.'

'Good. Hold still, we're nearly there.'

A moment later she stepped free, stumbling slightly. He steadied her. 'You should wash those scratches. Mrs Higgs will have some comfrey salve in the still-room.'

She nodded. 'Thank you, my lord.' Her breath came uncertainly. He still held her. Not to steady her now.

There was something intangibly different about the grip of his hands just above her bare elbows…something extremely unsteadying. She should step away. Should have already stepped away. Even as the thought flickered, his grip loosened, slid up her arms, his gaze questioning. And every speeding heartbeat she remained in his hold gave him the wrong answer.

'Someone in the bible found a lamb in a thicket, did they not?' His voice caressed. Hungry.

Oh, the temptation of that dark hunger! Not just his voice, but in his eyes. Her reason floundered for some sort of footing. 'Abraham,' she said. 'And…and it was a ram, not a lamb. He sacrificed it instead of his son.'

Heat flared in his eyes. 'As long as I am not expected to sacrifice you…'

Chapter Eight

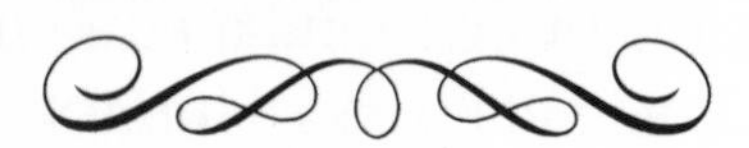

His blood hammered. Surely she knew where this was heading?

Awareness flared in her eyes. He took a deep breath. She knew, then. Knew and had not stepped back… Slowly he raised his hand to her face, brushing the backs of his fingers over the silk of her jaw, her throat…soft, warm…tawny tresses tumbled over his wrist. Any moment she would pull back, the golden, sun-warmed enchantment broken by reality.

Reality which said she was not for him. That she was respectable, unmarried, probably virgin—his sisters' governess, his stepmother's companion. In a word, forbidden. Dangerous.

Some dangers were worth risking. Behind the spectacles, her mismatched eyes were dazed. He drew her closer, one arm sliding about her waist, bringing her to him so that the small, rounded breasts just brushed against him. A taste. Just one taste of those sweet, berry-stained lips…

His intent was clear, and every instinct shrieked a warning to Christy. Folly! Exactly what she had guarded against. She should stop him. Say no… But she was discovering that virtue was a simple matter when there was no temptation to sin. And Julian Trentham was temptation incarnate. It glinted in the brilliant blue of his eyes, now blazing with desire, caressed her with fire in the touch of his fingers on her throat, and trembled within her at the hard promise of his body, so dangerously close as his lips sought hers.

One word—*no*—was all it would take.

His lips touched hers and her wits whirled.

A kiss. Just a kiss. She'd been mauled about before by an employer's son. *A bit of sport*, he'd called it. It had meant nothing to him, less than nothing to her. Only this man did not maul, and a kiss was definitely not just a kiss. Warm, firm lips feathered and caressed, promising ravishment, yet teasing with light touches before settling properly. The tip of his tongue traced the quivering seam of her lips, exploring, probing at the corner of her mouth. Gentle strength enveloped her, cradled her, all heat and restrained fierceness…and against all received wisdom, her head sank back against his arm as her mouth opened under his.

His control shook as he felt the flowering of her lips, the softening as they opened. Quelling the urge to ravish her mouth, he took it gently, absorbing the gasp of shock as his tongue penetrated the sweetness, sliding deep. Honey, sweet wild honey, intoxicating—her very hesitance, even clumsiness, made it all the sweeter. All the more dangerous… With his final, fading shred of sanity Julian broke the kiss. He stared down into her flushed face, and nearly lost control again as she blinked up at him from behind her spectacles.

'This,' he informed her, 'is not a good idea.' With difficulty he forced his arms to release her and stepped back, clutching a few returning shreds of common sense, not to mention honour.

'N…no.' She seemed to be having as much difficulty breathing as he was.

No man of honour seduced innocents. He hauled in a breath. This was neither the time nor place to say what he needed to say to Miss Daventry. Especially since he couldn't straighten his wits enough to think what that might be.

The blackberries she had been trying to reach caught his eye. Sweet, luscious and ripe. He stretched up, plucked them carefully, one by one, and deposited them in the basket.

'Your berries, Miss Daventry. I'll bid you good afternoon.'

Before he continued where he had left off and disgraced himself any further. She said nothing and, with a nod, he went to his horse and mounted.

Pushing Conqueror into a trot, he rode away, suppressing the urge to look back. Desire had been riding him with spurs for days, but kissing Christy Daventry was tantamount to insanity. Her birth and character rendered her untouchable. Or they should. Marriage was out of the question. Seducing her unthinkable.

But there were other open, honest offers that could be made to a woman. Offers that did not rely on the sweet lies and falseness of a cold-hearted seduction. He could have her as long as she understood exactly what was offered and was not permitted to delude herself with romantic dreams. As long as he didn't cheat her with lies.

Christy watched him ride away, shivering despite the warmth of the sun. She touched her lips. How could a kiss—just a kiss!—make her feel like this?

Like what?

As though she were about to melt. As though his hand still cupped her breast, and his mouth still plundered hers. As though her world had tilted on its axis and started spinning in the wrong direction.

Her world would be tipped upside down if she let him seduce her. She knew that. Why, then, was everything in her whispering that it might be worth the risk? It was worth nothing. The only guarantee was a parting.

So? that insidious little voice murmured. *He's rich. You could get a settlement from him that would mean you never had to work again...you would have what you want: security.*

She might also have a child, and not willingly would she start the cycle again. Oh, there were precautions that could be taken. She knew that. None better. She also knew that they were uncertain at best. Harry was proof of that. And there was further proof, a headstone in a Bristol churchyard...a little sister. She blinked back tears at the memory. She had been sixteen when eight-year-old Sarah died of measles. Sarah would be sixteen now, earning her own living. Worrying about scraping enough together to survive on. Perhaps it was as well…

She couldn't do it. She would not risk bearing a child with no rights. *Filius nullius.* A child who did not exist in the world's calculations. A child who would have to lie every time someone asked about her father. Whose father would not bother to attend that child's funeral… The old anger rose, but she forced it back. There was no point. There never had been. Even when she had said all that was to be said on the subject. Said it to the Duke of Alcaston's face.

And she could not bear to sell, for cold hard cash, what she had once refused to give for love. Desire was not love. This aching, restless need would not last. It would fade, as love had once faded. Until it did, her hard-earned and usually unshakeable self-control would have to do double duty.

Somehow all the delight had gone from the day, although around her the sun still poured golden, birds still sang, and blackberries gleamed darkly in the hedgerow. Bending down, she picked up the basket. She had enough in there. Some fruit was out of her reach; the rest was not worth the pain, and if she knew which ones Lord Braybrook had plucked, she would leave them behind for the birds.

After a long walk she should have been hungry. Instead, every spoonful of soup was an effort. The problem was sitting to her left, and he didn't appear to be off his food at all. Certainly he did not look as though he were aware that the woman he had kissed witless near a blackberry patch a few hours earlier was seated beside him. Not right beside him, of course, but a quarter of the way around the table.

There were only four of them that evening: herself, Lady Braybrook, Matthew and his lordship. Alicia and Emma were spending the night with Miss Pargeter. It should not have made any difference. Unlike her previous position where she had always dined alone if her employer had family or a visitor, she was expected to take her meals with the family.

She felt comfortable with them usually, except for the queer off-balance feeling that his lordship caused, but she ignored that, pretending it didn't exist. These family meals at the round table held little of formality, and it never seemed to matter who sat where. No one ever minded if the conversation bounced back and forth across the table and became somewhat noisy. The affection between them all glowed as golden and mellow as the candles on the table and in the wall sconces. Just being there and seeing it gave her a sense of peace, even though she was not really part of it. Not inside. It was not that they ignored her. Far from it. They made her welcome. But she still did not *belong*, although the light touched her.

Now, listening to Lady Braybrook explaining what needed to be done before the Summer Ball in three weeks, she knew what a fool she had been—that even while denying it, she had let herself believe that she *was* somehow included. The Incident—a cold, indifferent word chosen deliberately—by the bramble patch had jolted her out of her folly.

She nodded. 'Of course, ma'am. I will see that the bedchambers are prepared as well, if you wish to give me the list of guests staying overnight.'

Lady Braybrook smiled. 'Thank you, dear. It will be so much easier with you to help. I positively look forward to Braybrook marrying and his wife taking this sort of thing off my hands!'

Lord Braybrook looked up from his conversation about winter crops with Matthew. 'Serena, if the ball is too much—'

She waved him to silence. 'Nonsense. Not now I have Miss Daventry. Ah. Thank you, Walter.'

The servants cleared away the first course and brought in the second. Matthew's eyes lit up.

'I say! Blackberry pie! Excellent!' He grinned at Christy. 'Did you pick those?'

Her cheeks reddened. 'Yes.' She had delivered the berries to the kitchen, expecting them to be transformed into nicely anonymous jam or jelly. Not placed on the table before her, a tangible reminder of idiocy. Anger spiked. No doubt to his lordship they were merely blackberries. A tasty treat. Just as she would be if she weren't careful.

'A family tradition,' said Lady Braybrook cheerfully. 'One's first full basket of blackberries is always served for dinner. I gave the instructions this morning that if you came in with enough we were to have a pie.'

Christy felt the barbs dig into her again, mocking even as they drew her on.

'Looks jolly good,' said Matthew. 'Thank you, Miss Daventry.'

'They are…they are just blackberries,' she said. 'I thought they would be made into jam.' It was just their way. She would not fall into the trap of self-delusion again.

'Certainly not,' said Lady Braybrook. 'One's first blackberries should be memorable, Miss Daventry. Don't you agree, Julian?'

'Definitely,' he said. 'They look delicious, Miss Daventry.'

Cheeks hot, she met his gaze.

Beyond a polite greeting, it was the first remark he had addressed to her all evening. She wished he had refrained now. There was something disturbing in his gaze. Something that said he was thinking about the taste of more than blackberries.

She swallowed, cold and shaken as the blush ebbed. More than ever she felt apart, separate.

Matthew frowned. 'That walk was not after all too much for you, was it?' he asked. 'You're awfully quiet this evening. Pale, too.'

Aware of his lordship's intensified gaze, she managed a smile for Matthew. 'Nonsense. I am a little tired, but it is a nice sort of tired.' Or it would have been. 'And I saw a great many birds,' she added, desperate to change the subject. 'Just as you said. Only I didn't know what the half of them were.'

'Oh, we can't have that,' he said cheerfully. 'You'd better borrow Braybrook's bird books.' He turned to his brother. 'That will be all right, won't it, Julian?'

'Of course,' said his lordship. He turned to Christy. 'Indeed, there is something I wish to discuss with you, so if you come to the library after dinner I will give them to you.'

Oh, *God*! Why hadn't she bitten her tongue? She could just imagine what he wished to *discuss*. His etchings probably.

'Perhaps another time, my lord,' she said. 'I believe Lady Braybrook wishes to arrange the details for the Summer Ball, so—'

'Nonsense, dear,' said Lady Braybrook, cutting off her retreat. 'That can wait, but you do put me in mind of something.' She turned to her stepson. 'Julian—your marriage.'

Julian's wineglass paused halfway to his lips as he stared as Serena.

'My *what*?' he asked, in disbelief. Where the devil had that come from? They had been talking about blackberries. Sort of.

'Marriage, Julian.' Serena sipped her own wine. 'I am sure I can speak freely. Matt will not repeat anything and of course Miss Daventry would not.'

A quick glance told him that Miss Daventry looked as stunned as *he* felt. 'Nevertheless, it's hardly—' he began.

'It really is time you considered marriage seriously,' said Serena, ignoring his attempt to change the subject as she served some pie for herself and Miss Daventry. 'At thirty-two, it's high time you were settled. Before it's too late.'

He set his wineglass down with a distinct click. 'Are you telling me that I'm on the shelf?'

Matthew spluttered.

'Shut up, Matt.'

'Sorry.' Matthew didn't sound in the least bit sorry.

'Not precisely on the shelf,' said Serena. 'But if you leave it much longer they'll all be far too young for you. Think about it! All the eligible…that is, well-bred, well-dowered, *pretty* girls are snapped up at once.'

He stared at her.

'That is what you want in a woman, after all. Isn't it?' she said.

Those were precisely the qualifications that he had always taken it for granted that his *bride* would possess. Only right now he wasn't thinking about a bride. In fact, given his current intentions, discussing a possible marriage seemed highly inapposite.

'Have some pie, dear,' she said, passing it to him. His brain reeled. Those were still the qualifications he required. Blackberry pie had nothing to do with marriage…

'So,' continued Serena, as Julian helped himself to pie and then passed it along to Matt, 'it appears to me that as you have not met anyone suitable in London, then you might as well consider local candidates—the Summer Ball is a perfect opportunity for you to look them all over and make a selection.'

Good God! He took a spoonful of pie, its sweetness bursting in his mouth. She made it sound like buying a filly at Tattersalls! And he couldn't fault her for that, because, on the rare occasions he had considered the matter, that had been his own approach.

'Intelligent,' he got out and took another spoonful of pie. It was delicious, delicately spiced with nutmeg, and, violently aware of Christy's silent presence, he was enjoying it about as much as a bowl of dust and ashes.

Serena raised her brows. 'I thought that went without saying?'

And the rest *didn't*?

'Anyway, dear—give it some consideration. The obvious choice is Miss Postleton, but—'

'Anne?' asked Matthew, the serving spoon clattering against the pie dish. 'Shouldn't have thought she was quite Julian's sort, you know. She's not…I don't know…*kind*, really. Snubbed poor old Flint horribly in the village the other day when he asked her if he might dance with her at the Summer Ball. Liss spoke up to save his feelings and said *she'd* dance with him.'

'Oh, well,' said Serena. 'I do not say that I am set on Anne—that will be for Braybrook to decide…'

'Really?' he said with just the faintest hint of irony.

Serena sipped her hock. 'Don't be sarcastic, dear. I am merely pointing out that, unless you actually think about it, nothing will happen.'

'Better him than me,' muttered Matthew, casting Julian a pitying glance and pouring a generous dollop of cream over his blackberry pie.

* * *

Christy's faint hope that talk of marriage might have given his lordship's thoughts a more proper direction died as they rose from the dining table.

'Serena, if you will excuse me, I have some work to do this evening. If I may borrow Miss Daventry for a few moments, I will find those books for her.'

'Of course, Julian,' said Lady Braybrook, clearly oblivious to the possibility that her companion might have to defend her virtue. 'And, Miss Daventry, the ball can wait. This is still your day off, you know, and you look quite tired. I think you should go up early. Goodnight, dear.' She signalled to the footman who waited to carry her up to the drawing room. Matthew rose to wheel her out, saying, 'Goodnight, Miss Daventry.'

Once the door was safely shut behind them, Christy swung to face Lord Braybrook. 'You will excuse me, my lord. I have nothing to discuss with you. If you are happy to lend me the books, you may send them to my room. Goodnight.'

Devils danced in his eyes. Gritting her teeth, she turned to go.

'I'll bring them up myself, Miss Daventry. Just as soon as I find them. I suggest you don't prepare yourself for bed quite yet.'

'Wha—?' Recovering, she veiled fright and anger under frosty disdain. 'I *beg* your pardon?'

'Miss Daventry—I wish to speak with you. Now. You may choose the venue. My library. Or your bedchamber.' The corner of his mouth twitched. 'Or mine if you prefer.'

She went cold all over. Sometimes a man's kisses meant worse than nothing…

'On the whole I recommend the library,' he went on. 'You may sit beside the bell pull and I will sit far enough away to give you ample opportunity to use it should you deem it necessary.'

She stared at him. He might be lying, but she thought not. She simply couldn't imagine him telling a lie. Which might mean that her imagination was sadly lacking. 'The library, then,' she agreed. If he was lying, he would discover that she was not entirely without defences.

True to his word, Lord Braybrook made no effort to join Christy by the fireplace, but sat behind his desk.

'You know why we are here, Miss Daventry,' he said. 'But first let me assure you that I have no intention of seducing you here in the library, or indeed under this roof.'

'You don't?' Then what had that kiss been about? If ever a kiss had promised sinful indulgence…

'I wish to make you an offer.'

Shock robbed her of speech. He couldn't, it simply wasn't possible! And even if he did—

'I am offering you the position of my mistress.'

That on the other hand was eminently possible.

After a moment she said carefully, 'No doubt you will explain the difference between this and seduction, my lord, but—'

'The difference is honesty, Miss Daventry,' he told her. 'I am not offering lies about kisses and moonlight, nor about undying devotion. I am not tricking you into anything. I am not even trying to trick your body into anything. I desire you and wish you to be my mistress. After that kiss this afternoon, there is no point in denying our mutual attraction. Is there?'

She shook her head. One moment of idiocy. And God help her, the memory of it, the tender promise of his arms and kiss could still tempt her even in the face of his cool, businesslike proposition.

He was speaking again. Cold. Rational. 'Obviously you are not the sort of female to whom I can offer marriage—but you would be well provided for.'

She swallowed that without flinching. It was no more than the truth. Indeed, it was truer than he knew. She waited.

'I have several comfortable houses in nearby towns. A lease would be settled on you, along with an annuity, and I would visit you. Discreetly, of course.'

'Of course,' she echoed. *Discretion*, the duke's watchword. The reason he had not attended her mother's funeral, or Sarah's. Yet all her neighbours would know exactly what she was and she would live isolated except for his brief visits. Visits that would grow further apart until they ceased entirely and then one day she would receive a note from him to inform her of what her heart already knew: that it was finished. She would be her mother all over again. Mistresses were for bedsport only and when their charms faded, their lovers faded away too. Her mother had been lucky the duke had continued to support her.

'You would not find me an ungenerous lover, Miss Daventry. In any way. There would be a proper contract drawn up between us, including provision for any child. Nor would you be dismissed when I marry.'

'I see. A charming prospect for your wife.'

He actually flushed. 'You misunderstand. The requirements for wife and mistress are very different. In my world fidelity is not demanded, nor am I hypocrite enough to expect something of my wife that I am not prepared to give in return. Once the succession is assured, she may please herself discreetly.'

She had never heard it spelt out so brutally, and she had never heard of a contract, but she understood all about the difference between wife and mistress in his world. A wife brought breeding and fortune. A mistress was for bedsport. *And love…?* She choked that off. Love had no part in either arrangement, despite lip service in the marriage vows.

'Miss Daventry?'

She rose to her feet, conscious of aching regret, mingled with gratitude that he had made his offer openly, that he had not seduced her with sweet lies and kisses. Tenderness would have been the ultimate temptation. Now more than ever, she understood her mother's mistakes, understood her believing that it was different. Because the memory of this afternoon's kiss promised delight and tenderness. Even in the face of his cold, calculated offer, that kiss whispered of so much more. That with *him* it would be different.

'No, thank you, my lord. Goodnight. I will give Lady Braybrook my notice in the morning.'

'I beg your pardon?' He looked as winded as if she had landed a blow to his stomach.

'I am refusing your generous offer, my lord—'

'Yes, I understood that,' he said impatiently. 'But why are you leaving?'

She struggled for words. For coherent thoughts.

'My lord, you have offered me the position of your mistress. Surely you neither expect nor wish me to remain here?'

He frowned. 'I thought I made it clear that I was not going to seduce you? If you are refusing me, then that is an end of the matter. I'm not about to creep into your bedchamber to have my wicked way with you against your will. You have refused. So be it. Do not imagine, Miss Daventry, that I am fancying myself in love, nor that I am incapable of controlling my desires. You are perfectly safe under my roof.'

Safe? Perhaps in the way a mouse was safe from a well-fed, sleeping cat…but something about the very quietness of his assurance rang true.

He could be lying. But she still couldn't imagine it, and she liked being here. It was the most dangerous illusion of all, but here she felt comfortable. Which was stupid. His lordship's dishonourable proposal had showed her exactly how far from his world she was.

'Very well. I will remain.'

For now.

'Good.' He stood up and strolled across to the bookshelves, pulling out three octavo volumes. 'And you are quite sure that you will not reconsider your refusal?' As though he had offered to buy something material. Which perhaps he had.

'Quite sure, my lord,' she said evenly. 'It is not a life that appeals to me.'

He turned, the books in his hands, and frowned at her. 'I thought you were insulted, but you are not, are you?'

She considered that. Was she? Beneath the numbness she felt something, but she doubted it was anger. What right had she to be insulted? Even if he didn't know it, she was illegitimate, a duke's by-blow. She used the ugly term deliberately, reminding herself of reality. He had been honest with her. That in itself implied some sort of respect. He had not simply attempted to take what he wanted, either by stealth, or force. The choice was hers. She must make it wisely.

'No, my lord. You were honest with me. I appreciate that. But if it's any consolation, I have no experience or talents that would render me at all suitable as a mistress.'

He seemed to freeze, but an instant later laid the books on his desk, placing them with careful exactitude in the very middle. 'Ah. I believe these to be the volumes you wanted, Miss Daventry.'

'Volumes?'

Long, lean fingers brushed lightly over the calfskin, reminding her of the magic they could summon from a woman's body…

'George Graves, *British Ornithology*. In three volumes. Lady Braybrook will wish to know if you are enjoying them.' His voice was cool, remote. Aristocrat to humble dependant. Probably she would have been expected to call him *my lord* in bed… 'Matthew is our resident expert if you have any questions.'

She dragged in a breath, banishing fancy and regret. 'Of course, my lord. Thank you.'

The other subject was closed, then. Dismissed. No doubt from his mind as well as from discussion. Which was exactly what she wanted. Wasn't it?

Aware of his gaze on her, she came forwards and picked up the books. A slight movement behind the desk startled her. She looked up at him sharply.

'If you are not insulted, Miss Daventry, and you admit your attraction—will you tell me why you refused?'

His voice betrayed only mild curiosity, but something about the set of his jaw, the line of his mouth, had her backing away, heart pounding. And not in fear. Her mind was blank. Why *was* she refusing?

Words came without conscious thought. 'You warned me yourself, my lord.'

The black brows snapped together. 'Oh? When?'

'This afternoon. When you told me that no fruit is worth the pain of falling into the bramble patch.'

His mouth twisted. 'I see. Well, should you change your mind,' he said politely, 'you have only to say so and I will arrange it all.'

She inclined her head. 'You are all kindness, sir.' Then, clutching the books, she beat a dignified retreat.

Chapter Nine

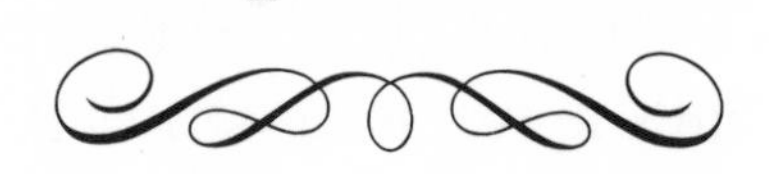

Julian shut his eyes and clenched his fists as the door closed. That was that. The refusal he had half expected. Without even bothering to find out what he was prepared to offer. What *was* it about Christy Daventry? She wasn't a beauty—but he had never wanted a woman more. She was honest enough to raise blisters when she abandoned her reserve. And the thought of her abandoning her reserve in bed raised something even more painful.

But she wasn't his usual sort of woman. She was neither one of his discreet aristocratic lovers, nor a woman he would set up publicly in London, an acknowledged ladybird—a voluptuous prize to flaunt before the world, at the opera, in the Park. He couldn't see her in that milieu at all. He wanted her all to himself. *His.* Here.

Well, not *here* precisely. That was impossible. But somewhere close to Amberley so that he could ride over and spend a few days with her at times…which was foolish beyond belief. He had never done anything like that in his life. When he visited a mistress it was to have sex. Not because he wanted to spend time with her. Damn it! Why had he wanted to sit down with those books and help her find the birds she had seen today? And suggest other birds to watch for. Why did he want to find out how to make her laugh, banish the sadness he sometimes saw in her eyes? Why did he even notice the sadness?

She had refused him. And it was not the sort of refusal that gave him the least hope she would change her mind. Her decision had been made, and voiced, with cool deliberation. No tears. No reproaches. She hadn't even been decently shocked.

No fruit is worth the pain of falling into the bramble patch.

That spurred something inside him startlingly close to shame. He knew damn well it was true. In these *affaires* all penalty was on the woman's side. Any social costs and hurt would be borne by her. Miss Daventry had decided that he wasn't worth the risk. And having assured her that she was safe from him, he must honour that promise. Her assurance that she had no experience didn't help in the least. Quite the opposite—he was doubtless about to spend a sleepless night imagining all sorts of ways in which he could redress her inexperience.

Enough! He had promised not to seduce her. Blackberries were off the menu.

For the next few days Julian buried himself in estate business either in the library, or about the estate, listing jobs to be done before winter. Cottages to be repaired, wood to be cut, a farmer's widow to re-house. He took Davy with him and spent as little time in Miss Daventry's company as possible. He saw her at breakfast and in the evenings, always in company with Serena or one of his siblings. She said *good morning, good evening*. Beyond that she scarcely even looked at him.

Which was a good thing, he assured himself as he tightened his horse's girth one morning ten days after the ill-advised rendezvous by the blackberries. Miss Daventry was doing the job for which she had been hired. She ran errands for Serena, helped with teaching Davy, supervised Lissy and Emma at their music, engaged in French and Italian conversation with them, and, according to Serena, was a great help with the arrangements for the swiftly approaching ball. This morning she had been sent off to the village shop to buy some embroidery silks. Serena had given her the errand at breakfast. He had been tempted to order his curricle instead of riding to his meeting with Sir John Postleton so that he might offer to take her up. He was an idiot.

Out of sight, out of mind. That's how it was meant to work. That was how it always had worked in the past.

This time dismissing a failed conquest from his mind was nigh on impossible, he thought, riding out of the stable yard. He snorted. Conquest? A more inappropriate word could not be imagined. Miss Daventry was not the sort of female one conquered. He still wanted her. Only that wasn't why he had thought of offering to drive her into the village. He had simply wanted to be with her. Talk to her. Perhaps tease her into one of her sharp comments. He must be mad. Barking, in fact. Especially since he was quite sure she would not have stepped into the curricle.

A bell clanged as Christy pushed open the door of the village shop. She blinked as her eyes adjusted to the dimness after the blaze of sunshine outside. The shop was crowded, shelves towering to the ceiling, laden with goods ranging from shoes to cheeses. More expensive wares, such as tea and spices, were stored behind the counter to be dispensed by Mr Wilkins on request. Flitches of bacon hung from the rafters and the whole shop breathed the yeasty warmth of new-baked bread.

Everything was spotless, from the windows to the floor, including the small, neat man behind the counter, subjecting her to a searching scrutiny. Recognising her, he relaxed and permitted himself a slight bow.

'Good day, Miss Daventry. May I help you?'

'Good day, Mr Wilkins,' she said. 'Some embroidery silks for her ladyship, if you please, and some cambric for myself.' She needed to hem new handkerchiefs.

Mr Wilkins bustled from behind the counter and in a very short time the embroidery silks were laid out for her inspection. Pulling Lady Braybrook's samples from her pocket, Christy began the painstaking task of selecting matches. Some blues were needed…that pale sky blue? Yes. But not that royal blue. This one? Perhaps… About to ask if she might take the silks to the window, she heard the bell ring again as the door opened. Mr

Wilkins, setting out some cambric for her inspection, looked up and his mouth pursed as though he had bitten into something unpleasant.

'What is it, child?'

The cold, dismissive tone drew echoes from the past, and Christy turned to see who had entered.

Shock slammed into her.

In the drawing room at Amberley there was a set of miniatures of Lady Braybrook's children. All painted as five year olds, all staggeringly alike with the Trentham dark hair and blue eyes, luminous on ivory.

It was as though the portrait of five-year-old Alicia had sprung to warm, glowing life and walked into the shop. The same glossy black curls and bright eyes—only this child's complexion was tinged golden with the sun.

'Well?' snapped Mr Wilkins. 'What do you want?'

There could only be one explanation for the child's resemblance to the Trenthams and Mr Wilkins's attitude. With condensing pain, Christy saw the little girl's nervousness.

'Please, sir—a paper of pins for Mam, and…and a pink riband.' The piping voice sounded breathless, and the child cast a quick glance at Christy. 'I've enough money.' She opened her tightly clenched fingers to show a shilling clutched there.

Mr Wilkins looked affronted. 'You'll have to wait. This lady is before you.'

Her voice indifferent, Christy said, 'There's no need for that, Mr Wilkins. I am not done with my selections. Serve the child.'

'Well—' Mr Wilkins found a paper of pins and wrapped them up. 'There. You can't have the riband. I'll not have you pawing through my goods, dirtying them.'

Within Christy long-buried rage uncurled, stretching its wings.

The little girl said nothing, just swallowed and handed him the shilling.

'Mr Wilkins,' said Christy in creditably neutral tones, 'I believe my hands are clean. Perhaps if I were to look through your ribands and the child were to point out the right colour?'

Purple, Christy reflected, was particularly unflattering on a man's face. 'There's no need, Miss Daventry,' began Wilkins, 'I assure you—'

The door jangled, but Christy did not bother to look around.

'Mr Postleton! Miss Anne!' Mr Wilkins started towards them, bowing low, his face wreathed in obsequiousness.

Miss Anne... Christy glanced over her shoulder—she had met Miss Postleton at church—briefly. Anne Postleton had acknowledged the introduction with a supercilious *oh?* and continued on her way. It was a wonder the shop ceiling didn't cave in with the shock of having the young lady under it along with the woman Braybrook desired as his mistress. Not to mention the child.

'Oh, Mr Wilkins!' said Miss Anne. 'I am in such a bother! The Summer Ball at Amberley, you know! And I am to have a new gown, so I should like to look at your silks, if you please!'

'But of course, Miss Anne!' he said at once, starting towards them, wreathed in unctuous delight. 'If you would just tell me which colours, I will fetch them down this instant!'

The final thread restraining Christy's temper snapped.

'The ribands, if you please, sir!'

Shocked faces turned towards her, and she shamelessly added, 'I should not care to keep Lady Braybrook waiting for her silks either, Mr Wilkins.'

Mr Postleton stared. 'What the deuce! Braybrook's governess, ain't it?'

'Miss *Trentham*'s governess,' Christy corrected him, willing herself to ignore the smirk.

A faint sneer curled Miss Postleton's lip. 'Oh, yes. The *governess*.' Oozing disdain, she turned back to Mr Wilkins. 'I won't keep you long, Mr Wilk—'

Mr Wilkins, however, had found the ribands and placed the box on the counter with a bang. 'Thank you,' said Christy, and turned to the little girl with a smile. 'A pink riband, was it not? And I don't think I know your name?'

The child looked up her hesitantly and nodded. 'Nan,' she whispered.

A stifled titter came from behind them. 'Oh, really! Ned! Do you see who it is?'

A muffled crack of laughter came from Mr Postleton. 'By Jove!'

The child, Nan, flinched. At the sight a slow fire ignited in Christy's gut. She remembered, oh, *how* she remembered the murmurs in Bath when she had been a child—the people who turned away, the shopkeepers who seemed not to see one. Whose arithmetic in working out the change had so often disagreed with hers. Then she had not understood. Now, she understood only too well. And this child…she was how old? Five? Six? And already condemned.

She summoned a smile. 'How do you do, Nan?' she responded. 'I am Miss Daventry. I work at Amberley.'

Selecting several different pinks from the box, she set them out. Beyond them at the far end of the counter, Mr Wilkins tenderly laid out lengths of silk for Miss Postleton. Christy ignored them, but Ned Postleton's occasional glances were an unpleasant itch between her shoulder blades.

The child, Nan, subjected the ribands to a close inspection, then, careful not to touch, she pointed and said, 'That one.'

It was a deep, rich colour, almost raspberry.

'Perfect,' said Christy. She could imagine it glowing in the raven curls. 'Is it for you? It will look very pretty.'

Nan nodded. 'Because I've been good.'

Such a simple delight, thought Christy. She put the other ribands back and looked toward Mr Wilkins, who was hovering over Miss Postleton, complimenting her on her taste as she scowled over the merits of jonquil yellow and palest pink. His back was firmly turned to Christy.

She dragged in a breath and prepared to do battle.

'Mr Wilkins—'

'Might as well serve the lady, Wilkins,' drawled Mr

Postleton, lounging against the counter and running his eyes over Christy. 'M'sister could be hours.' He gave Christy a wink.

Miss Postleton glanced up, cast a condescending glance at Christy and shrugged. 'Oh, as you please. I am sure it makes no difference to *me*!'

Mr Wilkins came over and grudgingly measured out a length of pink delight while Nan watched, breathless.

She paid for the riband and pins and then, stowing her treasure safely in a pocket, smiled shyly at Christy. 'Thank you, miss.'

With a jingle of the doorbell, she was gone, trotting off up the street. Christy watched her for a moment—torn between an aching sense of fellowship and a searing desire to hit the man whose careless pleasure had condemned his daughter to a half-life. Nan could have been herself all those years ago…or Sarah. Or her own child had she been fool enough to accept Braybrook's offer. An innocent, condemned by the world as tainted, impure.

Her chin up, she turned to Mr Wilkins. 'What a pretty child,' she said. 'Such blue eyes—I've never seen anything lovelier.'

Another titter escaped from Miss Postleton.

Let them make of *that* what they would! She knew exactly where those blue eyes came from and she would wager her year's salary that neither Mr Wilkins nor Miss Postleton had ever snubbed the father!

'Very pretty,' muttered Mr Wilkins, as though the words were dragged from him.

'And so well mannered,' continued Christy with malice aforethought, handing him Lady Braybrook's embroidery silks and her own cambric. 'One can tell so much from the way a girl conducts herself with others.'

Miss Postleton looked up from the dress lengths, her face stiff with outrage.

Casting discretion to hell, Christy continued pensively, 'Heritage does tell, does it not? Her parents must be very good sort of people.'

Mr Wilkins's mouth flopped open and closed like a fish on a very nasty hook, as he did up Christy's purchases in a neat parcel. Ignoring a stifled snort of laughter from Mr Postleton, Christy handed the money to Mr Wilkins.

Mr Wilkins gulped, and wiped his brow. 'Ah, yes. Jane Roberts…she's, er, widowed. As it were.'

'As it were, Mr Wilkins?' She tucked the parcel safely into her satchel. Never before had she quite understood the pleasure there could be in taking a pound or three of flesh.

The little man swallowed. 'Er, yes. He died—old Tom Roberts, her husband. Child was born a few months later.'

'How very sad,' said Christy. 'Such a misfortune. Well, thank you for your help, Mr Wilkins. Good day to you.' She nodded politely to Mr Postleton and his sister as she walked to the door.

A spiteful voice followed her. 'I dare say poor, dear Lady Braybrook will be *most* interested in the company her servants keep.'

Christy looked back. 'Oh, do you think so? I *had* thought her mind to be above village tittle-tattle, but if you think it will amuse her to know that I met you here, Miss Postleton, I will mention it. Good day to you.'

Without waiting for a response, she left the shop in a furious jangle of bells. She was shocked to find herself shaking. Not for years had anything slid beneath her guard; she had learnt to ignore that sort of jibe. For herself at least...only not since Sarah's death had she seen another child on the receiving end.

She pushed the memory away. Sarah was at peace in that little churchyard outside Bristol, a white rose dreaming over her. It *was* better that way. Or so she always told herself.

Out of the corner of her eye she saw his lordship riding into the village from the direction of Amberley. Rage bubbled up, scalding...all the things she wanted to say searing on the tip of her tongue. Just as they had boiled up at the Duke after Sarah's death. She had said it all then. She must not this time. She was not sixteen, and it was none of her business. Slamming the lid down on the roiling cauldron, she turned resolutely and forced herself to walk in the opposite direction. Fast. She ought to return to Amberley, but if she passed him, if he stopped and spoke—God only knew what she might say. All the years of self-discipline had incinerated in moments. She wasn't sure enough of her control to risk an encounter with him now.

And why on earth should she be surprised at this? It

happened all the time. Why this sense of disappointment? Would she have expected him to rear his illegitimate daughter with his younger siblings? Hardly!

A mocking catcall pulled her out of her abstraction. Fifty yards ahead a small group of village boys milled around a low stone wall. Pressing close, they shoved and jostled, apparently engrossed in something beside the wall. A puppy with a brick tied to its tail? A kitten? Something small and helpless they could torment? Christy's already swift stride lengthened.

'Givin' yerself airs, eh?' came a jeering voice. 'Yer just a little bastard, my dad ses, an' yer mam's nowt but a rich man's fancy piece!'

'Leavin's, yeh mean, Bob,' came another voice. 'Everyone knows he don't come next or nigh her no more. 'Ere! Gimme that!'

'No! They're me mam's!'

Christy broke into a dead run.

Unhesitatingly her hand fell on the shoulder of the largest boy, a tall, well-grown lad of perhaps thirteen, twisting him towards her. Caught off-balance, he staggered and bumped against another boy.

'Stop it!' she ordered. Her rage scorched. Nan cowered against the wall, her curls dishevelled, dress dusty and a trickle of blood showing on one leg. The little parcel of pins lay in the dirt.

The boys turned and eyed Christy in patent wariness. The big boy she had grabbed, shuffled and wrenched his shoulder loose, saying defiantly, 'We're not doin' no harm.' Ignoring that, she pushed him aside as she went to Nan, picked up the package and handed it to her. Then she turned to face the boys again, her hand on Nan's shoulder.

The big boy looked around at his mates, as if for reassurance and swaggered slightly. 'Just a bit of a game,' he went on, 'ain't it, Nan?' The others snickered in agreement.

The little girl, her cheeks tear-streaked, hesitated.

'Ain't it, Nan?' he repeated through gritted teeth.

'Yes,' whispered the child, pressing against Christy's skirts and reaching for her hand.

Disgust sour in her mouth, Christy stared hard at the boy, brows raised until his gaze dropped and his mates began edging away.

'Just a bit o' fun!' he insisted.

'Odd sort of fun,' came a deep voice, 'that leaves a little girl bleeding and in tears, wouldn't you say, boys?'

Christy spun around with the boys at the familiar voice.

Braybrook stood there, his horse's reins looped over his arm, his face hard, the mouth set in an implacable line.

He glanced at Christy. 'Thank you, Miss Daventry, for your intervention. I regret its necessity, and so will these lads once I have spoken with their parents.' His voice did not lift above its usual level, but the boys exchanged nervous glances.

'Just so,' he said quietly. 'You will, each and every one of you, apologise to both Miss Daventry and Nan.'

Under that cold blaze the boys shuffled past, muttering apologies.

When the last of them had gone, Braybrook seemed to relax slightly. Very slightly. When he turned to face them, tension remained in the hard lines about his mouth.

Yet his voice was gentle as he bent down to Nan. 'May I see that scrape?'

Despite her rage, Christy found his diffidence oddly touching. As though *he* were unsure of his rights. Still clutching Christy's hand, Nan nodded wordlessly, and with gentle hands Braybrook lifted her skirts to expose a skinned, bruised knee.

'Fell over running,' whispered Nan. 'Banged my knee.'

Braybrook said nothing, but Christy saw a muscle flicker beside his jaw. Without a word, he produced a handkerchief, and dabbed carefully at the graze.

'I've some water,' said Christy, finding her voice. She let go of Nan's hand and opened her satchel, bringing out the water bottle.

'Thank you.' Braybrook took the bottle and uncorked it, pouring a little water onto the handkerchief and using it to wash away the streaked blood and dirt.

'There,' he said at last. 'That's better. All clean now.' He straightened up, his expression unreadable.

Some of Christy's anger, momentarily deflected by his gentleness with the child, returned.

'All injury avenged,' she said coolly. 'I'll walk Nan home, my lord.' He might have come to the child's assistance, but she doubted that he would care to be seen walking through the village with her.

He looked down at her, frowning. Then, 'Yes. You do that. I have a couple of other things I must attend to.'

All of Christy's fury re-ignited.

It took every ounce of her self-control to say only, 'Of course you do, my lord. Good day to you.'

She held out her hand to Nan. 'Come along, sweetheart. I'll see you safely home. Do you think your mama will make me a cup of tea?'

Julian left the forge half an hour later, reasonably certain that not one of the boys would be able to sit down to his dinner. Whatever their parents might think of Jane Roberts, or suspect about her daughter's paternity, they had no doubts at all about the unwisdom of offending the lord of Amberley, who happened to own well over half the village.

Simple enough as far as it went. Which was not nearly far enough. His visit to Jane would not be simple at all.

Jane Roberts opened the door and flushed when she saw him. 'Good day, my lord.'

He tensed at the barely veiled hostility, but said politely, 'Good morning, Jane. How do you go on?'

Dark eyes wary, she said, 'Well enough. Is there something you want, my lord?'

He shook his head. 'No. Merely to say that I have spoken with all the boys and their parents and I doubt that there will be any more of this morning's trouble. I take it Miss Daventry explained when she brought Nan home?'

Jane's defensive air eased slightly. 'Yes. Thank you.'

'Tell me, Jane—has anything like this happened before?' he asked.

She shrugged. 'Only to be expected, wasn't it?'

'The hell it is!' he retorted. 'When you told me to stop visiting, I warned you about this sort of thing! Don't you think I'd have dealt with it, if I'd known?'

'Very obliging of you, I'm sure.'

'Obliging be damned!' he snapped. 'For God's sake, Jane! Would it not be better if you moved? Started somewhere else, where people won't take one look at Nan, and—'

'Call her a whore's daughter?' finished Jane. 'Why should I be driven from my home?'

'I'm not trying to drive you out,' he said wearily. Every time they spoke this came up. 'I want only what's best for both of you.'

Her face hard, she said, 'Twould make little difference. A "widow" with a child and a mysterious source of money, moving where no one knows her? Have me pegged in no time, they would. Might as well put out a sign sayin' "whore".'

'I'm sorry, Jane,' he said quietly. 'I wish for your sake it were otherwise, but—'

'Ten years!' she burst out. 'Ten years of marriage an' no child!' She bit her lip. 'D'you wonder I thought myself barren?' Savagely she said, 'An' even then it might not have mattered, if…if—'

'If she weren't the living image of her father,' finished Julian. 'May I see her?'

Jane hesitated, then shrugged. 'If you like. Nan! Nan!'

Flying steps sounded in the passage behind her and the small face appeared, peering around Jane's skirts.

He smiled down at her, feeling as always, absurdly

guilty. 'Good morning again, Nan,' he said gently. 'Are you feeling better now?'

The child nodded solemnly, but remained silent. Julian had heard the whispers, that she was slow, a dullard—the bright clear gaze belied it.

He persevered. 'I've spoken to Bob Pratchett and his friends. If it happens again, your mama will send a message to me. Yes?'

Again the nod.

'That's a very pretty ribbon,' he said. The deep pink set off the glossy dark curls. 'Is it a new one?' He had no idea whether it was or not, but it looked pretty, and she'd not been wearing it earlier.

'Yes.' The merest whisper. He had to bend to catch what she was saying. 'Miss Daventry helped me choose it. Mr Wilkins thought I'd dirty his things.'

'Did he?' Julian kept the anger from his voice with an effort. That was another call he'd have to make. Damn it all to hell and beyond! The person least to blame in this hellish muddle was Nan.

He straightened. 'I'll speak to Wilkins,' he said, more to Jane than to Nan.

She shrugged. 'You might also mention that I don't appreciate being charged extra in his shop.'

Anger tightened sharply. 'I'll do that.' He looked at her hard. 'In future, Jane, keep me informed. I don't shirk my responsibilities, but if you don't tell me, I can't help much.'

She flushed. 'You've supported us when you had no obligation. What more could I expect?'

Anger and guilt warring, he said shortly, 'Let me know next time there's trouble and you might find out.'

Her mouth twisted. 'Forget I said that. You've been good enough to us.' She frowned. 'One thing…that Miss Daventry—you'd best warn her not to call here. Don't rightly know that she understood how it was. Bringin' Nan back's one thing, but she did insist on coming in. Had a cup of tea an' all. Not that I grudge the tea. Kind, she is. But you warn her not to do it again. I don't want trouble for her after what she did.'

He snorted. 'Tell Miss Daventry what she may or may not do? If I survived the encounter, you'd have to scrape me off the walls!'

Chapter Ten

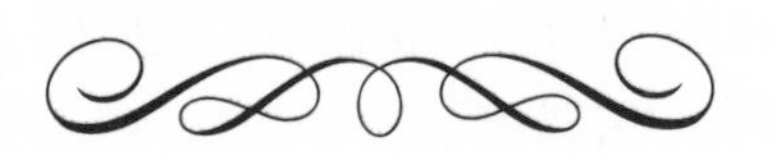

Julian rode through the village, conscious that he was late for his meeting with Sir John Postleton, and that the latest gossip would have circled the village at least twice.

The servant who opened the door bowed, saying, 'Good morning, my lord. Sir John is expecting you, but my lady requests the favour of a private word first.'

'Very well, but please inform your master that I am here.'

'Very good, my lord.'

Lady Postleton received him in the drawing room, her smile a polite fiction. 'Good morning, Lord Braybrook.'

'Good morning, Lady Postleton,' he said warily. Quite apart from Serena's comments on the subject of his marriage, he knew he figured largely in Lady Postleton's matrimonial plans for Anne. No doubt this interview was another skirmish in her ongoing campaign to secure the prize. Usually the young lady concerned was draped in a becoming pose around the chronically out-of-tune harp in the corner.

Seeing his eyes flicker to the harp, Lady Postleton said with a satisfied little smile, 'You are disappointed not to see Anne. I must tell you that she is laid down upon her bed with the headache, so overset was she about this morning's little contretemps.'

'Is she?' Julian waited. She couldn't have got wind of Nan's business and what affair was it of Anne's anyway?

'Yes.' Lady Postleton's smile glittered. 'And while I hesitate to upset poor Serena, it would be as well if you were to drop a hint in her ear. This Miss Daventry she has taken up is not at all the thing!'

Julian stiffened.

'I am given to understand that she was quite impertinent to my poor Anne this morning, putting herself forward in a most odious way and actually had the effrontery to insist on being served first in Mr Wilkins's shop!' Her mouth primmed. 'Quite the grand lady! I wish you will tell Serena that she is sadly mistaken in the young person's character and would be well advised to turn her off immediately.'

It took fifteen minutes of polite evasions to extricate himself from Lady Postleton's clutches. That he had done so without signing an agreement in his own blood to dismiss Miss Daventry the moment he laid eyes on her, was in the nature of a miracle. Of course, remarking on how much he personally would enjoy welcoming Lady Postleton to Amberley helped enormously.

Julian took his leave, conscious of a burning desire to know exactly what Miss Daventry had said to cause offence. Of course, it was also possible that Miss Daventry had a burning desire to box his ears, he realised, knocking on the door of Sir John's book room.

'Come in! Come in!'

The baronet looked up from his ledgers as Julian entered.

'Hah! Late!'

'I beg your pardon, sir,' said Julian. 'An urgent matter I needed to attend to.'

Sir John snorted. 'Don't bother sparing my blushes! Heard all about it already. Best to move the Roberts woman on. Don't know why you haven't. Not as if she's anything to you now. Just causes trouble. Pity it's so obvious, but if you moved her on, there'd be an end of it.'

Julian controlled himself with an effort. 'That is not my decision to make, sir.'

Sir John looked pained. 'Ought to be your decision, boy! That's the point. Your cottage, ain't it?'

Julian said merely, 'It is.'

'Yes, well. There you are. And of course my wife wasn't best pleased with Miss Daventry's actions in Wilkins's shop. Dare say that's what she wanted to speak to you about. Not Miss Daventry's fault—how was she to know who the child was?'

Julian froze. *Miss Daventry helped me choose it. Mr Wilkins thought I'd dirty his things.*

'Nan Roberts was in the shop?'

Sir John went slightly red. 'Er, yes. Dare say the lady wife didn't like to say. As I said, not Miss Daventry's fault. *She* wasn't to know.'

Miss Daventry not know? Did Sir John think she was stupid? Blind? Of course she knew. Or thought she knew…

Sir John pulled a pile of papers to the front of his desk. 'Fact remains, lad, if you moved them on, these situations wouldn't arise. Just as easy for you to provide for her elsewhere! And let's face it…' he cleared his throat, looking self-conscious '…awkward for your bride when you marry. Having it in her face, so to speak. Not,' he added hurriedly, 'that it's any business of mine!'

'Quite,' said Julian. 'Now, sir, I have the figures on the expected cider-apple yields. If you have yours to hand, we can see about this brewery.'

Clearing his throat, Sir John said, 'Oh, aye. I can take a hint. None of my affair, although—' He broke off. 'Very well, then—to business. Not a bad idea, you know, a brewery. A few more jobs. Stop some of 'em going off to the cities and getting into trouble. Bring up a chair, boy!'

An hour later, his head full of plans and figures for new plantings, Julian made ready to leave.

'Met that fellow Havergal yet?' asked Sir John.

In the process of ordering his papers, Julian stiffened. 'Not yet, sir.'

Sir John looked thoughtful. 'Seems to call out this way quite often. Visits Serena, Lady P. says. Odd sort of chap.'

'Odd, sir? In what way?'

'Hmm? Oh, well, as to that he's pleasant enough.

Taken lodgings in Hereford. Came before me on the bench t'other day.'

'*Havergal* came before you?'

'Yes—some young rascal picked his pocket, if you please. Bold as brass! Wouldn't have the boy charged, though. Just hauled him along for a warning. A warning, I ask you! He wanted the boy to attend some charity school. Waste of time, if you ask me! God knows where it will all end.'

'With one less child transported, or ending on the gallows?' suggested Julian.

Sir John gave a dubious grunt. 'He came to see me a day or so later. Told me the boy was at school and off the streets. Interesting chap. Been in India the last twenty-odd years. Just thought I'd ask if you'd met him. Since he calls on Serena.'

Deep in thought, Julian took his leave. Who was this Havergal? A fortune hunter? Surely he wasn't labouring under the misapprehension that Serena was wealthy in her own right? Like most widows, she lost her jointure if she remarried. He'd have to meet Mr Havergal, and make a few things very clear.

Christy left Jane Roberts' cottage, cursing her own folly. Once more Christy had stepped out from behind Miss Daventry, this time to deal a set-down to Miss Postleton. And her temper had still had the whip hand when Lord Braybrook appeared.

She walked back through the village, wondering if she had lost her mind. She had not bothered to hide her contempt. Oh, she might not have said anything, but her face, her tone of voice! She was an idiot. With a position that bordered on miraculous, she had jeopardised it by allowing her feelings to show. One thing to defend Nan. It was quite another to betray her scorn and contempt for Miss Postleton and her brother. Let alone her anger with Braybrook.

And she was, she realised, leaving the village behind and turning into the road for Amberley, still angry. Deep within fury and disappointment melded in a cold, bitter lump.

Disappointment? Anger, yes. But disappointment? That implied surprise, that she had expected something else. Yet what was surprising about a wealthy, handsome aristocrat taking his pleasure with a respectable woman, with no care for the consequences she would face if she bore his child? What was surprising about said aristocrat showing little interest in his child and leaving the mother to manage alone in a community that largely shunned both her and her daughter? Why should she have expected anything else of him? Had he not offered to take *her* as his mistress? And with just the same cold indifference to all but his own pleasure?

She was nowhere near finding answers when she reached the stile that gave on to the path leading through the woods to Amberley. About to climb over, she heard hoofbeats from the opposite direction and turned to see who was coming.

Around the bend came Harry on a tall bay. She was about to wave, but he saw her immediately and reined his mount in hard. For a startled moment his expression looked one of shock and fury.

Then he waved and rode up to her, saying with a friendly smile as he halted, 'It's not your day off, is it? Are you on your way to the village with an errand?'

Had she imagined the anger? 'Yes and no. I'm on my way back. Can your horse jump the stile? If you aren't in a hurry, you could walk me to the end of the path. It would be nice to talk.'

'Oh, er, no. Better not. Sir John will be expecting me, you know.' Harry flushed and for a moment Christy thought again that there was a faint hint of annoyance in his face. Then another smile. 'I'll call on my day off. And of course there is this party at Amberley next week—I am invited, did you know?'

'Yes.' She had helped write the invitations.

'Not having any trouble with him?'

'Definitely not.' Even if she *had* been tempted to succumb to the lure of his lordship's disgraceful offer, this morning's revelation had served as a timely warning.

'Well, that's good,' said Harry. He raised his whip in salute. 'Bye, Christy.' With that he pushed his horse into a trot and was gone.

Christy stepped down from the stile and set off towards Amberley. Her stride lengthened as her temper mounted again. This time directed at herself, for being foolish enough to think that Lord Braybrook was somehow different. That he was not the man to evade his responsibilities.

A more moderate voice made itself heard. *He did in-*

tervene with those boys. And looked after Nan's scraped knee.

She didn't want to think about the gentleness with which he had tended the child. Or the odd, blank expression on his face as he knelt in the road. Better to remind herself that he had left her, a stranger, to take the little girl home and explain matters to the mother. That he had preferred to limit his time with his daughter.

He is very protective of Lady Braybrook. And his sisters.

She dismissed that. Many men were protective of their sisters and mothers. Or stepmothers. Unfortunately they failed to make the leap to being protective of someone else's sister. Or wife.

Especially when the woman in question was lower in the social scale. Apparently it didn't count in those circumstances. And why that should be a surprise, let alone a disappointment to her, she couldn't begin to imagine.

Right now, even if she still had a position, keeping it might depend on her ability to cloak her emotions again. Miss Daventry, prim, proper, only-speaking-when-spoken-to Miss Daventry, had to mask Christy's fury.

Somehow she had to rebuild the façade. This was not a subject that ever needed to be raised with Braybrook. It was none of her business, and nothing she said would make a ha'porth of difference. Her business was to amuse Lady Braybrook, teach the younger children and keep an eye on— She stopped dead as she came around a bend in the path. The path ended at another stile which led into the park. Beyond it deer grazed, the pinky-brown bulk of Amberley rearing up in the distance against the summer sky.

Seated on the bottom step of the stile was Alicia—staring at her in consternation. Christy's brain whirled. No wonder Harry had been annoyed! Somehow they had planned this. Yesterday Alicia had walked to the village with Matthew and Emma. Lady Braybrook considered that safe enough. She opened her mouth, and closed it. She had no proof. It could be coincidence. And saying something might put Alicia on her guard.

'Good morning, Miss Daventry.' Alicia appeared to have recovered her composure. 'Have you been to the village for Mama?'

Christy hesitated. 'Yes. Embroidery silks. Shall we walk back to the house together?'

Alicia's gaze flickered to the path leading back through the woods. 'Oh. Er, yes. I…I was just going back.' She stood up and forced a smile. 'Did you see anyone interesting? In…in the village, I mean.' Again she cast a nervous glance back down the path.

'Your friend, Miss Postleton, was in the shop with her brother. And I ran into Harry.'

'Oh. How…how nice for you.' A telling blush crept over Alicia's face.

Christy decided to say no more. She would have to tell his lordship. And the last thing she desired just now was a private interview with *him*.

* * *

Julian arrived back at Amberley, still smarting from the unspoken contempt in Miss Daventry's gaze. Not unvoiced though. Her icy tones had been eloquent. He dismounted in the stableyard and loosened the girth.

Of course you could tell her the truth.

The truth? Why in Hades should he? It was none of her business!

It might make her think a little better of you.

Since when did he care for the governess's opinion? Even if she had agreed to be his mistress, her opinion was irrelevant—as long as it remained unexpressed. He removed the saddle and handed it to a waiting lad. 'Thank you, Billy.'

An interested nicker caught his attention. He glanced around and saw an unfamiliar face with a white blaze looking out over a half-door.

'Billy!' he called to the lad taking his saddle to the tack room for cleaning, 'Whose horse is that?'

Billy looked back over his shoulder. 'Beg pardon? Oh. That's Mr Havergal's Rajah. Called about an hour ago.'

'Ah.' Julian strolled over to look at the horse.

The nondescript bay gelding looked back. Average points, nicely put together—there was nothing wrong with the animal precisely—but there was no hint of quality either. An adequate hack, probably with comfortable paces. Several cuts above a job horse, but not an expensive beast. Rajah. An Indian prince. He patted the horse absent-mindedly. *Well, well, well.*

It shoved its nose at him hopefully.

At long last he was going to meet the mysterious Mr Havergal.

The drawing-room door was open, voices and laughter drifting through. Curious, he stood in the doorway. Serena, Davy and a man he assumed to be Havergal were sitting round a tea table, the backgammon set in front of them. Davy was frowning at the board.

Havergal was speaking. 'Look, Davy—this point has only one of my checkers. Land there and you force me on to the bar. Which means I can't do anything until I get off.' Average height, his hair grey and his face deeply lined and tanned—a man who had perhaps spent many years in a hot climate?

Davy grinned, and moved his checker. He looked up, smugly. It jolted Julian to see the likeness to Matt at the same age. And just as delighted to outscore an elder.

'That's it,' said Havergal. 'Now, I have to throw the dice so that I land on an unoccupied point in your homeboard—and since you have them nicely filled, I can't move. Your roll again.'

A shaft of irritation went through Julian. He'd taught Matt to play. Somehow he'd not yet got around to it with Davy and here was this…this *outsider*, this Havergal, doing it. Taking his place.

He watched unnoticed as the game continued. Their father had taught him. Would he have taught Davy too had he lived? He tried to be a father to Davy, not just a much older brother. Davy had no memory of their father… The grey head and the small dark one bent over the board in fierce concentration. An odd thought surfaced—what did Serena think of this? He glanced over and her face ripped him wide open.

She watched both of them, and in her eyes was regret such as he had never imagined. As though she were looking at something irrevocably lost to her. As though all the might-have-beens in the world mocked her. For a split second her fingers whitened on the arms of her Bath chair and she sagged back, her eyes closed…

Havergal's voice, instructing Davy, faltered slightly and he looked up. At once Serena's usual cheerful expression fell into place and she smiled at the fellow.

Julian's heart ached. Serena, infinitely cheerful, infinitely patient with her lot in life… He had known she must find her disability frustrating, but she refused to speak of it, was always so uncomplaining. She made it easy to believe her acceptance complete.

He must have moved slightly, because she looked around.

'Julian—there you are! Come and meet Mr Havergal, a very old friend of mine. We grew up together.'

An old friend…?

Havergal had risen and was holding out his hand.

'How do you do, sir?' said Julian, shaking Havergal's hand. What, precisely, was meant by an old friend?

'Very well, my lord. I am pleased to meet you at last. Whenever I call you seem to be from home,' said Havergal.

The merest glimmer of Serena's smile, and Julian

realised with a stab of shock that she had somehow engineered it that way. Hell's teeth! He thought back; on Miss Daventry's last day off, Serena had managed to get rid of the entire household!

'I don't think I recognise your name, sir,' he said mildly. Serena had been her father's sole heiress; he now owned the small estate and visited it on occasion—surely if they had grown up together the name Havergal should be familiar to him?

'My father was the Rector,' said Havergal.

'You are not in the church, yourself?' asked Julian.

Havergal shook his head. 'No. I was a great disappointment to my father there, but my uncle found me a place in his business.'

'Mr Havergal lived in India, Julian,' said Davy, his eyes shining. 'And he has a tiger! A real one!'

Havergal chuckled. 'You will be giving your brother a very strange notion of me, lad! A real tigerskin *rug*, is what I said. And I did *not* shoot the poor beast myself. It was a gift.'

'I should like to see it,' said Davy hopefully.

Havergal smiled. 'Another time, Davy. It would be a little awkward to carry while I'm riding. My poor horse would have a fit! Some time I shall hire the gig and bring the rug out for you.'

'Very kind of you,' remarked Julian. Obviously not a well-inlaid nabob if he had to hire the landlord's gig. It fitted with the quality of his horse.

'Can we finish the game, please, sir?' asked Davy.

'Of course.' Havergal sat down again. He glanced up at Julian. 'You will excuse me, my lord?'

'Certainly.'

Havergal, noted Julian, was obviously a very skilled player. While he won, it was by a narrow enough margin for Davy to be very, very pleased with himself.

'I'm improving, aren't I, sir? Can we play again next time?' he asked as they packed away the set.

'If your mother permits,' said Havergal, with a faint smile at Serena. 'I should be going now. Perhaps you will walk with me to the stables?'

Davy jumped up. 'Yes, sir. May I, Mama?'

'Yes, dear.' Serena smiled at him. 'And don't nag about that tiger!'

'I'll come with you as well, if I may, Havergal,' said Julian, rising.

Davy glared at him. 'I was only going to *ask*,' he said. 'It's all right to *ask*.'

Havergal chuckled. 'Quite right, lad. No harm in asking. But let's put your mother's mind at rest and consider me asked. I promise you shall see that tiger. Come along. You may ride Rajah down the carriage drive, if you like.'

He took his leave of Serena, and Julian's hackles rose at the way the fellow bowed over her hand. He didn't kiss it, but the way he held it, the intimacy of their parting smile, set alarm bells clanging.

Havergal bowed slightly to him. 'No need to see me out, my lord. Davy will do admirably.'

And as they left the room, Julian felt a sharp twinge of jealousy to see his small brother according a stranger the hero-worship usually reserved for his elder brothers.

'And what are your plans for the rest of the day, Julian?' asked Serena cheerfully.

He raised his brows. 'Manures. I have a new book on the subject to study. Shall I bring it up here in Miss Daventry's absence?'

'Not on my account, dear,' said Serena. 'I am sure she will be back shortly.'

'Serena—this Havergal—'

'Is a very old and dear friend,' she told him, her face closing up, and much of the remaining glow dimming. 'You need not concern yourself. I am neither planning anything foolish, nor indiscreet.'

'Of course not,' agreed Julian. In the face of such a clear *mind-your-own-business* sort of response, he dropped the subject. 'I shall remove myself to the manure heap, then.'

'You do that,' said Serena. 'And, Julian—remember, I am forty-two, not seventeen. And a widow to boot. As you are well aware, widows are not subject to the same restrictions as young girls.'

The book on manures failed to engage him. Bad enough having to worry about Jane Roberts and Nan. Like it or not, they were his responsibility. He had to find a better solution for them that Jane could accept.

And now Serena! *Widows are not subject to the same considerations as young girls*...hell's teeth, he knew that. None better. But...*Serena*? He just couldn't picture it—Serena taking a lover. And she was crippled! The doctors had spelt out the risks of another pregnancy after her accident. That was why…of course there were other possibilities, ways of giving and receiving pleasure, but… His cheeks scorched. Damn it! This was *Serena*! His stepmother!

Pushing these thoughts aside, he forced his attention back to his book and began taking notes. He had not made much progress before there was a knock on the door.

'Come in,' he said.

The door opened to admit Miss Daventry. Another, even more disturbing distraction. Whatever she wanted, he doubted it was to tell him that she had thought the better of her refusal to become his mistress. Meeting Nan Roberts would have settled that.

He laid down his pen, ignoring the immediate distraction in his breeches. 'Yes, ma'am?'

'If you have a moment, my lord, I wish to discuss Alicia with you.'

He repressed the urge to swear. 'Very well. Leave the door open.'

She flushed. 'If you wish. I do not doubt your word, my lord.'

He shrugged. 'Better safe than sorry.' He gestured to a chair. 'Please be seated and tell me what is troubling you.'

He listened in growing anger. 'You believe a meeting was planned?'

'Yes. They could have arranged it yesterday when she walked to the village with Matthew and Emma. A brief meeting in public—neither Matthew nor Emma would have thought anything of it.'

'Damn your brother!' said Julian furiously. 'He must have told her that he would be passing and cozened her into the meeting! Of all the dishonourable—'

'She agreed!' Miss Daventry replied. 'And Harry's intentions are perfectly honourable!' she went on. 'Which is more than I can say—' She broke off, her face crimson.

Julian snorted. 'I'd be better pleased if his intentions *weren't* honourable. Lissy wouldn't be such a little fool as to fall for that!'

'Thank you.' Shards of ice splintered in her voice.

He realised belatedly that he had expressed himself badly. Very badly.

'The cases are different, Miss Daventry.' Hell! That sounded even worse, and, judging by her narrowed eyes and flat mouth, Miss Daventry concurred.

'Quite, my lord. I have no aristocratic family to disgrace, do I?'

'No! That is...damn it! That is not what I meant at all!' he said, aware that he was digging an abyss. 'Lissy is my sister; I'm supposed to protect her!'

'But your protective instincts don't extend to other men's sisters.' She looked at him directly. 'Or wives. It doesn't matter to you that the consequences for a woman who becomes your mistress might be as disastrous for her as for Alicia if she marries unwisely.'

'Did you just call me a hypocrite?'

Silence hung quivering. Would she attempt to wriggle off the hook? Back down and apologise?

Her chin went up. 'Yes. I suppose I did.'

He breathed carefully, and tried to analyse the emotions pouring through him. Fury. Because her words stung. Her contempt burned. Admiration because she had the courage to hold her position. And through it all the lick of desire. The urge to find out if he could still kindle the same response in her. To reassure her that she was wrong. That she didn't understand…that he would look after her…the word *always* hovered. He shoved it away.

He *never* offered reassurances to women. Just a straightforward offer of intent. Take it or leave it. Definitely not pure, but very simple with no room for misunderstanding. And *always* had nothing to do with it. Ever. Yet with Christy Daventry he was in constant danger of overstepping these boundaries.

He changed the subject. 'Very well. What do you suggest we do about this situation, Miss Daventry?'

Her hands clenched. 'That I consider you a hypocrite?'

'No. Lissy's foolishness.'

'Why would you wish for my opinion?'

Why, indeed? Because she was so brutally honest that he valued her judgement? He shied away from that. 'So far you've had little hesitation in stating your opinion,' he said. 'Why stop now?'

'Leave it and remain alert,' she said. 'There is no direct proof. If I am wrong and you act, it will increase Alicia's resentment. If I am right and a meeting was planned, then the fact that it didn't work and they were so nearly caught might make her too wary to attempt it again. Especially if she is left uncertain about our suspicions and I keep her busy.'

'Say nothing?' he asked. 'Convenient for your brother.'

She stood up swiftly, jaw set and her eyes blazing. 'You asked my opinion. I have given it. And if I were concerned with protecting Harry, why tell you in the first place?'

He hung on to his temper. There was something else he had to say to Miss Daventry. 'Very well, ma'am—one more thing—'

She remained standing. 'My dismissal?'

His teeth ground audibly. 'No. My thanks for your kindness to Nan Roberts.'

She stiffened. 'Unnecessary, my lord. Visiting the sins of fathers on the heads of children is not a failing of mine. And I had a little sister—' She broke off, her face blank.

His gut clenched. 'Had?'

'Sarah died of measles when she was eight. I was sixteen.'

Her voice was expressionless. He could only guess at the agony it hid. He remembered the consuming fear when Davy had caught measles. 'I'm sorry,' he said. The fear had been bad enough…and Christy had not been spared the grief.

Her glare blazed straight through him. 'Sorry is an easy word. And in Sarah's case you have nothing for which to be sorry. *She* was not your responsibility.' She walked out with her head held high.

Julian stared out the window, his heart aching for the death of a child he had not even known.

Chapter Eleven

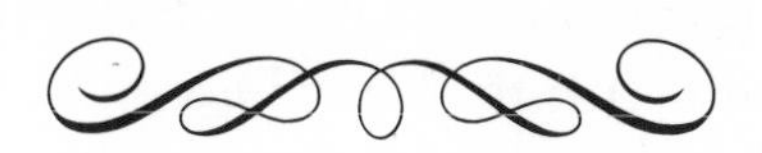

The next few days saw Amberley in uproar as the Summer Ball approached. Although it seemed to Julian that far fewer problems required his intervention this year, he saw far too much of Miss Daventry. She appeared to have a list permanently in her hand as she directed the staff scurrying about with furniture and linen for the guests who would remain overnight.

Alicia, too, seemed very much taken up with the arrangements. He found her in the library one morning going through menus with the housekeeper.

She looked up as he came in. 'Oh! I'm sorry, Julian. Are we in your way?'

'Not at all,' he said, bemused.

'Good,' said Alicia and turned back to Mrs Pritchard. 'The duckling, then, and green peas. And I think the apricot tart to round the course off.'

'Very good, Miss Alicia,' said the housekeeper, tucking her notes away and rising. 'I'll tell Cook.'

'Thank you, Pritch,' said Alicia. 'Tell her I'll come down later to see that all is well.'

'Very well, Miss Alicia.' The housekeeper dropped a curtsy and left.

'You're doing a good job, Liss,' said Julian.

Lissy flushed. 'It's not me. Mama handed it all to Miss Daventry and Miss Daventry asked me to help with the menus. I'm just doing as I'm told.'

She hadn't realised that she was being kept out of mischief, thought Julian. Miss Daventry had been right. A warning to Lissy would have resulted in sulking and fuming. Probably trying to come up with ways to sneak out and meet Daventry. Instead she was happily doing something useful.

'It's fun, really,' said Lissy, gathering up several pieces of paper. 'I thought it would be frightfully boring working out who should sit where at dinner, and what we should eat, but it's not.'

'You'll make some lucky man a very fine wife and hostess one day,' said Julian, pulling at a glossy curl as he passed behind her chair. Lissy giggled.

'More likely Miss Daventry would,' she said. 'I had the easy job with Pritch. Christy's out breaking the news to Hickson that he will have to provide flowers for the floral arrangements! I did warn her that he'd probably take a garden fork to her, but she said she could manage one crotchety old gardener!'

'Christy?'

Alicia shrugged. 'It's her name. Short for Christiana. I asked if I might use it, and she said yes.' She frowned. 'It's friendlier, and she's such a nice person.'

'I see. Well, if you finished your menus, I am going for a ride. Should you care to come?'

Her face fell. 'Oh, I'd love to, but I mustn't. I promised Christy that I would help with the sewing while she gives Davy his French lesson. Thank you, though.'

Nice? He thought about that after Lissy left the room. It seemed such a bland, boring word to describe Christy—*Miss Daventry*, he corrected himself. Stubborn, blindingly honest, kind. She took people as she found them, whatever society's opinion. Witness her response to Nan Roberts. Damn it, he supposed she was nice.

He doubted very much that she would return the compliment. Not that he was bothered by that of course, he assured himself. As a hired dependant she could count herself lucky to still have her position. He ignored an irritating little voice demanding to know how the hell he could have dismissed her for speaking the truth as she saw it. She was a companion, for God's sake! She wasn't paid to *have* a mind, let alone speak it. And it didn't bother him at all if she didn't think *he* was nice.

Nice. It *was* a boring word, and very likely closer acquaintance would prove it suited Miss Daventry admirably. Right now he was going for a ride. And he was not going to spare her another thought.

Hallam greeted him in the hall when he returned. 'You will find her ladyship in the drawing room, my lord. Mrs Pritchard is recovering from her turn, but she is of the opinion that The Creature will give Master Davy nightmares.'

'What creature, Hallam? What the devil are you talking about?' asked Julian, stripping off his riding gloves and dropping them with his whip on the refectory table.

'The Creature Mr Havergal brought,' explained Hallam. 'He met Mrs Pritchard on the stairs with it and she Had A Turn. Most unfortunate for the tea tray her ladyship had ordered.'

'I see,' said Julian, not seeing at all. 'I'll go up to the drawing room then, shall I, and see this, er, Creature for myself.' He started for the stairs.

'A very good idea, my lord,' said Hallam, gathering up the gloves and whip.

Julian found a scene of considerable confusion in the drawing room. Sprawled before the fireplace, snarling ferociously, was…a tiger, upon which Davy sat in glory, Matt and Emma scowling at him. Miss Daventry, seated beside Serena on a sofa, looked as though she were trying hard not to laugh. That cursed dimple flickered in and out of sight, causing his heart to beat painfully fast.

Seeing him, Davy leapt up, flushed, eyes sparkling. 'Look, Julian! Just look! And it's *mine*. Not Matt's or Emma's.' This last with a triumphant glare at his siblings.

'As if *I* want the horrid thing,' said Emma with an unconvincing sniff.

Matt didn't bother to deny anything. His lustful gaze at his small brother's treasure said it all. Julian was conscious of a twinge of envy himself. Of all the things guaranteed to thrill a small boy, a tigerskin rug, complete with snarl and positively lambent glass eyes, had to take the prize. He noted with some satisfaction that Tybalt had retreated to the back of the sofa behind Serena and was fluffed up to twice his normal size. Some very peculiar noises emanated from the affronted cat.

'Where the devil did that come from?' he asked Serena, who, to his surprise, blushed.

Davy answered. 'Mr Havergal brought it. Remember? He told me all about it last time, and I asked if I might see it? And now it's mine! He said it had belonged to another boy, but he didn't need it any more so he thought that I should have it.'

'I see,' said Julian, casting a very thoughtful look at Serena.

She returned his gaze, her blush deepening. 'It was very kind of Mr Havergal, Julian.'

'I'm going to have it in the nursery,' announced Davy. 'Mama, may I go into Hereford to thank Mr Havergal? Twigg would take me if I asked.'

Julian stared. 'I should hope you had thanked Mr Havergal when he gave it to you!' His mind was working furiously. Could Havergal, who was patently *not* well off, be misinformed as to the terms of Serena's jointure?

'I wasn't *here*,' said Davy. He cast Miss Daventry a very dirty look. 'I was in the schoolroom doing French verbs.' His aggrieved tone expressed to a nicety what a waste of time he thought *that*.

'Mea culpa,' said Miss Daventry. 'Unfortunately, Davy, no matter what you think of my ability to see out

of the back of my head, crystal gazing does not come within the purlieu of a respectable governess!'

Julian choked back a laugh.

'So he left it with Mama,' said Davy. 'He couldn't stay because he'd hired the landlord's gig to bring the rug out, and had to take it back. Really, Julian, don't you think that I *ought* to go and thank him?'

'Oh, I think so,' said Julian. Taking Davy to Hereford to thank Havergal would provide the perfect excuse to call upon the gentleman and apprise him of certain facts. Which, if he were not much mistaken, would see an immediate cooling of his attentions to Serena.

'In fact, Davy,' he continued, 'if Miss Daventry has drilled enough French verbs into your head for one morning, we shall go at once.'

Miss Daventry raised her brows. 'Can you doubt it, my lord?'

Serena laughed. 'Miss Daventry, may I trouble you to help Davy take the rug up to the nursery first? And Matt, Emma, you may take yourselves off. I require a word in private with Julian.'

His stomach clenched. A private word. About Havergal?

As soon as they were alone she went straight to the point. 'Before you visit Nigel breathing fire and brimstone, you should know that he has asked me to marry him and that I have accepted.'

Marriage?

He tried to assemble his thoughts. 'Serena, you know I only wish you to be happy. Are you—?'

'Perfectly sure,' she said. 'We were in love when we were young, but he had no money and my father would have disinherited me for making such a match. I chose not to be a burden on him and he went out to India. Eventually I married your father. Not a love match, but he was kind and very honest about his reasons for re-marrying. Convenience and spares in case something happened to you.'

He frowned. 'Serena—' he began, but she flung up a hand.

'No, Julian. You need to understand. We still love each other and there is nothing to keep us apart. He came home because he heard I was widowed—'

'How convenient.' He could hardly keep the cynicism from his voice.

Her eyes narrowed. 'We intend to be married very soon. He assures me that my lack of fortune will not be a problem, that he can support me comfortably.'

'And the children?' he asked. 'They are in my wardship. Where will you live? Here? That will make supporting you very easy! Can't you see? The fellow's using you!'

Sparks spat from the grey eyes levelled at him. 'If I could reach, Julian, I would box your ears for that! Listen to yourself! Don't think me ignorant of all the reasons it is unlikely anyone should wish to marry me. He knows that I bring nothing to the marriage—'

He snorted. 'So of course he'd assume I'd let you starve! He'd have me over a barrel, and he knows it even if you don't!'

* * *

Julian left his curricle and pair in the tender care of Jack Fichett, the head ostler at the New Inn and, hand in hand with Davy, strolled around to the cathedral. Mr Havergal, he understood, had lodgings nearby. Jack had been very informative. Mr Havergal had his own horse stabled at the New Inn, and indeed he had returned the landlord's cob and gig not an hour since. 'Pays his shot reg'lar, an' tips fairly. Horse ain't nuthin' special. Comfortable enough ride, I dessay, but not quality like your lordship's.' He stroked the silken nose of one of Julian's horses affectionately. 'Pair o' beauties, these lads.'

It all spoke of a man in modest circumstances. A man looking to better his situation. Bedamned if Havergal was going to attempt that to Serena's hurt. Better to choke this off now, before things went any further.

They found the house easily with Jack's directions. A solid timber-framed building, its cantilevered upper floors bulged over the street. A respectable-looking woman opened the door, took one look at Julian, and dropped a curtsy. Upon being informed that Lord Braybrook had called to see Mr Havergal, she became even more flustered, and conducted them up two pairs of stairs to the top floor and knocked on a door.

Havergal opened it and smiled. 'Ah. Good afternoon, Braybrook,' he said politely. Then he caught sight of Davy. 'Well, this is pleasant. How do you do, Davy? I understand Miss Daventry was doing her worst when

I called.' He turned to the landlady. 'Mrs Philpott, if it would not be too much trouble, could you bring up coffee for his lordship and myself, and milk for Master Trentham. And some cake?'

'Why, of course, sir,' said Mrs Philpott. 'It's no bother at all.'

'Thank you, ma'am,' he said courteously. 'Do come in, my lord. Come along, Davy.'

'Sir, thank you very much for the tigerskin!' burst out Davy as the door closed. 'It's splendid! I'm to have it in my room, and Matthew is as sick as a cushion about it!'

Havergal chuckled. 'Perhaps you might lend it to him on occasion? Please sit down, my lord.' He gestured Julian towards a chair.

Davy looked unconvinced. 'Well, I *might*,' he said.

They conversed for several minutes, with Davy asking as many questions as he could about India. 'I should like to go there,' he said.

'Later, lad,' said Havergal. 'The climate is not good for boys your age.'

The coffee arrived, along with the cake and milk for Davy. Julian sipped his coffee and watched his small brother with Havergal. Davy plainly liked the fellow, now telling him between mouthfuls what he had been doing and asking when Mr Havergal was going to visit again—fury soared through him.

'Oh, I'll ride that way again in a few days,' said Havergal easily. 'I am invited to your mother's party, too, but no doubt you will be abed.' He caught Julian's suddenly focused gaze and added, 'Davy, why don't you bring your cake and milk through into the other room. I've something there for you to play with.'

Julian watched in rising annoyance as his little brother's eyes sparkled.

'Another present, sir?' Davy asked.

Havergal laughed. 'No, Davy. These are mine—but you are welcome to play with them while your brother and I talk of boring grown-up things.' He stood up and held out his hand. Davy took it immediately and followed him into the other room.

A moment later Havergal was back, closing the door behind him.

'Here to warn me off, my lord?'

Julian set his coffee cup down with great precision. 'Do I need to?'

The corners of Havergal's eyes crinkled. 'That would depend on your point of view.'

'My point of view,' said Julian, 'is that I consider Serena to be in my care.'

'One does wonder what Serena said to that?' mused Havergal.

'That is neither here nor there, sir,' said Julian coldly. 'I am here to put an end to your pursuit of Serena.'

'How very gallant,' said Havergal. 'Would it allay your fears to know that my intentions towards Serena are perfectly honourable?'

'No. She told me of your offer. Cultivating Davy was very clever, wasn't it?' Havergal's eyes blazed, but he said nothing and Julian continued. 'You might like to consider that Serena's jointure is conditional upon her not remarrying and that her children are in my ward.' His gaze swept the room, taking in the modest furnishings and simple style. Bronzes and ivories were scattered about and there was a very fine rug on the floor. Interesting, but no doubt in India they could be picked up for a song. Havergal himself was neatly turned out, but his clothes were clearly well worn.

Havergal had straightened in his chair. 'Yes, she was at some pains to ensure that I understood that. More coffee, my lord?'

'Thank you, no.'

'Ah.' Mr Havergal poured himself some more and sipped, watching Julian over the rim of the cup. 'I have to inform you, my lord, that in this instance I am concerned only with Serena's point of view.'

'And your own.'

Havergal inclined his head. 'That too, but not quite as much as Serena's.'

Julian did not bother to repress a disbelieving snort.

'You become offensive, my lord,' Havergal informed him calmly. 'Let me assure you that Serena was most prompt to inform me of her circumstances. Nor did I give Davy that tigerskin to curry favour. I gave it to him because I thought he would like it and he reminds me of another small boy.' A slight pause. 'The boy who owned it originally was my son.'

His voice did not change, but Havergal's very stillness warned Julian that he was treading on dangerous ground.

He took a deep breath—damned if he'd back down. He spoke softly, but with lethal intent. 'I'll be blunt,

Havergal. Like it or not, Serena is in my care. And I'm damned if I'll let her be cozened by you or anyone else!'

Havergal's fists clenched. 'Admirable sentiments, my lord. Believe it or not, I am perfectly well to pass, and have absolutely no need to prey on wealthy widows to support myself!'

Julian raised his brows. 'Do you expect me to take your word for it?'

Havergal didn't answer. Instead he rose, went to an untidy desk and began writing. A moment later he sprinkled sand on the letter, stood up and handed it to Julian, along with a card.

'Authorisation to ask whatever questions you like of Hammerfield, my man of business. You may also wish to ask about me with the East India Company. I don't work for 'em any more, but they know all about me. I ask only one thing—that you don't tell Serena what you learn. I'd rather tell her myself.'

Julian stared at the brusque note ordering the unknown Hammerfield to inform Lord Braybrook of whatever he wished to know about Havergal's circumstances…and Havergal had been in India for over twenty years…was well known to the East India company…

If it wasn't a bluff, Havergal must be wealthier than he looked.

'Not all men choose to display their wealth, Braybrook,' said Havergal, apparently reading his mind. 'That brings its own inconveniences. Serena knows that I am well able to support myself, but I have not told her the extent of my fortune. She was having quite enough difficulty in seeing herself as a suitable wife for me.'

'A suitable wife,' repeated Julian. He shot a glance at the door to the other room, wondering if Davy was about to reappear. 'Havergal, a man with a fortune generally wants an heir. It may not—'

'Serena made that plain,' said Havergal quietly. 'I am not marrying for an heir.'

Julian frowned. If not for an heir, or money, then what the devil *was* he marrying for? It was not a question he could ask. As long as Serena was safe and happy—something else occurred to him.

'The children are in my wardship,' he said. 'Literally, my responsibility.'

Havergal smiled. 'We discussed it. I understand Serena chose not to move into the Dower House and of course she will no longer have a right to it, but perhaps you would lease it to me? Will that serve?'

Julian teeth clenched. '*Assuming* I am satisfied that Serena will be happy with you, then the Dower House lease is my wedding gift!'

He drove back to Amberley, returning automatic answers to Davy's chatter about the set of ivory elephants he had been playing with. 'Hundreds of them, Julian! Big ones and little ones. All in a big golden box. Only Mr Havergal said it was brass. And he says I may play with them again some day.'

Why did Havergal want to marry Serena? It defied all the logical, rational reasons for marriage.

He looked very hard at the question. From all angles. And discovered that he didn't much like the man who had asked it. Serena was a kind, attractive, loving woman. The sort of woman who would make any man a wonderful wife ...

She is crippled. She will never walk again. She cannot give him an heir, nor does she bring any money to the marriage.

Havergal didn't care about these things.

Love. That was the only reason left.

To Julian marriage was a matter of wealth and convenience. Yet at least two of his friends had married for love, shrugging at the lost opportunity to increase their wealth and position.

He liked their wives, too, and when he thought of the way Thea Blakehurst smiled at Richard, or the way Verity's eyes lit up when Max entered a room...it wasn't for him. He wanted an impeccably bred wife of suitable fortune, and a mistress for bedsport. And Christy Daventry, who declined to fit either compartment.

He forced his mind back to Serena's likely marriage. Havergal was taking her for no more than the use of the Dower House. He was also offering to find positions for Matt and Davy if needful. Julian didn't deny that having such careers laid out for his brothers would be a blessing. His first reaction had been refusal, but Havergal's expression had stopped him...

I thought that I would never return to this country...there was a native girl. Padma. She was to be burned on her husband's funeral pyre as is the native custom. I rescued her and, well, she couldn't return to her own family, they would have killed her. So I offered to take her, and she stayed with me. We had a child, a son. I would have remained with them, but they died of cholera some years ago...I told Serena when I brought the rug out this morning...

He glanced down at Davy, sitting beside him on the curricle seat, happily examining a little bronze tiger... Havergal's son had owned the bronze and the tigerskin rug. And had the boy or his mother lived, Havergal would never have returned. Even knowing that Serena was free, he would have remained in India, loyal to the native girl he had saved and their son...and Serena had loved him all these years, despite her marriage and unswerving loyalty to her husband and stepson. He faced a staggering realisation—and it went against all custom and received wisdom: if Havergal had not been wealthy enough to wed Serena regardless, he would still have ended up supporting the marriage, giving them the use of the Dower House and allowing Serena at least part of her jointure.

It was insanity. He could only be thankful that a merciful deity had probably spared him such foolishness. The Summer Ball was ten days away. If he sent urgent letters enquiring about Havergal tomorrow, he should have a response by the day of the ball. If Havergal's claims were borne out, then he supposed he would be making an unexpected announcement.

* * *

Amberley was ablaze as dusk fell on the night of the Summer Ball. With the weather set fair everyone who was anyone for miles around had come and laughter and chatter spilled with golden light from open doors and windows. The musicians hired from Hereford were installed in a corner of the forecourt to accompany the dancing and the Great Hall brimmed with merriment.

Julian looked around the Hall. Everyone seemed to be enjoying themselves. He glanced over to where Serena was seated by the refectory table, Havergal in close attendance. She caught his eye and raised a brow questioningly. He nodded. The waltz in the forecourt was nearly finished. After that it would be supper. He intended to make his announcement just as soon as the company was seated.

It would raise some eyebrows. News of Havergal's wealth had leaked out. Several matrons with daughters to establish had taken pains to make themselves known to Havergal that evening, parading their virtuous treasures under his nose. He'd muttered to Julian that he'd be relieved when the announcement was made and girls young enough to be his daughters stopped making sheep's eyes at him.

Lady Postleton had not swelled the hopeful throng, but probably only because she had Anne aimed at Julian's head. He had obliged by leading Anne out for one dance, and that was enough. He couldn't imagine why Serena thought the girl would suit him. Certainly she was well bred, well brought up, well dowered, dutiful and attractive...*everything you wanted in a wife, in fact.*

Except that, as Matt had said, she wasn't very kind. He tried to imagine her…*what*? Storming in to defend Nan Roberts from being bullied? Ridiculous. He had heard her not five minutes ago laughing openly at another young lady's unbecoming gown, encouraging others to laugh.

His gaze went to Miss Daventry. Gowned in soft grey cambric, she sat near Serena. Did she waltz? An irrelevant question. Even if she accepted, dancing—let alone waltzing!—with the governess would cause an uproar. And she would not accept. The only invitation she had accepted had been from her brother. Harry had lead her out for a country dance. She had declined all other invitations.

The Hall was filling up, most people were seated, only a few still looking for somewhere to sit down. He rang a small bell. 'If I might have your attention, ladies and gentlemen,' he said. The stragglers whisked themselves into whatever spots were left. 'First, thank you all for coming tonight. Lady Braybrook and I are delighted to welcome you to Amberley. And now, I have an announcement. Of a betrothal.'

There was a startled gasp and hum of speculation, swiftly suppressed.

'Yes, a betrothal,' he went on. 'For the past several years, Lady Braybrook has insisted that she wishes to retire to the Dower House and leave the running of Amberley to someone else.'

Another murmur. Speculative eyes rested on Miss Postleton, whose face was utterly frozen.

'Having now despaired of me ever making myself

agreeable enough for a woman to accept, Lady Braybrook has found another solution. I am delighted to announced the betrothal of Serena, Lady Braybrook, to Mr Nigel Havergal. I would ask you all to raise your glasses and wish them well.'

The shock had died down to speculative murmurs by the end of supper. Christy, looking for Harry, supposed the surprise was inevitable—most people seemed incapable of understanding that Mr Havergal's reasons for marriage might have more to do with the heart than monetary advantage.

'Well, Miss Daventry—your employment here will soon be at an end, will it not?'

Startled, she turned. Anne Postleton stood there, her gaze patronising.

'I beg your pardon, Miss Postleton? My employment?'

Miss Postleton smiled. 'My dear Miss Daventry, a newly married woman has little need of a *hireling* for company. And since David should be off to school soon and Alicia and Emma to Bath this winter—well, there is nothing left for you. My mama commented on it just now. Such a shame for you.'

'I pray you won't lose any sleep over it, Miss Postleton,' said Christy drily. There was no point in assuring the girl that Davy's departure for school was not imminent.

Miss Postleton smirked, turned on her heel and strolled off.

Supressing the urge to throw her reticule at Miss

Postleton's retreating curls, Christy looked about for Harry. Lady Braybrook had given her permission to retire for the night and she wanted to say goodnight. She frowned. Where on earth was he? Carefully she scanned the crowd. He wasn't in the Hall. Neither, when she went out on to the steps, could she see him in the forecourt...and nor, she realised on a surge of concern, had she seen Alicia Trentham anywhere.

'Looking for someone, Miss Daventry?' Matthew stood at her shoulder.

'Yes. My brother, and...my brother,' she finished.

'Oh. I saw him leave through the back of the Hall. Said he wanted a breath of air. Through the garden room, I think. Quieter out there.'

No doubt.

Christy stared at the door to the garden room. As a venue for an assignation it had a great deal to recommend it. Privacy. Well away from the party. No one was likely to want anything from it. And she hoped to God that she was a nasty-minded, spiteful old spinster and completely and utterly wrong.

Drawing a deep breath, she opened the door and walked in.

For a moment neither Harry nor Alicia realised she was there. They were completely involved in their kiss. They broke apart as she closed the door.

'I beg your pardon,' she said coldly. 'I think you had better return to the party, Alicia, before anyone else realises you are missing.'

'Damn you!' cursed Harry. 'You were spying on us! *Spying!*'

'And you were both breaching Lord Braybrook's trust!' she replied. 'Damn yourself, Harry. You claim to love Alicia, yet by arranging clandestine meetings you expose her to the risk of censure and ruin! If you cared for her in the least, you would see that!'

She turned on Alicia. 'As for you! Have you no common sense?'

Scarlet-faced, Alicia began, 'It is none of your—'

'Business?' suggested Christy, anger routing any tendency to mince words. 'Tell me—do you think being caught would force your brother's hand?'

Alicia's expression became mulish, and Christy swept on. 'Bear in mind that Harry cannot support you. What would you live on? *Where* would you live? His lodgings in the village?'

When neither of them returned any reply, she continued. 'Don't you realise Braybrook would be more likely to call Harry out for this, than permit you to marry him? And you tell me it's none of my business?'

Alicia paled. 'What are you going to do?' she whispered. 'Are you going to tell Julian?'

Christy considered. Now was not the right moment. 'Your mother's betrothal has just been announced. You should be with her. Go.'

White faced, Alicia obeyed.

'Full of orders, aren't you?' burst out Harry, as the door closed. 'Blast you, Christy! Just because you're such a damn cold fish—'

'Better than being a dead one,' she told him.

'Got orders for me, too?' he sneered.

'No. But this isn't the first time you've tried to meet Alicia, is it? The other day, when I met you at the stile.'

He shuffled. 'What of it? There was no harm in it!'

She held his gaze. 'No harm? It would have ruined Alicia had someone else caught the pair of you just now! Did you care about that at all?'

'Damn it, Christy! What am I supposed to do?'

She shook her head. 'Behave like the gentleman you claim to be, perhaps?'

His throat worked convulsively. *'Bitch!'* he spat at her, and slammed from the room. Christy leaned back against the wall with a shuddering sigh. There was no choice. Braybrook must be told the truth. Armed with that knowledge, he could ensure that Alicia no longer viewed Harry as a possible match. Heat pricked at her eyes. She hadn't wanted this. But what else could she do?

'Well, well, well,' came an amused voice from behind her. She whirled and found Ned Postleton standing in the open outside door. 'What a stirring scene, Miss D.' His eyes mocked. 'Dare say Braybrook won't be too happy, eh?'

Chapter Twelve

Fighting shock, Christy said nothing, but watched warily as Postleton strolled into the room, closing the door behind him.

'Very high in the instep about these things, Braybrook is,' he went on. 'Quite the fire eater. Nothing wrong with a fellow entertaining himself in the right quarters, of course.' He smirked. 'But Braybrook's sister ain't the right quarters. Eh?'

Christy found her voice—inextricably entwined with her temper. 'What are you suggesting, Mr Postleton?'

His gaze crawled over her and she felt unclean. 'Oh, I just thought you might like to devote a few moments to modifying my memory, eh? Amazing how a pretty woman can muddle a man's mind.'

'You think I won't tell Braybrook?'

He spluttered with laughter. 'Tell Braybrook? You won't tell him! He'd call Harry out! Think—Harry's tongue halfway down the chit's throat, his hand up her skirts fingering the goods.'

'That's a lie!' she exploded.

'Now, now, Miss D.' His eyes jeered. 'Think it over. It would make pretty telling.' He shrugged. 'Lose Harry his position, too. The Pater's quite the puritan over these things.'

He came a step closer and Christy snatched up a little gardening fork from the shelf beside her.

Postleton stopped, his startled gaze on the gleaming tines. 'Put that down!' he snapped, lazy mockery gone.

'When you leave,' said Christy. She stepped aside, indicating the inner door with her free hand and making sure there was room for him to pass easily. 'You'll want to be very sure of your story before you retail it to Braybrook.' It was a long shot. She had no idea which way Braybrook would incline, but if she could shake Postleton's confidence…

His expression twisted. 'You think he'll believe *you*?'

She assumed an attitude of amusement. 'A risk, isn't it? You see, he might wonder why *you* didn't intervene when you saw Harry taking such dreadful liberties. Why Harry isn't already sporting a black eye? And how you managed to see so much through a closed door?'

The stunned look on Postleton's face told Christy that this had not occurred to him. She held her breath. There were gaps in her bluff that you could have driven a coach and four through. But it might buy her time to reach Braybrook first.

'He's tupping you,' said Postleton suddenly. 'Braybrook's already dipped his wick! That's why you're so sure he'll believe you.'

She merely raised her brows, quelling the panic bubbling beneath the surface. The expressions he'd used were unfamiliar, but their meaning was clear.

'He'll tire of you fast enough' said Postleton. 'And then you'll be out on your ear, probably with his brat in your belly. Wouldn't be the first time.'

'Leave' she said. 'Now.'

His eyes narrowed. 'Oh, I'm going. I'm not fool enough to meddle with any wench Braybrook's bedding.'

He strolled towards the door and Christy tracked him with her eyes, moving to allow him passage, stepping back to remain behind him, the garden fork still levelled.

Then the door closed behind him and with a shudder she sagged against the shelves. Whatever riptide had seared her veins, allowing her to face him down, it had subsided to leave her cold and shaking. She stayed there, wrapping Lady Braybrook's old shawl close. The riot of birds, butterflies and flowers still shimmered, but now their loveliness served only to mock. She stared at the garden fork. Would she really have stabbed him with it, had he attempted to force her?

Yes. In a heartbeat.

On the thought the inner door opened behind her. Fury, spurred by fear, ripped through her and she levelled the fork as she whirled.

Julian retreated from the virago confronting him. 'Christy!'

Even as he spoke she sagged back against the shelves,

the garden fork clattering to the floor. He took in her white face, the trembling hands, heard her breath rush out.

'I...I'm sorry, my lord. I thought...I didn't realise it was you.'

The shaky words scorched him and he put it together in a surge of searing fury. Whoever she had expected she would have greeted him with a garden fork levelled at his guts...

'What did Postleton do to you?' He scarcely recognised his own raw voice.

She flinched. 'Postleton? How—?'

'Damn it, Christy! Trust me!' Then he forced his voice to gentle and said, 'He passed me in the hall. Look, if you were wielding a garden fork you were hardly a willing participant! What happened?'

Her eyes searched his face.

'Harry and Alicia were here too.'

'I beg your pardon? I thought Postleton—' Her words sank in. 'Harry and Lissy? Explain.'

She did. In a detached, clear voice, her gaze steady.

'Bloody young fools,' he muttered to himself. Then, realising he'd spoken aloud, 'I beg your pardon. Go on. Where does Postleton fit into this?'

'He threatened to tell you.'

'Not much of a threat since you've told me anyway,' he said.

'An exaggerated version.' Her cheeks flamed.

'Oh?' They were coming to the nub of it. For the first time her eyes wavered. Focusing on a point beyond his left shoulder, she said, 'He intended to tell you that

Harry had his…his tongue halfway down her throat, and his hand…his hand—'

'Very well,' he said. Her distress was palpable and he had the gist of it.

She went on. 'He offered to keep silent on certain terms.'

'What terms?' grated Julian, although he thought he knew.

She met his gaze. 'There is only one thing a gentleman wants from a woman of my station, my lord. As you well know.'

Anger roared through him. Anger at the thought of Postleton, or any other man, so much as thinking of touching her, let alone threatening her. And sheer, blistering hurt that she saw his own offer in the same tainted light.

'I did *not* attempt to coerce you!' he ground out.

'No,' she acknowledged. 'But there was no difference in what you wanted. Just that you wanted it for longer and were prepared to pay generously for your entertainment.'

Entertainment? This hot twisting in his gut was *entertainment*?

He opened his mouth, prepared to scarify her, rage at her…

'I'm sorry,' he said very quietly.

She stared, clearly confused.

She wasn't the only one. What was he sorry for? Postleton's insults? His own offer? All he knew was that behind the calm exterior she was hurt, upset. That she had been exposed to insult and danger in his house and he wanted to hit someone for it. Unfortunately, beating Postleton to a pulp would only cause more trouble. Quite possibly for her.

After a moment she cleared her throat. 'It doesn't matter, my lord. And this was certainly not your fault.' She swallowed, the movement of her throat convulsive. 'But there is something else I must tell you—'

'Whatever it is can wait until morning,' he said. The set of her jaw told him that whatever it was would cause her pain. 'You've had enough. Go up.'

She hesitated, biting her lip. After a moment she nodded. 'Very well. Goodnight, my lord.'

He meant to let her go. But as she drew level he saw the fine trembling of her mouth, that she clutched her shawl as if the warm night had turned chilly.

He muttered a curse and reached out a hand, laying it gently on her wrist. She stopped, but didn't look at him.

'My lord—please.'

He pulled her into his arms, felt the stiffness of her body, the shivering. He would just hold her for a moment. To comfort her. Nothing more. He slid his fingers into the warm silk of her hair and pressed her cheek gently against his chest. For an instant she resisted, her hands pushing back against his chest, but then with a little sigh, she relaxed, yielding to his embrace. 'Shh. It's all right,' he murmured, and rested his own cheek on her hair. It felt right. She fitted—against him, against his heart, in a way no other woman ever had.

He took a deep breath, trying to steady the rising beat of his blood, but breathing in was a mistake. Her soft, warm fragrance, mingled with the soap she used, slid into him and he was lost. He gathered her closer, turning her face up to his. Behind the spectacles her eyes were huge in a pale face.

'My lord?' she whispered again.

He should say something. Something reassuring. Comforting. But again all that came out was, 'I'm sorry.' And whether he was apologising for what he had already done, or for what he was about to do, he didn't know.

Slowly, giving her every chance to pull back or stab him with the fork, he lowered his mouth to hers.

Christy's mind whirled even as her lips softened, returning his kiss. She should say no, pull away. This was insanity. Steely strength surrounded her, yet it was not that which held her. His gentleness, his restraint, the aching tenderness of his kiss held her in thrall. She was cradled, not confined. He would release her if she wished it.

She did not wish it. Rather, as she felt the seeking caress of his tongue against her lips, she parted them on a sigh of longing and he took her mouth. His tongue slid deep, touching hers, possessing her, in a rhythm that sang in harmony with her beating blood.

A large hand drifted over her waist as though entranced with the curve, lifting to cover her breast. Even through her gown and chemise, the sturdier defence of her stays, she felt it. Her body leaping to life as her nipples peaked in a burning rush, pressing against the confining stays in a hidden plea so that she pushed against him. With a groan his kiss deepened, his arms tightening around her …

Lord, she was sweet. Her shy, untutored kisses set him ablaze as nothing else ever had.

A violent crash broke them apart and he broke the kiss to see the door bouncing off the wall.

'You bloody hypocrite, Braybrook! Get your hands off my sister!'

Harry Daventry's words and his contorted, mottled face as he glared at them from the doorway dashed over Julian like cold, dirty water. Beyond Harry, Ned Postleton's smirk mocked. Beside him, Christy tried to step away, a small sound of distress escaping from her. It pierced him and instinctively he caught her wrist.

'Dear me. Are we interrupting something?' drawled Postleton.

Julian's fists balled. 'Get the hell out of here, Postleton,' he said, stepping forwards. 'This is nothing to do with you!'

Postleton grinned. 'Oh, come, Braybrook! Hardly the first time you've slipped away to enjoy a lady's charms. Romance in the air tonight?'

'Romance?' spat Harry, advancing on Julian. 'I'm not good enough to raise my eyes to *his* sister, but mine is good enough for his amusement! Thanks for the tip-off, Postleton!'

'Harry! No!'

Christy stepped around him, facing her brother. Damn it! Was she protecting *him*? He caught her shoulders and pushed her behind him. 'Don't be an idiot!' he told her, and swung to face Daventry. At this point nothing mattered but protecting Christy from the consequences of his own stupidity.

'I'm willing to offer whatever satisfaction you like, Daventry, but this is neither the time nor place unless you *want* to see your sister's reputation ruined!'

'A fat lot *you* cared about—!'

'I say, sorry to interrupt, Mr Daventry, but have you seen my brother?' Matthew appeared in the doorway. 'Oh, there you are, Julian. Mama was wondering where you'd vanished…' His voice trailed off as his widening eyes took in the scene. 'Er—'

'I'll tell you where he'd vanished to!' roared Harry. 'Seducing my sister! That's where!'

A dull flush rose on Matthew's cheeks and he flung a hasty glance back over his shoulder. 'Um, George—why don't you go back? I've, er, found him now.'

And George Endicott's voice. 'Oh, ah, right you are, Matt. I'll see you later, then.'

Julian swore under his breath as Mr Endicott's footsteps retreated swiftly. Doubtless in a hurry to pass the story on to his sisters, who would tell all their friends. And so on. The story would be all around the ball within half an hour and all over the county inside of a sennight.

'Sorry,' said Matthew.

Behind him he heard Christy draw a shaky breath. He swung around, jaw set. 'We'll talk in the morning—' he began.

'Talk?' snarled Harry. 'What's to talk about! You'll marry my sister or answer to me!'

Christy's mind reeled. 'Harry—are you *mad*? I don't want to marry him!'

Braybrook shot a startled, measuring glance at her. Damn him! Did he imagine she'd marry a man who preferred her in the role of mistress?

Harry glared at her. 'You should have thought of that before he tupped you!'

'He didn't—'

'One more insult to your sister, Daventry,' snapped Braybrook, stepping forwards with clenched fists, 'and *you* will answer to *me*!'

Oh, this was ridiculous! They were like two dogs snarling over a bone! She had to stop it before one or the other of these *idiots* said something from which there was no backing down.

'Well, my lord?' growled Harry, 'Which is it? Pistols or marriage?'

'It will be neither!' said Christy. Dragging in a breath, she steeled herself to deliver the final blow. And saw Ned Postleton lounging in the doorway.

Her breath caught. There was still a chance that if she told Braybrook the truth privately, Harry could retain his position and she might scrape a reference. But if Postleton learnt the truth their ruin would be absolute.

'Get rid of him,' she told Harry, indicating Postleton.

Postleton's smirk intensified. 'No, no, Miss D. Independent witness, you know!'

'Exactly!' blustered Harry. 'Damned if I will. Postleton's stood my friend this evening, and—'

'He deliberately stirred up trouble!' snapped Christy.

'I'm warning you, Harry—it makes little difference to me, but it might make a difference to you.'

A split second of incomprehension, then Harry's face drained of colour. 'Christy, you…you wouldn't! You *can't*!'

'I can,' she said softly. 'Get him out. And make sure he doesn't listen at the door as he did to your tryst with Alicia!'

Harry stared.

'That's right,' she said, beyond caution. 'He tried to blackmail me over it!'

'A misunderstanding, Daventry,' Postleton assured him lazily. 'But we might as well leave the lovebirds to settle the date.'

With that parting shot, he strolled out. Harry cast a panicked look at Christy and followed.

'Daventry!' said Braybrook quietly.

He looked back from the doorway, his expression blank.

'You had better call tomorrow afternoon, or rather *this* afternoon, to discuss the matter.'

His face grey, Harry nodded and walked out, closing the door.

Letting out a breath he hadn't been aware he was holding, Julian turned to Christy.

Spear straight, she faced him. 'Wait a moment, then check that Postleton is really gone,' she told him.

He did so, but the passageway was empty, the only sound the distant drift of music and laughter. He closed the door again and turned back to her. His course was laid out for him, straight and uncompromising. Only he had never envisaged himself making an offer of marriage in the garden room on the heels of an argument and in the teeth of unprecedented scandal.

'Christy—Miss Daventry—' He broke off, searching for words, and settled on blunt formality. 'Miss Daventry, will you do me the—?'

'No.' She flung up a hand. 'There is not the least need for this, sir. You do not need to make me an offer of marriage.'

He sighed. 'Miss Daventry, we both know better than that,' he said. 'While marriage was not what I had in mind, I play by the rules. You are a gently bred lady in my stepmother's employ. By breakfast time, thanks to your brother, half the county will be speculating about our relationship.'

'You think he did that *on purpose*?'

The shock and anger in her voice was matched with clenched fists.

'That is irrelevant,' he told her. 'What is relevant is that either I marry you, or your reputation in this neighbourhood is destroyed.'

'If it doesn't matter to me—'

'It matters to me,' he told her. 'I am sure you do not expect me down upon my knees, so—will you make me the happiest of men, and do me the honour of becoming my wife?'

'No.'

He suppressed the urge to swear.

'Miss Daventry, we have no choice in this.'

'You may not. I do. No.'

Some of his certainty vanished. His offer to take her as his mistress was one thing. He could understand her refusing that. But he was offering marriage now. An offer far beyond anything she could ever have dreamed.

'Miss Daventry—'

'No!' She flung the word at him, took a deep breath and continued, 'Harry and I are illegitimate, my lord.'

'What?'

'Precisely, my lord. The Duke of Alcaston is our father, not Harry's godfather. That circumstance relieves you of any obligation. It should also dampen your sister's enthusiasm for marriage with my brother.'

He stared at her, dumbfounded. She faced him unflinching, her chin up, cheeks burning with embarrassment.

'That is what I was going to tell you earlier. Now, if you will excuse me, I must begin packing.'

She walked towards the door, the shawl clutched around her. Stunned, he let her go. She was illegitimate. Her brother was illegitimate… Even Lissy would acknowledge that that rendered Harry Daventry ineligible. And as for Christy Daventry, that simple statement was his salvation; no one in their right mind would consider that he owed her marriage now.

Serena's grey eyes resembled nothing more than twin gun barrels after the house was quiet and he confessed to what had happened and told her the truth of Christy's birth. Nigel Havergal, seated beside her, said nothing and his expression said less. But Julian had never seen Serena angrier.

'I have very little choice, Julian,' she told him quietly. 'And apparently Miss Daventry herself knows it if she has said that she is leaving.'

'No.'

Serena raised her brows. 'What else is to be done? With her reputation destroyed, I cannot employ her without damaging your sisters' reputations.'

'It wasn't her fault!'

Serena laughed mirthlessly. 'Julian, in these cases it is *always* the woman's fault. Especially when it isn't. You know that. All I can do is give her a reference. And even that won't help her once the story is out, whether you seduced her or not—'

'I didn't!' He dragged in a breath. 'She refused me.'

Serena raised her brows. 'A pity you didn't listen to her. There is nothing I can do, Julian. Unless you have another solution?'

He slept badly. Time and again he woke from dreams in which Christy was gone. Vanished into a swirling fog that consumed even her memory as if she had never been. Each time he reminded himself that he'd given instructions that no carriage was to be ordered for her unless *he* ordered one.

Unless she walked, without her possessions, she couldn't leave. He'd told himself that each time he woke sweating. Now it was time to face the day. And the consequences of his idiocy.

He saw Alicia first. Pale and subdued, she came to him in the library.

'Mama said you wished to see me.' Her voice was husky, as though she had been crying.

'Yes.'

She swallowed. 'I'm sorry. Mama told me what happened, and…and about Harry…that he's—' She took a shaky breath. 'I'm sorry, Julian…I didn't mean—'

'It's all right,' he said quietly. How could he allow Lissy to apologise when his behaviour had been much worse?

'Mama is writing to Aunt Massingdale in Bath, to see if I may visit earlier than planned.'

It was probably a sensible solution, but…'What do you want to do, Liss?'

She stared and a tear trickled down her cheek. Dashing it away, she said, 'I agreed it would be best. So Mama said I should leave straight after the wedding. But Julian, is it—?'

'Wedding?'

Her cheeks reddened. 'Well, Mama's wedding. Julian—you…you aren't going to challenge Harry? Are you? Please, say you aren't—I couldn't bear it!'

What the hell could he say? There was every chance he would end up facing Harry over duelling pistols. 'I hope not.'

'Will you have to marry Christy?'

He gave her the best answer he had. 'I don't know, Liss.'

* * *

His fingers drummed on the desk as he waited for Christy. They had to settle this. Gossip must be flying already, by tomorrow the hunt would be up, with Christy the prey to be coursed and torn to pieces… *Yes, my dear—quite shocking…Of course, I knew how it would be. Always the same, girls of that order—cunning. Out for what they can get.* There would be plenty to join the cry. *Dreadful! Poor Serena! Carrying on the affair right under her very nose. Still, she should have known there was something more to it when Braybrook employed the girl. Dare say the slut will be gone by now…* The men would take a different perspective…sniggering, speculating… *Bit of sport, eh? Shouldn't have thought she was quite the type, but these quiet ones…eh?*

He stood up and went to the windows, staring out at a golden late summer's afternoon. He could step away from the situation. Christy's illegitimacy rendered his offer null and void. Drop the fact of her birth into the flood of gossip and the thing was done. She and her brother would be disgraced, and there would be no expectation that he should respond to a challenge from Daventry with anything but derision.

That was how the world would see it. There was even the possibility that with her character destroyed and nowhere to go, she would consent to becoming his mistress and no one would breathe a word of censure.

A light tap came on the door.

'Come in.'

Christy entered, and it was like a punch to the stomach. Even across the room he could see how strained she looked. How tired. As though she had not slept any better than he had.

'My baggage is in the hall, my lord,'

She was even making it easy for him…

Chapter Thirteen

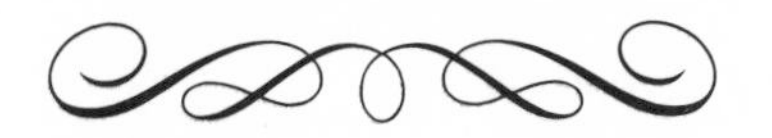

A headache thumped behind Christy's tired, scratchy eyes. Sheer exhaustion had induced an hour or so of nightmare-ridden sleep. Dark, twisting streets in which she wandered alone, lost, searching, always searching for something that remained misty and formless.

Braybrook stood by the window. With the light pouring in behind him his face was shadowed and unreadable. She was unsure why he had sent for her. She supposed he might wish to dismiss her formally with her quarter's wages. Unless her altered status made her fair game for seduction now. Please God she still had the courage to refuse.

He came forward and she saw the gravity of his expression. 'Miss Daventry, my offer of marriage stands.'

Her world spun out of control, all her certainties reeling. Barely able to breathe, she stared at him. Against all precedent, all expectation, he was still offering marriage. She could neither speak nor think for the confusion storming through her.

Then, 'Why?' she whispered. 'Why would *you* be prepared to marry me knowing that, when even—?'

She broke off too late. Braybrook frowned, his gaze slicing through every barrier into her memories.

'Who was he?'

She struggled to rebuild the barriers. 'That is nothing to do with you, since I have no intention of marrying you.'

'Who was he?'

Anger stirred. 'Why? Are you worried in case I'm not a virgin?'

He frowned. 'Should I be?'

'Not unless I agree to marry you, and even then I doubt you have the right.'

His expression hardened. 'Since we *are* going to marry, I'd say I have every right!'

'Didn't you tell me once that you were not hypocrite enough to demand something of your bride that you were not prepared to give?'

He was silent for a moment. 'Very well. Shall we agree that I have no rights, merely a lamentable curiosity? Christy—who was he?'

Perhaps it was better to get it over with. Like cauterising a wound, or digging out a splinter. She shrugged. 'No one you would know. Jeremy was the son of a merchant. Not wealthy, but rising. I had been at school with his sister and…' she swallowed, barely able to say it '…we fell in love.'

'And?'

'He asked me to marry him, so I told him the truth.'

Braybrook nodded. 'Whereupon you never saw him again?'

Oh, how she wished that were the case!

'On the contrary, he came to me a week later.' She forced the words out. 'He still wanted me; only his terms had changed. I was to take lodgings for which he would pay.' She stopped, unwilling to go on. Of all men, he would know where this sordid tale was going.

'Did you?' There was no accusation in his voice.

'No.' She had wanted to crawl into a hole and die of shame. He had spoken to her differently. *Looked* at her differently. As though she were something to be bought. As though she had no right to want, let alone expect, something better.

'So why are you refusing to marry me?'

She stared. 'Why—? *You* wanted me to be your mistress too! Do you think I wish to marry a man who sees me that way?'

His fist clenched. 'Touché,' he said harshly. 'But you refused my offer. As well as refusing the man you apparently loved.'

She shivered. Had she loved Jeremy? How could she tell now? She had thought that she loved him. She had certainly liked him, had wanted to marry him. He would have been a safe husband. But love—?

'I refused because I was angry!' she snapped. 'Not because of any particular virtue!'

His mouth twitched. 'Yes, I'd imagine that you were angry.'

'Not because he declined to marry me,' she said. 'I

understood that. I told him to give him that chance. It was because he wanted to have his cake and eat it.'

His lordship's eyes widened. 'He—? Of course.'

'And I did *not* refuse your offer because I was holding out for a better one!' She couldn't bear him to think that. 'All you need do is let the truth be known. No one will censure you.'

'Except me,' he said.

'You?'

'After refusing my original and dishonourable offer, you made sure we were never alone together again,' he said. 'In fact, you took pains to avoid me as much as possible.'

'What has that to say to anything?' She ached with weariness.

'It matters because you made it clear you did not want what I was offering despite the attraction between us.'

She didn't want to think about that. About the way her whole body, heart and soul had echoed in harmony when he kissed her. About the way he had made her believe, or wish to believe, that his kisses meant something. That *she* meant something beyond a passing fancy.

'Perhaps I was being coy,' she suggested.

'Coy?' he repeated. 'Christy, you are probably the least coy woman of my acquaintance!' He laughed wryly. 'Except possibly Serena.'

She was trying not to think about Lady Braybrook. 'The fact remains, my lord, that—'

'That you made it clear you would not have me, and I gave you my word you were safe. Instead, I ruined you.'

Her eyes blazed. 'You did not!' she shot back. 'It was a *kiss*, nothing more!'

'Your reputation, then,' he amended. 'Unfortunately, that is enough.'

'You *can't* wish to marry me,' she whispered. It was impossible that he should do such a thing.

His mouth twisted. 'Christy, this is not what either of us wanted,' he said quietly, 'but, there is little choice. I'm not going to announce your illegitimacy.'

She dragged in a breath, fighting to block all emotion and view the matter rationally. She could marry him, or leave in disgrace. If she refused and Braybrook would not use her illegitimacy to defend himself… She swallowed. Harry would challenge him. *One of them at least would die because you were too missish to accept a marriage that is entirely to your advantage…*

'You would have to meet my brother, would you not, my lord?'

Shock slammed into Julian.

'Christy—you can't think—! His quarrel with me is justified! I would—'

'Fire in the air?' She shrugged. 'Where's the difference? Harry is a very fine shot. Very well, I will marry you. You are not the only one with an inconvenient conscience, my lord.'

His breath caught. She understood he would not kill her brother. So if she had not agreed to marriage to protect Harry—his brain felt sluggish, clogged—it was *his* life she was concerned about. She had agreed to marriage to protect *him*. The realisation left him reeling.

You are not the only one with an inconvenient conscience, my lord.

'We are well matched after all, aren't we? Shall we say, in four weeks?'

She nodded, turned around and left the room without a word.

Julian stared at the closed door. He had wanted a bride without any romantical notions to complicate matters. It seemed he had got that with a vengeance. He had also gained a penniless bride with worse than no connections.

Now all he had to do was write a discreet letter to inform Alcaston that his unacknowledged, illegitimate daughter was about to become a viscountess.

'My lord?'

Julian looked up from his account books to find his butler fidgeting in the doorway. 'Yes, Hallam.' He frowned back at his recalcitrant column of figures.

'My lord, I thought you should know his Grace, the Duke of Alcaston, has called.'

'What?'

He straightened and set his pen in the holder. 'Alcaston? Of course I should know! Show him in!' He'd received a note from Alcaston's secretary acknowledging his letter and heard nothing more. By now he had assumed that Alcaston was going to ignore the matter.

Hallam swallowed visibly. 'I'm very sorry, my lord, but he said he'd see you afterwards—'

'Afterwards? After what?' demanded Julian, pushing his chair back.

'After he had seen Miss Daventry,' explained Hallam. 'He insisted.' Hallam hesitated. 'Not my place to say, my lord, but his Grace…well, he looked angry.'

Suppressing the urge to swear, Julian nodded. 'Very well. Thank you, Hallam. Where are they?'

'The drawing room, my lord.'

'Lady Braybrook is there?'

Hallam shook his head. 'No, my lord. Her ladyship went down to the Dower House with Mr Havergal to see the new furnishings.'

Christy stared, shocked at the duke, whose cold eyes surveyed her. 'I don't know what fairytale you spun Braybrook, girl, but if you thought I'd let it pass, then you're more of a fool than I imagined!'

She stiffened her spine. 'Fairytale?' She was going to remain calm and in control of herself. She wouldn't let him win.

Alcaston's eyes surveyed her coldly. 'How'd you do it? Trapped him? A mere compromising situation? Or did you play your only trump card?' He gave her a measuring look. 'I dare say that's it, isn't it? You let him swive you.'

She said nothing. She didn't care what he thought of her, and it would have made no difference anyway.

'I nearly let it go,' he told her. 'After all, if he's fool

enough to marry a girl without connections or a penny to her name, let alone one who'll let him bed her, then he deserves what he gets.'

'So why are you here, sir?' She was mildly surprised to discover she felt very little for him.

A harsh laugh escaped him. 'Couldn't do it, could I? Couldn't let a man pollute his line when I could stop it!'

Once those words would have hurt. She would have felt rage. Shame. Now there was only emptiness. She could not think of him as her father. His seed had gone into her making, but she felt nothing. Not even regret for the void.

'And how will you stop it? Stand up in church and denounce me?' she suggested. 'It's hardly in keeping with your policy of discretion.'

His face mottled. 'I won't need to, girl. I'll give you one chance—tell him you've changed your mind. Break the betrothal quietly and I'll settle some money on you. Otherwise I'll tell him the truth myself and you'll get nothing!'

He thought she had deceived Braybrook. Lied by omission.

'You may go to hell, sir,' she told him.

For a speeding instant he looked stunned. He recovered swiftly. 'Words, girl! Do you think he'll marry you once he knows the truth?'

'What truth, your Grace?' came a cool voice.

Alcaston swung around. Christy's breath caught. Braybrook stood in the doorway. Tall, dark and somehow menacing. The planes of his face were hard and cold, the brilliant eyes fixed on the duke. He strolled forward. 'I do beg your pardon, your Grace.' The urbane voice belied the chill in his gaze. 'I am at a loss to understand why my butler should have shown you in here rather than bringing you to me. Most improper of him since Miss Daventry is not yet mistress of Amberley and Lady Braybrook is out.'

There was a pause. To Christy's amazement Alcaston looked chagrined. Even diminished.

'I believe I indicated to your man that I wished to see—that is, that I—' He broke off, jaw working. 'No matter,' he growled.

Braybrook's cold gaze never wavered and Christy was torn between admiration and horror. Alcaston was a *duke*, for pity's sake! Had Braybrook taken leave of his senses?

He spoke again. 'Obviously you read my letter at last. I dare say you were eager to wish Miss Daventry happy. I hope I see you well?'

Alcaston recovered the use of his tongue. 'Aye. I'm well enough,' he snapped. 'And I read your letter three weeks ago! You're damned lucky I decided to do something about it in the end!'

Braybrook raised his brows. 'Do something?' He reached Christy and took her hand, setting it on his arm, covering it with his other hand in a heart-shakingly protective gesture. 'I have already made a generous settlement on Miss Daventry, but of course if you wish to see the documents—'

'The devil I do!' growled Alcaston. 'I'd like to speak to the girl alone, if you please, Braybrook!'

'I don't please,' said Braybrook quietly. 'And you will mind your language in front of Miss Daventry,' he added.

Alcaston's jaw worked. 'Mind my—' He looked at Christy and his eyes hardened. 'Very well. I offered her a chance, but only to spare your feelings. I don't know what lies she's told, Braybrook, but she's no more fit to marry a man of rank than is a mongrel bitch. The truth is, she's a bastard. Her mother was my mistress. Sorry to be the one to break it to you, but—'

'Why would you assume I didn't know?'

'Because—' Alcaston broke off, jaw slack. 'You *knew*? Your letter didn't—'

'I was being discreet.' Braybrook's voice was icy. 'For your sake more than mine, I might add. I assumed your secretary would read the letter, so I referred to Miss Daventry as the sister of your godson. Naturally I am aware of Christy's birth.'

'How? How could you have known?' he rapped out. 'No one ever knew! Their mother passed as a widow.'

Fury at the memory of the lies her mother had been forced to live sang through Christy. 'Because I told him!'

The hand covering hers tightened. 'Leave this to me, sweetheart,' he murmured. Her heart shook at the endearment.

Braybrook's voice became colder. Harder. Yet his fingers still caressed hers reassuringly. 'You see, Miss

Daventry was more honest with me than you were with her mother, Alcaston.'

Alcaston's eyes bulged and a vein stood out at his temple. His face was mottled. 'You'll marry her and soil your bloodline?'

Braybrook's voice lashed. 'I'll admit the thought of *your* bloodline doesn't fill me with delight. But since there is clearly very little of you in your daughter, I'll risk it. Was that all you came for?'

'Damn your insolence!' spat Alcaston. 'I take the time and trouble to warn you, and you meet me with insults? She's no daughter of mine, and you'll get not a penny from me!'

'You relieve me,' said Braybrook. 'Perhaps you might also relieve us of your presence?' Christy stared up at him, shocked. He had snubbed a duke for her. One of his own class. Under the sleeve of his elegant coat, in the hand covering hers, she could feel every muscle hard and corded. His jaw resembled solid granite and her heart's defences shook.

'You *fool*!' ground out Alcaston. 'Go to the devil your own way!'

He stalked out, slamming the door.

Julian clung to the remaining shreds of his self-discipline. Frogmarching Alcaston through the house and flinging him down the front steps was out of the question. Instead he turned to Christy.

She looked calm, unmoved, as though her father had not just denounced and disowned her without so much as speaking her name. As though nothing had shifted in her world. Perhaps it hadn't. Yet he could feel her fingers digging into his arm. Fury? Hurt? As though reading his mind, she relaxed her hold.

'Thank you, my lord.'

'You're welcome. Come, sit down.' He urged her to a chair and then turned away to a small side table and poured a glass of brandy from a decanter there. 'Here—drink it. You'll feel better.'

She sniffed it suspiciously. 'I don't need it.'

'The hell you—' He broke off.

'Lost for words, my lord?'

He ran a hand through his hair, smiling ruefully. 'Having just called your fa—' Something in her eyes stopped him. He rephrased what he had been about to say. 'Having called Alcaston to account for swearing in front of you, it would be the outside of enough to do it myself.'

Behind the spectacles something glimmered. He swallowed, turned away to pour himself a brandy.

'He's no father to me,' she said softly. 'My father would have attended Sarah's funeral.'

Sarah? Her sister? His heart twisted. 'I don't blame you,' he said. 'Christy, you've never told me about your mother. I didn't want to pry, but—'

'You have every right,' she said. He wasn't entirely sure that was true.

'After all,' she continued bitterly, 'she might have been a back-alley whore or a notorious courtesan.'

He shook his head. 'Unlikely. No back-alley whore could have raised you to be what you are—a lady. And if your mother *had* been a notorious courtesan, then it's unlikely Alcaston could have kept your existence quiet. Nor,' he added, 'would your mother have had to pretend to be a widow. Tell me.'

She was silent for a moment, but he did not think it was the silence of refusal. Her eyes were distant, remembering, thinking. At last she met his gaze and sighed. 'This is only in part what Mama told me. Some of it I pieced together from old letters and her diary.'

He nodded, and she continued. 'Mama was the daughter of lesser gentry living near Alcaston's principal seat. Her name was Catherine. Catherine Louisa Daventry.'

'It was her real name?'

She frowned. 'Yes. There were a couple of letters from my grandfather, and a diary she had kept before and just after her elopement.'

'Good.' Safer to ask. A false name could call the validity of their marriage into question later.

'From the diary she believed that Alcaston intended to marry her, but since the previous duke had contracted enormous debts, he contracted to marry the only daughter of an extremely wealthy merchant. Naturally he did not tell my mother this when they eloped. By the time her family found her, Alcaston was married to his heiress and I was on the way.' She shivered. 'There was a letter from her father disowning her.'

'They cast her off?'

She frowned. 'I think…when I was about six—it was after Harry was born—a man came to visit. We were in Bath by then. I think he was Mama's brother; she said at first to call him Uncle Harry, but that made him angry. After he left Mama said we'd be all right now. I suppose he gave her money. There was an annuity that died with her.'

He nodded. 'Did Alcaston support her?'

She bit her lip. 'After a fashion. He didn't visit often after Sarah was born. That was when he moved us to Bristol.' Her cheeks reddened. 'Easier to maintain the "widow" fiction if he moved us during each pregnancy.'

He didn't know what to say.

She continued. 'After Sarah died, he tired of Mama, but gave her the Bristol house.' Coldly, she added, 'Guilt, probably.'

Julian thought back over all he knew of Alcaston. Fear of exposure might have had something to do with it. It was common knowledge that Alcaston's father-in-law had been particularly strict on such matters. He'd have pulled the ducal purse strings uncomfortably tight had he suspected this. Probably Catherine's family had used that to force Alcaston to support her.

'Do you wish me to approach your mother's family?'

Some of her brandy spilt. '*No*. I wrote for her when she was ill, dying. A note came back from a Henry Daventry saying that he had no sister. I wrote again when she died and received no reply.'

He nodded. Families hid a daughter's disgrace at all costs. And sometimes the innocent paid.

'We'll ignore them,' he told her.

The ghost of a smile touched her lips. 'I doubt they'll notice.'

'Their loss,' he said lightly. And meant it.

Two days later Christy faced the altar of the village church as the Vicar expounded the reasons for matrimony, the words she had already heard that morning piercing her.

'Thirdly, it was ordained for the mutual society, help and comfort, that the one ought to have of the other, both in prosperity and adversity. Into which holy estate these two persons present come now to be joined…'

Early that morning Serena had married Nigel Havergal with only the family present. Their faces had been alight with happiness, the rightness of their union unquestionable. The Vicar's words had been a blessing, a confirmation of joy.

But now those same words sounded a warning…

'Therefore if any man can show any just cause why they may not be lawfully joined together, let him now speak, or else hereafter forever hold his peace…'

She half-expected Alcaston to reappear. Folly. There was no legal impediment to the marriage. Merely social convention. She dragged in a breath to give her responses. Was she doing the right thing? Harry's belligerence suggested her chances of talking him out of challenging Braybrook had been non-existent. Braybrook himself appeared completely unmoved, and for some unstated reason Serena was delighted, welcoming the betrothal, dismissing her birth.

Unfortunate, but since you are exactly what he needs there is no point dwelling on it. It is nobody's business but your own.

Kind, generous words, but how could a bastard, a woman he had wanted as his mistress, be what he needed in a bride?

Harry was placing her hand in the Vicar's. A moment later the Vicar gave her hand into Braybrook's keeping. He took it in a firm, steady clasp. Just that formal touch demanded by the ritual, and her senses sang with awareness. His height, his strength, the hard line of his jaw, the hint of sandalwood and the spicy, masculine tang that was *him*. Every nerve thrummed with a terrifying anticipation…

The Vicar was speaking again.

'Wilt thou have this woman…?'

Had it been a foolish impulse on his part? Did he regret his decision already, or would that come later? A shiver ran through her.

Beside her, he frowned, the dark brows snapping together. She lifted her chin and met the piercing blue gaze.

'…and forsaking all other, keep thee only unto her, as long as ye both shall live?'

The frown deepened…then his fingers tightened.

'I will.'

Her heart shook as he made vows she doubted he intended to keep. Yet, unbidden, her fingers returned his clasp, and trembled as his thumb stroked gently over the back of her hand.

* * *

The wedding guests were gone except for those staying in the house and Christy stared out of her bedchamber window. The western sky flamed pink and gold on deep, deep blue, the trees beyond the park standing black against the glowing embers of day. The whole world, the very air was flushed golden pink. She leaned out, pushing the casement wide. It was still relatively early. Far too early to be in her nightgown. But her newly appointed maid had been waiting when she came up, had seemed to think that she ought to be arrayed in her nightgown. Ready.

Acquiescence was easier and a hot bath was unaccustomed luxury even without the various oils Beth the maid tipped into the steaming water.

Her ladyship—Mrs Havergal, that is, gave them to me specially, my lady. For tonight. A conspiratorial smile had accompanied the words.

There had been soap as well, its delicate fragrance a match for the bath oil. She would have loved it, even with Beth hovering, making sure everything was just so. But the rising, scented steam reminded her mercilessly that this was a ritual, that she was being readied. Adorned. Made fit for her husband.

She had rebelled, though, at the gauzy froth of silk and lace laid out for her on the downturned bed. Serena had given it to her, but the thought of appearing before Braybrook in the intimacy of her bedchamber half-naked sent panic skittering down her nerves. Her husband had been bedding London's beauties for years.

She had no idea of inviting comparison. Instead she had folded it carefully away, selecting instead plain, modest, high-necked linen. It gave at least the illusion of safety.

A fragile illusion. Braybrook's chamber was next to this one with a connecting door and she had heard faint sounds of movement. Indistinct male voices. She had dismissed Beth at once, and the maid had departed with a curtsy, and barely concealed smile at the closed connecting door. That had been bad enough, but had Braybrook appeared with the maid still in the room…

A throat was cleared. 'Christy?'

Chapter Fourteen

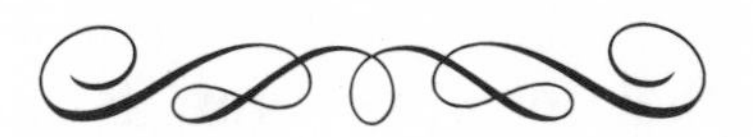

Julian watched her from the door as she leaned out of the window, limned in light. The way she was seated sideways on the window ledge had his blood heating. One bare foot remained on the floor, steadying her; the demure nightgown—which should have concealed, but instead hugged breast, slender waist and curving hip—had slid up to expose a dainty ankle, part of her calf, graceful, shapely… She was half-turned away, her face hidden as she gazed out.

Desire bucked, but he hesitated; she had been nervous in the church. Yet during the hours since her composure had been absolute. A façade, he knew, something that could be broken. He had once wondered what it would take to break her quiet self-possession.

A wedding night was almost guaranteed to leave her self-possession in tatters.

And what about your *self-possession?*

He dismissed that. *His* self-possession had never been in doubt. Not with any woman. It was not now.

He cleared his throat. 'Christy?'

She did not move, yet where she had been still before, her stillness now held the quality of force. And when she turned to face him, the control in her movement cried tension. In the dimly lit room and with the flaring sky to frame her, he could not read her expression.

'My lord?'

That stung.

He came further into the room as she slipped from the window ledge and the nightgown fell around her in modest concealment. He gestured towards the door. 'Shall we?'

She looked blankly from him to the door. 'I beg your pardon?'

'Our wedding night. Or had you forgot?'

She flushed. 'Of course not! I…I just thought—' Her gaze flickered to the turned-down bed and he saw where her confusion lay.

'My bed,' he said quietly. Tonight at least it seemed fitting.

Her eyes widened, the faintest chink in her calm. Without a word she moved around the room, snuffing candles until the only light was from the window and the doorway behind him. She made to catch up the dressing gown lying across a chair.

'You won't need that,' he informed her. She wouldn't need the nightgown either, but he supposed it would be a bit much to tell her to leave that behind. As it was, she stilled and her head came up.

For an instant her hand hovered over the dressing

gown, then dropped and she came towards him. He stepped back to allow her to pass through the doorway. Roses and honeysuckle, and soft, warm woman drifted by, the fragrance humming through him. He hardened his jaw against the instinct to haul her into his arms there and then.

What was the matter with him? She was a woman like any other. Why did she burn at his self-control? He forced his arms to remain at his sides. Better not to give her any hint of his urgency. She was probably nervous enough. Besides which, without a measure of control he would hurt her more than was inevitable in the loss of her innocence. And the thought of hurting her in any way lashed at him. How could he keep this marriage on a manageable footing when the thought of that unavoidable, and probably slight, hurt knotted his gut?

He remained at the door, watching as she crossed the room. The chaste gown hid everything. In the dancing firelight there was not the slightest shadow cast through the heavy linen. No hint of the lissom body he knew was there. The long, slender legs, the rounded bottom and swell of her hips, made for a man's hand to slide over and possess. Why did he want *her* more than he had ever wanted another, so that desire itself burned anew?

He had always assumed that he would desire his eventual wife and enjoy taking her to bed. In a friendly, comfortable sort of way. Rather like his aristocratic lovers, but without the inconvenience of constant discretion. He'd also assumed his wife would be a woman of his world, bringing wealth and important connections to the marriage.

Christy was different—she brought nothing to the marriage. And all the power was his, to give or to withhold whatever he pleased. So why did he feel so at sea? As though he were in the grip of something larger than either of them? Something that swung him to and fro, bobbing like a cork in a tempest.

And why the hell did he feel that in some odd way, without even realising it, his powerless, inconvenient bride held the reins? Because he couldn't take his eyes off that demure nightgown? Because just watching her walk unhestitatingly straight to his bed had him hard and aching?

Christy stopped at the bed. Shock at being summoned to his room had propelled her across the vast expanse of his bedchamber. It was not sufficient to get her into that enormous bed.

Her legs rebelled and refused to go a step further.

Nothing in her experience gave any clue to what she should do next. She took a deep breath and another. But her insides still quaked. She knew what happened in the bed, but how was she to get into it? Climb in? Wait to be invited? She felt a complete fool that he'd had to summon her to her duty, but how was she to know where they were to…she didn't even know what to call it. *Making love* seemed inappropriate in the extreme. Consummate the marriage?

She turned and swallowed; he wore only a banyan.

Beneath the heavy crimson silk was bare chest. She stared. His feet were bare too. Presumably he intended to remove his robe. Would he remove her nightgown? Or should she take it off?

Suddenly he looked larger, more powerful, his face harder, etched in shadows. A trick of the firelight, surely. He might resent the marriage, but he was not a man who would use his physical strength against a woman.

She supposed he would be careful in…in taking his pleasure, that he would not hurt her intentionally. There was nothing to fear—except even now, with him still on the other side of the room, she could feel her body's treacherous yearning, the melting heat. The memory of his fingers on her breasts sent heat curling through her. Would he expect her to touch him? Or would it disgust him?

She felt cold. Lost.

He had wanted her as his mistress. And had been forced to take her as his bride. She knew, none better, the yawning gulf between the woman a man would take as his mistress and the woman he would take willingly as his bride.

His gaze raked her from head to foot. And still he said nothing, made no move towards her. Perhaps she didn't look pretty enough. Perhaps she should have worn that confection of lace and gauzy silk—except she would have felt more exposed than if she had been naked. Bad enough standing here before him in this all-enveloping linen.

She still wore her spectacles. Slowly, hands shaking slightly, she removed them, and set them carefully folded on the bedside table. The room dissolved into a firelit blur, her husband—oh, God! her *husband*—an indistinct shadow near the door.

Julian took an uncertain breath as she laid her spectacles down. In a career dotted with beautiful women draped in various alluring poses and degrees of undress, he had never seen anything more erotically tempting. His bride, shrouded from neck to toes in plain, white linen, her soft tawny curls confined in a single braid hanging over her left shoulder almost to her breast. Christy, blinking at him uncertainly without her spectacles. His mouth dried.

She said nothing. Just waited. She was his, and his blood burned with wanting her. Every law and precept, all custom and tradition, said she was his. His by undeniable right. He started towards her, half-expecting her to step back. She didn't, but he could see the tension, the self-control she exerted not to do so. Instead her arms came up to cross defensively over her breasts.

He stopped, desire a heated ache, thickening in his groin. A hunger that he would soon assuage in the soft body of his bride.

She stood before him—a pale offering against the dark hangings of his bed.

'Our wedding night, Christy.' The words were out before he knew it, leaving him wondering why he had said them at all.

Silence stretched between them.

'Yes.' Her voice was quiet, expressionless. As if she merely agreed with his statement of fact. But something about her very stillness told him it was more than that. That in one word she had voiced her acceptance, her submission to what would take place in the shadows of the bed behind her.

Desire flexed its claws and he took the final steps to stand directly in front of her. She met his gaze unflinchingly, but her throat moved convulsively, the tip of her tongue moistening soft, trembling lips.

He fought the immediate, feudal urge to take and possess that mouth, ravishing it utterly. His self-discipline hung by a thread—if he touched her now, let alone tasted her, they would be on the bed. If he didn't just tumble her to the floor and take her there. He forced desire back into its cage. She was his bride—he had all night.

Slowly he raised one hand and set it to the ribbon securing the neckline of her nightgown. A gentle tug, and the bow surrendered. Need clawed at him. A row of buttons marched down the bodice of the gown to disappear under her tightly crossed arms. One by one he encircled her wrists in a careful grip, lifting them away from her breasts. Her eyes widened, dilating as he drew her hands down, holding them slightly away from her body. He kept his touch light, aware of the tension flickering through her, although she had not resisted.

'I wish to see you.'

Her breath came and went in a rush. She nodded and

he released her wrists. Her hands remained at her sides. Without the protection of her arms he could see the veiled hint of sweetly rounded breasts. Soon he would taste them. Soon he would have her beneath him. His own breath shortened. Soon. Very soon.

Her chin lifted, exposing the slender column of her throat. So vulnerable, so tempting. He leaned forwards, touched his lips to the hollow at the base of her throat, flicking out his tongue to taste. Soft female fragrance exploded through him.

He straightened, and saw that her eyes were closed, lips slightly parted. His blood drumming, he set his fingers to the top button of her nightgown and undid it, forcing himself to be slow, deliberate. One by one the buttons fell victim until the gown hung open almost to her waist.

The sight had his blood roaring in his ears. Dainty, rounded breasts, half-hidden by the gown. He set his hands to her and pushed the garment off.

A startled gasp escaped her as she clutched at the gown, catching it at her hips. A simple matter to pull it away, leaving her fully exposed…instead he traced the curve of a creamy, uptilted breast with shaking fingers. Dear God, she was lovely—soft, silky flesh that begged his touch, shadows and firelight dancing over her.

Lightly, he touched one pink nipple; it tightened in reaction. He nearly forgot to breathe as he stroked again. A strangled sound brought his gaze back to her face. Her eyes were tightly shut, her lower lip caught between her teeth.

His conscience murmured. Slamming a door shut on

the unwelcome voice, he slid his hand lower, over the gentle swell of her stomach, feeling taut muscles flicker. Pushing beneath the gown at her hips, his fingertips found the soft curls nestled at the juncture of her thighs.

She froze, every muscle locking.

He stopped, no longer able to ignore the truth. She was afraid.

She was his wife. She had not protested. Had not taken so much as one step away, let alone tried to stop him. His fingertips still rested on those soft curls.

Yet even as he watched, a tear slipped from beneath her tightly closed eyelids.

His conscience rebelled.

You can't! Not like this.

Why not? She is my wife. She has not refused me, and even if she had—she is still mine to take.

You can't do this. No matter that law and custom say you can. No decent man would take her like this.

He looked at her. She was shaking with the effort to hold herself still, her lower lip still gripped between her teeth.

There was no equivocating. No matter that he had every legal right to take her—he couldn't do it. It didn't matter that she had consented, that she was not fighting him, or even protesting.

She was not willing.

She has not refused me.

His conscience scoffed. *Why would she? She knows the law as well as you. She has no rights. She is yours and she knows it.*

He took a long look at the sweetly enticing body of his bride. Never in his life had he taken a woman who was anything less than eager.

With a savage curse he withdrew his hand and turned his back.

'I can't do this,' he said tautly. 'Cover yourself and get back to your room. Quickly.'

Before he changed his mind and tumbled her to the bed. He tasted bitter self-loathing as he realised how close he was to doing that. The temptation hammered in his veins. Every muscle and nerve, every fibre growled in frustration as he listened to the flurry of movement behind him, heard the swift padding of bare feet, and the thud of the door.

Christy stood shaking in the darkness of her bedchamber. She leaned on the panelled door, clutching her spectacles, barely able to stand for the trembling of her limbs. He didn't want her, had ordered her out.

I can't do this.

Her breasts ached with need. He had scarcely touched her and she felt…she didn't understand what she felt. Or did she? Weak—liquid heat pooling low in her belly. An emptiness that cried within her. Body and soul, she felt as though something had been ripped from her core, leaving her cold and desolate.

Her eyes stinging with unshed tears, she faced the truth: he had scarcely touched her and she had wanted him. She had felt her whole body melting, like heated honey, at his light caresses. Her cheeks burned in the darkness. It had been all she could do to stand, unresponding, and not press against him.

His touch on her breasts, sliding over her belly, lower and lower, had been terror and delight. Knowing that he would soon touch her *there*, where she ached. *There* where she felt...with shaking fingers she touched herself, gasping at the bolt of sensation—*there* where she was wet and hot.

She was his wife, not his mistress.

Shame scorched her body. Had he reached just a little further he would have found that slick heat. He would have known. Known that she *wanted* him to touch her there. He expected his wife to behave as a lady. Which she was patently incapable of doing. Perhaps he had known, despite not touching her. Known and been disgusted.

She drew a shuddering breath. Foolish to remain here shivering all night. The room was pitch dark. She strained her eyes, staring into the emptiness, trying to remember where things were. The bed was directly opposite the door. She moved cautiously towards it. And stumbled over a chair.

There was a tinderbox near the fireplace, she recalled. Only the way her hands shook, she would probably end up burning down the house if she tried to use it.

She found the bed, fighting her way through the hangings, and dragged in a sobbing breath as she huddled under the bedclothes. In all her nervous imaginings of this night, it had never even crossed her mind that she might end it as she had begun—a virgin. He had expected her to do her duty, but apparently he had been far too disgusted to do his.

Julian stared up at the shadowy canopy of his empty bed. It was some sort of judgement on him, he supposed, that after years of seducing other men's wives, he now couldn't seduce his own. His closest friends would be hard pressed not to chuckle at his predicament.

He swore and punched his pillow as the clock on the chimney piece chimed endlessly. Midnight. Over two hours since he'd sent her back to her room. By now, if he'd behaved like any normal husband, his marriage should have been consummated, his bride irrevocably his.

Instead he was lying here, wondering if he should have continued gently and got the deed over and done with. He would have to do precisely that eventually. His stomach clenched at the memory of her white face. Never before had a woman feared him. Never. It was not a pleasant feeling.

It looked like being a very long night. And then there would be tomorrow. He was taking her down to Abbey House, a small manor he owned in Monmouthshire. It was a quiet, secluded place near the river. Ideal for a newly-wed couple head over heels in love. Precisely the impression needed to stem the murmur that a scheming little adventuress had trapped him. She didn't deserve that.

But what the devil did he say to her? How could he reassure her that he would not press his rights immediately? And what was he to do about this marriage all together? A marriage of convenience was what he had always intended and there was no reason he could not have it. Desiring his wife was perfectly convenient. As long as he didn't allow it to rule him.

As long as he remembered that a wife and a mistress inhabited two different spheres of a man's life and it was not wise to combine the roles in one woman.

Chapter Fifteen

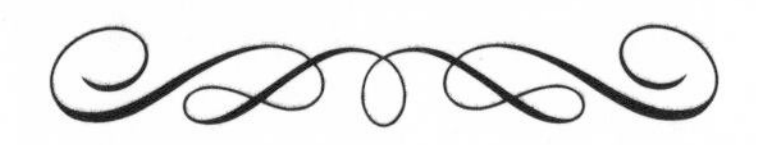

Julian trod up the worn stone stairs of Abbey House the following evening, shielding his flickering candle from draughts. Had he been mad to choose this shabby old manor for the bride trip? It held memories of mad boyhood summers, when he and the Blakehurst twins had come here with Serena and run wild fishing, climbing trees, riding their ponies all over the place and not always coming home at night. Carefree holidays when all that mattered was who caught the biggest fish, jumped the highest fence, or climbed the tallest tree, and the next day might see the record fall to a new victor. Days his memory insisted had been endlessly sunny.

Why had he brought Christy here? Shouldn't he have taken her to Bath? Shown her off publicly as his chosen bride? Surely she would have preferred Bath where she could shop, meet people and be acknowledged as the new Lady Braybrook. Yet when he had suggested it she had demurred, saying she would prefer a quiet place. So he had thought of this house. But what would she do here?

And why hadn't he sent instructions for a second bedchamber? The housekeeper here, Mrs Braxton, was a farmer's daughter. In her world husband and wife shared a bed. A flash of memory came—when his father had joined them in the summer holidays he had always shared Serena's room. No, it would never occur to Mrs Braxton to prepare two rooms. Not for two newly-weds.

He reached the upper corridor. Who would he find in that bedchamber? The self-possessed woman who had bid him goodnight an hour ago? Or the terrified bride of the previous night? If the latter, he wasn't sure he could bear it.

He found his bride ready for, but not yet in, bed. Closing the door behind him, he surveyed his property. Never before had he questioned the legal decree that a man's wife was literally his property. Now he did. It seemed absurd. Even wrong.

Christy was…Christy. Herself.

She sat curled up in a wingchair beside the fire, wrapped in a pink silk robe. A wine table beside her held an oil lamp and a tumble of bright embroidery silks. The mellow light shifted and gleamed on the thick tawny braid hanging over one shoulder as she looked up from her sewing. Something flickered across her pale face, instantly stilled.

'Am I disturbing you?' he asked.

Her surprise was palpable. 'Of course not. This is your room too.'

He frowned. Was her calm real, or feigned?

'I did not like to say anything tonight,' he said, 'but

tomorrow I shall speak to Mrs Braxton about a separate room for myself.'

Again that indefinable something flickered.

'You must do as you please, my lord.'

'Dammit, Christy! We're married! This is our bed-chamber—you may call me Julian!'

He dragged in a breath. Yelling at a nervous bride wouldn't help.

'Does our marriage give me that licence?'

He stared. 'Of course it does!' He thought about it. 'In private, at least. Publicly you would call me "Braybrook" or "my lord" and refer to me with anyone but family or a very intimate acquaintance by my title.' He added, 'I think.'

'You *think*?'

Laughter welled up as he went towards a screen set up across a corner of the room. Of all the things to be discussing! 'That's just it,' he said. 'I don't think about it. It's automatic.'

'Bred into you, in fact.'

He shrugged. 'Yes.' And saw the barely perceptible withdrawal—if a woman as reserved as Christy could withdraw any further. Belatedly he saw where the conversation had gone as he stepped behind the screen. 'It's not very important, Christy,' he said from behind it.

'Not to you,' she agreed.

But to her most definitely. He eased his coat off and untied his cravat. The story of their suspiciously swift marriage was buzzing about with a sting in its tail. Any slip she made would be magnified and bandied about in every drawing room from Hereford to Ludlow and beyond. Discussed with smiling malice between ladylike sips of tea. A raised brow here. A knowing look there. The inevitable way of the world, he acknowledged as he unbuttoned his shirt and hauled it off over his head.

Sitting down, he pulled his boots off. The only reason a man of his rank would willingly marry a woman like Christy was if he had fallen head over heels in love. Ergo, in the eyes of the world, he had not been willing and Miss Daventry had trapped him most cleverly. Never mind that the whole damn thing had been his fault, he thought, stripping out of his breeches and drawers. A ewer of water and basin stood on a night table. He poured water and washed before donning the nightshirt left ready and walking out from behind the screen.

He didn't have to spell it out to the woman sewing in the pool of light. She knew. For the first time he wondered if she would be happy. He'd taken it for granted. Rank, wealth, security. What more could she want?

Climbing into bed, he looked at his bride. She was still sewing. Quiet, industrious—she appeared to be embroidering a handkerchief. Firelight flashed off her spectacles. Memory tossed up an odd scrap of knowledge gleaned from Serena—the light…didn't seamstresses often go blind sewing in poor light?

'Shouldn't you stop sewing soon?' he asked.

She finished setting a stitch and looked up, her face still. 'If…if you wish it, I will come to bed now.'

His stomach clenched. Did she think he was ordering her to his bed?

'That was not a command, Christy,' he said quietly. 'I was concerned that sewing in this light would hurt your eyes.'

'Oh. I thought—'

'I know what you thought,' he said shortly. 'And you need not worry. I've never taken a woman who was less than willing, and I'm damned if I'll start with my wife.'

Christy, sliding her needle into the handkerchief, looked up sharply. 'Last night,' she began, 'I thought you…that it was because I…that you did not want—' her face flamed, but she held his shocked gaze '—that I had somehow—'

'No!' He found his tongue and stumbled into speech, searching for words to reassure her. 'No. That was not a problem,' he said in careful understatement. 'I wanted you.'

She looked disbelieving.

'You were frightened,' he said simply.

She was silent for a moment, then nodded and said, 'But not unwilling. Just nervous.'

Nervous? She'd looked terrified.

'Nor am I unwilling now.'

Nor was she… His heart skipped a beat over the sudden, slow, heavy rhythm of his blood. Light caught in the thick braid over her shoulder, silken tawny fire. He could almost feel his fingers sliding through the mass, tumbling it over the pillow…her mouth, lush and sweet; his to ravish and plunder… No. That way lay madness with her. Her kisses, for all her inexperience, were incendiary and kisses were not necessary when making lo—having sex—he didn't want that intimacy, especially not now when it threatened to tear him apart.

'My lord?'

He drew a ragged breath. She was a virgin. He must not lose control and hurt her. 'Julian,' he corrected her softly.

She nodded. 'Julian, then. We must do this, must we not?'

'Yes.' His control would not increase with waiting—rather, the opposite.

An indrawn breath, as though she braced herself. 'Then I would prefer to get it over with sooner rather than later.'

Not the most flattering invitation he'd ever received from a woman, but tension cried out from every taut line of her body. And she was being as honest as she knew how. Painfully so.

'Come, then.' He flipped back the covers on the other side of the bed, his eyes never leaving her. She nodded and began to put away her embroidery. He watched, not missing a movement of the careful, clumsy hands that fumbled over the simple task, the heightened colour of her cheeks, or the way the silk robe flowed around her.

Dear God, he was hard to the point of pain, just watching her. Finished, she stood up and doused the lamp, leaving only his candle and the firelight. Slowly she slid her robe off, laying it neatly across the chair. Either the same demure gown as last night, or its twin, enveloped her.

His breath shortened. Familiarity wasn't helping. He remembered those buttons, the softness and fragrance of creamy, rose-peaked breasts. His groin ached.

'Come,' he repeated. If she could not come to him of her own free will, then he had no business taking her.

Panic shuddered through Christy. His expression was unreadable. He was very still, but there was no hint of relaxation in the corded tendons of his neck, and his eyes possessed her darkly.

If she could not walk to that bed and climb into it, she would have another day of strain to face. Folly! If she knew anything about him, she knew he was not a brute. That she remained virgin bore testament to that.

The room was not large. A shaky breath and a few steps took her to the bed. She circled the foot, startled when he leaned over to blow out his candle. Just the firelight now. She reached the other side of the bed. Steps led up into it. A mountain to be climbed.

Trembling, she climbed up and slid under the covers beside her husband who lay propped on one elbow now, watching with dark intent…*and the two shall become one flesh*…he was so still, a statue, not flesh and blood at all…*one flesh*… Steadying her hands, she removed her spectacles and placed them on the bedside table.

There was a sudden movement beside her and she jumped.

He stilled again. 'Christy?'

'It's all right,' she whispered, but he made no move.

The previous night he had unbuttoned her night-gown… Clumsily she undid the top button.

'No.'

Embarrassment burned her. No?

'That's my privilege.'

He thought it a privilege?

Banners of heat unfurled as large, gentle hands took over, opening button after button until her bodice hung open and he carefully cupped one breast, stroking his thumb over the suddenly aching peak. She sat rigid, fighting her body's melting response to his caress and hot, hungry gaze. His free hand tugged at her nightgown, sliding it up over her legs.

'Lift up,' he said.

She suppressed an instinctive protest and wriggled so that the nightgown came free to be taken off over her head. Her breath caught and she slid lower into the bed. But he sat up, hauled off his nightshirt and came to her, pushing back the bedclothes. Skin to skin. Hot flesh to hot flesh…sparks flickered and leapt under her skin. She lay still, trying to control her trembling, reminding herself that he would not hurt her, that he would be gentle…but she was *naked*. And *he* was naked—lying against her, looking at her, touching her, undoing her braid, freeing the thick, unruly mass. She gasped as he pressed a knee between her legs, *opening* her. Her breath shortened as fires danced beneath his warm hands sliding, feathering over her so that she ached *there*, between her legs where she was becoming moist and warm as she had the night before. The same fear shook her—would she disgust him?

'Ssshhh,' he murmured. 'Relax.'

Relax?

She lay half under him as he leaned over her, one powerful thigh wedged between hers, holding her open for his hungry gaze and wicked, invading fingers on her inner thigh. She felt vulnerable, helpless. No—not helpless. One word would stop him, and she didn't want him to stop… Oh, but she had to force herself to lie still, wanting to touch *him*, fighting the surging need to lift her hips against his hand in restless wanting—and then his fingers were *there*, where she ached, sliding easily on slick flesh.

'Good,' he murmured, smiling down at her.

So he didn't mind the embarrassing wetness, it pleased him…it felt strange though…it should have felt immodest, but it felt good… Her whole body jerked and quivered as one finger pressed, and slid just inside the hot, slippery ache. She gasped, tensing against the cataract of sensation, of stretching.

He stilled.

'Does that hurt?'

'N…no.' She wanted…*more*.

He lowered his head to her breast, kissed the taut nipple, then drew it into the shocking heat of his mouth and sucked. She bit back a cry as bright pleasure speared from her breast to where he so gently penetrated her body. Involuntarily her hips lifted, her body winning free of her control to arch towards him, around him.

And she had *more*. Fierce strength took her, covering her, and she cried out in shock as his hard weight pressed her into the mattress, her thighs pushed wide, wider than she could have believed. Hot pressure at her core, stretching her, burning as he came into her and she gasped, biting down on sudden pain, closing her eyes against it.

A ragged curse, and he stilled.

Then, harshly, 'I'm sorry,' And he thrust the rest of the way.

Pain cut, tearing a choked cry from her throat, and he was still again. Blessedly still. She lay quietly, forcing herself to breathe, half-surprised that there was room for breath, she felt so…full. He was deep, so very deep inside her, pain easing to discomfort.

'Are you all right?' His harsh voice. At odds with the gentle, clumsy fingers sliding into her hair; *he* was shaking, she realised on a burst of shock. Actually shaking as he brushed moisture from her cheek…she was crying? She opened her eyes.

'Christy, are you all right?' His expression was urgent, taut. As though *he* were in pain.

'Y…yes,' she lied, shifting to ease that shocking fullness.

A groan tore from him. 'For God's sake—stay still.'

She tensed, staring up at his hard face, the blazing eyes. Sweat beaded his brow, a muscle flickered in his jaw.

He groaned again, shutting his eyes, and pulled back so that she sighed in relief, only to catch her breath on a gasp as he pushed in again. And again. Slowly. His eyes shut tight and sweat sheened his face. That first flash of pain over, she could bear it now. And he slid more easily, it was almost…almost pleasant, despite a lingering soreness. But he was distant. Closed away. Shut eyes in a taut mask. He was moving faster, his breath hoarse and ragged. Harder, faster so she felt the push and pull within her where his body invaded hers, until with a groan he pushed deep, his whole body shuddering and convulsing, before he collapsed on to her, burying his face in her hair.

Shudders rippled through him, and her arms curved around him, holding him safely to her, enjoying his weight, her hands shyly stroking his shoulders where muscles bunched and flickered beneath hot, damp skin. Briefly he turned his head and pressed his lips to her temple. Heat stung her eyes at the caress. Somehow she had thought kisses played a bigger part in the marriage bed.

She drew a breath. It was done. She had survived. She hoped he hadn't found her too gauche and ignorant. He was still inside her, his weight shifted slightly to one side, utterly limp in her arms. *In her arms.* Her arms still encircled him, held him to her. She was clinging to him. Carefully she released him, forced her arms to fall to her sides.

His head lifted at once. Heavy lidded eyes opened, piercingly blue. Please, God, he could not see her thoughts, know that she felt wanton. Bracing his weight on his elbows, he withdrew from her body and rolled away to lie staring up at the canopy.

She swallowed. There seemed nothing to say. A stolen sideways glance showed his mouth set hard.

Anger? Disappointment? Perhaps she had done something wrong, but she had no idea what and no way of finding out. She was all for plain speaking in this marriage, but she baulked at asking her husband how she had erred, not five minutes after resigning her virginity to him.

She wondered if he would fall asleep soon. She wanted to wash. She felt sticky and tender there. *There* where he had been. And she supposed there would be blood...

He sat up, pushing back the bedclothes, and she watched out of the corner of her eye as he left the bed and shrugged into a robe, stepping behind the screen. She heard water pouring, and flushed. If she was sticky, then... Moments later he reappeared in his nightshirt and robe, a flannel in his hand.

Her breath jerked in as he came around the bed to her and reached for the bedclothes. She sat up, clutching them to her.

'My lord? Julian?' She pulled herself together. 'Thank you', and held out her hand for the flannel. Cheeks hot, she held his gaze.

His mouth twisted. 'As you wish,' he said, handing her the cloth and turning away.

Snatching up her discarded nightgown, Christy dragged it over her head and scrambled out of bed, trying not to wince at the ache between her legs.

Julian took a shuddering breath as she disappeared behind the screen. What the hell did he say? Apologise? Promise it would be better next time? Could he keep that promise? None of his lovers had ever had cause to complain, but they had all been experienced and had come to him willingly, not acquiescing because he owned them body and soul and they had no choice. Nor had he ever lost control like that.

He felt like a brute. A rutting brute. She had been a virgin and he hadn't even aroused her sufficiently not to hurt her, let alone bring her to pleasure as he ought to have done before taking her. Some pain had probably been unavoidable, but his conscience lashed him—she had cried. There was no need to look for blood where she had lain. The blood on his body had been accusation enough.

It had not been even remotely good sex. Certainly not for her. And yet he had never felt such fierce pleasure sliding into a woman's soft body, nor experienced such a shattering release.

Frustration. He'd wanted her too long. She had been a virgin too. He had never lain with a virgin. *Nothing like novelty to pique the appetite*, a sly, cynical voice murmured. Damn it! He'd never *wanted* to lie with a virgin before! And he hadn't wanted that now. He'd just wanted Christy, beyond all rhyme or reason. Because she was Christy? He pulled back from that thought. Of course, he had not had a woman for months. Not since leaving London. Logical answers, explaining everything. His loss of control. His response.

It didn't help. What sort of brute was he to have felt pleasure when Christy had felt only pain?

She reappeared from behind the screen, her colour high, her eyes shuttered.

He managed a smile. 'Come. You must be tired.'

Quietly she climbed into the bed and lay down. 'Goodnight.'

The catch in her voice tore at him. Unthinking, he leaned over and kissed her gently on the mouth, cradling her jaw, brushing his thumb over her cheek.

He felt shock leap through her and prepared to pull back, but her lips softened, parting, and he was lost. With a groan he accepted the invitation, his tongue surging deep. Fire exploded through him impossibly, searing every vein as his body hardened. So soft, so lovely. It would be better for her this time. Slower—

Damn it!

He released her mouth. He'd just taken her virginity, for God's sake! Bad enough to hurt her; rutting on her again would be unforgivable.

'Enough,' he said tightly, forcing himself back to his side of the bed. 'Goodnight.' Staring up at the canopy, he felt her roll away from him.

Reality crashed in on him. This was his wife. In his bed. Or was he in her bed? Christy had been a virgin, but this part was new to him. He'd never slept, actually slept, with a woman. When he spent the night with a mistress, it didn't involve sleep beyond brief dozes between bouts of sex. His aristocratic lovers had been literally drawing-room affairs—quick interludes snatched on a *chaise longue* fully clothed. This was different, lying sated and sleepy, listening to the whisper of a woman's breathing, feeling her weight depressing the mattress, aware of her warmth and the hot, musky scent of their lovemaking. Very different, and perhaps not wise…

He awoke in the middle of the night to realise that someone else was in the bed—the warm, sweet fragrance of woman mingled with roses was all about him. Sleepily he reached out and gathered her to him. Christy. His. With a sigh she snuggled into him and he felt the soft huff of her breath through the linen of his nightshirt. Complete, he sank back to sleep.

Christy awoke, warm, safe and comfortable. She dozed, aware of nothing but the sensation of being cradled, cherished… She snapped awake to realise that she was in her husband's arms, her cheek resting on the nightshirt covering his broad chest, and her nightgown around her waist leaving her shamelessly exposed, with a powerful thigh pushed between hers and a ridge of unyielding male flesh pressed into her hip. She felt that strange softening inside—the ache of…emptiness?

She looked up and met a hot blue gaze. Her breath shuddered out and her whole body turned to honey.

'M…my—Julian?'

A queer look, almost revulsion, crossed his face. He pulled back, disentangling them, and adjusting his nightshirt.

Her cheeks fiery, Christy straightened her own nightgown, pushing it down around her legs where it belonged.

'I am sorry. I…I am not used to—that is, I must have forgotten you were there, and rolled over.'

He stared. 'No. I—' He broke off. Then, 'No matter. What would you wish to do this morning? Ride?'

Christy hesitated, wondering what *he* would prefer.

He reddened slightly. 'No. I suppose not.' He reached out to brush the backs of his fingers over her cheek. His mouth twisted. 'I'm sorry.'

Her face heated. 'I'm not…I'm quite all right.' That other ache deepened, intensified at the gentle touch of his fingers.

He looked unconvinced and drew back, saying, 'Tintern Abbey is close. We could walk there, or drive if you are tired.'

His tone was polite. Friendly, even. But distant. As though she were an acquaintance—not the woman he had spent the night with. As though they had not awoken in a warm, drowsy tangle. Yet there was that hesitance, an underlying concern in his voice and eyes.

It's all right. I'm not sore.

The words froze on her tongue. Ridiculous, but she couldn't say it. It was too intimate, entwined with another ache whispering hotly deep within her.

'Tintern would be lovely,' she said, sitting up. 'And I should like to walk.' Surely that would reassure him their wedding night had not crippled her?

Polite, friendly. That would be the rule for their marriage and her idiotic, romantic longings for *more* were to be squashed flat.

Polite and friendly. Considerate. Attentive. By the close of the day Christy knew she had nothing to worry about. Her husband was courtesy itself. And she had never felt more alone. Which was ridiculous. He had spent the entire day with her. Being kind. Friendly. And distant.

She stared at the closed door of her bedchamber. Now most definitely *her* bedchamber. Julian had spoken to Mrs Braxton and arranged another chamber. Ten minutes ago he had wished her a polite goodnight at the door and continued down the hall to his own room.

She felt as though she had intercepted a bucket of icy water. Surely she hadn't been secretly hoping he would come to her again? Oh, yes, she had. All day. And lying to herself. Pretending she didn't want him, as if in doing so she could prevent him from ever realising that he had married a wanton.

Chapter Sixteen

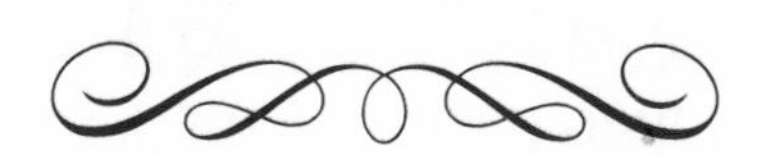

Christy awoke alone on their last full day in Monmouthshire. Just as she had each morning after the first day. Although they had spent at least part of each day together, Julian had not come to her again at night. He had begun teaching her to drive a gig, they had ridden and walked. In the evenings he had read aloud while she sewed. Last night she had played the old harpsichord in the parlour while he listened. In some ways she knew him better now. She knew what he liked to read, what music he enjoyed, and that he loved apples. She knew he cared for his tenants and looked on his rank as more responsibility than privilege.

She knew *things* about him. She did not know *him*. And it seemed that was how he preferred it. His very courtesy was a barrier between them that she did not know how to breach. Or even if she should. She had thought consummating the marriage would make things easier.

They were not. Several times yesterday she had caught him watching her surreptitiously, his gaze so intent she had wondered if she were doing something wrong, or had a smudge on her nose. And still he had politely bidden her goodnight at the door of her bedchamber and gone to his own room, leaving her restless and far from sleep.

And now she was awake in a grey dawn. She pushed back the covers and went to the window. Outside mist rose from the river and birds rejoiced at the day's return. It could not be much past five, but sleep was far away.

Further down the river the dreaming arches of the abbey soared above the mist, as though nothing could ever disturb the ivy-clad walls and tumbled masonry. Later the ruins would echo with the voices and laughter of visitors, as it had the other day. It would be different now, lying at peace in the misty curve of the singing river. There would be the same stillness and belonging she had found on that day high above the river. Before Julian had kissed her for the first time, and the world had changed for ever.

It was only a mile to the abbey. She would be back in time for breakfast at eight easily. If she went now, it would just be herself, the birds, the murmuring river and the mist.

Julian blinked as the slender cloaked figure hurried out through the damp garden below towards the river path. In the pale light she looked insubstantial, a creature of the mist and dawn.

Yet he knew, none better, that she was a woman of flesh and blood. Last night he had nearly gone to her, tempted by the siren lure of warm, yielding softness. He had resisted. She had seemed edgy, restless. He thought he knew why; all day he had been watching her, wondering if it were too soon to take her again. It had probably made her nervous.

He flung off his nightshirt, washed and began to dress. All week he had taken her about, walking, driving, riding. Frustration aside, he had never enjoyed a week more. Just being with her had been a delight. He had taken her down to Chepstow one day to explore the castle. She had loved it, even crying when he told her about the final siege when Cromwell's forces took the place and shot the commander on the spot.

Can we come again?

There probably isn't time this visit.

Next time?

He hauled on his boots and stood up. He desperately wanted a next time, but without this frustration and guilt. All week he had avoided the subject of that night. Ashamed of himself, worried it would embarrass her. Hoping it would sort itself out was idiocy. His was the experience, however illicitly gained. If anyone was to put this right, it would have to be him.

He followed her easily, her tracks clear on the damp path leading from the house towards the river. He thought he knew where she was going. The abbey would be peaceful now, before visitors arrived.

She was seated on a fallen block of masonry, her expression calm, distant, as though fixed on something beyond the river in its misty cloak. He hesitated, wondering if he should go back, or just wait until she returned from wherever it was she had gone.

Before he could step back, she swung around and her eyes widened as she came to her feet. 'My lord? Julian?'

She still found it difficult to use his name, despite the fact that hers came to his lips so easily. He walked towards her.

'Is something amiss?' She flushed. 'I suppose I ought not to be here alone—is that it? I am doing the wrong thing?'

He stared. Did she expect a scold? He supposed it was true enough—she ought not to be here alone.

'No,' he said. 'I was awake and saw you leaving the garden, but I just wanted to talk to you.'

'Oh.' She relaxed a little.

'You like it here?' He sat down on the block she had vacated, leaving room for her.

'Yes.' She sat down again. Perhaps he had not left quite enough room. She was very close. The fragrance that had haunted him all week wove around him, insubstantial as the morning mist.

'Christy?'

She looked up.

The stilted little speech died in his throat. Very carefully he lifted one hand, brushing the backs of his fingers along the line of her jaw, tracing her lower lip with a knuckle. Her lips parted and he heard the uncertain breath as her eyes widened.

Somehow his arms were around her and he bent his head and took the kiss he had not known he was aching for. With other women kisses had been pleasant, but not necessary. With Christy, he realised on a wave of tenderness, kisses were vital. Perhaps for both of them. Her lips clung, the sweetest invitation. He fought the urge to deepen the kiss. For now this was enough—warm soft lips trembling under his, her body pressed to his, her arms holding him. This was right. But before there could be anything else he had to find the right words. Gently he broke the kiss and rested his cheek on the top of her head.

'I wanted to apologise for hurting you,' he said quietly. They were not the words he had planned, but they came easily. Like the kiss, they felt right.

'Hurting me?' She pulled back a little and stared up at him.

Denying the need to kiss her again, he brushed his lips over her temple and pulled her back against him. Somehow feeling her relaxed and trusting in his embrace made this easier.

'The other night.'

A tremor ran through her and he held her closer. 'Exactly. I wanted you to know that when I…when we come together again, it will not be like that. It won't hurt again. You don't need to fear me. I'll leave it to you to decide when you wish to come to me.' She stiffened, and he pressed a kiss on her hair. 'No, you don't have to say anything. Just come to me. And I'll do my best to make it good for you. That's all. I'll leave you in peace now.'

He released her and rose. 'I thought I might fish today, if you do not mind. I believe Mrs Braxton was going to show you some of her special recipes?'

Christy nodded. 'Yes. This morning.'

He smiled. 'I'll see you at breakfast then.'

He walked away. And prayed he had said enough.

Christy spent a glorious morning in the kitchen with Mrs Braxton and had a notebook full of jams and preserves as well as stillroom recipes. She had been busy and occupied, but her mind kept drifting back to that early morning tryst. Julian's gentleness. The sweetness of his kiss, and the reason he had not come to her bed again. She should have overcome her idiotic shyness that morning a week ago. Told him in plain words that she was perfectly all right.

She thought about it after lunch as she set out for a walk. He thought she feared him. Physically. That their coupling the other night had left her unwilling. So he had stayed away from her and spent a week worrying that he had really hurt her because she had been embarrassed. She followed a path she knew led to a quiet backwater partially shaded with willow trees, hidden from the main river. It would be peaceful there, and she could think.

She didn't doubt he had told her the truth. One thing she could count on with Julian—he always gave her the truth. She might not always like it, but that did not diminish the value of the gift.

He had left the ball in her court. She would have to

go to him, and tell him when she wished him to come to her again because he did not trust himself. Something else he had said shifted beneath her worry about *how* to tell him.

Just come to me. I'll do my best to make it good for you.

Those words thrummed through her with all the glorious promise of his hands on her body the other night, his mouth hot and demanding, his body burning against hers. Did he mean *she* was to enjoy it?

She came out of the woods into the clearing and saw the familiar, black horse grazing. Conqueror. And then she saw her husband standing on the bank, facing the river.

She gulped. Julian had been swimming. It was the only possible explanation for him to be dripping wet and stark naked.

She could always retreat. He had no idea she was there. But she stayed, her gaze riveted to his back. That one night, what with firelight, bedclothes and her own shyness, she had not seen him properly. Not like this. Broad shoulders gleamed wet, tapering to narrow hips and the taut curve of his buttocks, the long powerful legs. She had not realised that beauty could be masculine, encompass such power. She had not equated beauty with strength. She did now, and her heart pounded as heat rose inside her.

I'll leave it to you to decide when you wish to come to me.

He hadn't meant here on the river bank, for heaven's sake! But she could tell him…tell him what? She reminded herself to breathe. It would be all right to tell him that she wouldn't mind him coming to her bed again. Tonight, perhaps? Could she manage that without making a fool of herself? Without letting him know the mere sight of him had that hot ache twisting in her belly, and lower.

He should return to the manor, but the sun on his back was glorious after the chill of the river. As long as no one came along. But this backwater was very much on his land. Screened from the main river, few people knew it was here.

Conqueror whinnied, and Julian turned to see what had disturbed him. And found his wife, her eyes wide with what he assumed to be shock. They widened even more as her gaze moved down his body.

Naturally he did the only thing possible. He slid straight back into the river.

The chill was as shocking as ever, but he managed to find his voice. 'Were you looking for me?'

'Er, no. Not exactly. I mean, I didn't know you were here, but I'm quite glad to see you.'

She'd probably seen a damn sight more than she'd bargained for.

'Are you going to swim again?' She came towards him.

He gritted his teeth. 'No. I was about to get dry.'

'Oh.' She stopped. 'Do you…should I go away?'

Something about her voice suggested she was deferring to *his* sensibilities. Not that he had many. Except he didn't want to frighten her and right now, despite his assurance that the next time would not hurt, the sight of him probably *would* frighten her. Which confounded all precedent. Never before had he been violently aware of rampant, hard-edged lust while standing up to his chest in a distinctly chilly river. Only, he didn't want her to go.

And she didn't sound as though *she* wanted to go.

'Pass me the towel and shut your eyes,' he said.

She did as he requested and sat down, closing her eyes obediently. Right where he planned to get out.

He heaved himself out of the water and dried himself quickly. And carefully. He'd never realised quite how erotic a towel could feel. Swearing silently, he hauled on his drawers and breeches, and discovered a new problem. While he had on occasion been wearing breeches when this problem arose, he'd never had to button them up around it before. He struggled on, desperately ignoring the muslin-clad temptation beside him.

Finally succeeding with the breeches, he reached for his shirt.

Temptation spoke. 'May I open my eyes yet?'

He shut his own eyes. She sounded exactly like a little girl with a present. He wondered if he would survive the experience of being unwrapped by her.

Swallowing raw desire, he managed to say, 'If you wish.'

He couldn't help watching as she opened her eyes. Watching as her gaze travelled over him, the oddest smile trembling on her lips. A smile that made him long to kiss her, feel her lips flower and part for him. He breathed deeply, fighting to retain his sanity, clutching his shirt. If he kissed her now, it wouldn't end as chastely as it had this morning.

His shirt. He started to put it on.

'You don't need to put your shirt on, do you?'

The shirt dropped, forgotten, as disbelief radiated through him.

She reached out, curious fingers skimming his shoulder, the light tracery on bare skin shafting fire straight through him. He braced himself against the urge to take her in his arms and kiss her senseless. To ease her down into the grass and make love to her until she moaned with pleasure. Need slammed through him in slow, hot waves, mounting with every heartbeat.

Jumping back in the river wouldn't help. After all, he'd got into this state standing in the water. Instead of dousing desire, there would be steam rising off the water.

'Julian?'

'Yes?'

'When you kissed me this morning—well, I liked it.'

His heart began to pound. 'Did you?'

'Yes. I…I always like it when you kiss me.'

'You do?' A slow, hot, heavy beat.

'Yes. So, would you…would you kiss me again? Now? Please?'

Would he…? As he reached for her, she removed her spectacles carefully, folded them and set them on a convenient log.

Julian was drowning. Drowning in her taste, the sweet, wild response of her mouth, yielding to the passionate demands of his lips and tongue; drowning in the delight of her pliant body shifting beneath him, rounded arms drawing him closer.

Shaken to the core, he caressed the curve of her hip under the flimsy muslin and discovered that his fingers were bunching the material, pushing it out of the way.

He shouldn't do this. Not here. Not now. But his body refused to obey the dictates of mind and conscience. Tenderly he kissed her, drinking the soft cry as he caressed the silken skin of one thigh. Easy, so easy to part her thighs, but if he did… No. He mustn't. Not here. He hung on to the sliding reins of control.

She opened to him anyway. He forced his fingers to stillness, struggling for sanity. Her hips lifted. Very slightly. Just enough for him to feel the silent plea. This was the response he had wanted from her. Here. Now. His. All his for the taking.

With a groan, he surrendered. To her desire, not his, his seeking touch finding a softness that blossomed in liquid fire as he caressed her with growing intimacy. And she touched him, shy hands exploring and discovering, curious fingers finding his nipples, lingering to tease when he groaned in aching pleasure.

This was the sweetest kiss he had ever known. And then he remembered.

Would you…would you kiss me again?

She had asked him to kiss her. Not seduce her! And she was so damned innocent, she didn't have the least idea what she was doing to him! Where this would lead. Furious with himself, he tore his mouth free and sat up, shuddering with the need to tear his breeches off, push her thighs wide and sink into her wet, scented heat. Instead he grabbed his shirt, hauled it over his head and began to do it up with clumsy shaking fingers.

'No more,' he said, frustration roughening his voice. He tried not to look at her, but even so there were scorchmarks on the remnants of his self-control.

Forcing himself to his feet, he took several painful strides towards the bank.

'Cover yourself,' he said shortly. God help him if he turned and saw her lying there, dishevelled from his lovemaking. He shook at the thought.

She was his wife. She deserved better than to be tumbled on a river bank when all she had asked for was a kiss, just because he had all the self-control of a rutting stag.

'I'm…I'm sorry. I won't do it again.'

He didn't dare look at her. 'Won't do what?'

'That. Here. I mean, I won't—'

Her voice broke and he turned.

'Christy.'

The sight of her quiet self-possession dissolved into tears lanced through him and three strides had him beside her, all control shattered by the need to comfort her.

'Christy, sweetheart, it's all right. I'm sorry. I never meant it to go so far. You don't have to be frightened of me.' His voice cracked as he rocked her. 'No matter how much I want you.'

She wriggled free and faced him. 'You *do* want me?'

He nodded, not trusting his voice, desperately trying to banish the memory of Christy yielding beneath him in the fragrant grass, her mouth soft with his kisses... Helpless, his fingers traced the line of her throat, feeling the warmth, the flickering pulse leaping to his touch.

'Then, why did you stop?'

Why? Directness was the only possibility. 'I stopped because you had no idea what you were doing,' he informed her. No idea she'd reduced his control to smoking ruins.

She reddened. 'I know, but how...how can I know what pleases you, or...or how you want me to behave, if—'

'What?'

The small part of his mind retaining a semblance of rational thought observed that her blush had deepened.

'Christy, I didn't stop because I wasn't enjoying what you—what *we*—' Dammit! Now *he* was blushing!

'I was enjoying it so much,' he told her, 'that I was within about two heartbeats of taking you.' It might have taken him a little longer to remove his breeches, but not much.

'Then, you...you didn't mind that I...that I was enjoying what you—' The break in her voice turned him inside out. There was light now at the end of a very dark and mystifying tunnel. He had no idea what was out there in the light, but if he went just a little further, committed himself to chance—

'Christy—I loved that you were enjoying it.' Her eyes widened and it was as though he had opened a gift early, breaking it in clumsy greed. But then someone had taken the broken gift and wrapped it again, renewing it, giving him a second chance.

A humming silence spread around them in which the golden late summer air fizzed and sparkled, rippling like the river, alive with promise.

Then she said, 'Well, you did say this morning…and I…I suppose there must be worse places, must there not?'

His mouth dried. He had told her this morning that he would leave it to her to decide when she wished to come to him. And what did she mean by *worse places*? Was she deliberately…?

He forced himself to ask. 'Worse places for what, Christy?'

She looked at him uncertainly. 'You didn't mind?'

'No, I didn't. Trust me. Worse places for what?' he repeated, unbuttoning his shirt again, just in case he was right.

She reached out and fumbled with a button. His heart contracted.

'Worse places to…to…' She floundered to a halt, obviously uncertain of what to say, what to call it.

'To make love?' he suggested, capturing her hand and taking it to his lips, drawing her to him.

To make love. He had never used those words. Not to any woman. Always, always it had been sex. No more. But the words sounded right with Christy in his arms, just as kissing her was right.

She hesitated and his heart nearly stopped beating. 'Only if…I mean, it's not the sort of thing you expected of your wife, is it?'

His heart tried to catch up and failed. He hauled the shirt over his head and dropped it.

'No,' he said, easing her down to the grass. 'I have to admit it never occurred to me I'd be lucky enough to marry a woman who would seduce me on a sunny river bank.'

'And you don't mind? Even though I am your wife—'

Pardon?

'—not your mistress.'

Wife, not mistress?

The painful words rocked him to the core, the wound he had dealt her laid bare. He heard his own cynical voice outlining the roles of wife and mistress—he had convinced her that a woman's passion was something furtive and shameful, only acceptable in a mistress. That in his wife it was unwanted. That *she* was unwanted.

'The only thing I mind,' he said, sinking on to the grass beside her and taking her in his arms again, 'is that I was such a damned fool. This is what lay between us, isn't it? You thought I didn't want you to be like this?'

'Yes.' The merest whisper, as though she could barely draw breath.

He took her lips, teasing the sensitive curves with his tongue until she opened to him and he could ravish the sweetness within. By the time he lifted his head she was soft and yielding, half beneath him, and his senses were reeling again.

Dear God. All he'd had to do was kiss her?

'You thought wrong,' he murmured, and kissed her again.

Dazed by his kisses, Christy was still aware as wickedly skilled fingers unbuttoned her bodice, that he had lifted her in his arms and peeled the muslin away, leaving her in her stays and chemise. She blushed, but it was too late for modesty. He had turned her and was loosening her stays. Heat flooded her at his hot breath on her nape, his lips brushing warmly over the curve of neck and shoulder and her lungs seized as he nipped gently at her ear.

'Julian—'

One arm slid around her, drawing her against him, still nibbling as he fondled her breasts. 'Do you want me to stop?'

'No. Oh, no,' she breathed. She no longer cared about being a wanton hussy.

The arm tightened, his tongue traced the curve of her ear and her mind and body melted in delight. 'Thank God.'

Moments later her stays and his breeches were gone and she was in his arms, only her chemise between them. He cupped one aching breast through the fine linen, his thumb stroking lightly over the urgent nipple. Lightning shot through her and she cried out, arching. This time there was no need to hold back.

Slowly he lowered his mouth to her breast and kissed it, his tongue laving the sensitive peak until the fabric clung wetly.

He drew the taut crest deep into the heat of his mouth, suckling gently, then, as she cried out in pleasure, harder before turning his attention to its twin while one hand slid down her body, sliding up under the linen to tease gently over her belly.

Shaking hands stripped away that last barrier. Caressing. Learning. Loving.

His hand moved lower, reaching between her thighs and her breathing fractured as he cupped her and stroked gently into slick, aching need. Pleasure, bordering on agony in all it promised, rippled through every vein in torrents of fire. And at the centre of it all a shattering emptiness, crying out to hold him within her. Her hips lifted involuntarily against the wicked play of his fingers.

His control quaked at the pleading dance of her body, all soft, wet temptation, burning him alive. Lifting his mouth from her breast with a groan, he gripped her hip, stilling her. 'No. Just lie still.' Any more and he'd be buried in her, and he wanted to take his time, make it right for her…

She tensed, pulling away, and he knew what he'd said. With aching care he brought her back, gathering her close. 'No, Christy,' he whispered, feathering kisses over her face. 'Not that. Never that. It's just…I want you too much.' He kissed her, his tongue plundering gently until she sobbed in need and her hips lifted again, seeking, urgent against his teasing fingers.

He lifted his head, breaking the kiss. 'I want it to be right for *you*,' he said, tightly, continuing to ravish the slick heat that lured him. Groaning, he slid one knee between her thighs, opening her, feeling the sweet tremors shake her body as he settled in the intimate cradle. He braced himself on one elbow, reaching down between their bodies to guide himself to her.

'Julian?'

He kissed her. 'Yes, sweetheart. You're soft, wet—do you want me?'

'Julian…oh, God! Yes. Please!'

'Where, love? Here?' He pressed carefully against the hot entrance.

'Yes, oh, yes. There. Inside.' Her voice broke as he pressed into her, feeling the clasp of her body.

'Slowly,' he whispered as his control shook, whether in reassurance, or to remind himself, he couldn't have said. He withdrew a little, waiting. And it came—the urgent lift of her hips, following his retreat. He hung on, shaking, as her response, hot liquid silk, welled up, her breath trembling on her lips.

Her eyes opened. 'Please…now,' she whispered.

He lowered his mouth to hers, consuming her soft pleas as they fell from her lips. One thrust, deep and true, and he lay buried to the hilt in her sweet sheath. And held utterly still as her cry stabbed into him.

Her eyes were shut tight, her breasts rising and falling in trembling breaths. He hung on to control as she softened, hot and sweet around him. Slowly her eyes opened again, and he saw the dawning knowledge, the realisation of him buried deep within her body.

'Christy,' he whispered. 'Oh, Christy.' This then was what he had wanted. He had wanted her to let go. Steel bands contracted savagely in his chest. He had been forced to let go first. Tenderly, he pushed back a tumbled curl from her face, threading his fingers in the silken skeins, and feathered his lips over hers.

There were no words to express how she felt. She didn't know what she felt. Never in her life had she felt so helpless, so vulnerable as she did lying impaled beneath him, her body captive to his. It did not hurt this time. She had trusted him that it would not. But she had not thought, had not realised, that feeling him so deeply within her, filling her so tightly, a *part* of her, might be joy itself. She had not thought desire could leave her shaking, frantic with need, longing only for his utter possession.

She had not thought it could feel like this—his weight a heated intimacy, mingling with his musky masculine scent, lean fingers tangled in her hair, his thumb clumsily brushing tears from her cheeks…all her nervous embarrassment gone, replaced by aching need, to feel him move within her, to move herself. To give until nothing was left, except the need to give.

She had not thought at all.

Certainly she had not thought to see her own vulnerability reflected in his eyes, or hear it in his voice as he soothed her, nor expected his hands to tremble as he cradled her face.

'Julian—' Her voice broke as he shifted slightly within her, fire streaking through every vein. She wanted, needed, more.

He stilled, tension pouring from him—evident in the flickering muscles of his shoulders, the corded tendons of his neck.

'Am I hurting you? Do you want me to stop?' His

voice, harsh with restraint, pierced her to the core. She could hear the need in his voice—taut, hungry; see it blazing in his eyes; feel it in the minute, helpless shifts of his body, ravishing hers, melting her senses in fiery delight. Those tiny movements, splintering in fierce pleasure, told her what she needed.

'No,' she whispered. 'Never. I want you.' And shifted against him.

He was lost. The silken caress of her body raked him with fire. So hot and soft and tight around him. The chains of control snapped and his mouth came down on hers, taking her sobs of pleasure as he began to move, claiming her, urgent and possessive. Yet still, at the very depths of his desire, one gossamer thread held true, stretching, never breaking, binding him as surely as iron chains; he took her with a fierce tenderness he did not understand, and had never imagined could exist.

She had not known, had never imagined it could be like this, her body winged, frantic for release, as he possessed her deeply, irrevocably in a rhythm that sang with time itself. Above her, on her, within her, he took her spinning into the heart of fire. The very edge of madness.

She tried to hold back, her fainting reason crying out, warning her that from this point, if she went any further, there would be no going back.

He would not let her hold back. He took her to the brink and held her there, breaking, then went with her as she shattered, her body dissolved in delight.

Chapter Seventeen

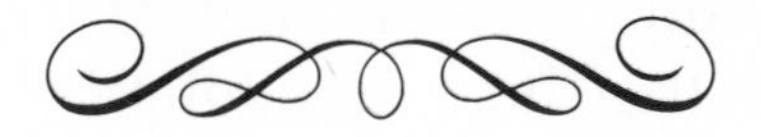

He lay, Christy asleep in his arms, staring up through the sun-dappled green, hearing the hum of insects and the call of birds. A faint splash from the river told him a trout had risen. The air fizzed gently. Alive. Glowing. He felt part of it as he never had before. As though heaven and earth had contracted to the space occupied by their bodies and infused them.

Something nameless within him had broken loose.

His arms tightened, and she wriggled against him with a sigh, sending shards of rekindling desire splintering soul deep. Whatever it was that had got loose shook again. The other night she had given him her innocence. Today, here on the river bank, she had given him herself.

Neither of which gifts he deserved. Could they start again? Could they have the marriage he had always intended for himself? True, she had not brought any money to the match, but she was intelligent, caring. She was interested in the estates and his people. Now their misunderstandings were largely behind them, surely they could create a solid, rational union.

A wry voice suggested the passion unleashed between them had nothing to do with rationality.

Christy stared at the book in her lap. The pages might as well have been blank. Even though she was alone in her bed, everything was different now, wasn't it? She had come up half an hour ago. Julian had been reading a report sent down by his bailiff.

It had been such a lovely evening. They had talked. Really talked. She had asked him about this house and he had told her about all the summers he had spent here as a boy. About his friends. About himself. She knew so much more about him now. It was as though what had happened on the riverbank had breached his barriers. It was not just the lovemaking…

It never occurred to me I'd would be lucky enough to marry a woman who would seduce me on a sunny riverbank…

She blushed. Had she really done that?

No, it was not just the lovemaking, although it had been… She searched for a word—beautiful? Shocking? Exhilarating? All of that. But now there was an intimacy between them. Julian—his name came so easily now—was so much more relaxed, as though he had been on his guard before. She supposed the same could be said for her. Indeed, she knew it; making love like that left all of herself, all she kept hidden, exposed to him.

It was terrifying.

Because that complete, unreserved, nothing-held-back physical intimacy had revealed her own unacknowledged longings. For tenderness.

For love.

She was falling in love with a man who had married her only because he had to. Worse—only because *he* thought he had to. His world would not have cared a scrap about her fate. His sense of honour, the unexpected streak of kindness, disarmed her. He hadn't cared about the world's opinion. Only his own.

He didn't love her. She must remember that. Only his tenderness *felt* loving…his kisses…the gentle way he'd touched her, held her afterwards—close, as though he couldn't bear to release her. But her mother had warned her men were different. They could feel only physical pleasure where a woman felt as though her heart had left her breast.

That was my mistake, dearest. Don't repeat it.

Other women must have felt this way about him. Jane Roberts, perhaps. Coldness gripped her. Jane and her daughter, Nan—did he have other children? There was no point resenting his past involvements; she was the product of such a union herself. It was just that she was falling, or had fallen, in love. She was jealous. Possessive. She wanted him to be hers alone from now on, and he never would be. He had been very honest about that.

She had tried not to let this happen—even this afternoon she had tried to hold some small part of herself apart, inviolate, but afterwards he had coaxed her into the river, teaching her to swim, endlessly patient and encouraging. And, oh! The touch of his hands on her body through the wet, clinging chemise. She'd been too shy to swim naked, but in the end the chemise had been worse than nothing. A tremor coursed through her—it had not just been his hands, but the sensation of his wet, powerful body sliding against hers, and the hot, hungry touch of his gaze, and his laughter. His encouragement of her efforts and his delight when she could keep herself afloat and swim a few strokes.

She had to remember that to him it was nothing more than kindness.

They had walked back to the house, his horse trailing behind, hand in hand like lovers.

We are lovers, she thought. But only in the physical sense.

The opening door scattered her thoughts.

The sight of her husband seized her breathing. He stood just inside the open door, his expression serious, the dark hair tousled and slightly damp. Beneath his robe she could see only bare, muscled chest. Her lips parted on a soundless gasp—he hadn't bothered with a nightshirt. She steeled herself against possible disappointment; perhaps he had merely come to say good—

'May I come to you?'

Shock slammed through her. He had every right to take her whenever he chose. That even now he had not taken her consent for granted—the last little bit of her that she had tried to hold back was lost, utterly lost.

Joy flared, blocking her throat.

'Y…yes,' she stammered.

Then, seeing his hesitation, she repeated in a despicably wobbly voice, 'Yes, oh, yes—please.'

His eyes darkened. The door shut with a thump and he came to her.

Her mind shattered, dazed with pleasure, Christy opened her eyes to stare down at her husband, her lover—the man who lay beneath her, one strong hand on her hip more to share her rhythm than to guide, while his hot gaze and free hand caressed and loved her. He was so hard and deep inside her and she was burning, dying with need, yet she could not find her way over… *Please! Please!*

'Like this, sweetheart. Come to me, love. Now.' The hand at her hip tightened, bringing her down hard just as his questing fingers found that place, the special place hidden in her damp, soft curls, and pressed so the storm within her broke. She cried out, convulsing helplessly around him as her release swept through her and he was holding her, rolling her beneath him and the firestorm redoubled, roaring through her again as he drove to his own climax.

He had called her 'love'.

She lay exhausted in his arms, thoughts and emotions tumbling through inextricably tangled, but through the whole shimmering web one thread wove brightly…

I love you.

His arms tightened and she realised sleepily that she had spoken aloud. That the last barrier had fallen, and he had said nothing.

He should return to his own bed. But an hour later Julian lay sleepless, listening to Christy's quiet breathing.

I love you...

The sleepy words haunted him. Had she meant them? Or believed she meant them? Hell! Had she even been awake? Other women had spoken those words to him. Especially in the throes of passion. Often they thought love was the only ladylike reason for their own sexual desire. He understood that. But sometimes they actually believed it. He always tried to pull back gently from those *affaires*. It did not seem fair to tacitly accept a woman's love when he was not prepared to return it in any way. As he grew older he had learnt to recognise and avoid women likely to believe they had fallen in love, and he had been careful not to use the word *love* as an endearment. Nor to call what happened in bed *making love*. Sex was safer. Less open to misinterpretation.

He could not avoid Christy, though, and all his rules had flown out the window. He had called her *love*. The word had just come out, and he had called sex *making love*. Now he had to explain as gently as possible the terms of their marriage. After all, a marriage of convenience would be the safest thing. For her especially, he told himself. As long as he could assure her that her response to him was nothing to be ashamed of, that it delighted him, and she did not need to excuse it in any way.

I love you...

But the memory of the words, her sleepy, unfocused voice, pierced him. It was highly unlikely that she meant it. Making love—having *sex*—could be like too much to drink. One could find oneself saying and doing things one would not dream of normally. She might not recall saying it in the morning.

He should return to his own room. That was what one did in a marriage of convenience...he yawned and her fragrance sank deep...one bedded one's wife and returned politely to one's own bed to sleep. His eyes drifted shut...he supposed he ought to leave...rolling towards her he hooked an arm around her waist, drawing her against him. She came with a sigh and a wriggle, all soft curves, and drifting curls tickling his nose. Brushing one aside gently, he breathed her sweetness and slept.

Sleeping with her had been a mistake. He'd meant to make an early start. And he had. Only it hadn't involved getting out of bed. He hadn't meant it to be like this.

Like what?

This...this warmth. The pleasure of looking forward to her company on the journey. The remembered intimacy of lying with her this morning, her silken body snuggled against him, limp with pleasure.

This was dangerous, Julian realised as he handed Christy up into the curricle. Bedding her, yes, but not sleeping with her. And he'd intended to ride today while Christy travelled in the coach. Somehow he had to create some distance between them. But she had barely touched her breakfast and he'd remembered her tendency to carriage sickness. Her unwillingness to make a fuss about it.

'Thank you,' she said, smiling down at him as she settled her skirts.

His wits fractured and he dragged in a breath.

Lust. Reduce everything to its component parts, and she was an attractive, innocently sensuous, responsive woman. He'd have to be dead not to desire her. But that didn't explain the aching tenderness, or splintering joyous agony of holding back to ensure her pleasure. Oh, he'd always been careful to please his partners. That was only fair. Part of the exchange. And their pleasure also increased his own.

He stepped up into the curricle and nodded to his groom to release the horses.

It was not like that with Christy.

He wanted *her* pleasure. For *her*.

Duty and his own gratified lust had little if anything to do with it.

He glanced at her as he set the horses in motion and guided them out into the lane. Her cheeks were softly flushed, and her mismatched eyes shone. His breathing shortened as he remembered those same eyes dazed and unfocused, the aftershocks of pleasure trembling through her this morning…and last night—those sleepy, haunting words…

I love you…

His blood surged and the horses snorted and tossed their heads as his fingers tightened on the ribbons. Quickly he eased the pressure on their mouths. He wasn't a green youth to be addled by a pretty smile or passion-induced declarations of love. He *had* to put this marriage on a proper footing. Bed was now satisfactory for both of them. Surely he could arrange everything else as neatly?

They liked—yes, *liked* and respected each other. The marriage would work, and it was time his bride—he stole another glance at her—understood how.

He drew a deep breath and began.

Christy listened to her husband's careful detailing of family finances, her gloved hands gripped painfully in her lap. He seemed quite unmoved as he explained his responsibility as head of the family to ensure everything was passed on intact to succeeding generations.

By marrying her he had made his task a great deal harder. Not that he had actually said that.

She glanced up at him. He was watching the road, as calm as though he had told her what he liked for breakfast. Not as though he had just explained why marrying her was the greatest mistake of his life.

She bit her lip.

He flicked a glance at her. 'You needn't look so downcast—I merely wished you to understand how things work.'

'We should not have married.' It was all she could say.

'I beg your pardon?' His voice was frosty.

'You can't afford me.'

The horses slowed.

'What the hell do you mean?' Anger incinerated the frost.

She struggled for the right words. 'When Harry insisted on that enormous settlement, and—'

'It was the right amount. What I would have provided for you without Harry's intervention,' he informed her. 'What do you mean—I can't afford you?'

'I brought nothing to the marriage,' she said. 'No dowry to provide for myself or my children. The money settled on me is money you should be using for your brothers and sisters. And for your property. Isn't it?'

His silence told her she was right, and she risked looking at him. He eased the curricle around a farm cart.

Safely past, he said, 'None of that matters. I didn't say I regret our marriage!'

No. He was far too polite. But it could not be far from the truth. From his explanation she had understood that what was left of Serena's dowry would provide for Lissy, Emma and the two boys. How were her own younger sons to be provided for? Where would *her* daughters' dowries come from? For Julian to hand on his lands and wealth intact he had needed a wealthy bride. Instead, he had her. Penniless, illegitimate Christy Daventry.

'How can you not?' she whispered. What a fool she was to have thought that what they had found together was something more than sex. And she had been fool enough to speak words he did not want to hear.

He pulled the horses into the hedge, transferred the reins to one hand and his free arm came around her. 'Damn it, Christy! How can you believe that I regret it?' he demanded. 'After yesterday afternoon! And last night!'

She forced herself to meet the blue fire of his gaze, and swallowed, heating at the memory of his passion, her own passion leaping to meet it. The soul-wrenching delight as they made lo—

'You heard what I said last night, didn't you?' she asked painfully.

His mouth tightened. 'Yes. It's all right, Christy. You have never had a lover so you are unused to…physical pleasure. Naturally I understand why you said it, but it is not necessary.'

Nor wanted. Worse, it was actively unwanted.

'Then it is just…just—sex,' she said. 'Not—' She broke off, forced the choking lump from her throat and continued, 'You could find that with any woman.' Dragging in an aching breath, she added, 'You have always done so. I expect you will continue to do so. That was clear when you asked me to be your mistress and said that I should not be dismissed when you married.'

Blue fire froze to icy chips.

The arm withdrew and the horses were set abruptly in motion. She shifted away from him, not daring to look after saying something so shameless.

He drove on into the golden haze of sunshine and birdsong. The hedgerows towered above their heads, full of song and bustle. Beyond the hedges a cow lowed, a boy's voice called in the distance. It was all hollow—empty.

Eventually he broke the gaping silence. 'You are reconciled, then, to the possibility that I will be unfaithful to you?'

She fought the urge to deny it as heat mantled her cheeks. She did not have the right. She had known the truth before she agreed to marriage. 'Yes.'

'And will you be unfaithful to me?'

I am not hypocrite enough to demand something of my wife that I am not prepared to give in return. Once the succession is assured, she may please herself...

She was silent for a moment, trying to imagine herself in that situation. She couldn't imagine it. But what if Julian were to be unfaithful? Would she be able to imagine it then? Perhaps that was what marriage vows were for? To hold you firm when you *could* imagine such a thing. After all, her decisions about her behaviour were *hers*, were they not? Why should they be dependent on *his* behaviour? Those vows had been made not only to him, but to God.

'No. I do not intend it.'

He sent her a swift unreadable glance, but said nothing.

She gritted her teeth. He had not offered a similar reassurance. Nor would she ask. If he gave it, she would not believe him, and she would have pushed him into a lie to save her feelings. The one thing of value they had between them was honesty. She was not prepared to squander it.

Four mornings later Christy walked to the village for embroidery silks. She had spent the past two days receiving bride visits. News of their return had spread and it seemed everyone wished make the acquaintance of Amberley's new mistress.

She felt like a beetle pinned to a board for constant scrutiny. Oh, everyone was polite enough. Offering felicitations, saying how delighted they were to make her acquaintance—and all the while she could imagine the conversations once they were safely back in their carriages.

My dear! What did he see in her? No wealth! No connections!

It's true, then? She trapped him?

Who had trapped whom? Did it matter? She was married. Safe. Secure. Her husband was kind to her. He was honest. Too honest to permit her to deceive herself with dreams of love.

He was being very careful to make his position clear. Despite coming to her bed each night to make—for *sex*, he did not remain afterwards. He bedded her passionately and skilfully, leaving her limp and exhausted with pleasure, and then he left. As though he wished to make sure his behaviour mirrored what he felt: nothing.

One day she might learn to be grateful for his honesty, rather than feeling as though a small piece of herself died every time he left her sleepless in an empty bed.

What mattered now was that they had an invitation to dinner the following night at Postleton Manor.

I should be delighted if you could attend, had gushed Lady Postleton. *It is not to be a grand occasion. Just a few people who would be honoured to make your acquaintance.*

The hypocrisy sickened her. *Not my acquaintance. It's the new Lady Braybrook they want...* Nothing would give her greater pleasure than to decline the invitation, but that was impossible. Julian had been pleased. *Good. You'll soon be established.* If they ever found out what she was, she would be unestablished in a heartbeat.

The bell jangled as she entered the shop and predictably Mr Wilkins greeted her with oily subservience, bowing low. To her annoyance he followed her around the shop, rubbing his hands together. By the time she left with her embroidery silks, having arranged the delivery of several dress lengths, she was urgently needing fresh air.

In the village street she saw Nan Roberts. On an impulse, she stepped across. 'Good morning, Nan. Are you well?'

Nan went pink, nodding shyly.

'And your mama? Is she well?'

Another shy nod. 'Yes.' Then in a rush of confidence; 'I've got a kitten. T'other Lady Braybrook gave her to me.' Nan bit her lip. 'You can come an' see her, if you like.'

Christy swallowed. Jane had been Braybrook's mistress. It might be awkward, but the child was looking up at her hopefully. It was not Nan's fault and Julian's previous *affaires* were none of her concern. She pushed away the thought that his future infidelities were also not to be her concern. 'I should love to see your kitten. If you are sure your mother won't mind?'

'Oh, no!' Nan assured her. 'Mam said you was nice.'

Which didn't necessarily mean Jane would welcome a visit. Christy thought Jane Roberts looked anything but pleased when she saw who had come to call, but she greeted her politely enough.

'Her ladyship wants to see my kitten,' said Nan.

Jane heaved a sigh. 'Does she now? Well, you find Puss quickly, then.

'You ought not to be callin' on me,' she informed Christy bluntly as Nan went off to find the kitten. 'Folks talk and his lordship won't like it.'

'If that's all that's bothering you, let me worry about it,' Christy told her. 'Has Nan had any more trouble?'

Jane shook her head. 'No. Thanks to you and his lordship. Didn't mean to sound unwelcoming, but I don't want trouble for you. Not after you were so good to Nan. But since you're here, you might as well come out in the garden. Should you care for tea or my blackberry cordial?'

'Oh, the cordial, please.'

Jane bustled about setting a small tray with glasses and a bottle of rich, dark cordial. Nan came back with a ball of wool and a tiny striped kitten, bearing a strong resemblance to Serena's Tyb. She showed the kitten to Christy with pride.

'She's all mine, an' she's going to keep all the mice an' rats away.'

'If she's ever allowed to walk anywhere, an' not carried and cuddled half to death!' said Jane wryly. 'Nan-love, you take her ladyship through to the garden, while I bring the tray.' Christy followed the child out into the small garden and sat down on a bench in the sun. Flowers and vegetables grew in garden beds and insects buzzed everywhere. At the end of the garden an old plum tree leaned against the wall, its leaves just beginning to turn. Nan took the kitten down there and played in the shade.

Jane poured a tumbler of cordial for each of them. 'I make this each year. No need to worry. It's not strong liquor.'

Christy sipped, tasting sunshine and blackberries as she watched Nan trailing wool for the kitten to pounce on.

'She loves that kitten,' said Jane. 'Good of her ladyship to bring it. She's always been kind, despite things.'

Christy said nothing. Of all women, she couldn't imagine Serena holding Jane to account because of Julian's affair with her. She just wished there was more she could do for Nan and Jane.

She turned, trying to think of something, something to say, to offer…and saw the wasp on the edge of Jane's tumbler. She reached out to knock it away, but it was already at the other woman's lips.

'Jane—!'

With a gasp of pain Jane dropped the tumbler and batted at her mouth, knocking the wasp away. Angrily it buzzed back and Jane cried out again. And again.

'Mam?'

'It's all right, Nan,' called Christy. 'Just a sting.'

She looked back at Jane. It wasn't all right. Jane's mouth looked queerly misshapen. Swollen. Swelling further as she watched.

'Jane! Does that hurt? Can I fetch something?'

The woman felt her mouth and looked dazed. 'Hurts,' she said in a queer constricted voice. 'My throat…can't swallow properly…'

Her throat… Christy felt the blood drain from her face. 'I'll send Nan for the doctor.'

Dr Wharton stared down at Jane Roberts, now fighting for breath, her face and throat impossibly swollen. 'Good God,' he muttered, bending over the bed. Christy had assisted Jane inside and applied a cool compress, but it hadn't helped. Jane was losing consciousness now as she wheezed, her face purple.

'A wasp, you say?' said the doctor.

'Yes!' said Christy. 'It was on her cordial glass.'

The doctor swore under his breath. 'There's nothing I can do,' he said. 'I'll stay with her until it's over. Keep the child out.'

Christy stared. 'What? Until…' Her stomach lurched. 'She's going to die?' she whispered.

The doctor nodded. 'Some people react badly to wasp or bee stings. Especially around the mouth and especially if it stung several times. I've seen it twice before.'

Jane's eyes opened, dazed, terrified. Her mouth worked, but only a desperate wheezing came out. Her tongue was impossibly swollen. She tried again, a frantic, choked sound, her eyes clinging to Christy's.

Christy knew what she was trying to say. What she herself would be frantic about if she were Jane. She went to the side of the bed and took Jane's hand. The woman clung with shocking, dying strength. Her own eyes blurring with tears, Christy choked, 'I know, Jane. It's…it's all right. I swear I'll keep Nan safe for you. Is that it?'

The dying woman nodded, tightening her grip.

'She will be safe,' repeated Christy. 'I'll look after her.'

Jane squeezed her hand again and then released it.

Christy looked up at the doctor.

'Go,' he said. 'You can do nothing more.'

Chapter Eighteen

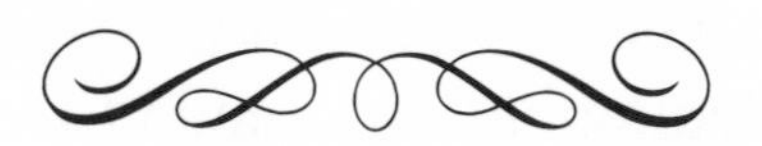

A quarter of an hour later Dr Wharton came out of the bedroom, his face grim. Christy's unspoken hope faded. Nan, clinging to her, burst into tears at the doctor's expression and Christy held her, conscious of her own tears. There was nothing she could say.

'I'm sorry,' said the doctor. 'There was nothing to be done.' He looked at Christy and the sobbing child in her arms. 'Kind of you to ease her worries, but I'm aware of how embarrassing this could be for you. I'll make arrangements for the child, Lady Braybrook. No need to concern yourself. An orphanage will take her if her mother's family won't do it. My housekeeper will look after her tonight and I'll see to it all tomorrow.'

Sick understanding came to her, as Nan's grief-stricken sobs redoubled.

'You misunderstand, sir,' she said, rising to her feet with Nan still in her arms. 'Those were not empty words to comfort a dying woman; I meant it. By all means speak to Mrs Roberts's family, but unless Nan's maternal relations can provide her with a safe and happy home, she will remain with me. If…if you would speak to the Vicar to…to arrange the funeral? I will send a servant to collect Nan's belongings. She will come home with me now.'

The doctor's eyes widened. 'Ah, Lady Braybrook, it may…er, have you fully considered? His lordship—!'

The door crashed open, and Christy, her arms full of the still-weeping child, turned to find her husband in the doorway.

'What the devil is going on?' he asked. 'The village was full of some story that Jane is ill. Christy?'

Wharton stepped forward, his face stiff with embarrassment. 'My lord—a most tragic occurrence, but I fear her ladyship does not quite—'

'What tragic occurrence?' snapped Julian.

'Mam! Mam!' sobbed Nan.

A queer look crossed Julian's face and his hand stretched out to the child. 'Nan?'

Doctor Wharton spoke again. 'Jane Roberts is dead, my lord.'

The hand fell. Julian turned to the doctor, his face white. '*Dead?* How?'

Christy intervened. Nan did not need to hear the details. 'My lord—is your curricle outside?'

'My—?' He looked at her. 'Yes. Yes, it is.'

'Good. Nan and I shall await you in it. Please bring her belongings and don't forget the kitten.'

His jaw dropped. 'Bring her—'

Doctor Wharton flushed. 'As I was saying, my

lord, her ladyship does not comprehend the, er, *delicacy* of the situation. I can make all arrangements for the, er, *housing—*'

Christy moved towards the door and Nan, realising, screamed, *'Mam! I want Mam!,'* fresh tears pouring down her face. Christy's eyes burned as she held Nan securely, her own voice choking on useless words of reassurance. What comfort could there be? She stepped out into the small garden strip. It seemed impossible, wrong, that the sun still shone, that a blackbird was whistling in carefree abandon.

Julian's groom, Twigg, stared at them in surprise and Christy noticed a gaggle of curious villagers standing at a distance. She ignored them and went to the curricle.

'Stay at their heads,' she told Twigg, and lifted Nan to the seat, stepping in after her and lifting the child back into her lap. All she could think was that the child needed to be held. Her screams had died to a low sobbing, and she lay limp in Christy's arms, her face stained and her eyes reddened.

A short time later, Julian came out with the doctor. Between them they carried a small trunk. In addition, Julian held a small closed basket. The trunk they placed in the boot, but Julian handed the basket up to Christy. It yowled indignantly.

'The kitten,' he said in an expressionless voice.

Nan stirred at that and Christy spoke gently. 'Best to leave Puss in the basket so we don't lose her on the way home.'

In the act of stepping into the curricle, Julian looked at her sharply, but said nothing. Nan nodded, and lay, silent now, in Christy's arms.

'You'll make the funeral arrangements with the Vicar, then, Wharton,' said Julian. 'You may leave the rest in my hands.'

Wharton nodded. 'Yes, my lord.'

'Let 'em go, Twigg!'

'Where is Nan?'

Julian didn't turn around as he asked this question, but continued staring out of the window unseeingly. After arriving home he had told Christy to see to Nan and then to come to him in the library. That had been an hour ago.

'In the nursery. It seemed the best place for her.'

He turned, and his chest constricted at the pain in her white face and red-rimmed eyes. He braced himself to deliver the blow she must be expecting.

'Christy—this was unwise. She cannot remain here.'

Her eyes sparked defiance. 'Then Nan is unfortunate in her father!'

A blow straight to the heart of the matter.

Grimly, he reminded himself that his wife should have no say in this. He didn't even owe her an explanation—least of all an explanation she was almost certain to dismiss as a lie. And yet…

'You're quite correct,' he said quietly. 'Nan was unlucky in her father, but, contrary to what most people believe, she is not my daughter.'

Christy's eyes widened in shock. 'Not—?' she began. 'Oh, *please*—!'

He steeled himself against the bitter disbelief. Pain banded his heart. There was no reason for her to believe him. He did not doubt that in the end she would accept his word, but in the meantime—

'Your *father*?'

The icy bands around his heart snapped, and his fist clenched on the table.

'You believe me?' he asked.

'Yes,' she whispered. 'You've never lied to me. Not once. Why would you lie about this? To me of all people?'

He sighed. 'Yes. Nan is my half-sister,' he said. 'But most people believe her to be my daughter. You remember Jane was married to a farmer? His second marriage and he had three daughters by his first wife. Jane's marriage was barren. Naturally Tom blamed her.'

'How surprising,' said Christy with more than a touch of sarcasm.

Julian continued to explain. 'The fellow did have three daughters from the first marriage, remember.'

Christy didn't respond.

This was the tricky bit. 'Has Serena told you much about my father?'

She shook her head. 'No. I've, er, gathered he was somewhat autocratic.'

'He was indeed,' said Julian.

'A family trait, perhaps?'

Ignoring that, he went on. 'He was one of the old

school. A good man, though, and after Serena's accident when the doctors said it would be extremely dangerous for her to have any more children, naturally he looked elsewhere for his—' He stopped, unable to think of a polite way of putting it.

'Amusements?' suggested Christy. 'Entertainment? I've noticed men do tend to think of women in those terms.'

Stung, Julian said bluntly, 'Shall we say sexual release, then?' Dammit! Did she believe he thought of *her* as entertainment?

She blushed crimson, but her chin lifted a notch. 'If you wish. It is at least honest. Do please continue.'

'My father had an affair with Jane and she became pregnant. She told him she was pregnant, and broke off the affair. Neither of them was particularly concerned. In fact, it was impossible to know for certain then who *had* fathered the babe. Jane was married, Tom still bedded her regularly and he was cock-a-hoop to think he'd finally got her with child.'

'And when Nan was born? What did he think then?'

'He was dead,' Julian told her. 'Nan was born in the winter, and he had died in a tree-felling accident the previous autumn. Under the circumstances, and Tom having been one of our tenants but with no son to take on the farm, my father provided for Jane with the cottage and a pension. When he died three years ago, I continued the arrangement. But by then it was obvious that Nan could not be Tom's daughter.' He hesitated. 'The resemblance—'

'Is remarkable.'

'Since Jane was my father's only indiscretion for many years, people assumed I was the father. My father asked me to let it stand.'

'Why?'

'He was fond of Serena. He didn't want her to be hurt, especially after her accident—and everyone assumed me to be responsible anyway.' he shrugged. 'My reputation helped.'

'And Lady Braybrook?'

'I assume she believes Nan to be mine.'

'I see.' She was silent for a moment. 'But this makes no difference. She is your half-sister instead of your daughter. As much your sister as Emma or Lissy.'

He had to make her see what it would cost if she kept the child. 'Christy, we are to dine at Postleton Manor tomorrow. Can you imagine the conversation? By then people will know of Jane's death, that you were with her and have taken her daughter. If you keep her, then people will whisper that I thought no better of my bride than to ask her to raise my by-blow! There has been enough talk about our marriage without that!'

She went white and an appalling silence echoed.

'And I suppose,' she said after a moment, in unconvincingly calm tones, 'someone might even discover that you had been obliged to marry someone else's by-blow?'

The ugly word festered between them.

'Damn it, Christy—I didn't mean it like that.' But how the hell *had* he meant it?

She appeared to share his scepticism. 'Oh? I wouldn't

have thought there were so very many interpretations,' she said quietly. 'You will excuse me, my lord. I ought to return to Nan.'

Gritting his teeth, Julian managed a brief nod and watched as she left the room. Would Serena be able to talk sense into Christy? Make her realise the gossip she would face with her position already so precarious. Curse it! He was trying to protect her!

If he could arrange a decent home for the child…a decent home with Jane's brother and his wife. Carter was a good, upright fellow, if a trifle unbending. His wife was known for her good works, and they had older children. Nan would be safe with them. God knew he wanted her safe as much as Christy did. He could provide a weekly sum for her upkeep, even a capital sum in trust to serve as her dowry… He'd arrange it now and send for the Carters. If Christy met them, surely then she would see it was for the best.

And why the hell was he even hesitating? It was his decision and it *was* for the best. Particularly for Christy. He strode over to his desk and sat down, pulling paper and the standish towards him. He'd settle this here and now. A groom could deliver his letter and wait for a reply.

Christy found Nan still huddled in the chair she had left her in with the kitten sleeping in her lap, petting it, her face blank. Beth got up from her own chair as she came in.

'She's not said a word, m'lady,' whispered the maid. 'Just sits there stroking the kitten.' She shook her head.

'Poor little thing. What'll happen to her? Tisn't like anyone will want her, what with all the talk.'

Something inside Christy that had been close to breaking, stiffened, hardening into renewed resolve. *I want her.* 'Nan will be cared for.' She said it firmly, strongly. As much to convince herself as anyone else. She had given Jane her word.

'Shall I fetch some mending, m'lady?' offered Beth. 'I could sit with her a bit. She shouldn't be left alone, should she?'

'No, she shouldn't,' agreed Christy softly. 'I'll stay…' She hesitated. 'Fetch that mending, Beth. It would be nice to have someone to talk to, or I might have to leave.'

Beth dropped a curtsy and left.

How did you comfort a child whose mother had just died? She noticed the untouched bread and butter on the table. 'Do you want your bread and butter, Nan?'

A quick shake of the black head, but she said nothing. Only the small hands moved, stroking the kitten.

There were toys in the room, a plethora of them. A large, battered, dapple-grey rocking horse. In one corner stood a collection of wooden swords, ranging from quite well-carved efforts to a very simple one consisting of a short piece of wood nailed at right angles to a long one. A table with a dolls' house, elegantly furnished. An old Noah's Ark. A bookcase stuffed with books. Here were dreams and fantasies for a dozen children. But not this little girl whose small, safe world had fractured into nightmare.

Christy looked around desperately. *She* didn't know what to do. What did she know about small children? There had been Sarah…what had she done when Sarah had been sad? She had held her. Let her know she was safe and secure. And when Sarah had died, her small frame racked with fever, she and their mother had held her then too. So there should be someone to hold Nan. Someone to comfort her. What was God *thinking* to do this to the child? If He was going to take her mother, then He damn well should have provided someone else for her!

He had provided Christy.

So she walked to the chair, bent down, lifted Nan into her arms and sat down. There was a moment's frozen stillness and then Nan fought her, screaming, the unnatural calm broken into glittering shards. Shocked, the kitten leapt to life, scuttling for cover under a table.

Christy hung on, ignoring the feet battering her shins, holding the child's arms close to her body, speaking softly…nonsense…anything…aware her own tears had escaped, that she was crying as hard as Nan and that something inside that she had tried to hold inviolate had shattered irrevocably. And it hurt far more than she could have possibly believed.

Running footsteps sounded and Beth burst into the room, her eyes wide.

'Oh, m'lady! Here—I'll take her!'

Christy shook her head. 'No. I'll manage.'

At last Nan had fought and struggled herself into exhaustion and lay limp and sobbing in Christy's arms. Christy just held her silently, stroking the tangled black curls with a shaking hand. She had no more reassurances to whisper, and Nan seemed not to need it. The storm had passed for now and the child drifted towards sleep, the small body growing heavier in Christy's arms.

Beth who had sat quietly in a corner occupied with the mending, looked up.

'Asleep, is she?'

Christy nodded.

'Likely she needed that.'

'Yes.' She had screamed and raged after Sarah's death. At their father. Blaming him. For everything. For her life. For Sarah's life. Even for Sarah's death, which had certainly not been his fault. And hating him for not caring enough to attend the funeral. For being more concerned about appearances. He had ignored her after that.

Beth spoke again. 'I made up Miss Emma's old bed. It's all ready. No need to undress her. Just slip her shoes off. Even popped in an old dolly of Miss Emma's. Something to cuddle.' She shrugged. 'Better'n nowt.'

'Yes.' Bracing herself, Christy rose, Nan a limp weight in her arms. Together she and Beth tucked Nan safely into bed and stood looking down at her.

'You'll sit with her, m'lady?' Beth asked.

'Yes.'

'I'll fetch some tea for you. Anything else?'

She started to refuse, then a picture on the wall caught her eye. A portrait. Rather amateurish, but recognisably Serena. Without answering, she stepped closer. It was signed, *ET*—Emma Trentham.

'Yes. Yes, there is something, Beth. My sketching things.'

Before memory faded for her or Nan.

It was dark before she had finished and the lamps were lit. Beth had brought her meal on a tray along with some soup for Nan, who had woken for long enough to be changed into a nightgown and tucked back into bed after having the soup.

She had fallen sleep clinging to Christy's hand, the kitten on the pillow beside her. Eventually the viselike grip had eased and the small hand relaxed on the covers. Now Christy sat staring at her sketchbook, knowing it was inadequate, but unable to do better.

'Will you remain here tonight?'

The deep quiet voice from the doorway startled her, so that she nearly dropped the book.

'Yes,' she said turning to face her husband's disapproval. He didn't look particularly disapproving just now, but he'd made his attitude clear that afternoon. 'She's only a little girl. Someone should stay with her.'

'One of the servants—'

'She trusts *me*.'

His mouth twisted. 'Sensible of her. Your maid told me what happened. Are you all right? She didn't hurt you?'

She thrust away the warm little feeling of delight that he'd asked. Duty. Cold, hollow duty. 'I am quite uninjured, thank you.' The sin of *her* birth could be hidden. Nan's couldn't. That was the only difference.

He came and squatted down beside her chair, reaching to cover her hand with his. His presence nearly overwhelmed her.

'You're sure? Your maid said the child was beside herself.'

The warmth of his hand stroking. He was only touching her hand, yet the gentle caress awoke other memories in her body. Fingers sliding on slick, wet flesh, seeking the hot, fierce joining of their bodies… It was only sex. It was not important and she was a fool to wish otherwise.

'Christy?' His lips spoke her name, but all she could think of was the dark, heated demand of his mouth on her breasts. Her own hunger answering his. And the longing and hunger that he did not answer.

'I'm perfectly all right,' she managed. She tried to focus on Nan, asleep in the bed.

'What's that?' Before she could stop him he had twitched the book from her lap and was examining her truly dreadful portrait of Jane Roberts. She had only met Jane twice and those last terrible memories had kept intruding, so that she had finally given up in despair. Just as she had with the sketch of Sarah… It was as like Jane as she could make it.

Julian was utterly silent as he looked at the sketch. Silent and unnaturally still. Would he understand why she had done it? To give Nan a way of remembering Jane clearly and knowing that someone else remembered her mother?

He handed the book back to her and stood up.

'Did you draw Sarah?'

Her throat ached. 'Yes. Before I could forget.'

Something passed across his face.

'I sent for Nan's aunt and uncle. They will come tomorrow. They are willing to take her.' His voice was distant and expressionless.

Pain sliced soul deep. She was going to fail in everything, then?

He went on. 'No doubt you will wish to meet them, assure yourself they will care for the child.'

Soothe my conscience? 'Thank you, my lord.'

He frowned, but did not correct her. Instead he reached out to stroke Nan's cheek with a careful finger. She didn't stir, but the sleepy kitten yawned pinkly and dabbed at his hand with a lazy paw. He touched it with that same finger and straightened.

'Goodnight, Christy.'

'Goodnight, sir.'

He left the room and she heard his swift strides on the bare boards of the nursery, the sound of the outer door closing behind him. He was gone, and she wasn't going to cry. She *wasn't*, curse it!

Julian forced himself to focus on his agent's report. He had an hour before the Carters could be expected and he ought to spend the time profitably. Workers' cottages. Needing repair. Before winter. Estimates of cost. Which had to be balanced against the money he had available for the repairs. It could be managed. With Serena remarried, the estate no longer provided for her.

But his thoughts refused to focus. He'd scarcely slept. Without Christy his bed was cold and empty. Which was ridiculous! It was no emptier, or colder than it had been before his marriage. It was exactly the same bed, with the same blankets and exquisite linen. Not to mention the same richly embroidered counterpane. Besides which, Christy had never been in his bed. He'd been going to her bed and returning to his own to sleep. Or not.

It wasn't only last night he'd slept badly. He kept waking and reaching for her in the night. When had he ever done that after leaving a woman's bed? When had he ever wanted to hold a woman—just hold her—while she slept? Why was everything suddenly so damned complicated? If only Christy would fit into the neat little box labelled 'wife'.

What was she doing this morning? He assumed she was still with Nan. He shut his eyes, trying to banish the image of his wife sitting by the sleeping child's bed. Of course Christy would sympathise with Nan's predicament. But it didn't alter reality.

He shoved his chair back from the desk and stood up. Why was he so on edge about a simple question of duty? He was doing the right thing in ensuring Nan's well-being. He was being generous in making a financial settlement on her. Providing a separate allowance to her aunt and uncle for her upkeep was more than generous, and adding a little extra as an incentive for them to treat her well was more than anyone would expect of him.

Except his wife.

He understood that. With her experience she did not see things in the same way.

Coldly?

Rationally. The solution she had proposed was unthinkable.

No. Not unthinkable. Royal bastards have always been well provided for.

I'm not royalty, and she isn't my daughter!

No. She's your sister. And it didn't matter a damn to Christy when she believed Nan was *your daughter.*

That in itself staggered him. Believing Jane to be his ex-mistress and Nan his daughter, Christy had still befriended them.

He walked over to the window, staring out at a blustery day. He was doing the sensible thing. The right and proper thing. Only he couldn't forget the blank, shuttered expression in Christy's eyes as she applied the term *by-blow* to herself.

By-blow—with all it implied. Tainted. *Filius nullius*—a child with no legal existence. Better unborn. Or dead. Like her sister.

He saw again Nan's pale face against the pillow, her eyes red-rimmed, and Christy sitting beside her. His Christy, sweet and affectionate. So blazingly honest and independent. Did he really want to contemplate his world without Christy in it? It might have been an easier world… No—it was too late for that. Christy was his.

I love you…

The opening door interrupted his churning thoughts.

'The Carters have arrived, my lord.'

His gut clenched. 'Show them in, please, Hallam. And send a message up to her ladyship asking her to bring Miss Nan down.'

'Certainly, my lord.'

A moment later the Carters were ushered in, dressed in what Julian assumed to be their Sunday best. Prosperous. Respectable.

Julian knew them by sight and reputation. Carter was Sir John's tenant, not his. He knew them to be well thought of. Upright. Decent.

He went forwards, holding out his hand. 'Carter. Mrs Carter. Thank you for coming. Please sit down. Lady Braybrook will be down shortly.' He hoped.

Carter frowned. 'Very kind of your lordship.' His wife murmured her agreement, and they sat down on a sofa, perching on the extreme edge and looking excessively uncomfortable.

'Please accept my condolences on the death of your sister, Mrs Carter,' said Julian politely.

The woman flushed and Carter spoke sharply; 'As to that, it's all for the best, no doubt. We're decent, God-fearing folk, an' there's no denying that Jane—' He broke off, eyeing Julian in some trepidation. Julian said nothing, and Carter went on in a hard voice. 'Well, she's dead now, and a body shouldn't speak ill, but there's no cause for grief. The Good Lord moves in mysterious ways.'

Julian wondered if Carter felt God's wasp had left half the job undone. Hoping to reduce the tension, he began to talk about the harvest.

Carter was expounding his views on the advisability of planting more apple trees when the door opened and Christy came in, hand in hand with Nan.

While Julian had not expected Nan to rush forwards with shrieks of glee to greet her relations, it came as a kick in the gut to see her shrink closer to Christy's skirts at the sight of them. Shy, he told himself. She would adjust soon enough. But how did a child adjust to guardians who openly described her mother's death as divine retribution? He rose to present them to Christy.

The Carters greeted her civilly, but Julian caught the surreptitious and curious glances. Like the rest of the county, they were doubtless wondering exactly how she had prevailed upon him to offer marriage.

'And here is Nan,' said Christy, urging the little girl forwards gently. 'Come, Nan.'

Nan's murmured greeting tore at something in Julian. He smiled at her, but her eyes were downcast.

Carter grunted. His wife remained silent.

Christy's chin lifted. Julian stiffened, but her voice remained calm. 'She is a little shy at the moment. I am sure you understand her distress.'

Carter cleared his throat. 'As I was a-saying to his lordship, sometimes these things are all for the best. 'Tis hard on a respectable man to knowin' his sister-in-law isn't no better than—'

He caught Julian's eye and subsided. 'Well, mum for that. I'm sure your lordship has more important matters to see to. I understood from your lordship's note that you wish to put the girl under our care?'

Julian nodded, and said slowly, 'Yes. That did appear as the best solution.'

Carter's heavy shoulders squared. 'We'd best discuss ways and means, then. No denying it'll mean an extra mouth to feed.'

Christy spoke again. 'Mrs Carter—the care of Nan must come upon you. What do you think?'

Carter cleared his throat. 'Beggin' your pardon, m'lady, but I'm master in my own home,' he told her bluntly. ''Tis my decision, and no other's.'

'Carter!' Julian's voice slashed.

'My lord?'

'You will remember, Carter—Lady Braybrook's sole concern is Nan's well-being.'

Carter's face reddened. 'Beg pardon, my lord. I meant no disrespect.'

Julian nodded. 'Very well. Naturally I am prepared to contribute a weekly sum for Nan's board. In addition, a capital sum will be held in trust for when she weds, or comes of age.'

Carter scowled. 'Well, now. I don't say something for the girl's keep would come amiss,' he said. 'But there's no need for the rest. Setting her up over my own childer. Don't seem fitting somehow for a child like that.'

'Fitting?' Christy's voice had lost all semblance of gentleness, slicing into the sudden silence.

Mrs Carter spoke up. 'A child of sin,' she said. 'We don't need paying to do our Christian duty.'

Julian flinched. The word *duty* had never sounded

colder. And Nan had shrunk back against Christy, as though someone had raised a fist to her.

'Of course not,' said Christy, her hand going to Nan's shoulder. 'But St Paul believed that without charity, *love*, that is, even giving your body to be burnt would be an empty act.'

Mrs Carter's lips pursed. 'We've said we'll take the girl and do what's right,' she said in a low, hard voice. 'Bring her up strict among godly folks. 'Tis only right we do our best to make sure my sister's sin don't go no further. Look at that ribbon in her hair! Vanity!' She almost spat the last word.

'That ribbon,' said Christy, 'was her mother's last gift to her!'

Carter turned to Julian. 'Best we take the girl now, my lord. She'll forget quick enough.'

'No.' Christy's voice was sharp. Peremptory.

Julian took a deep breath. They couldn't have this conversation now. Not with Nan present.

Christy rushed on. 'A note came up from the Dower House, my lord. Your stepmother wishes me to take Nan to visit her. I sent a note back promising to do so.'

For a hastily concocted excuse, Julian thought, it was superb.

Carter frowned. 'Better not, my lady, beggin' your leave. Give the girl foolish ideas above her station. Best she comes with us now.'

'Aye,' said his wife. 'Start as we mean to go on.'

It made sense. Julian knew that. It was the sensible, rational way forwards, only—

'I am afraid my stepmother would have Lady Braybrook's head on a pike,' he said politely. 'And Nan's belongings will not be packed.' He couldn't believe he was saying this, and, judging by their expressions, neither could the Carters. 'I will send a message when all is arranged. Thank you again for coming. Let me show you out.'

Chapter Nineteen

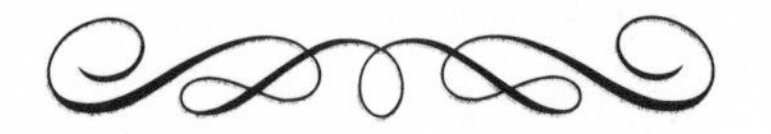

When he returned to the library Christy was alone, sitting in a wing chair by the window.

'Where is Nan?' he asked.

'Don't you mean *the girl*, my lord?'

Never had he heard such bitterness in her soft voice.

'I sent for Beth to take Nan down to Serena, with a promise that I would follow.'

So it hadn't been an excuse.

'How *can* you?' she burst out.

'Christy—'

'How could you abandon any child, let alone your *sister*, to people like that?'

'The Carters are reputed to be honest, hardworking—'

'They didn't greet her, or speak to her. They didn't even use her name!' blazed Christy. 'Carter as good as said in front of her that Jane *deserved* her death! How do you imagine they will treat her? Even the ribbon in her hair was a crime!'

Anger flared. 'They will have me to answer to if she's not cared for!' he said. 'Once they understand their allowance is contingent—'

'Money!' she spat. 'Do you really think it can buy what Nan needs? Even if they don't mistreat her, how happy can she be if no one loves her? She's lost her *mother*! Don't you understand? You could settle a fortune on her, force people to be polite, fight a duel over it—and it would all be empty. Worthless!'

She stood up, her shoulders somehow slumped. She looked exhausted, defeated. 'You will excuse me, my lord.'

'Where are you going?' he asked sharply. The despair in her voice lodged deep inside him.

'To visit Serena,' she reminded him, walking towards the door.

Perhaps it was better to let her go and discuss the whole thing again when she was less upset. 'You recall we are to dine at Postleton Manor? We need to leave by half past four.'

'Of course, my lord.' She reached the door and looked back. 'If you believe me fit for such exalted company.'

'Hell's teeth, Christy!' he growled. 'That's ridiculous!'

'It is the truth,' she told him, opening the door.

'You're my wife!' he said.

She shivered. 'Yes. And perhaps it would have been much easier had that wasp landed on my glass, not Jane's.'

The door closed behind her with a terrible finality.

He'd read the blasted report and written instructions about the cottages. He'd been through his accounts and written a letter to Modbury about investing in shipping. He had responded to the Vicar's message setting Jane's funeral for the day after tomorrow. Bereft of excuses for avoiding the issue any longer, he shoved the standish away with unwonted force.

Did Christy really think he would have been relieved if she had been the one to die? Logic told him that she was hurt and had lashed out. But he had been the one to hurt her. And he was forced to admit a certain logic in her reasoning—her birth was, in truth, no better than Nan's.

But damn it all! He had defied her father, the Duke of Alcaston, condemned him for his behaviour to her…her father who had disowned her without ever speaking her name. Just as the Carters had not spoken Nan's name?

Was there nothing more binding them than duty and honour? And the passion they shared in bed? Was it just sex? She had said that the other day, and it had hurt, hurt unbearably. He had felt as though the world had emptied, become barren and void. What had Christy said to the Carters? It niggled at him—something about St Paul.

He pushed his chair back and strode over to the window, staring out over the parterres and park. From here he could see the Dower House, nestled in its trees. On the grass he could see small figures, faintly hear shrieks and yells as they batted the shuttlecock back and forth. Emma was there, with Matt and Davy. Not Nan. No doubt she was with Serena and Christy beneath that oak. He could see two people sitting there.

The shade made it impossible to see properly, but he thought there was a smaller figure too.

Christy had said something about St Paul… He pushed the thought aside.

What the hell did he do now? Christy was right. He couldn't let Nan go to the Carters. His conscience wouldn't allow it. Would he have realised it if not for Christy? Without her he would have arranged everything at a distance. He might not have even seen the Carters in person. He had done that to reassure Christy.

And they were not bad people. Just unyielding. He did not think they would be intentionally cruel to Nan, but…he remembered his own confusion when his mother had left. No one had spoken of her. Her portrait had been removed and his father had ordered him to forget her. He hadn't. He'd just pretended to because it was easier. And then his father had remarried. He'd wanted to hate Serena, but that had proved impossible. Later, when the news came of his mother's death, it had been Serena who had comforted his forbidden, unspoken grief.

He'd been older. How could a little girl of five be forbidden to speak of her mother? Forbidden to remember her with love.

What had Christy said about St Paul? Irritated, he went over to the corner where the family bible was kept. He lifted it down, bracing himself against its weight and took it over to his desk. Lord, he was as bad as Ricky Blakehurst when a stray quote bothered him this much.

St Paul… He riffled through the New Testament. Something about love, or rather charity…he found it in Paul's letter to the Christians at Corinth…exhorting them to love…*if I have not charity…I am nothing…though I bestow all my goods to feed the poor…give my body to be burned, and have not charity…*

Charity. Love.

Hell and the devil! Not even the Vicar would interpret the passage in that way.

Christy had, though.

He went to stare out of the window again at the little group by the Dower House. There appeared to be some disagreement over the shuttlecock game. Davy was jumping up and down, a sure sign that he was cross about something.

From the chimney piece, a delicate chime rang out twice. He frowned. Two o'clock. Christy should be back soon if they were to leave on time. Perhaps he should walk down and bring them back.

How happy can she be if no one loves her?

The words flayed him.

Halfway across the park he realised that the adult under the tree with Serena was Havergal. Nan was there, sitting close beside Serena. She looked to be sewing and Serena was bending over her to guide and help, but Christy was nowhere to be seen.

She must have stepped into the house… He was within a hundred yards of the group when he noticed there was no chair set out for her. Davy had seen him and came tearing up, yelling and whooping.

'Have you come to play? Play on my side!'

Julian swung him up. 'Steady there. What are you up to?'

'Shuttlecock. Couldn't you *see*? Nan isn't playing. She's sitting with Mama and Uncle Nigel, because Mama says she's too sad.'

'Yes. I saw that. And where is your Aunt Christy?'

'She doesn't like being "aunt",' Davy informed him. 'She said to call her Christy.'

'And where is she?'

Davy wriggled and Julian set him down. 'I don't know. In the house? Are you going to play? Emma and I have been playing against Matt.'

'Perhaps.' In the house? Not very likely. If she were, Serena would be with her. Had she gone back to the main house already? But why leave Nan here?

'There's lemonade,' said Davy. 'Come and have some.'

Serena looked up, frowning as they approached. Havergal smiled, brandishing the lemonade jug. 'Your tipple, Braybrook?'

'Thank you, sir.' He smiled at Nan. She looked back gravely, saying nothing.

Serena said gently, 'You are doing very well, Nan. Keep the stitches nice and even, just like that.' She smiled at Julian. 'She is a far better pupil than Alicia and Emma were. Are you looking for Christy? She went for a walk. I am sure she will be back soon.' She reached for her parasol. 'In the meantime, you may take me for a walk.'

Havergal handed him a glass of lemonade, which Julian drained.

'Very well, Serena.' No doubt she was about to tell him why he could not permit Christy to raise Nan. She smiled, picked up her parasol and opened it.

Julian was used to pushing Serena's chair, but it was always disconcerting to converse with a pink, tasselled parasol.

They were barely out of earshot when she said calmly, 'I discussed the matter with Nigel, after Christy left, and if you really feel unable to take in your sister, she may come to us.'

Julian stared at the parasol's tassells fluttering in the light breeze. He supposed one day Serena might lose her power to shock him, but he couldn't imagine when. Hauling in a breath, he said, 'You *knew*?'

Hidden by the parasol, her expression could only be guessed at, but her snort was eloquent. 'My arithmetic is quite good, Julian. At the time Nan must have been conceived, you hadn't been anywhere near Amberley for months. In fact, I have letters from you in Paris for that period! Of course I knew. From the very first, as soon as I heard the talk. I asked your father and he admitted it. But he insisted that the story of your responsibility stood, because he didn't want me embarrassed.' She frowned. 'I didn't like it, but it wasn't hurting anyone, so I agreed.'

Good God!

All he said was, 'And you are prepared to raise her?'

The parasol snapped shut and Serena glared up at him over her shoulder. 'The person I was cross with was your father! Not Nan. Of course I'm prepared to raise her! Although I'd probably let the lie about her being your child stand. Then I'll appear a saint, not a fool. Naturally, if you and Christy are to keep her, we shall let the truth come out and I can be a martyr while you and Christy appear saintly.'

The idea that one day Serena might cease to shock him died a swift and painless death as he started to laugh helplessly.

'The trick, dearest, is not to give people the least reason for thinking *you* are at all perturbed by the situation,' she told him, putting up the parasol again. It twirled, tassells aflutter. 'Once you have decided, let me know. For now I suggest, since you and Christy are to be out for dinner, that you leave Nan with me. The poor child will be better for some company. Christy's maid may bring some things down for her.'

'Very well,' said Julian. 'I will think about it.'

The parasol twitched. 'Well, make sure you do think. Don't just take your prejudices out for exercise. That isn't going to help your marriage either. Now you may take me back to Nigel and Nan. And then you had best return to the house. I'm sure Christy will not be far behind. She had her watch in her pocket.'

But she did not return. By three-thirty Julian was concerned. Half an hour later he was panicking. They ought to be leaving soon. Where the hell was she?

He stared at Twigg. 'You're sure she isn't in the park?'

'Aye, me lord. Looked everywhere, we have. I've sent lads down along the river, but—'

Julian didn't hear the rest. The river. She didn't swim very well. If she'd fallen in… No. This might be her way of avoiding the dinner party. She'd been upset, suggesting he must believe her unfit to be in such company. She was angry with him. His fear eased a little.

'Bring Conqueror around,' he told Twigg. 'I'll look for her myself.

Four hours later, he hadn't found any trace of Christy. His voice was hoarse and fear crawled coldly in his veins as he stared around a clearing he had already been through twice—she might be home already. He needed to check. Wheeling Conqueror, he pushed him into a trot, heading for Amberley.

Reaching the edge of the woods, he rode out into the park and stared across the tree-studded expanse at the house. Dark against the deepening sky, it stood ablaze with lights.

If she hadn't returned, he'd go out again. But where? The forest was huge, stretching for miles. If she had left the path in there… His stomach churned. They might never find her.

He pushed the gelding to a canter. He was a hundred yards from the house when a yell went up. Hope unsheathed itself again, slicing at him, as he saw one of the undergrooms running towards him from the stables.

'My lord! She's here. Just gone up to the house!'

He had Conqueror in a flat gallop within six strides. He pulled up beside the lad and flung himself from the saddle.

'Is she hurt?'

The groom took the bridle and said cheerfully, 'Don't think so, my lord. Just went for a walk in the woods, she said. She's got a—'

He didn't hear any more. He was running for the house.

She'd been in the woods. And, having frightened him half to death, she'd reappeared too late to attend the dinner party.

He strode into the house by the side door and met Hallam. *'Where is she?'*

Hallam eyed him with some misgiving. 'In the Hall, my lord. But I think—'

What Hallam thought he didn't wait to find out. His whole mind was occupied by the blistering reprimand he was going to give his wife the moment he saw her.

Curse it! He'd been worried sick, and she'd been hiding in the woods because she didn't want to go to a dinner party. Did she think he wanted to go, damn it? Not likely. All he wanted was a chance to—he slammed the lid down on his preferred alternative. Reprimanding his bride while wreathed in lascivious visions of seducing her would be damn near impossible.

He stalked into the Great Hall and found his bride crouched over something on the hearth.

'Where the devil have you been?' he roared.

Belatedly he noticed the presence of his housekeeper and an assortment of maids and footmen.

'Out.' Couched in deadly soft tones, the command encompassed all of them. His boots echoed on the stone flags as he approached his kneeling bride. It was tempting to think her submissive posture betokened an attitude of becoming repentance, but, knowing Christy, he could imagine nothing less likely.

Sure enough, she glared up at him as he approached. At least, he assumed she was glaring at him. With candlelight glinting off her spectacles and her thick hair collapsing half over her face, he really couldn't be sure. And somewhere in his confused and befuddled mind, part of him was relieved to see she wasn't cowed. There was not the least hint of fear in her attitude.

Then he got a good look at the state she was in, and forgot all about whether or not she was glaring at him. His prim and proper, never-a-hair-out-of-place bride was a complete and utter mess.

Quite apart from her dishevelled hair, her cambric walking dress was torn and looked as if she had been lying face down in the mud. Her arms were scratched and filthy, and her hands—he blinked—she looked as though she had been digging with them. They were black, the nails, or what was left of them, encrusted with dirt. Fear lashed through him, all the worse for knowing it was too late for him to do a damn thing about whatever trouble she had landed herself in.

'What the *hell* have you—?'

The whimper stopped him cold, and he saw the dog. Well, he supposed it was a dog. A half-grown pup, actually—but its ancestry beggared the imagination. Thin, scruffy, its filthy white coat splotched with brown, one drooping and one flyaway ear—for a moment Julian was speechless.

Then, 'Where did *that* come from?' he demanded.

'He,' said Christy, with what Julian considered undue emphasis, 'is a dog. And *he*—'

'Are you sure of that?' asked Julian sarcastically. He should have known better.

Cheeks flaming under the grime, Christy said, 'Perfectly sure. Even I know bitches don't mark trees.'

Julian took that one on the chin. 'Thank you,' he said, suppressing the urge to throttle her. Or kiss her. 'And what evidence can you present that this…*thing*…is indeed a dog?' Seeing that she was silenced, he swept on, 'And where did you find this dog? For want of a better term.'

'In the woods,' said Christy in oddly muted tones. 'He…I…we were playing, with a stick, and chasing rabbits. At least, he was—'

'And you *conveniently* forgot the time. You decided playing with a stray mongrel was more important than fulfilling your social obligations, so you stayed out late—worrying me half to death in the process!' he finished savagely.

'Worrying *you*?'

She sounded as though the idea struck her as ludicrous.

'Of course I was worried! What did you imagine I'd think when you didn't come home? But much you care! You were out disporting yourself with a dog who should have been shot for trespass!'

'Stop yelling at me!' said Christy furiously. 'Can't you…can't you see he's hurt? And you're frightening him!'

Her voice shook, and to his horror a tear slid down her cheek, leaving a track in the dirt.

All his anger dissolved, leaving exposed the fear he had lived with for hours. His stomach clenched again, painfully. And tightened further as another tear fell.

'Just go away,' she said in a very wobbly voice.

He stared down at her, half-turned away from him. How indeed should she have known that he would worry about her? How could she know that his conscience was like a raw wound with salt burning it? How could she know he had spent the day going over his dealings with her and finding himself completely at fault?

'How is he hurt?' he asked quietly.

There was an aching silence. Then, 'His back leg,' she whispered.

Julian crouched down, eliciting a growl from the frightened pup.

'Gently, little fellow,' he murmured, holding out a lightly clenched fist for the pup to sniff. It snapped, and then whined piteously. He kept talking in a lazy sing-song voice, uttering nonsense, knowing only the tone mattered.

Christy herself was caught, enthralled by the change in him. Dazed, she listened to the soothing voice.

'You're lucky she found you. What stupid mess did you get into? Hmm?'

The pup sniffed cautiously at the outstretched hand.

'Yes, that's better. I don't really eat dogs—there. Yes, that's a good spot, isn't it, laddie? Softly, then.'

The lean, powerful hand scratched gently behind the

pup's ears. Christy gulped, recallng the effect those caressing fingers had on her.

'Now, let's see…ah, so there's the problem. How did you do it, you silly creature?'

'What has he done?' asked Christy softly.

'Dislocated the hip,' replied Julian. 'Nasty. Never mind, little chap. How did it happen?'

It took Christy a moment to realise that he was asking her.

'Oh. I was on the way home—with him,' she added defiantly. 'And he chased a rabbit. There's a tree down in the woods. Just on the edge of a bank. He got in among the roots chasing it, and…' She hesitated. He was going to be furious.

'Go on.'

She took a deep breath. 'Well, it was odd, but there seemed to be tunnels in the bank, behind the tree, and—'

'What sort of tree?' he asked sharply. The pup cowered and he moderated his tone. 'Easy, little chap. What sort of tree, Christy?'

'Um, an oak. It was awfully smelly.'

'I know the place. It's an old badger sett that foxes use now,' he said grimly. 'Go on.'

'Well, he didn't come out when I called, but I could hear him barking…and then there was a sort of rushing noise and he was still barking, but it was muffled.' She shivered, remembering.

'You mean part of the sett collapsed?' asked Julian in a queer, tight voice.

She nodded.

'So how did he get out?' His eyes raked her ruined gown. Clearly this was not the behaviour a viscount expected of his bride.

'I…I climbed in over the roots and dug him out,' she said.

His face drained of all colour, and he said in a carefully expressionless voice, 'You're telling me you crawled into a badger's sett, in an unstable bank, that had already collapsed *twice*, to dig out this…this misbegotton excuse for a dog?'

Anger and hurt flared. 'I wasn't thinking about his ancestry at the time,' she said. 'No doubt you would have left him to his fate and strolled home without a care in the world!'

She didn't realise she was crying until shaking hands cradled her face and a gentle thumb wiped clumsily at a tear.

'Christy, he's just a dog.' His voice sounded strange. 'You could have been trapped! Killed! We had no idea where you were!'

She knew he was right, but— 'I couldn't just leave him!'

His breath came out in a groan. 'No. I don't suppose you could. Very well. We'd better patch up him.'

'How?' she asked. 'It looks dreadful.'

He grimaced. 'I can assure you, it doesn't feel very pleasant. I think we'll find Twigg knows how to put it back. He put my shoulder back in for me once when I was a boy. Ring the bell. We'll send for him.'

She reached up and tugged on the bell pull. Then she looked at her husband, sitting on the hearth, comforting a mongrel pup, his hands gentle.

'Julian?'

He looked up, his blue eyes somehow bruised.

'I'm sorry about the dinner. I don't suppose you will believe me, but I was coming back for it. Truly, I was.'

His jaw dropped.

Once he'd been sent for, Twigg appeared promptly. Julian rather thought Hallam hadn't been far away, given the swiftness of his response to the bell. Probably wondering if he would have to intercede on his mistress's behalf, thought Julian in self-disgust.

I don't suppose you will believe me…

Ice had condensed in his stomach at those words. She didn't expect him to believe her? What the hell could he say? He'd already said quite enough and there was the pup to look after now.

Twigg took one look at the shivering pup. 'Well, well. That's a nasty mess an' no mistake.' He grinned at his master. 'You'd know what that feels like.'

'Only too well,' said Julian drily. 'Can you put it back?'

'Oh, aye. Easy enough, if so be as you and the mistress can help. I could get a couple of the lads, but I dessay he'll feel better without too many strangers messing round with him.'

Christy swallowed. 'What do you want me to do, Twigg? I don't know anything about dogs.'

He smiled. 'You'll do just fine, m'lady. Now, first thing—since I can't tip a quart of brandy down his throat like I did with you, Master Julian, you'd best hold his head and shoulders.' He grinned at Christy and added confidentially, 'We'll give him that job, then it'll likely be him as gets bit.'

'Thank you,' said Julian wryly. 'Did you want a reference, or not?'

But Twigg's shrewd old eyes were on Christy's wrist. 'Looks like you already got a bit of a nip, ma'am.'

Julian focused sharply on the puncture marks. 'Damn it, Christy! How did that happen?'

'When I pulled him out,' she said. 'I must have hurt his leg. I could see it was all wrong, but the tunnel—' He drew a savage breath and she broke off, 'I was in a hurry.'

She was avoiding his gaze and his blood congealed. 'The bank collapsed again.' He felt cold, frozen to the marrow. If she hadn't got out…she wouldn't have stood a chance with the weight of the earth and possibly the fallen tree on her. She would be dead by now. Buried. They might never have found her. A world without Christy?

He gave vent to his feelings in a few blistering words that turned the air blue and earned him a dressing down from Twigg.

'Yeh talk nice in front of her ladyship,' he admonished. ''Taint no way to talk to any woman, leave alone your bride!'

He turned to Christy. 'Now, m'lady, once his lordship's got the pup firm, I want yeh to lace yer fingers together, and link them under his thigh—like so.' Gnarled old hands guided hers into position. 'That's it. With you bracin' him, I can twist the leg easier to get the joint back in. See?'

Christy gulped.

Twigg looked sympathetic. 'Just shut yer eyes. No need to look at what I'm doing. Happen he'll make a bit of noise, but it can't be helped.' He grinned. 'That'll just be dog talk for a few of the things Master Julian said a moment back.'

Christy managed a shaky smile. 'Very well.'

'Good girl,' said Julian softly.

Steadied by this praise, she felt better.

She did shut her eyes, but nothing could shut out the pup's terrified yelps. Tears ran down her face, but she hung on, and suddenly felt a click under her hands, and heard Twigg's triumphant, 'Ah! There 'tis! Well done, lass. We've done it!'

Sick to her stomach, Christy opened her eyes.

The leg was back in right relation to its owner.

'Now, he'll need to be kept warm and quiet for a few days,' said Twigg, with a glance at Julian. 'I can take him down the stables with me while that leg heals. What'll you do with him then?'

The question took Julian by surprise. He looked at the pup and repressed a shudder. 'Ask roundabout if anyone owns him; if not, I suppose someone might like him for a child. One of the farmers, perhaps.'

Beside him, Christy's breath jerked in and she froze to utter stillness.

In a very diffident voice—one she used, he was fast learning, to conceal hurt—she said, 'May I not keep him?'

Chapter Twenty

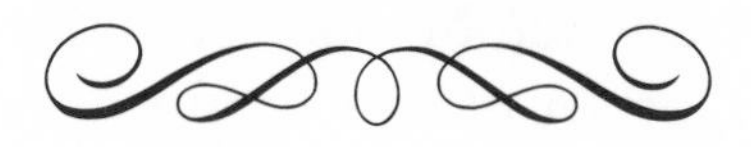

Julian stared. Keep the pup? Rescue it—yes. Tend its injury—by all means. But keep a misbegotten pup that looked as though it had strayed off a dust heap?

'Christy, if you want a dog, of course you may have one,' he said. 'A proper dog. Not—' He broke off.

'Is breeding so important, my lord?'

'Well, yes. At least—' He stopped—heard what he was saying.

Christy's odd eyes met his unflinchingly. 'Then he is quite dog enough for me. He has a tail to wag when he sees me, ears to prick when I call him, and eyes to tell me—' She stopped, blinked several times and then went on, 'That is sufficient for me. I fear I am not quite so nice in my requirements as you, my lord.'

He felt sick. 'Christy, I didn't mean…' But he had once meant it, and her eyes told him that she knew it. The pup…Nan…Christy herself.

'You really want him?' He could see his reputation going straight down the sink.

She nodded.

He sighed. 'There can be no objection. He'll have to be trained, though, if he is to be a house dog.'

Her smile broke through like sunshine after rain. Hesitant and wonderful.

Twigg grinned. 'I'll deal with that. My missus'll like havin' the pup to fuss over and he can come back up here to the house when he's learned his manners nice.' He turned to Christy. 'You come down each day to visit him and take him for a walk when that leg's ready and he'll learn who's mistress quick enough.'

Delight flooded Christy. The pup was hers. She stood up, wanting to thank Twigg, but staggered as the Hall spun, a crazy blur of light and stone…

'Christy!'

Strong arms caught her.

She came to herself seated at the long refectory table, Julian beside her, holding her close. Twigg and the pup were gone.

'Christy—are you all right?'

'I'm…I'm quite all right, my lord. Just tired. I should go up now.'

'In a moment,' he said. Still with his arm around her, he looked into her face, frowning. She must look a complete fright. She blushed as his gaze travelled to her scratched and filthy hands. He touched one gently and she trembled.

She felt dizzy again. Julian seemed to realise, because his arm tightened. She shut her eyes, leaning against him. Perhaps in a moment he might let her go up to bed. She didn't like to think about how she was going to get that far.

A moment later she felt herself being swung up into his arms and carried upstairs. Whispers and movement penetrated the haze. And Julian's harsh voice ordering a bath to be drawn, cloths and warm water to be brought along with supper to her bedchamber. She sighed and rested her head on his shoulder.

She roused as she was lowered with infinite gentleness into a chair before the fire in her room.

'Here. Let me.' His voice was a soothing murmur, but her eyes snapped open as a warm, damp cloth touched her face. She was beyond protest as he bathed her face, then her arms and hands. Light, caring touches that insensibly eased her and cleansed more from her than dirt. It sponged away hurt and fear.

Behind them Beth bustled about, directing the footmen where to place the bath. It didn't interest her. The strong hands cleansing her held her utterly spellbound. She closed her eyes again, surrendering to his care, and a powerful arm cradled her close. It felt so good to be cared for in this way. Not since she had been a little girl and skinned her knee had anyone tended her like this.

It was not safe. His warmth and strength seduced her senses—she could withstand that. But his tenderness tore at her heart. It would be much easier if he were the cold, arrogant aristocrat. But behind the pride and chill was a man who could ravish the heart from a woman without even knowing, or wanting it.

He was being kind now because he felt guilty about hurting her. Desperately she reminded herself that he wanted a dutiful bride to give him an heir. He enjoyed her passion and her body, but the emotions battering at her held no value for him.

Folly to weave dreams around simple kindness, to imagine that his hands had trembled as he sponged away dirt from her face, that the long fingers had grazed her throat on purpose. She fought the urge to nestle closer, burrowing against him.

Beth's voice broke into her daze. 'Comfrey salve, my lord. Best for those scratches.'

'Thank you.'

Salve was rubbed in with a feather-light touch. Face, hands, arms.

By the time he had tended Christy's scrapes and the bite, Julian ached with arousal. He breathed carefully. Kissing her senseless in front of her maid was more than slightly inappropriate. Especially since he would end by carrying her to his bed and… He halted the train of thought right there. She was exhausted; she needed sleep.

Never before had he realised how deeply it was possible to desire a woman. And it was not just that he wanted her *more* than any other woman. He wanted her differently. He wanted all of her. Everything he had pretended was unimportant. Her barbed tongue as well as her sweetness. Her blazing honesty that never backed down. Her pride.

He wanted *her*. Christy. His wife.

'Beg pardon, my lord. Bath's ready.'

He looked around. Christy's maid stood beside a steaming bathtub by the fire. Towels lay over a chair.

It required an effort of will to stand up.

'I'll be in my room,' he said. Everything in him roared a protest, that he should dismiss the maid and care for Christy himself, but he couldn't trust his control. He would come back when she was safely in bed to make sure she was all right.

Christy submitted to Beth's ministrations, clumsily washing herself with her left hand, but permitting the maid to wash and rinse her hair. Her bandaged right wrist ached, but overlaying the pain was the memory of Julian's gentleness as he had cleansed and tended it.

When Beth asked, she stood to be rinsed with a bucket of warm water. Once dry, she pulled on a robe and sat by the fire to rub her hair dry. Food was brought. A hot, rich soup, bread and cheese. She ate hungrily.

Beth took the tray when she was finished, saying gently, 'Bed, my lady?'

Bed. Obediently she got into bed and Beth drew the bedhangings, leaving a small gap so Christy could reach the bedside table.

Slight sounds came to her. Hushed voices as two footmen removed the bath. Beth tidying up.

'Will there be anything more, my lady?'

'No. Just snuff the candles. Thank you. I will ring in the morning.' She felt as though she could sleep for days and still be tired. It wasn't just her body, tired though it was. Her very spirit felt weary, as though she had been confronted with something that she could neither walk away from nor ultimately win. She lay back against the pillows, listening as Beth moved about snuffing candles. Bit by bit the room darkened.

She had to be sensible. Not moping because she…because she what? Had a husband who worried about her and lost his temper when she had frightened him? Because she could depend on him to look after her? Because he would follow an honourable course no matter what?

The darkness swelled as Beth doused the lamp on the dressing table.

She had nothing to mope about. She had aimed at the moon and she had tripped. That was all. She hadn't hurt herself badly. Only broken a useless dream. Countless girls and women were sleeping in doorways tonight, and, but for Julian's sense of honour, she might well have ended up among them.

'Leave this one, my lady?' Beth was back, looking at the candle on the bedside table.

'Yes. Thank you. Go to bed.'

'Yes, my lady.'

Another door closed. The world seemed full of closing doors.

She had lost nothing. Only a dream she had never really believed in. Not for herself. It wasn't practical, or even safe to dream that particular dream. She would manage without it. Compared to her failure to keep Nan safe for Jane, it wasn't important.

She sat up, took off her spectacles, and leaned over to blow out the candle on her bedside table. Darkness poured over her. And with it, fear. Blind, unreasoning fear. Of the dark. Panic. Black, choking, as the tree shifted, earth and stones sliding around her, pattering over her, and she heard their hungry growl, knew she had only instants, seconds to get out before the consuming dark took her…

She forced herself to breathe. Clean, free air. She was safe. Safe in her own bed. Julian was in his room. If she called, he would come. But she would not call. Knowing that she could must be enough. Better if he didn't see any more of her weakness. A bright moon had been rising earlier. Moonlight was safer than falling asleep with a lamp or candle.

Flinging back the covers and hangings, she got up and went to the windows. The curtains rattled as she pulled them back. The clear, bright sky drove panic into retreat.

She turned away from the window and cried out in terror as a shadow moved by the door.

'Christy!'

He was across the room and had her in his arms before she could take another breath. His heat infused her, warming, comforting. Beneath her cheek his heart thudded. One hand held her close, the other traced her jaw, her lips, throat, and slid shaking into her hair, pressing her closer to the reassuring beat of his heart.

'Shh. It's me. I needed to see that you were all right. That you weren't frightened.'

She tried to summon a lie. Tell him she hadn't been frightened. But her trembling body betrayed her.

'You…you startled me. I wanted light…it was so dark. And it smelt awful—' She was babbling, unsure whether she meant her room or the sett. 'I'm sorry about the dinner—I was coming back for it. Truly.'

His arms hardened instantly. 'I thought I'd lost you.' His voice was rough. 'Then when you told me what had happened, and I knew how close you'd been to—' He broke off, and she felt a shudder rack him. Strangely, it steadied her. 'The things I said—I'm sorry. The dinner wasn't important.' His mouth brushed clumsily over her temple, her eyes. Then he released her and stepped back, his face etched hard in silver and shadow. 'Is there anything you need?'

She swallowed. Pride would help here. Pride would allow her to assure him that she was very well. That she had only needed fresh air…that she hadn't been frightened…

'Just you.'

Her voice was the merest breath, but she saw her words strike. Saw the shock in his expression.

His voice neutral, he said, 'You wish me to remain with you for the night? Just hold you?'

It would be easy to let him believe that was all. Safer. And untrue.

'No,' she said. 'I need to know that I am still alive. I need *you*.'

'Christy.'

It was all he said before his mouth claimed hers.

Words were impossible, unnecessary, consumed in the fierce desperation of their kiss. Then she was swept up in his arms, being carried past her own bed and through the door to *his* room and *his* bed and tumbled on to it. There was scarcely time to gasp before he was with her, his weight, hot and hard, covering her, swift hands banishing her nightgown, his robe, until nothing remained between them. Nothing but fiery need, all restraint and distance incinerated.

Julian couldn't speak. There were words he needed to say, but his throat was hot and tight, choking him. Because she was kissing him, her cheeks wet with tears. And her hands, hesitant and a little clumsy, were a burning, soul-deep delight. Every shy touch echoing the words in his heart, the ones trapped in his throat.

He wanted everything. He wanted to give her everything. Everything given and received. Everything taken and offered. Because it had nearly been too late.

He kissed his way down her throat, licking and caressing, finding the frantic pulse beating at the base. Adoring the high, sweet curve of her breast, coming to the taut nipple and drawing it into the dark heat of his mouth to suckle fiercely so her body arched wildly and she cried out, a strangled sound of pleasure. Pleasure stabbing deep in his own body, driven by her response.

He shifted, burning, and reached between restless silken thighs. 'Open.' His voice harsh, demanding. But she obeyed and he pressed shaking fingers to hot, liquid silk as he took her mouth again, kissing her deeply in searing promise.

Everything.

He stroked and teased, finding the hidden nub, circling so that she moaned and pushed against him, pleading for more. He slid one finger inside, felt her body clench wildly, and pressed with his thumb. She convulsed, her cries spilling into his mouth as release took her, leaving her limp and trembling.

So easy, so tempting to take her now. But he'd wanted to give everything.

He slid down her hot, quivering body, kissing every slick inch. Breasts, sweetly curving waist, the gentle swell of her belly, flaring hips and finally the soft cream silk of her thighs, pushing them wide, wider, with his shoulders. She gasped, a high, shocked sound and tried to push him away. He captured her hands gently.

'No. Don't fight me. Trust me. Let me love you.'

The words stilled her startled resistance and Christy's mind fractured at the hot, open-mouthed kisses on her inner thighs, at the harsh sound of his breath… the warm caress of his breath…there—there where she was aching and burning again. It terrified her…the intimacy, the emotions pouring through her.

Let me love you…

Oh, please, please…

Strong hands held her hips captive, tilting her for an impossibly tender, shockingly silken caress.

Her hips bucked as dark pleasure speared her and her throat burst with a raw, choked scream at the hot pressure of his mouth. Her hands sought him, clutching, sliding through the silk of his hair. It shattered her, terrified her. It was unbearable, it was wonderful. She would die if he didn't stop. She would die if he did stop.

She broke, crashing into oblivion as ecstasy poured through her again, consuming her in a fiery cataract. She hardly heard his tender, loving words as her tears spilt. And she wanted more, she ached, felt empty.

'Please.' Her voice shook. 'Please. I want you...all of you.'

With a harsh sound he surged up her body and she opened fully to him, felt the hard press of him at her entrance.

Shaking, on the brink of madness, bathed in her taste and scent, part of him clung to sanity, to safety. He should be gentle with her, take her carefully.

She was having none of it. Even as he fought for restraint she lifted against him, hot, wet softness claiming the head of his shaft, long slender legs wrapping around his hips. Nails raked his shoulders and her voice broke on his name.

Control exploded into ruin as he thrust into her welcoming body and buried himself to the hilt. Lost, he took her again and again, feeling her pleasure as his own, feeling her catch and match his rhythm so that their bodies sang together. He knew when the end was upon her, when he could let himself go and be swept with her into the final crescendo. Consummation took him, all dark, fierce pleasure as he spilt deep within her convulsing body, blind and shaking.

With a groan he collapsed on her, and slid to one side, still holding her close, unwilling to let her go. Ever.

With his last remaining strength he pulled the bedclothes over them, sinking into a warm cocoon in a sweaty, sated tangle of limbs, Christy safe in his arms.

He woke to bright sunlight. Somewhere outside, high above, a lark was pouring its gift of winged song back to the world. He rolled over, reaching out, and made an unwelcome discovery—he was alone. She might be in her own room. He got up, pulled on his dressing gown and went to look.

There was no sign of Christy, but her maid's eyes first widened at the sight of him still tying his robe, and then dropped modestly to the floor, her face scarlet. He felt his own ears burn. Damn it! Why the hell hadn't he put on his nightshirt? The entire staff would be laughing over this.

He cleared his throat. 'Do you know where your mistress is?'

'Oh, yes, m'lord.' Was that a flicker of amusement? 'She went down to the Dower House to fetch Miss Nan. She's up in the nursery with her.'

'Thank you, er, Beth, isn't it?'

'Yes, m'lord.'

He beat a hasty retreat.

The nursery. He was going to have to face them both.

Back in his own room, Julian realised that at some undefined point either last night or this morning he had made a decision. Two decisions. About his marriage and Nan's future.

'I don't know, sweetheart.'

Christy's tired, defeated voice sliced into him. 'It…that may not be possible, but I…I promise you will be safe and well looked after.'

He tensed at the uncertainty in her voice as she made the promise. Was she wondering if she would be permitted to keep it?

An indistinct murmur followed—a child's voice. Nan. His sister.

'Yes. It must seem strange. I don't fit in very well here either.'

Not fit? His fist clenched on the door frame until his knuckles whitened.

Again, Nan's indistinct voice.

'Of course not, Nan! No one will mind if you ride it!'

He'd heard enough. He pushed open the door and walked in.

His old rocking horse had been pulled into the middle of the floor, and Nan was clearly attempting to dismount as Christy tried to stop her. Scarlet faced, Christy turned as Nan's eyes widened and her breath jerked in on a gasp at the sight of him. She slid off the horse and stood stiffly, her eyes downcast.

He felt sick, clumsy and completely useless.

What the hell could he say? To either of them?

Christy met his gaze. 'My lord. You should have sent for me.'

'Actually I wanted both of you.' He looked at his sister, who was still staring at the floor. 'Good morning, Nan.'

A quick glance up, a mumbled greeting.

'Am I interrupting your ride?' he asked very gently.

A silent shake of the black curls answered him.

He looked from the stiff, averted face to the rocking horse. He'd been a year younger than Nan when Twigg's father made it…Starlight. Named for the diamond blaze on the wooden face. Dapple-grey paint, chipped in places, worn and rubbed in others. The leather reins were soft and supple, the padded leather saddle showing where four gallant riders since himself had sat brandishing wooden swords, urging their noble steed to death and glory.

He reached out to touch the arched neck, remembered holding Lissy and Matt for their first rides. He supposed they had done the same for Emma and Davy. The once-flowing mane under his fingers looked a trifle ragged now, as did the tail. Probably due to five pairs of hands, firmly taught to care for their mount first and foremost.

At Nan's age he'd half-believed Starlight a real horse, enchanted to look like a toy by day, but resuming his true form once the house slept. So many dreams. He'd been Starlight's first owner—was he special to Starlight? The painted eyes had faded, but there was something about the expression… To a creature like this, all children would be special, a flying weight of dreams on his back, and small, loving hands grooming out yet more of his mane and tail every year. He accepted them all.

He gave the proud neck a last rub and stepped back. 'I called him Starlight,' he told Nan.

For a moment there was silence. Then, 'He's yours?'

He thought about it. 'No. Not really.' Any more than Amberley truly belonged to him. Perhaps it was actually the other way around. Or he was merely a guardian. Starlight had passed happily to other children now. As one day he hoped Amberley would pass to his son.

He looked around. His eye fell on Noah's Ark, set out on a low table with the animals dutifully lined up in pairs, being shepherded into the Ark by Noah, his wife and their sons. Only the lion, at the head of the procession, was alone. The lioness had fallen to lie forgotten beneath the table.

He crouched down before the table, and held out his hand. 'Come and look, Nan.'

She came hesitantly.

'This,' he told her, 'was made for our great-grandfather.'

He heard Christy's startled intake of breath, but his concentration now was on the child looking at him, uncomprehending.

'Your great-grandfather, sir?'

'Yes. And yours.' He drew a deep breath. 'I remember him. Just. When he was a very old man he used to let me bring the Ark down to the library after dinner. He said our father, yours and mine, had liked it too.'

Her hand had remained at her side, but now Julian

reached out and took it. She looked at him, the blue eyes so like his own full of bewilderment.

How the hell did one explain something like this to a child?

He tried. 'There was a time, you see, Nan, when your mother and our father were both very sad and became friends. Your mother was very kind to our father, and you were born. I've always known that, but your mother obviously wanted you with her. And that was right and proper. But now—'

He stopped. Nan's eyes had spilled over and his own throat felt thick. Uncertain if it was the right thing to do, he put an arm around Nan and hugged her gently. Fumbling in his pocket, he found a handkerchief to wipe her eyes and blow her nose.

'It…some people would say what they did was wrong, because they were both married to other people—but that is in the past and is not your fault,' he said carefully. 'And it means you are my sister—my half-sister, like Lissy and Emma. And Davy and Matthew are my half-brothers. We all have the same father.'

He couldn't look at Christy. He didn't dare. A few days ago she had told him that she loved him—and he'd flung it back in her face. Reduced her gift to mere sex. Because her honesty had frightened the hell out of him. It had been easier to deny what she felt—deny *her*.

Just as it would be easier to let Jane's family raise Nan, and contribute to her upkeep, holding aloof from further entanglement. Easier. Safer. For he did not delude himself that his chosen path would be easy. It would not. There would always be people to censure him for this step and look down their noses at Nan. He couldn't help what they thought, but, by God, he would protect his sister.

'So, these toys, Nan,' he said. 'Some of them were made for me. Some for my father and aunts, and so on. They don't seem to mind which children play with them. They just belong here. Like the children. No doubt you'll have Davy coming over rather often, and in a year or so there might be another occupant—' He risked a glance at Christy, but she had turned away, was folding some clothes in a basket. With a deep breath he looked at Nan. 'You might have to share, but I don't suppose you'll mind that. They're yours to play with for as long as you want them, because this is your place now, and you belong here, just like they do.'

Nan said nothing, but she wriggled out of his hold, leaned forwards and picked up the fallen lioness. With careful concentration she set the creature upright beside her mate.

'That's it,' said Julian, his throat unaccountably tight. 'They'll be happier together.' He was aware that Christy had turned around, was watching them. 'Poor old Rex probably felt a trifle lost without her. He'll do better now he's got her to show him the way to go on.'

He looked up and met Christy's gaze.

Her breath caught in her throat at the smile in those blue, blue eyes. She was being foolish, imagining too much into his words. He had decided to accept Nan—that was all. No—it was everything. The most wonderful thing that could have happened. Far more important than her foolish romantic dreams.

She said nothing and after a moment he murmured something to Nan and gave her shoulder a squeeze. He rose in a lithe surge and came to her. She forced herself to remain still as memories of the previous night washed over her. His fierce passion, his tenderness—it had just been sex. That was all. For him.

'Come,' he said, and led her from the room into the empty passage.

He spoke softly. 'Sometimes we have trouble seeing what's right in front of us.'

She took a careful breath. He was all around her, the musky scent that had wreathed her all night faintly overlaid with the sandalwood soap he used. He was right. Sometimes it was difficult to keep sight of things that were laid out clearly. Like the difference in their feelings. Last night had not been about love. Not for him.

Yet his touch, careful and light on her cheek, the gentlest tracery, said otherwise. *Let me love you.* Not more than physically. He was a consummate lover and once was quite enough to make a fool of herself in that particular way. And it shouldn't matter so much.

She stood rigid, trying not to let her heart show in her eyes under his magical touch. Yet still her heart yearned, not so much to hear him say it, but to be able to say it. To say it and not have it dismissed as a woman's excuse for enjoying sex. As gratitude.

Just dismissed. As something almost distasteful and rather vulgar. It was as though she had finally opened a door she had never wanted to approach, only to find herself trapped on the threshold, barred from the wonderful new country she had not even suspected.

'Christy?'

She managed a smile. He meant she had helped him to see the truth about Nan. He would never have done this simply to placate her. Rather he had listened, really listened. And he had changed his mind. She had his respect and that would be enough.

Only the bright world she could see through the door blazed and beckoned. She could still shut the door and turn away. It would be safer to do that. Far more comfortable to close it.

He reached for her hand, enveloping it as though it were infinitely precious. Her left hand, weighted with his ring, the symbol of their contract. Duty and honour. Cold, empty bedfellows, but they would have to be enough. She dare not ask.

'What was right in front of you?'

She scarcely recognised her own voice. It came from a great distance, as though she were not quite in control. As though some foolish, rebellious part of her had stepped out to take one last risk.

He lifted her hand to his mouth and kissed the heavy ring.

'That quote you flung at me yesterday—eventually I looked it up.'

Her mind tripped over the image of her rakish husband searching for a Bible passage.

'St Paul was somewhat unequivocal on the subject

of love, wasn't he?' said Julian, a wry smile tearing at her heart. 'There was nothing there to let me off the hook. Even if I didn't have the courage to acknowledge my own feelings, I had no right to cheapen and dismiss yours.'

'Your feelings?' she whispered, hardly daring to believe what he was saying.

He drew her into his arms, into the warmth and safety. And it was he who sighed in pleasure first as she settled against him.

'Yes,' he said. 'I spent a great deal of time and effort trying to convince myself that there were many excellent reasons for wanting you and marrying you. Desire, duty, honour.' He kissed her gently. 'But in the end I had to admit I was being a fool. Oh, I desired you right enough, but it became so much more.' He broke off again, seeming to search for words. 'I care what you think of me, I care about *you* and I don't give a damn about your birth, unless it causes *you* hurt. Yesterday, when I realised how close I came to losing you—' his arms tightened around her '—it terrified me.'

He held her slightly away from him. 'Tell me it isn't too late, sweetheart—tell me you still love me.'

'Yes, I love you,' she whispered. 'So much. I just wish…' Her voice faltered.

'What do you wish, sweetheart?'

She struggled for the words. 'That I was not…my birth…'

Gentle fingers stopped her lips. 'No,' he said. 'Don't wish that. Don't wish to be anything other than who you are and what you are. That's the woman I love. The woman I will always love.'

Her eyes were blinded, the room dissolving into mist. But he caught her chin and lifted it, then gently removed her spectacles, slipping them into his pocket. Through the blur she saw his mouth twist.

'You gave me those words, and I didn't have the courage to accept them, let alone return them. So I hurt you instead.' He kissed her tenderly, on the eyes, the cheeks, capturing the silvery tears. 'I'm not worth these,' he whispered.

She smiled through them. 'Not even tears of happiness?'

'Just as long as I don't cause you any more of the other sort,' he said, holding her close.

More tears fell, but through the mist of joy she could see the gleaming world stretching out, limitless. Full of mysteries and unseen paths, probably not a few sorrows, dangers and pitfalls, but it was theirs to tread and explore. Together.

HISTORICAL

LARGE PRINT

HIS RELUCTANT MISTRESS

Joanna Maitland

Lord Leo Aikenhead – renowned rake and expert spy – has finally met his match. For opera singer Sophie Pietre will be no man's strumpet! But these are dangerous times in Vienna and Sophie's tempted both by his offer of protection and – she can no longer deny it – even more tempted by the offer of a place in his bed…

THE EARL'S FORBIDDEN WARD

Bronwyn Scott

Innocent debutante Tessa Branscombe can't help but be intrigued by her guardian, the arrogant Earl of Dursley. But the Earl has no time for girls – Miss Tessa Branscombe, in particular, is trouble. She tempts this very proper Earl to misbehave – and forbidden fruit always tastes that much sweeter…

THE RAKE'S INHERITED COURTESAN

Ann Lethbridge

Sylvia Boisette, daughter of a Parisian courtesan, is shocked when her guardian's will decrees she become courtesan to his nephew! Christopher Evernden is appalled – he knows he should rid himself of his disreputable charge. But Sylvia's beauty and surprising vulnerability make him wonder – could his inherited mistress become his rightful bride?

HISTORICAL

LARGE PRINT

THE RAKE'S WICKED PROPOSAL

Carole Mortimer

Lucian St Claire, one of the wickedest rakes around, needs an heir – so it's time to choose a wife! Opinionated Grace Hetherington is definitely not the wife he wants. Yet there's something irresistible about her – and, when they're caught in a rather compromising situation, he has no choice but to make her his convenient bride!

THE TRANSFORMATION OF MISS ASHWORTH

Anne Ashley

Tomboy Bethany Ashworth's innocent dreams were destroyed by Philip Stavely's betrothal to her cousin. Years later, Bethany has grown into a beautiful woman, tragedy has left Philip knowing exactly what he wants – he's now determined to marry the woman he should have swept up the aisle six years ago!

MISTRESS BELOW DECK

Helen Dickson

Wilful Rowena Golding needs Tobias Searle's ship to chase her kidnapped sister, but the boarding price he's asking is one night in his bed! Rowena is determinedly immune to Tobias' lethal charm and so, dressed as a cabin boy, she's prepared for the dangers of the high seas…but is she prepared for the notorious Tobias Searle?

HIST1209 LP

HISTORICAL

LARGE PRINT

THE PIRATICAL MISS RAVENHURST

Louise Allen

Forced to flee Jamaica disguised as a boy, Clemence Ravenhurst falls straight into the arms of Nathan Stanier. The heat between them sizzles, but honour demands Nathan resist Clemence. However, she seems determined that their adventure will be as passionate as possible!

HIS FORBIDDEN LIAISON

Joanna Maitland

To restore his reputation, rakish Lord Jack Aikenhead undertakes a covert intelligence operation in war-torn France. However, silk weaver Marguerite throws his plans into disarray! Jack needs the French beauty's help on his mission – though she will be hopelessly compromised…

AN INNOCENT DEBUTANTE IN HANOVER SQUARE

Anne Herries

Debutante Helene has one season to find a husband and save her family. Her compassionate nature leads her into the path of handsome, secretive rake Lord Max Coleridge. He's intrigued by innocent Helene – but with his life in danger, how can he put her at risk? Max determines to solve the mystery – and make Helene his bride!

HISTORICAL

LARGE PRINT

THE BRIGADIER'S DAUGHTER

Catherine March

Having married her sister's bridegroom, Miss Alexandra Packard is shocked at her own daring. The sensible, logical part of her urges her to speak up. The other part – the romantic, womanly, lonely part – keeps her silent. Secretly, she very much wants to find out what it would be like to be Captain Reid Bowen's wife in *every* sense…

THE WICKED BARON

Sarah Mallory

Luke Ainslowe's reputation as an expert seducer precedes him. Most ladies are torn between outrage and desire for the most dashing rake London has ever known! But innocent Carlotta refuses to become the Baron's next conquest – she has lost her heart to Luke before. However, what if the Wicked Baron refuses to take no for an answer?

HIS RUNAWAY MAIDEN

June Francis

Rosamund Appleby is dressed as a youth and fleeing to London when she meets Baron Alex Nilsson. Intrigued by this "boy" and suspecting the truth, Alex seeks to protect her. But, now hastily married to Rosamund, Alex begins to wonder which is more dangerous: his enemies – or the seductive lure of the woman in his bed…

HIST0210 LP